SATURNINE

BY PAMELA DICKSON

Four Watt Press

🜊 FOUR WATT PRESS

ISBN: 978-0-9965247-0-4 paperback
ISBN: 978-0-9965247-8-0 ebook

This book is available in print at most retailers.

For Mom and Jimmy

SATURNINE

"One can say that the content of the menippea is the adventures of an idea or a truth in the world…"

PROBLEMS OF DOSTOEVSKY'S POETICS,
MIKHAIL BAKHTIN, TRANSLATED BY CARYL EMERSON

BOOK I

ONE

"YOU STARTLED ME," she said. Her husband filled the doorway.

He walked in, picked up a piece of parchment, and read aloud, "The zeal they turned on the world." He continued reading to himself, then looked up at her. "You wrote this?"

"Yes," she said. She'd made tangible that which even as thought was subversive, criminal.

He dropped the parchment; it circled to the floor. "Lord Lupicinus is here. Prepare and join us." He gave a nod and went out. He did not need to say more than the name: Lupicinus, powerful advisor to the bishop of Rome. This was Lupicinus's first visit to their domus, and she knew her husband expected something, some position with the Church. Lupicinus, and by extension the pope's church itself—as it was called—had taken an interest in Victorinus.

Flavia, the maidservant, entered and paled when she saw Saturnine with her scrolls and parchment. "You were careless!" Flavia said in the low voice she used when they were alone.

Saturnine gathered the parchment and rolls and placed

them in a worn leather sack. "I needed him to know," she said. "Never mind. Prepare me to receive Lupicinus, our guest."

Flavia lowered her head and went out.

A cynical smile came to Saturnine's lips. Lupicinus, the great churchman, had come to their domus just when her husband had discovered her words, her writing against the Church. Saturnine felt enveloped in secrets, as if her whole life were criminal, secretive.

Flavia returned with a silk wrap—silk, the secret of China, and the tall hairdresser now stood at the door with a belt of utensils. Saturnine and Flavia exchanged guilty glances. Saturnine went to the stool. The hairdresser's tongue stuck out, and her eyes narrowed with the concentration of an artist as she worked on Saturnine's thick, unwieldy hair.

Christians think I'm going to hell, Saturnine thought. How could she know if they were right? The complexity of life astounded her. Even the act of dressing baffled her. She could not recover the right air. In writing, she'd been in a primordial state, the Saturnia Regna, the Kingdom of Saturn, oblivious to time, to sundials and water clocks. She had to remember how to behave. Ten years, she thought. In two days, *Mars, five Kalends of Martius*—the day would mark ten years from the night this god-filled city had burned Philo alive.

TWO

I MUST NOTE certain things.

I call myself Lupicinus. It's what I can manage, adopting this wolfish name and speaking of myself as if of another. Perhaps I'm not the man I write about, Lupicinus. That is, perhaps I'm him no longer. What matter? We're characters to ourselves. We learn who we are by watching what we do, as if from a remove. We see how we've acted in the world.

I write of Saturnine, Kharapan, and others, and of Lupicinus too, as if I know their thoughts, for don't I? I know enough. I have Saturnine's work, and the work of that woman of Hellenica called Metis, including her codex *Kingdoms*. I say now: I do not intend to relate what happened after the events of the few months I describe, and yet I believe this will be clear enough. More clear to those souls of the future. Perhaps our lives, what is gestured at—what we become, how we live, Saturnine and I—hold what meaning there is to be found in this chronicle.

As for Saturnine, I say: at the time my chronicle begins,

Saturnine would not use the word *atheos* to describe herself or (God forbid!) add it as a surname, as certain ancient philosophers have done. Yet, disbelief has a long and distinguished history. Disbelief is as old as thought. But in our time, centuries after Lucretius's godless poems, disbelief thrived underground, so to speak. Saturnine knew that Rome would use the word *atheos* against her.

Saturnine—born in the year of the last pagan emperor, dying in the world of the one Catholic God—her life, her lived years, mark a transformation from a world filled with gods to a world of God. In the year of Saturnine's birth, a panegyric to a new Christian emperor could still state: "You must be aware that a king cannot compel his subjects in everything... there are some matters which have escaped compulsion... the whole question of virtue, and above all, reverence for the divine. The impulse of the soul is unconstrained and is both autonomous and voluntary. God made the favorable disposition toward piety a common attribute of nature but lets the manner of worship depend on individual inclination. The clash of different views energizes society."

Emperor Theodosius issued his edict after Saturnine turned sixteen, four years before the events of this chronicle took place. Emperors west and east, Gratian and Theodosius, issued a joint edict proclaiming the Nicene faith, but Theodosius's edict sent a shudder throughout the relevant part of the world. He would enforce the Nicene Creed. He would unify even the thoughts of men.

EDICT TO THE PEOPLE OF CONSTANTINOPLE.
It is our desire that all the various nations which are subject to our Clemency and Moderation, should continue to profess that religion which was delivered to the Romans by the divine Apostle Peter, as it has been preserved by faithful tradition, and which is now professed by the Pontiff Damasus and by Peter, Bishop of Alexandria, a man of apostolic holiness. According to the apostolic teaching and the doctrine of the Gospel, let us believe in the one deity of the Father, the Son and the Holy Spirit, in equal majesty and in a holy Trinity. We authorize the followers of this law to assume the title of Catholic Christians; but as for the others, since, in our judgment they are foolish madmen, we decree that they shall be branded with the ignominious name of heretics, and shall not presume to give to their conventicles the name of churches. They will suffer in the first place the chastisement of the divine condemnation and in the second the punishment of our authority which in accordance with the will of Heaven we shall decide to inflict.

All in the Roman Empire, perhaps beyond, had to profess the Nicene creed: one deity of the Father, the Son, and the Holy Spirit, in equal majesty and in a holy Trinity. One substance, consubstantial, *homoousios*. The powers of empire, of emperor and law, and of Church, bonded to form a unified Christian world.

Enforcement ensued, but never complete, not in the time

I speak of. Theodosius issued letters directing his praetorian prefects to impose the Nicene faith across their provinces. Those not professing the Nicene Creed surrendered churches to Nicenes. The law declared its aim: that catholic churches in the whole world be restored to orthodox bishops who hold the Nicene faith.

It would seem, given the uncertainty of the times, barbarians breaking in, Theodosius hoped to strengthen the Empire by enforcing unification of belief. But in the years after the edict, we in Rome heard endless news of uprooting and violence against heretics within. Old laws against astrologers and diviners accused of *maleficium*, sorcery, were used to condemn bishops and heretics to death. The emperor constructed a list of heresies: Arians, Macedonians and Apollinarians, Novatianists and Sabbatians, etc. The law would target books of heretics and require codices be burned; it would ban all books except orthodox texts—but this would come after events I describe in my chronicle.

This new statement of the creed by an emperor, by Theodosius, supreme representative of God on earth, an emperor divine for centuries past, this new creed of an emperor and the network of bishops worked its way into the past as well. Those Christians in the centuries, including intellectuals or those declared 'saints' in the past, all those who had not professed the Nicene creed, even as it became known later, were declared heretics and evil and wiped clean of history. They disappeared in the march forward and backward of the record of those who conquer.

I see the power of words. In the world of the Trinity, the wrong word can turn the tide of an Empire against one, or against one's enemies. The right word. Unscrupulous bishops could cause other bishops to be banished, all the riches of the diocese coming into their hands.

The astonishing innovation of Theodosius's edict, an idea of unity of belief, true, but one deeper and mysterious and more subtle, more powerful: an idea of unity by "faith alone." I am sure even he was not aware of it. The Trinity could not be proven by the words of scripture. It was this that gave it its power and changed the 'culture' of an empire, one might say. The Trinity became the Empire's myth, its *core*, Kharapan would say. Words, only these could be asserted, those regarding the Trinity that could not be "proven" by words of scripture, and anyone who spoke otherwise, who attempted a rational explanation or argument about the Trinity, who were not in perfect alignment with the creed, he or she was branded "evil" and subject to prosecution, banned from society, status, jobs, reputation, all. This new myth, and its enforcement, expanded like the sun over thought, over debate and ideas, which diminished and disappeared. A single truth that can only be grasped by faith—challenged the entire Greek and Roman world, including its long intellectual tradition.

In the distance of years, looking back, Theodosius's edict and its consequences did not surprise me. I intuited a Kingdom of God from the age of thirteen. The Nicene myth formed an Empire, an authoritarian rule of Kingdom, a bond between church and state. No one could counter such power. If there is a God, even a Jesus as God, I shudder at judgement day: at the power asserted by an emperor of Rome, by a network of church institutions, by words of man, forcing everyone to believe! But there it is.

I note: Emperor Theodosius, in referring to Damasus, bishop of Rome, as Pontiff in his edict, gave Damasus even greater authority and power. Damasus had long called his church the "apostolic see," and those of Rome referred to his church as the pope's church.

In the time of my chronicle, although the emperor declared the death penalty for heretics and forbade divination, outlawed all unorthodox thought, still, much of the Empire, particularly in the west, in Rome itself, remained if not free, relatively free, a hotbed of ideas. Those in Rome looked on in astonishment at news of the empire in the East, but, naively perhaps, could not believe there would be one rule of thought, one creed imposed on belief, that there would ever be, in effect, a Roman Empire of One God called the Trinity. Even in the year of my chronicle, four years after Theodosius's edict, Rome had a large pagan population and senate. And yet, still, a mood of looming threat infested Rome.

I note, looking back—yes, I had no doubt that the Church would have its Kingdom. I desired nothing more. But as I write, in spite of everything, even what I've witnessed since, the march toward unity, the suppression of thought, at least of words, libraries dwindling from thousands of texts to hundreds owned by a few, those approved orthodox texts, still I say: I don't know. I don't know if there will ever be one Christian Kingdom, one that dominates all single unique individuals. And in the gap of not knowing, of *agnosis* Khara-pan would call it, I admit, complexities flow as if a fresh wind. Even I find a moment of joy in wonder—if undeserved.

In the time of my chronicle, Rome, once the city at the

center of the world, thought to hold the flower of mankind, rational creatures combining extremes of North and South in one harmonious clay, discerning creatures meant to rule the world, in my time, Rome was no longer the center of Empire. The Empire's Capital had moved to Constantinople over fifty years before Theodosius's Edict. But churches rose in Rome, as grand as the most luxurious bathhouses. And four years after Theodosius's Edict, the time of my chronicle, a magnificent bathhouse was transformed into one of the largest and most resplendent houses of worship ever known: a Christian Church, with its Man-God called Christ.

Saturnine had not converted, even then, the year when events of this chronicle take place. It's not entirely clear how much her husband, Victorinus, knew or understood her cast of mind. I believe he didn't know of her written work until that fateful day that marks the beginning of this chronicle. It seems she had been engaged for some time writing a work exploring how the Empire, a world full of gods, became an Empire of God—even then, when no one in Rome could believe such a thing.

For a time, Saturnine wrote in secret at the domus that had once been her family home. However, in early morning hours while her husband Victorinus was at the senate, she had begun to write in the domus where they lived. She sat at a small desk in her bedroom under a window, gazing out through slender trees on the hill, looking over a simmering city, writing about the hierarchy of churches that had spread across Empire.

But this is Rome, Saturnine thought or might have thought.

The air thick, redolent of sewage that rushed in a great, dark river beneath Roman streets. Humidity held Rome as if motionless. The dim winter light made the city amorphous. Umbrella pines webbed the sky in shades of light and dark. Carts pounded over stone streets, faint voices hummed. The city shimmered as if from a great smokeless fire.

Here, then, was Rome, its sky the home of gods. Earthly desires stretched upward to paint the sky, to catch the gods' attention and bring them down.

THREE

SATURNINE FOUND THE men on the porch. Flavia stood directly behind her. It was an unusually warm day for winter. Victorinus introduced her as 'Cornelia'—this was the name he'd given her himself, her real name too near old gods. Lupicinus, a small, gray man, bent his balding head and squinted at her. Saturnine gave a brief bow. Rufinus, at the table too, a heavy man, a pagan senator, a friend and frequent guest, gave Saturnine a conspiratorial smile.

Saturnine took a red-cushioned chair, glad the men continued their discussion. Lupicinus thought he noticed something odd about her, although she might have been dressed well enough, her hair acceptable or acceptably hidden.

Victorinus spoke loudly, smiling broadly: acts of senate—emergency meetings, a crime against Empire (someone from Carthage), the Altar of Victory.

The kitchen slaves brought out grapes, cheese and bread, dark wine, and a large bowl of water for the servants of guests to dip a cup into. The damp and cool air, disturbed by a recent burst of rain, made them pull in their cloaks. Heavy drops fell from early camellias in bloom. The crumbling capital, the edge of the Palatine, loomed in the distance like a ghost.

As Saturnine sipped her wine, a smile and a sense of mockery grew in her. The wind blowing through their white togas whispered "uselessness." No one let on. 'We're at the center of the world,' senators exclaimed on street corners. A Christian emperor who'd never been to Rome humored senators when they cried to return the marble goddess of war, the Altar of Victory, to the Curia in Rome.

Lupicinus caught Saturnine's attention. "Christians will become a majority even in the senate," he said as if he knew the plan of the world.

In the pause that followed, the mirthful fates found a chance to intervene. Saturnine considered Lupicinus. Although intimate with the bishop, he had no official role in the Church. She'd heard he'd been advisor to a line of bishops supporting the Orthodox position for some thirty years. Rumor told he had fantastic wealth, and that his conversion to Christianity followed a miracle. Was he a Christian saint? He had a bland, ugly face, yet it held something interesting in it. A smirk, though not visible on his thin lips, in the seeming forced immobility of his gaze.

Victorinus regretted the turn of conversation. The lack of the Altar in the senate—he'd called it "a symbol of the past"—weakened morale, but he feared Lupicinus would think he went too far in support of the Roman religion. His wife's soft voice interrupted him as he opened his mouth to speak.

"There are three reasons for Christianity's rise to power," she said, looking at Lupicinus.

The men looked at her in surprise. Victorinus's hand went to his chest.

"What reasons, my dear?" Lupicinus said. He had a reputation for composure. Lupicinus particularly admired this aspect of himself.

"The Altar should be destroyed once and for all," Victorinus said, color rising.

Rufinus lowered his head, pained at Victorinus's remark but intuiting something of his predicament.

"I'm interested to hear Cornelia's three reasons," Lupicinus said. He lifted his lips as if in a smile.

Saturnine paled. She hadn't intended to speak her mind. Words danced off Victorinus's tongue as pieces in his mosaic of power and control, but for her, words expressed a person's truth and she had never grown used to using them otherwise. Silence had been her means of performance and her rest, her sanctuary. But she'd revealed her mind and now must explain, and to one close to the bishop, that man called pope. Her heart pounded. Her eyes turned to the floor, but she suddenly felt reckless, angry. Fine, let it out, it has to end. To loosen her tongue was to fall from grace but she had never been graced.

"I will tell you my three reasons," she said to Lupicinus, pulling her cloak close. "First, we rational creatures are susceptible to superstition." She peered boldly at Lupicinus. "The art of controlling fear—and it's just that, an art—must be practiced, but no one manages fear. Christians practice an opposite art, the art of invoking fear—by threat of hell, and otherwise—to increase their membership."

Saturnine couldn't help a glance at her husband. *Impossible*! showed in his eyes.

The exclamation, "Jupiter," escaped Rufinus. He put his hands on his thick thighs. Lupicinus, glancing at Rufinus, traced the cross over his chest.

"Saturnine," Rufinus said, ignoring Lupicinus, understanding Saturnine only in part, "the gods, even the Christian God, not only invoke our fear but also our hope and love. They guide us in the way everything is connected."

An old friend, Rufinus had known her parents: he still called her her given name. Lupicinus gave an interested look.

Saturnine gave Rufinus a bare smile. For Rufinus, and her parents when alive, the behavior of animals, seeds, and tides proved that all parts of the cosmos were linked by a natural affinity, a sympatheia. The secrets of the stars, the science of Ptolemy and Hipparchus, added to their insights.

"Your other reasons?" Lupicinus said.

"The content of your doctrine," she said. "You promise eternal happiness in heaven if one believes in Christ, the only requirement to membership, and pain and suffering in hell if one doesn't believe. The choice is ours, but what a choice! And the miracles, the benefit while one is alive, the possibility of being raised from the dead, and the punishment for refusing or simply being unable to believe."

She studied this gray, cold man, thinking: he might be one of the Christians' raised dead.

Lupicinus cleared his throat and spit on the floor. A slave ran over and wiped it up. "And your last reason, my dear?"

"With a Christian emperor the Church has the power

of armies, that and the hierarchy of the cult. Churches are connected throughout Empire." She paused. "It'll have its Kingdom."

She flushed and burned in the silence that followed.

Lupicinus's slightly open mouth revealed dark teeth (I speak the whole truth!). "Yes, the Church will have its Kingdom," he said. "Are you thinking of converting, casting your vote to ensure an afterlife?"

Saturnine gave a laugh but grew solemn. "No," she said. "I'm excluded by nature. Belief eludes me. Your God needs even our thoughts to reveal our faith."

Lupicinus breathed in. He interlaced his fingers and laid his hands in his lap. He noticed Saturnine's oily hair, a lock out of place. Although some might consider her beautiful, she was oblivious to physical charm, her own or that of others. Her simplicity disturbed him. A man's wife revealed a man, and this wife gave Lupicinus a clear idea of the guidance Victorinus needed.

"Consider where your reasoning leads," he said. He paused as if everyone would see the obvious. "Tell me," he continued, "what world would we have without superstition? Civilization is based on a common belief in gods. Your position would do away with all religion, my dear, even with the Roman Empire itself." He paused. "The Orthodox church will surpass the work of paganism: it will form the greatest, most unified, civilization ever known, even beyond the boundaries of Empire. It will bind together minds, the very thoughts, of men. I agree with you, we will have our Kingdom.

"If rational creatures were godless," Lupicinus went on,

sitting back, "we'd be worse than barbarians. Even they have gods. We'd be cats prowling squalid hovels, exhausting our desires in alleyways."

Rufinus snorted, and even Victorinus smiled.

Saturnine pursed her lips. "Cats," Saturnine said, "yes, perhaps it's true, perhaps there's no community among disbelievers."

She didn't notice the look of surprise in Lupicinus's face—it had not occurred to him to think of her as an atheist, that rare creature, a true *atheos*, a disbeliever in all gods. For Saturnine, Lupicinus's mention of barbarians, and perhaps the near anniversary on *Mars*, brought to mind that extraordinary night long ago, the night Philo died, and Kharapan, a barbarian, a disbeliever apparently, saved her life. It might even be that Kharapan's country, Hellenica, what he called Chi, was a civilization without gods.

Lupicinus's stiff fingers straightened in a near undetectable lengthening over his legs.

Saturnine peered into the distance. "I don't know," she said. "Maybe we'd be better off admitting that we don't know much about gods. Maybe we'd still have civilization, an even better civilization."

"Where's your evidence?" Lupicinus said, extending a thin arm toward the city.

They all looked out. An orange mist hovered above the gold triangle roof of the Jupiter Capitolinus. They could see the rough edge of what had been a bath, now a Christian church, the largest and most brilliant house of worship ever known. Gods were in every breath of air. A breeze rustled.

Clouds thickened and cast shade and light over the god-swelled city.

"Even so," Saturnine said, "I can't force myself to believe, even if society, Empire, wishes it and wants to domesticate me. But I am honest, Lupicinus. I say that. For failing to believe only harms me. Your God threatens me with hell for failing to believe. And failing to pretend to believe only harms me in Rome." And in my own home, she thought, not daring to look at Victorinus.

Lupicinus's chair jerked. It scratched the tiles and startled Saturnine. Victorinus looked at Lupicinus with concern.

"Your honesty is treachery," Lupicinus said. "It's not worthy. It's treachery. You—those like you—weaken the minds and faith of men and threaten civilization itself."

He gave Saturnine a piercing stare. He had once seen a monkey with its claws tearing into the back of a lion racing around the arena. He imagined it on Saturnine's head, clinging to her face.

Saturnine grew pale. Blotches of red appeared on her face. Victorinus looked down at Hercules's snake-like hair in the mosaic tiles.

After a time Lupicinus said, "There is no moral life but the Church." He rose. They all rose.

Victorinus went to Saturnine and took her arm, making a show of tranquility and, to the extent of his powers, stateliness. For Saturnine, the silent pose she might have taken in the past transformed into painful demure. She could hardly hold up her head.

Lupicinus bowed to Saturnine. He and Rufinus took leave of Victorinus and Saturnine.

FOUR

VICTORINUS DID NOT release Saturnine's arm after Lupicinus and Rufinus left. He led her to the cold, dim library. He did not call a servant to start a fire or light a lamp. He closed the heavy door. Saturnine leaned against a thick leather couch, crossed her arms, and looked at him with what he took as a determined expression.

"What have I done to make you want to ruin me?" he said when she remained silent. He struggled to keep his voice low.

"How can I help my thoughts?"

"You can hide thoughts, but you speak them, you write them down."

She had a slight turn to her lip, a sarcastic smile, he thought, but it marked her inner struggle. "What made you imagine you should speak your mind? To Lupicinus?" She'd been strange since her father's death. He thought it was grief.

Saturnine felt her heart pound.

"If you consider it rationally," she said, peering at him, "how can my thoughts be the stuff of outside rule? I once heard a man on the street. He was a philosopher, I don't know of what school. He had the sound of conviction in his voice."

She paused but continued before he could interject. "I've been writing for years," she said. She continued: she'd stopped writing when they married, believed she would stop and did for more than two years; but she'd started again after her father's death. She realized, she told him, that she had to write. "I can't keep it a secret any longer." She stared at him, eyes wide.

"Impossible!" he said. "Do you want to expose us?"

"I didn't always write about the Church. After Philo died—"

"Philo? The one executed for black magic?"

She flushed and looked away. In the face of Victorinus, in the face of the world, the old doubt blossomed. Writing words considered subversive by the entire world—for the world is Rome—what purpose? particularly words written by a woman, the wife of a Christian senator of Rome.

"If I don't write," she said, "I become the walking dead, like the walking dead."

Victorinus turned away from her and grabbed an unlit lamp from the wall and threw it. It hit the wall behind her with a crash.

Saturnine could hardly breath. Shocked tears started from her eyes.

"I don't know who you are," he said. "I don't know who I married."

She couldn't speak, could hardly swallow.

"Tell me you'll stop."

Saturnine gave a strained nod. Besides the violence of the moment, a new idea shook her: he might divorce her. He had tried to mold her in the past but had never threatened to abandon her, had never threatened their marriage, but she thought she heard that threat now. Impossible. She could not even imagine a life alone in Rome, in Empire.

Victorinus straightened his robes as if throwing the lamp had been a reasonable and passionless act. He looked at her, noticing what finally appeared to him to be remorse. He loved her. He knew something of her mind—she had an irrational fear of faith, an obsession with doubt—but he believed, had always believed, that she would convert for his sake, for the sake of their lives in Rome. She would, if she must, pretend to believe. He didn't think he would be asking for much. Her keen intelligence made him uncomfortable at times. He thought of her with a certain fearful admiration.

"For God's sake, Cornelia, you spoke your mind to a man intimate with the pope. It may be that you write in secret, it may even come to my attention, but to speak to Lupicinus…"

Saturnine heard retreat in his words: he would mold her to his will, but he would not leave her. His loyalty shamed her. The cold damp air felt thick. Saturnine shivered, her body trembled. Victorinus felt the impulse to go to her, to hold her, but he repressed it.

Saturnine resisted the old feeling—relief. But a part of her felt relief. Victorinus saved her, he saved her from herself. She felt as if waking from a dream—for which is the dream? Empire? Or passion, mere thought?

Almost three years before, at her father's party celebrating a Charioteer, the son of one of her father's guests caught her arm and whispered, "You'll fall in love with me." His dark eyes were intense. Saturnine affected an arch glance and feigned a laugh, but his eyes had been ominous, and she couldn't dismiss that pause in which it was as if something important had passed between them and been understood. Victorinus's grandfather had been an ordinary businessman, a spice merchant. But his father turned the business into a major enterprise and owned four ships. The young man's oiled dark hair and white dress exuded status, but he lacked elegance and natural grace; his well-toned muscular body was rigid and square. At the time, he'd recently returned to Rome from Athens, where at the insistence of his father, he'd been taking instruction from a famous teacher. His father had written to him telling him that his mother had died.

Victorinus hadn't known his mother was sick but found out that she had been ailing for a long time, and grief and anger at her death left him unable to focus on his studies. At the time he met Saturnine, he didn't care about the future. He'd attended the party reluctantly, at his father's request. His father had ambitions for Victorinus's career, and even then was negotiating a place for him in the senate. But Victorinus liked the exotic look of the daughter of his host's domus, and her name and status would satisfy his father, he thought. As the only legitimate son, Victorinus carried the weight of his father's dreams.

Saturnine resolved to resist him, but her body wouldn't listen, and resolve made more of him than she had intended. His stare unnerved and excited her against her will. He visited her daily. It seemed that from the moment he predicted her love, he'd cursed her, caused a physical change. Her parents had once chosen Philo for a husband; since his death, they sometimes discussed marriage. But she resisted, nor had she found anyone to love, perhaps absorbed in her secret life, though love was in vogue in Rome. But she had to marry; she never doubted it.

As if fate claimed Saturnine for him, Victorinus said they'd marry. He had a power over her. He grew teary-eyed when he spoke about his mother's death and admitted that he wanted to be someone in Rome: being a senator was a step to greater power. Saturnine understood that Victorinus was suited to Rome. It seemed to Saturnine as if he had no thought contrary to the world that was their city, nothing subversive, nothing contradictory to its values or customs. He would take a wife with him into the heart of Empire. She was entranced. She felt relief at the idea of being saved, saved from herself. She could envision a life in Rome.

"What have I done?" she whispered.

Victorinus looked away. "Lupicinus will forget," he said. He felt weary. Surely, a woman could cause only limited harm.

"Lupicinus will come to dinner on *Mars*," he said. "It's to be an intimate evening—you'll join us for dinner. If the hours go well, if he comes, all will not be lost."

He would go to Lupicinus, he thought. He would explain his wife's momentary derangement and confirm dinner on *Mars*. He thought of Cornelia like a child. "It would be best, especially now, Cornelia, if you converted," he said.

Saturnine lowered her eyes. She felt instinctive danger.

If she converted, she would lose whatever gleam of spirit she had left, but what spirit could she have left? She recognized, if with despair and loathing, that she might convert. There were reasons to sacrifice oneself: love, safety, duty.

"Did you hear me about *Mars*?" he said.

"Dinner will be perfect," she said in a mix of fear and relief. She had a limited reprieve; she did not have to promise to convert.

"I'll go to my bath," he said. He hesitated. "You should destroy that writing—burn it."

Saturnine bowed her head, gave a bare nod.

Victorinus went to her and put the back of his hand to her cheek. He looked at her with wondering eyes but then his face grew sad and severe. He went out.

Flavia roused Saturnine when she came into the library. Saturnine could see Flavia's form in shadow.

"There are dangers…" Flavia said, her voice low. "You aren't aware what you risk."

Flavia had her own secrets in mind—irrevocable events of the past that she long believed put Saturnine at risk.

"You think I'm mad," Saturnine said, not understanding. "You've always been afraid for the soundness of my mind." Saturnine suspected Flavia feared for her sanity, given what Saturnine wrote and her secret life. And now starting to write again. In fact, the fear Saturnine attributed to Flavia terrified Saturnine herself. Her fear of her own nature, her lack of courage to rise and live that nature, was perhaps stronger than her fear of the world.

I note, perhaps to myself: it is possible that I paint

Saturnine in these pages, this chronicle, in her worst light—weakness, fears, faults, evil, yes evil. Or worse, perhaps, a character unformed, crushed by Rome, a thing like the 'walking dead' Kharapan spoke of, until she chooses that life, inhabits herself, so to speak, until she lives, that is. She is not yet that writer of Alexandria. And yet, I document the soil as it were—from which that creature, that character, would rise or free herself. Someone once said: clouds pass and the rain does its work and all individual beings (*might*, I add) flow into their forms.

But who am I to say? I who…. The mere words of an awakening of an old man.

"It doesn't matter. You won," Saturnine said, passing but not touching Flavia as she went out.

FIVE

I MUST PAUSE. I must go back ten years, more, to certain events leading to the night Philo was killed, to the night itself when Saturnine, ten years old, was rescued by Kharapan from the Bakers of Rome—I will say Kharapan saved her life, but it is more correct to say her life was saved much later, by what this chronicle relates or perhaps can merely touch upon.

Saturnine, six years old, in the library with Philo, her tutor and friend, wriggled and laughed when he teased her about being adopted. She, with her olive skin and dark hair, couldn't help knowing, like others must, that she'd been abandoned as a baby at the pope's church. It was what one did with unwanted babies. No one except Philo mentioned any abandonment or adoption.

"Probably your father," he whispered, handing Saturnine a drawing of a man with curly dark hair wrapped in the red cloak of a Christian priest. His comments would infuriate her parents. Although she laughed, his joke gave her an odd feeling she often had. If she had been born to her parents, she might fit in better. Still, she had Philo, and her maidservant Flavia, and with them she felt she had a place in the world, though she could not have expressed it that way at the time.

Her parents surprised them. Saturnine rolled the papyrus, but Theanis and Constance, caught in some excitement, hardly noticed her.

Theanis took a chair and Constance sat on the footstool, since Theanis wouldn't let go of her hand. Her green silk bunched on the floor. Theanis dropped her hand and put his hands to his face and when he removed them, the white outline of his fingers remained. Saturnine leaned back on couch pillows, spread her legs wide like a street boy, and studied her parents as if puzzling the customs and mannerisms of strangers.

"Hear this," Theanis said when Philo stood to go.

Philo sat down. The son of an ex-Prefect of Rome, twelve years old, Saturnine's parents expected him to marry Saturnine one day, and he approved of the idea himself.

"The other day, during the hot hours," Theanis said, "a donkey climbed the steps of the fountain and brayed. It was an ominous sign." He paused. "Today, three men were hung."

Saturnine's eyes narrowed. When concentrating, especially when in doubt over something, she looked angry. Her father often dramatized events of his day, but events he described sickened her, and his apprehension seemed real. Her mother sat stiff and unmoving.

Theanis continued in an even voice. A former vice-prefect and his wife complained to the urban prefect that three men—an organ maker, a wrestler, and a soothsayer—conspired to kill them with poison. Because the urban prefect was sick, they petitioned Maximin, the Christian prefect of the corn supply, a man who'd never had the power of a judge. Maximin heard the case and ordered the men hung in the span of an hour.

"They hang by their necks in front of the Arch of Titus, with the letters 'C' and 'S' scratched into their chests. Conspirator, Sorcerer."

He put his hand on his wife's head but pulled it away. Strands of her hair flew up as if in excitement of his touch. He went to stand in front of the fire.

"The Gods will protect us," Constance said. The passion in her husband sometimes shamed her; for his part, her lack of emotion exasperated him.

"Maximin will never relinquish power," Theanis said.

Saturnine crossed her arms, anticipating her father's outburst, but her father turned to her.

"It is her destiny in the long years I worry about," he said. Saturn, the father of the gods, wise and understanding lord of contemplation, keeper and discoverer of mysteries, would protect his daughter. But there had been inauspicious signs. From the first, he believed it inauspicious to take babies from the church, and inauspicious that Saturnine—for that was what he had named her given her pensive eyes and the state of the world—was born in the year that Emperor Julian, the lover of Rome's Gods, had mysteriously (and traitorously, no doubt) died. But the masses abandoned their babies at the Church of Savior at Lateran, the pope's church it was called. And he had wanted this dark-haired baby. He had convinced his wife—the monk hadn't had to utter a word—that they were destined for a girl, for this girl.

Saturnine flushed. She couldn't help feeling excited by the thought of the gods considering her in their plans. But her eyes turned instinctively to Philo.

Theanis returned to the domus with the rank smell of blood. He had sacrificed goats and asked the gods to forgive Christians for failing to pay homage to them, but his worship didn't impede the forces of civilization. Maximin had sent a missive to Emperor Valentinian warning of an infestation of magic, sorcery, and treason in Rome. He wrote that the city had been left on its own for too many years. "The aristocrats of Rome are more treacherous than the fiercest barbarians. They betray your Lord from within, from the very heart of the Empire," Maximin wrote.

The Catholic emperor Valentinian despised elite pagans, but even those close to him had no assurance of life. He feared magic, the spells that foretold the future and raised the dead. He gave Maximin full power over Rome "to rid the city of evil." Valentinian gave Maximin license to torture high-ranking citizens who'd been exempt under previous legislation.

Maximin summoned powerful people to court and held quick trials. He accused Senator Cethegus, a short stocky man with a laugh like a donkey, of adultery, and had him beheaded. Maximin convicted a celebrated soothsayer of making sacrifices for a nefarious purpose and ordered him clubbed to death. He accused highborn women of adultery.

Soldiers in full armor took women from their homes, stripped them and wrapped them in animal skins, and threw them into the arena to be killed by wild animals, although the soldiers were later punished for impropriety. The torture and killing of the rich enthralled the masses. Amphitheaters filled with hysterical, enthusiastic crowds.

In the years that followed, Maximin's terror reigned in Rome. Hundreds were hanged or burned after short mock trials. The citizens of Rome destroyed thousands of scrolls for fear they would lead to suspicion of sorcery: philosophical texts, prophecies of doubtful source. The shelves of libraries grew bare.

Many turned informant in the hope of saving themselves. Torture produced evidence for the most improbable crimes. Prisons overflowed.

Winters turned into warm, humid, rainy springs. The festival of Floralia passed and passed again, watched from sidelines by Christians. Flower petals scattered by courtesans rotted in the streets. Saturnine, turning ten, had yet to experience the worst of the trials.

"It is a dark magic," Philo said, examining his hand, his outstretched, slow-moving hand.

At sixteen, Philo considered himself a Neo-Platonist. He noticed Saturnine's wonder-filled eyes.

Fundamental questions rose in him. He had to trust in a rational world, in a world that allowed a man to struggle with reason, mind, nature, or he wouldn't have any space to live at all. Saturnine never asked Philo to stop what he did. He copied from a philosophical text. It was a philosophical exercise: Magic is what the mind produces due to appearances. Consciousness is different from what is seen, it isn't the action, the presence, but the reasoned reflection, the thing after the event: reason is the illusion of appearance and cause, the magic. The master of illusion is Natural Being; human reason is a magician of relationships and societies, but one might move outside of it, one might have moments beyond time.

Saturnine had written poems herself even then—poetic aphorisms in the form of questions. A child might exercise an authentic character and talent but might lose the natural skill, might come to know herself less, might repress or forget what she is as she encounters the restrictions and limitations of a world.

I shouldn't have used the words 'dark magic,' Philo thought. But, he considered, Saturnine did not fear out of superstition. She feared powerful people. She feared Rome.

Philo hid his scrolls and texts and concealed his studies, but he might have been careless. He might have felt safe. His father had been the Prefect of Rome. Maximin had accused, even killed, powerful men and women but none of such high status, no sons of such men.

A rumor spread that Theanis had conspired with a charioteer to lose a race. Rome worships its charioteers. Conspiracy amounted to treachery. Theanis waited in fear of Maximin's summons. Saturnine brought him wine and sat on the couch near him. "Bellona storms our eternal city," he murmured.

The cry of birds foretold the gods' anger. But the summons never came. Theanis had been passed over. A different accusation attracted Maximin's attention.

On the morning of *Mars, five Kalends of Martius*, Saturnine went into the garden. She pretended to be a spy, to spy on those who plotted against her family or who used their position to obtain favors from the powerful.

A servant pushed open the wooden door that led into the garden, and Saturnine ducked to hide in bushes that scratched her and she suppressed a laugh.

"Philo?" a servant whispered. "His father was Prefect of Rome."

"They say he writes on black arts. One of the servants knew. The boy's in hiding. Maximin ordered him to appear."

The voices faded.

Saturnine, stunned, trembling but still, remained in the bushes for a long time. At last, she crawled out and went to her room.

In her small bedroom off the open center of the domus, an iron-framed bed took up one wall, and she had a round backless chair. If she stared at the mosaic on her wall, rough-cut glass—Mercury, fat and dancing, his toes in a blue stream—the picture blended into a play of color. A water fountain trickled in the center open courtyard.

She stared at the tiled floor. Philo had come to her room one early morning not long ago, called out her name, and knocked on the shutters. She opened the window, and he climbed in and held up the scrolls. Generations past on her mother's side owned this domus in Rome. Rumor circulated that it had secret treasure and passageways. They'd made a game: knocking on walls and floors. On discovering loose tiles and boards on the floor in Saturnine's bedroom, Philo said he'd use the space beneath to hide his work, and then he came that morning not long ago, throwing aside the rug. "No one will find it," she had said, lying on her side, watching him. He came to the bed and put a hand on each side of her head. He treated her like a child, but there'd been times when he'd taken her hand, when he'd leaned in close. She felt breathless. He wouldn't kiss her, not yet. Neither of them smiled. In two years, when she was twelve and Philo eighteen, they would marry. They would marry for love. Nothing could stand in the way of such a perfect match.

Philo suddenly appeared at her window now.

"Philo," she mouthed.

"Where've you been? I've been waiting," he said, as if they had been playing. He climbed through the window. "Yes, I'm in trouble," he said, seeing in her expression and manner that she knew, his face pale but resigned. He sat next to her on the bed.

"Why hide?" she said. "Give them what they want. It is philosophy not magic."

He gave her a curious smile. "They have my writing," he said. "Some servant stole it to earn a profit." He paused. "They say I practice dark magic. There's nothing I can do."

He saw her defiant look and took her hand. "No matter what happens, regardless of what they say, know this: philosophia guides you to a good life."

"I know," she said. But she had terrified tearful eyes.

"Leave what work is there hidden," Philo said, motioning

to the floor. "Let years pass." He stood and peered at her face. "I would have liked to see what you will become," he said.

"You will!"

He gave her a smile as if to encourage her in the more difficult pursuit of life. He took up her hands and held them briefly, then let them go and turned and crawled out of the window. She watched him run to the cover of the trees.

Silence consumed the domus. No one would say Philo's name. Even Flavia wouldn't speak of him. When Saturnine pressed her, Flavia told Saturnine to consider the Fates, to know that she, Saturnine, had no control over destiny, but that Saturnine could try to stay away, to let the world pass as it must.

One day at their meal, Saturnine's mother said to Theanis in a low voice, "They've found Philo. They're taking him to the Curia right now."

Saturnine stood, confused, panicky. She ran to the edge of the grass where she could see the black Tiber River twisting through Rome. A moment later she crept into Flavia's room and took Flavia's coarse old cloak. It was the first time she'd been out of the domus alone. Half hidden in the cloak, she ran on cobblestones next to the great marble wall of the Circus Maximus. A crowd filled the wide road that led to the forum. She pushed through in time to stand in front of oncoming guards. She saw thin Philo in a dirty beige tunic walking between two guards in full armor.

His gleaming eyes held hers. She ran alongside him on the street. The guards took Philo under the marble Arch of Titus. At the far end of the forum, they climbed the steps and went inside the Main Curia.

It is a tall rectangular building, ugly and permanent. Inside, narrow sheets of light streak in through small windows above, shedding a thin light on interior shadow. With the great dark doors open, one would likely see Maximin at a long table on a raised platform in front of what he despised—the Altar of Victory.

In the small comidian outside people crowded and pushed. Saturnine leaned against the cold marble at the base of the building. Two guards came out. It had not taken long. The people grew quiet.

One guard bellowed, "Philomanius Agrippus Theavanius is guilty before the public and sacred Gods of Empire of dealing in black arts and will be burned on the stake at dusk in full view of the people of Rome."

Saturnine cried out and fell against the wall and wretched dryly. An old woman touched her arm but afraid of sickness moved away.

Saturnine's legs barely held her weight. She didn't feel the cold. The dark cloak dragged behind her. No one noticed when she entered the domus

Flavia entered Saturnine's bedroom and seeing her own cloak on the bed next to the girl, grew grave. She felt Saturnine's cool face. "I'll tell your parents that you're unwell; we'll stay in your room together this night."

"No," Saturnine said. "You'll excuse me from supper, but you'll leave me."

Flavia didn't respond.

"Don't," Saturnine said, in a hard voice she hadn't used with Flavia. Saturnine sensed and knew Flavia's devotion—a concatenation of concern and loyalty that surpassed even the duty Flavia owed to her parents. She didn't understand it, perhaps didn't try, or took it for granted.

Flavia had a severe expression but only gave Saturnine a penetrating look before going out.

In the early evening, Saturnine left the domus in Flavia's cloak.

In the forum, the stake loomed in front of the Curia, waiting in the setting sun. Piles of kindling covered the base. People milled about, growing in number until a tired mob made way for a procession of guards. Maximin walked in front, a small, narrow man, dressed in layers of royal blue. Four guards held torches and surrounded Philo. Silence swept over the crowd. Philo looked ahead. Saturnine watched from a distance. His face seemed calm, even fresh somehow. The guards lifted him, limp in their arms. They tied his legs to the stake at the base and his arms behind. Maximin directed the guards to light the wood, and four torches lit the corners of the kindling.

The fire started. It reached Philo's legs. He wailed, a hollow piercing sound.

The ground rose. People stepped on Saturnine as the stench of burnt skin floated on the cool evening air. She ran out of the forum and into the labyrinth of a city. Smoke rose thick behind her. She ran.

The city glowed under a large moon as if the day only dimmed in horror of what it had witnessed and wouldn't dare full dark. The stricken hollow faces of street creatures hovered in shadows. Saturnine found herself in a dark corner between two buildings and sank against the cold wall to the cobbled ground as if wanting to become part of the marble and stone and not be alive.

The night was not done with her. She didn't know how long she'd been on the ground; she might have been asleep. When a man's fish-smelling hand covered her mouth she couldn't understand at first. He pulled her up and held her in strong arms. Men wander the streets at night looking for children, men who work for the Bakers of Rome, an organized, powerful, and secret society. They kidnap children, and, after raping them, make them serve as workers or sell them overseas. Saturnine struggled, pulled free for a moment and made a garbled cry before he covered her mouth. In a moment she knew her world had changed, but it came to her, too, that she had already lost her life.

A man's deep voice broke the night. "Let her go," he said.

The man's hold slackened. He dropped Saturnine and walked away. The other, a tall black-skinned man, bent down to her. He had the darkest skin Saturnine had ever seen. He smelled like fresh straw.

"I'm sorry," he said, his natural voice deep and sonorous, "about Philo."

She could hardly understand—who he was and why he spoke to her—but Philo's name on his lips penetrated, as if piercing her.

"Saturnine," he said. He had to say her name several times before she responded.

At last she looked up. "You know me?" she said.

He smiled. "I am Kharapan," he said, as if she must have

heard of him. "I'm a friend of your… maidservant, Flavia."
He paused. "She asked me to follow you tonight, to watch
over you."

"My maidservant knows you?" Saturnine couldn't
understand.

Kharapan sat on the ground, his long arms resting on
bent knees. "I've known her a long time," he said, as if to
himself. "Of course, I wasn't supposed to introduce myself,
but the world…"

Saturnine felt confused wonder: the pale, dutiful woman,
her own maidservant, had this exotic secret friend.

The night mixed with silence. To Saturnine it seemed as
if she and this strange man were alone in a new awful world.

"He studied philosophy," Saturnine said after a time.
"Not magic. He needed to think and work. He thought better
to die than not to think at all, not to live." She stared defiantly
at the dark man.

"His life, his passion, is a model to us," Kharapan said.

"I know," she said with a vehemence that made Kharapan
smile. She was also surprised at his words and grew silent.

How strange this night, this moment—and its consequences. But Kharapan felt conflicted. To Kharapan,
knowledge resided in lives, in Saturnine's father's life for
instance, the father she did not know about. He would have
liked to speak of Flavia too—the maidservant that was Saturnine's true mother. But given events of the night, besides all
of the rest, he could not. Still, with Saturnine at last, he had
to speak while he had the chance, in spite of the night, no,
because of the night and all that had happened.

He told her Philo would have loved Chi, his country, it's official name Hellenica. The people of his country, he said, believed that individuals had a core or essence in the nature of a 'supreme fiction'—a particular passion that led and guided one to the good life. There were as many cores as rational creatures, and no core was better or worse than another. It didn't matter if a rational creature loved being a blacksmith, scholar, politician, or something less easily defined.

Civilization has its own core, its own supreme fiction, he said. "A man might find that his core conflicted with the core of his civilization. The core of my country is different from Rome's. Chi has a core of mystery, if I can put it that way, of trying to develop what we don't know. In fact, we are a godless people, one might say."

Saturnine's thoughts touched the hard shell of meaning, if not meaning itself; she sensed the mysterious dark inside.

I am sure he told her something of the following: that if one didn't follow his core and work to know himself, he put his life at risk. One could die in spirit, be the walking dead. A person risked more by failing to live his core, even if it didn't seem that way to her now: he put others at risk and even failed to serve civilization. The pursuit of our passions, Kharapan likely told her, moved society toward freedom. The passionate engagement with one's core pushed against the restrictions imposed by laws (those abstractions), and provided the space, the freedom for each rational creature to live. One who did not follow his core failed to make the right moral decisions, as well as ruined or wasted years of his life. The danger was severe and remained hidden; that is, without practice in remaining true to one's core, one couldn't know the nature and extent of the danger until it was too late. One might look back on one's life, but it would be too late, and then one would look back with regret.

Saturnine might have been surprised at his words and his serious manner but events of this night made her believe him a spirit-savior.

Kharapan didn't know if she grasped what he was saying, or if it would be of any use to her. She had her head on her knees, and she watched him. He would have liked to have given her an example of how events could compromise one's integrity. He thought of his own experience of moral failure. To speak of it would give Saturnine an example of what could go wrong, of what one risked. He hated secrets, but one secret within him seemed to have the force of nature, this secret he had kept so many years. The experience and 'the secret' involved the murder of a monk in Chi, and Kharapan's role in events. He kept this secret because it involved the welfare and safety of Chi itself. But the need to keep these events secret did not prevent him from telling Saturnine; rather, the circumstances involving the monk seemed too close to what he couldn't say or would stumble over. The monk's death and the death of Justin, her father, though separate, tangled in his mind.

"What is this place, Chi?" she said.

"It's called Hellenica, and it's south of Roman Egypt."

"Not in Rome?"

"No."

It seemed to Saturnine that worlds broke. He was a barbarian. She'd heard barbarians were savages but to her it made him seem an even more exotic spirit-savior.

Kharapan reached into his sack and pulled out a dark object. "It's lead," he said. "A kiln transforms lead as wisdom transforms thinking. Ach! The more I learn, the more I know how little I know." He held out the lead and dropped it into the small hand that reached toward him. "I'd be wiser if I could be happy knowing I know nothing."

Saturnine held the cold substance, even blacker than Kharapan. She bent her head and cried.

A golden cat paused in front of them and stared with burning yellow eyes. A rumor told that Cleopatra brought the first cat to Rome.

Saturnine wiped her eyes and said she would return to the forum. They stood. They walked side by side, a small girl in a black cloak, and a tall man moving evenly with his walking stick, his sack flung over his shoulder, his rust-orange clothes loose and easy about him. A few stragglers wandered the streets. The forum was deserted, the buildings shadowed in darkness. A long time ago the buildings had been inaugurated, after which the augurs said that the buildings had been "defined and freed," but it seemed, even to the augurs, that the gods had abandoned the buildings.

Saturnine had lost her sandals, and barefoot she stepped on damp cobblestones. A pile of burnt wood and ash were the only indication of the night's events, a mound of thin black leaves, some floating without breeze. Saturnine bent near the ash. The damp smell of smoke permeated their senses and clung to their skin and clothes as if the remains of Philo made an alchemical attempt at life.

The sun slipped through night. The moon disappeared and left them in the tentative first morning. Saturnine knew to leave. People would think they had conspired with Philo or were involved in the black arts. Indeed, rumors spread that evil spirits congregated near the stake where the boy had burned, only disappearing with the light of day.

Kharapan took Saturnine to her domus, and when he left she believed she would see him again, even the next day, but she did not. She believed—all through the ten years that passed, even if Flavia wouldn't speak of Kharapan or admit anything—that she would see Kharapan again, that he was a guardian like a spirit in her life.

Six

THAT SAME DAY, after Lupicinus's visit to Victorinus's domus, he saw Victorinus at the bath and gave him a curt nod. Victorinus cringed, thought he secretly cringed at Lupicinus's small wrinkled potbellied body. The comparison of Lupicinus's flabby figure to his own manly form probably gave him courage.

An old manservant paused before disturbing his master. Lupicinus rocked back and forth on his red lounge, unaware of being watched. "Truth. Honesty," he whispered. He spat in his urn.

The manservant knocked and approached. "You have a visitor, my Lord. Victorinus Marcus."

Lupicinus didn't respond for a time. He waved a hand, disturbed by the rustling of the slave's robe. "Bring him here."

"Your red room, sir?" He retreated at Lupicinus's threatening look.

Lupicinus rose, brushed his robes, and looked at his reflection in the small hand mirror at his desk. His eyes, when he forced them open, were a little bright, but otherwise his face revealed nothing of his mood. He replaced the mirror, returned to his lounge, and turned when Victorinus entered. But he did not stand.

A downpour had followed the balmy day. Gusts of rain hammered against red terra cotta shutters. Victorinus closed the door behind him. He felt sudden anger at his wife for forcing him on this awkward errand, and he wondered why he hadn't forced a promise from her to convert. He walked with a controlled stride to the shutters and stood next to them as if contemplating the outdoors. He listened to the rain.

The small elegant red room felt stifling and too intimate for Victorinus's taste. He was surprised by, and dismayed at, the sudden intimacy. The furnishings included one lush red lounge studded with gold and jewels, a small round backless chair at the glistening wooden desk, curiously missing a Bible. The room had no Christian symbols or markings, and the walls were covered in red. The room glowed a soft crimson in the lamplight. It had a familiar smell, a dank smell that Victorinus associated with old men. And yet, he couldn't help wondering whether Lupicinus was saintly. A fire in the intricately carved portable iron heater made the small room too warm. My name isn't old, Victorinus thought—but he was a popular senator and was ascending toward even greater status in Empire.

"I came to apologize about my wife," he said, facing Lupicinus.

"Husband and wife should be a model of Christian fidelity and friendship," Lupicinus said.

The smaller man sat perfectly still. He had no lines of laughter or anger, nothing to reveal the range of emotion in a man's life. Victorinus envied this outward calm and thought it evinced goodness. He was suddenly almost glad for the way his wife had rattled Lupicinus.

"Her father died recently," Victorinus said, walking across the room, holding his white toga close. He understood the pain of losing one's parents, but he hated the weakness he suspected he had inherited from his mother. Grief affected him too much like a woman.

"You need a son," Lupicinus said.

Victorinus stood still, awkward without a place to sit, and yet, he thought, I am beautiful. He tried not to be a man of reflection, but the oppressiveness of the room turned his thoughts inward. It's true, he thought. Cornelia hadn't borne him a son. Was Lupicinus suggesting divorce? His heart quickened, and he held back a desire to touch his neck to feel the throb of his heart. He would not be faulted for divorcing her if she were barren. But what of love? Cornelia had slipped into his life, an exotic colt, unpredictable, unformed. He loved to make love to her and to consider her as his own. He knew she was faithful, and he was more faithful to her than many men, many senators to their wives.

Forgetting himself, he turned from Lupicinus and rubbed his hands, generating an eruption of sound. He stopped abruptly, frustrated at his own display. He imagined amusement in Lupicinus's face, but whatever Victorinus might have seen faded, and he couldn't be sure of anything.

The thought that something unholy infested his wife's

thoughts made Victorinus uneasy. He liked the image of Christ, a man. The fact that Cornelia mentioned Philo that day didn't ease his fears, and yet, Christians believed that demons infested all non-orthodox minds.

One murky thought rose above other murky thoughts. Where is truth? Was it in his love for Cornelia? Was it in success, his place in Empire? Was it in Christ, in this man called God?

Some grasp truth but briefly, as the touch of wind on a leaf, a cold breeze that can't be grasped. Truth becomes a memory that is misunderstood. Others have to work hours every day in search of a truth, any truth, and might find one that they cling to for life. Sometimes a man's truth turns out to have been false all along.

"Constantine's sons only threatened him in the end," Victorinus said, stupidly he thought. He was only one and thirty, and Cornelia only twenty; they had time yet for children.

Lupicinus said nothing, a pause that weighed heavily on Victorinus.

Lupicinus smiled. "There's no problem with *your* person, Victorinus. There was a great man named Saturninus, a Christian Martyr in Carthage." Lupicinus paused. "The name is not the man: calling her Cornelia doesn't change her essence."

Victorinus bowed his head. "There are many mixed marriages in Rome," he said.

Lupicinus was expressionless.

Victorinus wasn't sure what had just passed, but he felt the conversation at an end. "You'll come to dinner on *Mars*, my Lord," he said, wincing at his uncertain tone.

Lupicinus confirmed that he would go. Perhaps he looked forward to the dinner. It was true: the church had an interest in Victorinus. The man was tractable. But Lupicinus wasn't thinking of Victorinus.

"You won't be disappointed," Victorinus said, his eager voice betraying relief. He paused before going out. He hoped Lupicinus would mention the Church's interest in him or make a request, but Lupicinus said nothing.

"Please know that I am at your service," Victorinus said with a low bow. He was glad to leave. He breathed easier outside in the dark humid air.

Lupicinus lay back after Victorinus left.

He thought of Saturnine (with that name, even then). He couldn't stop thinking of her in the way one's thoughts touch upon some old, menacing, irrational feeling. In trying to understand his discomfort and feeling annoyed at the power she had over him (in making him think of her), he suspected his discomfort was related to his past, the time before he converted to Christianity when as a Godless boy he had been filled with simple ambition, hope, and plans to speak his own mind. He'd sacrificed this dream of truth. Saturnine dared to speak her atheist mind; she even believed it honorable. It was this, he thought: his old life, his old thoughts, his old dream, his sacrifice that she brought to mind as if fresh within him.

Peronius, a tawny-complected boy, entered. Lupicinus unfolded his robes and raised a hand to call the boy over.

Lupicinus reflected. Since his conversion to Christianity at thirteen, even before, since that meeting of the bishops, his dream had changed. Since then, he dreamt of civilizing the masses. This was not, perhaps, the highest dream a man such as Lupicinus might have. His was a dream of order and unity, one in which the extravagances of men would be subdued— "tamed," Lupicinus would say. Christianity would tame the people and bind them in civilization. Civilization.

SEVEN

IN BED THAT night, Lupicinus let memories expand. He gave himself over to them mostly in grief, but also with some satisfaction.

He'd converted to Christianity at thirteen as a result of a striking insight. One day he saw a large number of bishops enter the former imperial house owned by a family friend, the presbyter Vitus, representative to Bishop Julius. Lupicinus, small for his age, slipped in with the bishops. It turned out that they had been summoned from all over the empire to hold a council to discuss accusations against Athanasius, the bishop of Alexandria.

Athanasius had been expelled for his orthodoxy, which was in opposition to the Arian creed of the emperor. Lupicinus listened in astonishment at the explosion over a word: Arians argued that Christ was of like substance to the Father, homoiousiou. The orthodox, like Athanasius, argued that Christ was of the same substance and same being, homoousions. Lupicinus struggled to understand. But then he did.

No one cared about the man, about Athanasius. Some feared: how would they go to heaven if they didn't have the right word? But the rage, a contagious rage, came from the idea of the secular power dangling before them, a limitless earthly glory if one side had bishops in power and an emperor on their side. And power depended on putting forth the right word, the word of God.

A sinking sensation came over Lupicinus. The thought— This is a world power—came to him with such force it was like the voice of God. He'd imagined Christianity filled with fanatics, powerful but irrelevant, on the outskirts of the true power of Empire. He saw that he'd been wrong. Christianity, he understood, had the potential to control every man's thoughts, a power even above an emperor's, if Christian emperors now use this same power and enforce it. They had God's word. Christians who held the right word, God's word, would rule minds. A Christian Kingdom would constitute a civilization for all people, surpassing the Roman Empire itself.

After the bishops' meeting, that night long ago, in front of the fireplace in his bedroom, an unfamiliar sensation came over Lupicinus. He trembled as he felt on the verge of a decision he knew would change his life. He had two not-quite-equal forces at work within him. He stood in front of sweet food unable to restrain himself from taking it, lacking fortitude, even if he knew that restraint would result in a greater reward in the long run, the promise of a moral, open, and honest life. Perhaps he had not received enough practical experience to know himself and the meaning of a good life. He sensed a valid and deeply intriguing challenge to oppose the Church, to expose what he believed was absurdity. He could be a noted intellectual. Even then he knew his powers. But such a life would banish him to the margins of society. The Church would acquire power regardless of his small life, regardless of his truth or his lies. Instead, and this was the other force working in him, he could share in the power of the Church. He felt weak in the face of such temptation.

Lupicinus justified his decision and believed throughout most of his life in his justification. That night in his youth he formed the foundations of an idea that would last almost all of his life. As he aged, his idea only became more sophisticated. Later, when he looked back, he couldn't be sure how much he'd understood as a boy. Regardless, he never doubted (not for most of his life): if he made the decision to convert due to desire for power, still, he convinced himself, the decision had been inevitable given what he'd understood, given his powers to understand the nature of the world.

If Christians owned the word of God, Lupicinus thought, then it was they that defined what human beings must believe. They provided the rules and subject matter for each person's innermost thoughts, created a bond of community, a community of mind unknown before in human history. Christianity stood to create a civilization so unified that it invaded and conquered the minds of men. Other religions claimed to know God's truth but didn't have God's words, didn't force people to believe, only to worship, didn't have the hierarchy of the Church. (Here, he had to admit Saturnine's relative perspicacity.) With emperors, armies, and law behind the Church, everyone would at least have to pretend to believe or be destroyed. One might wish to be rid of religion if it had such a cost. But Lupicinus believed, felt convinced at the time and for a great many years afterward, that culture couldn't exist without God. Individuals might question the existence of God, but the godless did not shape civilization. And if humanity had no choice but accept God, to submit, then the Christian church with its one God, the mythlike power of the Trinity, might be seen as religion's pinnacle. Christianity would form and contain the highest civilization for man.

Christianity left no place for truth. He recognized that. A great man must sacrifice his own truth and devote himself to society, to the masses and empire. He must lie to protect and preserve the faith of others for the good of a unified world, for civilization. This, the lie of faith, became the highest moral good to his way of thinking.

So formed the hard parts of his mind.

The boy, Lupicinus, went to Vitus in the early morning following the bishop's meeting. He boldly strode into Vitus's office ahead of others and shut the door, leaning against it, his face full of wonder.

"Lupicinus. What is it?" Vitus knew the boy's family, which, like his own, moved in the highest circles.

"I was at the meeting of the bishops."

Vitus shrugged. "You're welcome." He smiled politely at the pagan boy, thinking of some urgent business that he had to attend to.

In the pause Lupicinus might have said nothing. But he stepped forward. He committed himself to his first lie. "Christ came to me last night," he said.

Vitus paused. "How did Jesus visit you, in what form?"

"He told me to learn the teachings of Athanasius, he made me swear never to accept another's." Lupicinus placed his faith in orthodoxy from an intuitive understanding of its vision: in orthodoxy one had to go through the Church to have access to God; this gave the Church tremendous power. Besides, he guessed that Vitus supported Athanasius.

Lupicinus saw the sparkle in Vitus's eyes.

Lupicinus explained how he'd dreamt awake, not sleeping, but dreaming still. Christ floated above him. God's words entered his mind and warmth spread through his body. Tears filled his eyes as he spoke.

Perhaps Vitus didn't believe Lupicinus, but that didn't prevent him from announcing the miracle of Christ's visit to a pagan boy. Christ visited an innocent pagan boy, and sent the boy, a new believer, to them as a sign, he said, so that they would clear Athanasius of the accusations against him. Whether the bishops believed this tale, whether certain bishops suspected Vitus of inventing this rather brilliant idea, didn't matter; the miracle shifted favor to Athanasius. Others gave in. Lupicinus's first move in the Christian world reestablished a bishop in Alexandria. The boy's name spread across Empire. Lupicinus couldn't help wonder if Christ *had* visited him.

They baptized Lupicinus. As a Christian without faith, the lies, the words he used that he diligently studied in what they called canonical texts, transformed Lupicinus's life and caused a revolution in his relationship to others. He had to hide his true mind. As he grew, as he studied Christian texts and gained control over their words, there seemed to be no end to the power he might command. The closer he identified with Christianity, the more cloaked in public goodness, merit or truth irrelevant, the greater influence he had over Empire. Lies built upon lies thrusting him on his path like a vessel carried by currents. Christ's willing vessel. His rise seemed to confirm the accuracy of his vision: his attachment to orthodoxy proved more insightful as the orthodox gained power, and orthodoxy unified the Church. Over time, he fortified the reasoning behind his decision to convert, until he thought of himself as the Guardian of Civilization.

The bishop of Rome and his advisor, Vitus, brought Lupicinus into their inner circle. When someone made a passing biblical comment, Lupicinus murmured the citation to the gospel like God in the back of the room. He became a personal favorite of a succession of bishops. In his twenties, when the Arian emperor Constantius II exiled the orthodox Bishop Liberius to Thrace because the bishop refused to condemn Athanasius, Lupicinus advised Liberius, and three years later, Liberius returned to Rome and his bishopric. Lupicinus convinced Liberius to compromise his position at the council of Sirmium, to pretend that he no longer supported Athanasius. They would bide their time, like a black widow before she strikes. Lupicinus learned to monitor the movement of opinion like a sailor at the top of a mainsail testing the winds.

Lupicinus understood how his first lie to Vitus sealed his fate to some extent. The exercise of justifying that original lie made it easier for him to justify other immoral acts. He hadn't strengthened moral rigor but opened a floodgate of justifications. However, if he committed inhumane acts, he might be said to have humane reflections: he looked into the face of himself. At times, he wondered: What is moral pain in a world that is empty of God and empty of meaning? Whatever its purpose, he accepted his punishment, this pain, this guilt. Pain meant nothing, he told himself; it meant nothing in or to the world. All of the violence to build a Kingdom was necessary for the good of a civilized world.

Truth simmered within him: he learned to grapple with the impulse to confess. In the early days, he hid behind the fortress of a squint. His vision grew worse with age. He no longer needed to force a squint, but perspicacity grew as his eyes became weaker. The body ages, but reason doesn't depreciate with age: two and two make four, regardless of a shriveled body, Plato said. Lupicinus earned a reputation for a somber demeanor.

But the dead lived in his fluids, and the pain didn't cease.

In the prime of his life, history turned to favor orthodox Christians. After pagan emperor Julian's death, and a short rule by Jovian, Christian sects scrambled in intense opposition to know the creed of the new emperor: homoousians, Arians, semi-Arians, eunomians, anomoeans, homoeans crowded the streets and crossroads in a holy race. Valentinian, an Orthodox Christian, became emperor. Tall and majestic, cruel and superstitious, he enacted laws against magic and bloody sacrifices; he promoted soldiers and bureaucrats, but his instatement gave rule to the Orthodox, the power of an Empire. At the time, the bishopric of Rome became a prize: an Orthodox bishop would have enormous power with a Catholic emperor behind him. Battles raged in the outer territories against barbarians who threatened the Empire, but another battle roiled in the heart of Rome. To them, what took place in Rome was the world and meant the world. Lupicinus himself had not been innocent in the murder of a hundred people in the Basilica of Julius, slaughtered with machetes. Catholics, with Bishop Damasus as their ruthless general, fought a war as fiercely as necessary. Catholics won the prize. Damasus became bishop of Rome. Lupicinus could not even remember all of the violence he'd plotted or encouraged, but besides this, he'd played a more intimate hand in death.

Lupicinus had been in his forties, sure of his powers, heedless, when Maximin's trials had begun in Rome—evil, sorcery, black magic. The trials resulted in the execution of many Christians but most by far were pagan. After quick trials, one after another, man or woman of old pagan name was burned at the stake, head chopped off, or made part of the gory fair at the amphitheater. The trials, these events in Rome, masked and overshadowed the Church's own violence and internal wars. The Church would emerge glorious and unscathed, and the trials proved that rich pagan men and women had no stronghold in Rome. The trials purged pagan Rome, if not to eliminate them entirely, at least they stoned the terrain like Roman roads to enable Christians to march in and conquer. So Lupicinus believed.

One day, Lupicinus made a show of being a dutiful son and paid a visit to his mother, a staunch but godless pagan, who performed the outward duties of her religion but was not attached to belief. He noticed a gaunt, but attractive slave boy.

"Who is that boy?"

His mother, small and attractive, prouder of her keen intellect than her name, wealth, or clothes, admonished him—didn't he recognize Achaleus? Achaleus's father had been the slave that Lupicinus and his brother and sisters called Doctor, an intelligent man, knowledgeable in arts, medicine, bookkeeping, well read in classics, and proficient in rhetoric. Achaleus was the Doctor's son.

His mother's gaze made him uneasy. As the youngest child, the youngest son, he'd spoken freely to her before he turned thirteen; she'd loved his mind and more than tolerated his godlessness. She had been shocked by his decision to convert. But he couldn't bear to tell her the truth. Perhaps he feared that if he told her his mind, she would convince him to take a more upright path. He suspected she knew that he lied. Since his conversion at thirteen, their relationship had been strained. Recently she'd asked why he'd never attempted to claim the title of bishop. He didn't want it. He admitted to himself that he'd never wanted the administrative duties or show, that he kept his freedom and strengthened his power without title. His vague role gave him an aura of mystery; and his lies about faith, or, often more accurately, the silences he kept, distanced him from others and added to the myth, the myth of himself. In fact, Lupicinus might have admitted: he wanted to be thought a saint—to be remembered and documented in the annals of history as a saint! Besides, he could engage in Church affairs, direct its course, but retreat to his domus where he worked on studies of his own.

He didn't stay long on any visit with his mother and

avoided his family as much as possible, but his interest in Achaleus lured him to his mother's domus. Lupicinus thought only of his own desire. His mother must have been distressed by the trials and the deaths of friends and acquaintances; she must have feared; she had burned scrolls and codices, but he didn't speak to her of the trials—at first, because it was dangerous to speak out loud, and later because he could see the benefit of the trials to the Church. His family thought him equally at risk, but he had too much power. Maximin would not accuse the pope of a crime or the one shrouded by the pope's right hand.

Achaleus wasn't classically beautiful, but he had a way of moving that captured Lupicinus. Achaleus's naïve belief in love enchanted and unsettled Lupicinus: a love where one shared everything. Lupicinus didn't know at the time that this would destroy them.

Lupicinus advised Achaleus on books to read; they discussed literature and philosophy and art. Achaleus bent to his will when Lupicinus made sexual overtures; bewilderment overshadowed joy. Achaleus looked to Lupicinus with such respect, he could hardly speak. And for a time, they had an ecstatic love. Achaleus went to Lupicinus's domus often and Lupicinus begged his mother to free him—she promised to do so in her will—but she assumed Achaleus was one of Lupicinus's temporary pleasures. Lupicinus made her give Achaleus a private room so he could go there, and Lupicinus often snuck in and out by a back door like a street creature.

The nagging lie of his faith in Christ created a chasm between them. Achaleus felt it from the first, although he didn't understand. Achaleus thought Lupicinus a pure and devoted man; because of his love for Lupicinus, he had a natural, gentle curiosity about Christianity, but his questions pained Lupicinus. Lupicinus didn't want Achaleus to convert. Achaleus took it as an insult. For a long time Lupicinus didn't tell Achaleus the truth.

Achaleus began to change toward him. Achaleus thought that Lupicinus had power over him, but Lupicinus didn't want power. He felt Achaleus had the true power. Achaleus became filled with spite. He bought statues of gods from the market—coarse, gaudy things; he filled his room with them, but it only made Lupicinus laugh; he thought they had a certain disgusting charm. Achaleus spoke against the Church, and that hardly bothered Lupicinus. Then Achaleus painted a devil on the wall, behind his mirror and showed it to Lupicinus. Lupicinus understood and warned him of the danger to the domus, but his warning only inspired Achaleus to more foolish acts. He piled half-burnt books—writings by charlatans—in the corner of his room, barely hidden beneath a rag.

Achaleus found another way to upset Lupicinus. He went to the forum where boys gathered around a man who called himself a philosopher; this philosopher professed to be a poet and took an interest in Achaleus. He guided Achaleus, eager for knowledge. Lupicinus grew jealous. He feared that if he didn't tell the truth, Achaleus wouldn't have a chance to love him; Achaleus would never truly know him. Instead Achaleus became infatuated with a mediocre poet.

Lupicinus told Achaleus the truth about his lies. At last,

Achaleus understood. At first he felt sad for Lupicinus and begged him to give up his duplicity. Achaleus didn't understand Lupicinus's refusal, and again they were unreconciled. Achaleus threatened to tell his mother and others; he repeated his threat even when they weren't fighting. He'd get a glint in his eyes and ask, as if innocently, what the bishop would think if he knew about Lupicinus. Lupicinus laughed and told him that the bishop was an atheist too. But, in fact, Achaleus disturbed Lupicinus.

Lying in bed one night, Lupicinus reflected that Achaleus was the mistake of his life. Added to the discomfort of Lupicinus's constant jealousy was the thought of how he would be the subject of ridicule, vulnerable to a servant boy. The world's view pierced him. He felt an old man, his invincibility pierced. The arguments had exhausted him. Lupicinus had begun to take on other lovers, even if he had no joy in them. The idea came to him and grew stronger that one more death would be nothing. It seemed a reasoned decision and not one of passion.

He acted quickly, without questioning himself, as if he knew that doubt, hesitation, would hobble him. He rose one night, took his knife (it had been his father's), and went to his mother's domus. There he found Achaleus sleeping. As he watched his peaceful face, anger and rage filled him. He stabbed Achaleus in the heart. Achaleus gasped and opened his eyes: he put his hands on Lupicinus's hands holding the knife. Achaleus's body shook. Lupicinus turned the knife in the boy's flesh.

I must pause, for a moment.

Lupicinus thought he had control of his reason. He took the knife out of Achaleus's body. He saw nothing, thought nothing. He walked out of his room and returned home. He didn't even hide the knife dripping bloodily at his side. He'd forgotten, or had not thought of, the statues of gods or the drawing of the devil or the half-burnt papyri in Achaleus's room. He thought everyone would know who killed Achaleus, and he suddenly didn't care. But that's not what happened, although his mother knew the truth.

A servant found Achaleus. More than an ordinary clamor occurred; the domus, overlooked before by the powers of Rome, inevitably attracted notice. Servants discovered strange texts in Achaleus's room, and when they cleared furnishings to be cleaned and made whole, they uncovered Achaleus's scratched devil on the wall. Fear overcame the household. Wreaths circled the domus to ward off evil spirits. Maximin ordered an investigation.

At first, Lupicinus felt stunned. Quickly, quickly, it all went so fast—Maximin held brief trials and sentenced his mother and others in the household to death for conspiring in black arts. No one blamed Lupicinus or even mentioned his name. Lupicinus existed like a shadow in the background of worldly events, pushed there it seemed, but when he thought it through, he understood and felt powerless. The death of an evil demon might be a holy act. If he admitted killing Achaleus, he might be considered a hero for protecting Rome. Bishop Damasus would place the story in that light. If he cried for them to punish him, or tried to save his mother, he'd be respected for his honesty, his natural feeling.

If he admitted everything—explained that he'd lied about his faith, how it angered Achaleus and how Achaleus tried to hurt him by playing with hell's fire—his admission would either be ignored or would convict him too of conspiring with the devil. He'd be killed like his mother.

Lupicinus convinced himself that the death sentence of his mother, by the time it happened, was beyond his control, beyond what he could be held responsible for. He convinced himself that it was beyond him spiritually, in a sense. He had a new family in his followers, the people of Christ; it wasn't hardness but truth. In the strange carnival of the world, Rome, Empire, everything was turned upside down. Everyone pretended, and lies became the thing that was wholly believed and true—as events in the world proved.

He'd been angry with his mother, too, at first. His mother had no right to cling to the past and no right not to see the future, Rome itself, in the Church. He'd felt guilty relief (I will reveal all): for if they killed his mother, they would also eliminate that knowing, penetrating look.

One cannot foresee one's bodily burdens. One doesn't know how the dead cling to one. If so, one might do anything—even join death—to avoid that burden.

Lupicinus watched his mother's execution. A silver blade caught a glint of light. He thought he saw the defiant look on her regal face, the honest face of ancient Rome. The blade hesitated in the canvas sky. Her head dropped into a peasant basket.

Horror filled his marrow, thick and consuming. Time, he guessed, would enable him to stand it; time would wash his memories in brine, scrape horror thin; but time didn't conform. As years passed, there might have been hours, perhaps days, when he didn't think of his mother or Achaleus, but memory was more than a brutal shudder. One death and then another sank into his being like pebbles, not only that of his mother and Achaleus but countless others, the people of Rome. They sank into his being like pebbles. He vowed not to go mad, not to kill himself. He had no right. He would live until he died of a natural cause or at someone's hand. One day, he thought, he would become the harmless material of dust. But even ashes—the ashes of those called saints—might have immortal power and continue the lies of the Church.

Could Lupicinus have acted otherwise? He tortured himself with what might have been. He relived details, moments, events formed of immutable acts. The danger of his faults—how he gloried in his power—had gone unperceived. He hadn't had the sense to be cautious. If, when he was thirteen, he'd entered Vitus's chambers and didn't tell that first lie…. But, no, he convinced himself: that first lie couldn't have been otherwise. He had seen the truth of the Church and civilization. He had no choice, having seen. But he might have sensed danger; he'd had a heedless belief in his illimitable power; he might have been more cautious and wary. His faults heightened to a crescendo, to an explosion of lust, power, and shame, and thrust him into a heightened level of lies and immorality.

And yet, Lupicinus had merely been devoted to an idea, as devoted as any ordinary Christian who killed for what he called faith. He'd cut Achaleus's life short—made the decision so that he, Lupicinus, could live and continue his lies in support of the Orthodox Church.

Lupicinus, along with his brother, inherited great wealth on his mother's death. He donated large sums to the Church and helped build a monastery in the Egyptian desert. His reputation grew. The people of Rome, of Empire, thought him a generous honorable man. Lies upon lies, a conspiracy of lies, the world wanting his lies, insisting on lies: and the contract he'd made with his Idea, he knew, was irrevocable. If his vision had been wrong, if the Church crushed men rather than granted a unified world, if the Church would not create in the end a great civilization for man, then his vision of himself, of his entire life, all he'd done, would have to change. He would have to recognize himself as evil. He would have to see himself as a savage. Yes, events solidified his dependence on his Idea: believing he was correct about the Church's capacity to form a world civilization allowed Lupicinus to hold up his head. And he was too old for grand reversals and revelations. So he thought—even up to the time of this chronicle and for many years after.

The events of his past changed nothing, so Lupicinus believed: not the stream of fate, not the development of the Church, not the fact that the Church served as foundation for civilization. What had happened pained and tortured Lupicinus, but there was no salvation. One might have an image of an ideal, the sage, and judge every scratchy fault against such a smooth exemplary ideal. Lupicinus was gouged, but he wasn't ruined. He held onto his Idea, and the Idea was true. It existed apart from him. It existed in the world.

EIGHT

MARS, FIVE KALENDS *of Martius*, the first light of day: slaves labored in halls, buckets clashed, lamps tinkled, and Saturnine thought, here is the noise, the bee making, the fungus. The tide of hours moved them steadily on the path forged by Rome.

Flavia set a plate of dried fish, garum, bread, and a flask of water next to Saturnine's bed. The day, the anniversary, ten years after the day Philo was killed and Kharapan saved Saturnine's life, made them both think of Flavia's secrets. But for Saturnine, it would be the first anniversary she would not let herself even pay homage to Philo by reading his work or burning one candle to his memory.

Birds chirped and dived as Saturnine, Flavia, and the female slaves walked to the bath. The smell of damp earth rose as they joined the march of women, wealthy and poor, slaves and citizens of a great civilized world. Mosaics of multi-colored glass covered the walls of the magnificent front chambers of the bathhouse in the shape of the Pantheon.

Through an archway, Saturnine saw women conducting games and exercises on an expanse of grass and, farther back, wrestling with each other in mud. Strolling down the great hall, she acknowledged acquaintances, wives of those who could benefit Victorinus; she paid respect to a great lady and spoke of the weather and the games. A brown skinned, full-bodied slave, wrapped in a tunic, escorted her and the servants to the cloakroom and gave them towels. They undressed and paused at the sudatoria, slipping on sandals before stepping onto the hot floor. When Saturnine grew faint, the servants followed her into the calidarium, a large room with a tub of hot water. The full-bodied bath attendant asked to scrape Saturnine with a strigil and took up Saturnine's limbs, scraping each one with absentminded courtesy, flicking the scrapings onto the wall, onto the black-green rot that the doctors collected for medicines. Saturnine and her servants continued past the tepidarium to the frigidarium outside where Saturnine walked into an extensive cold pool, submerging herself, surrounded by the light and dark blue tiles of Neptune. She relaxed in the corner of the pool, wondering why she didn't find everything she wished for in this good life.

But the day, thoughts, memories of Philo and Kharapan and the years that followed, haunted her; she sunk in the water of that life, that *disappearance*. She saw Flavia at a distance near a wall and stared at her, even after Flavia looked away.

In the early days following Philo's death, in anger, in defiance of a world, in loyalty to Philo, in the nearness of Kharapan's words urging, compelling, her to know herself, Saturnine had taken out Philo's scrolls. Her hands had trembled—and while Flavia monitored the door, she sat at her small desk and copied Philo's words into a parchment book of her own. Anger gave Saturnine a sense of being all-alive in the world. As years passed, she continued to write, even when Rome became eminently less dangerous if never free. Her anger grew weak in uncertainty and sadness. Still, the writing, her secret realm, a place outside of Rome, outside of cities and empires made her feel as if she existed. Later, the secrets she kept caused an unbearable strain, an intolerable abyss between her interior and exterior worlds.

After Philo's death, when Kharapan didn't return, after Flavia's refusal to speak about him, the thought of Kharapan, of what he'd said, his manner, made her suspicious, but of what she wasn't sure. She came to believe Kharapan had a special interest in her. While at first the idea gladdened her—like a spirit waiting to mark her future—she came to worry about a more mortal truth. She wondered if Kharapan had been Flavia's lover. Questions came to Saturnine's lips, but a look from Flavia silenced her. A person can stop another's words with an aura, an expression. Saturnine had a tingling fear, a sense of a truth she should not dare discover, and Flavia's manner inhibited any investigation. Later, Saturnine told herself that although Flavia might befriend a barbarian, she could not; moreover, it was proper to both her position and Flavia's that she didn't learn the details of Flavia's intimate life. Saturnine might reveal every nuance—every crime. But it was improper for Flavia to reveal the details of her life to her mistress. Now, in the cool water, she wondered; she felt somehow that these secrets between them amounted to a failure, another failure of her own to pursue the truth. And the thought that followed—'what matter'—felt like another failure.

After leaving the pool, she took a massage, after months of forgoing one. In a small room, warm from heated floors, Saturnine lay face down, naked on the tall bed. The dank air covered her like a blanket. A half-naked young man, a slave, entered.

He started to work on her back. She felt the movement of hands on a body that seemed to have forgotten its physical existence. "Wine," she said, and when he handed her the cup she drank quickly and handed it back.

She turned over when he beckoned, naked, exposed. He started on her legs, the oil making his hands melt into her skin. Her eyelids fluttered; she couldn't stop their mad flutter. It seemed to her she couldn't remain true to the role Rome determined for her, couldn't understand her position as a thing solid and true.

At last, he covered her with a soft towel and left.

She rolled on her side, curled on the bed.

Victorinus and Lupicinus arrived with their servants to the sound of a flute in the garden. Victorinus smiled to see his wife dressed in gold silk over a beige silk embroidered with gold flowers, wearing thick gold arm and neckbands inlaid with emeralds. Her dark hair was woven in complex waves— a preparation, Saturnine thought morosely, as her husband greeted her, that took up the entire day.

"You look beautiful," Victorinus said, taking up Saturnine's fingers in a formal gesture.

Lupicinus gave her a polite, restrained nod. But she didn't

have to make him love her, she thought. She had only to be demure and hope that he admired her husband.

Saturnine insisted they sit in the garden before dinner as they had on Lupicinus's first visit. She did not say so, but she insisted to overlay and obliterate Lupicinus's prior visit from everyone's memory. A fire burned in a portable iron heater. The three sat on pillowed chairs. The servants laid out delicacies and served a dark nectar-like wine. Lupicinus's servants stood in the background. Flavia stood near the wall behind Saturnine.

An expanse of time passed as they sat in the cold air. Victorinus, when speaking, paused to include his wife and Lupicinus, in case he had something to add.

Lupicinus couldn't restrain himself, and in such a pause said casually to Saturnine, "And how does a cat occupy her day?"

Saturnine, not understanding at first, flushed. She noticed Victorinus's face stiffen.

"I'm not sure what you mean!" she said. "If it's to remind us of our previous conversation, please don't. I wish it had been otherwise."

"If it causes you pain, I'll not say another word," he said. "However," he hesitated, "I wonder that you think the conversation so abhorrent when you merely expressed your beliefs, or should I say lack of belief."

She remained silent; she looked out at the grass. She could not deny it: she might burn her work and never write, but godless thoughts even now threatened her tongue.

It was then, I believe, or not long after, when a strange,

dark-skinned man emerged through the bushes and stood on the grass. Tall, calm, in spite of his dirty white robes, holding a walking stick, a leather bag over a shoulder, he seemed a creature metamorphosed out of an ancient past, a sage or prophet come to pass judgment on them all. The white robes, as dirty as they were, magnificently accentuated his dark skin. Perhaps in looking back I am making too much of him, this first time I saw him. Mud matted his curly hair, but his face was clean, and he wore a close, though not perfectly cut, beard. He studied them as if expecting something or expecting nothing at all.

"What's this?" Victorinus cried. "Get rid of that savage," he commanded a manservant.

"Stop," Saturnine said, standing.

The man's dark skin, walking stick, his loose clothes, and the meaning of the day, plus a glance at Flavia, head down as if frozen, confirmed Saturnine's suspicions. Ten years doesn't change a man as much as it does a ten-year old girl. In fact, Kharapan was always going to appear, it happened fatefully just then.

Saturnine, partly in fear, partly incredulously like a child, walked out on the grass.

"Cornelia," Victorinus said. Saturnine paused but did not look at him. She went to Kharapan.

A thickness of expectation fell over her. Kharapan's Ethiopian skin and woolly hair gave her pause, even a small shock. He smelled fresh, of saltwater and seaweed. The sun had burned his face red-black, and scales and fish blood blended with the dirt of his white dress.

"Kharapan," she said.

Eyes that studied her replaced his uncertain look. "Saturnine," he said, that gentle and deep voice. She smiled, felt tears, embarrassed tears, and blinked to hide them.

She instinctively held out a hand, as if to an acquaintance in Rome. A barbarian! She was struck by the wide gap between her adult world and her childish notions. She had not considered it, had not had to, but speaking to such a man… and yet, here she stood.

He took her hand, but she dropped her hand and blushed.

"You…." he paused, shaking his head. The need for lies already tangled his tongue. He couldn't control his wide smile. "A woman!" Of course, but it was an effort to join the girl and this woman in his thoughts. In fact, he was not so much older than her, perhaps fifteen years. "I arrived in Rome today," he said. "I realized the significance of the day within the hour and walked up the hill. I didn't take time for a bath. I didn't even dare that. And here you are."

He seemed quite astonished. "Flavia is there," she said confusedly. Both looked over, but Flavia would not look at them. Victorinus and Lupicinus sat in silence, staring at them. This moment seemed a pause, outside of a world, infinite, dark, timeless.

Saturnine turned away. She felt the old feeling: this man knew something about her, held some unaccountable, impossible role or relationship to her. She feared truth, feared it now. This day, this anniversary, meant something to him too. But as she faced the man himself, she felt foolish for her old fears, foolish and ungrateful. Of course he would remember that night; of course it would have been eventful for him as well.

"You made a deep impression on me," she said. "As a girl, I was sure I'd see you, or hear something…"

He looked pained.

In truth, Kharapan had remained much a part of her thoughts in all of the years that had passed since she'd met him.

Saturnine felt ashamed. She might have invested more meaning in him than facts warranted. Her imagination might have made him larger when, a friend of her maidservant's, he'd merely shown kindness to a girl, a maidservant's ward and young friend.

In an awkward silence between them, Saturnine bent her head. A new feeling filled Saturnine, an idea. She could not continue to stand in the grass, but there was more. She thought, here might be proof. Kharapan had come to mind during Lupicinus's last visit. Kharapan might offer a contrast to Lupicinus's view that there would be no civilization without God. Kharapan could tell them about the godless people of Chi. She hesitated still. Did she dare invite a man such as Kharapan—a barbarian!—to the table of a man such as Lupicinus? And yet, she felt she must. In the strangeness of the moment, she felt she had no choice. The moment, its elements, the anniversary, the conversation she'd had with Lupicinus, in which Kharapan was not far removed, all this conspired in her decision, if a decision it was. It seemed fated.

"Join us," she said in a low voice, more command than invitation.

Kharapan, surprised but with a conspiratorial smile, nodded. He might have noted Saturnine's courage in inviting him to join her senator husband and guest, but he didn't appreciate its extent, didn't know he'd meet a man of Rome with an ancient pagan name, a man intimate with the pope.

Saturnine, walking on the grass in front of him, paused and turned back, and said under her breath, "I hope you won't disappear before we have the chance to talk in private."

"I won't," he said, and his grave tone and look gave her a chill.

NINE

How can I relate that first meeting, that first conversation, which had such a profound effect on me, which led to events I document in this chronicle—those events I describe, even if history itself will fail to note them? I should say, to be clear—events began with Saturnine, our first meeting, first encounter, and even this encounter with Kharapan was her doing.

Kharapan knew that a man or woman of Rome would likely be curious about him. Over the years, he adopted his own style, a mixture of the clothes of his homeland—the billowy blue, orange, and green robes of the philosophic schools—with those of the Romans. For many years now he had worn white. No one is born in the city of Rome, the people said. The people of Rome might imagine him a peasant from Alexandria. But the elite of Rome, Kharapan knew, especially those who had indeed been born there, looked askance at anyone born outside of Rome and could hardly fathom the humanity of a barbarian.

Flavia, pale and severe, gave Kharapan a bold, unsurprised look before staring at the sky.

Saturnine returned in a strange rapture: flushed, smiling, shaking her head.

"Cornelia," Victorinus said in a low voice.

A look of confusion passed across Kharapan's face at the name he called her.

"It's Kharapan," Saturnine said in a low voice. "Kharapan. He saved my life ten years ago to this day. I have not seen him since."

"The barbarian!" Victorinus gasped.

As if a pure act of will, eyes glowing but deeply serious, Saturnine turned to Lupicinus. "The last time we met you said: what evidence that civilization exists without God," she said. "Here is my evidence. Kharapan is from Chi, or Hellenica it is called, a godless country, a country of cats. Isn't it so?" she turned to Kharapan, afraid suddenly that she'd misremembered, afraid too of throwing Kharapan at Lupicinus in this way as a kind of introduction! But she had little control of circumstances or herself.

Saturnine looked at Kharapan with fear, but Kharapan laughed. "I'm not sure about being a cat," he said, "but one might say that the people of Hellenica are more godless than your Epicureans, if that is what is meant. We meditate on *agnosis*, the unknown and unknowable." He shrugged. "There isn't much room for knowing one way or another about gods when one seeks to know or contemplate what one doesn't know."

Kharapan had smiling eyes. He looked from Lupicinus to

Victorinus. He was long experienced in conversations of this sort, arising in part from the contrast in him, a man of Hellenica and those of Rome. He delighted in discussions of this kind and was pleased to find himself having one, invited to it by no less than Saturnine on this day. Kharapan's manner, intelligence, and open sweet laugh silenced those around him and excited their curiosity. His charm undercut the precarious nature of his words. A few servants crossed themselves.

I am sure our pagan servants, let alone the Christian ones, looked upon Kharapan with amusement, even bewilderment. Pagans didn't quite know what to think of a man who disbelieved in gods. Atheism—the man who doesn't believe, who denies that gods exist, or denies that they take part in a human world, didn't amount to a crime in pagan Rome. It had been a crime to refuse to join the rites and festivals of the gods, to fail to make a show of worship, even if one didn't believe. Thoughts had not much mattered to them. But Christians cared very much about the thoughts of rational creatures. The Church had not officially acknowledged atheism. At the time, atheism was not documented by a religion that otherwise categorized and detailed every kind of thought. Atheism, at the time, had not yet been made a crime, perhaps because it had not yet been sufficiently understood as a threat to the Church (and yet atheism is the ultimate threat, I always understood that). At the time, and for a hundred years or more before, the Church had been focused inward, engaged in inner turmoil, one Christian sect battling another to prove and control the ultimate word of God. For many years, however, in Rome, the Orthodox Church, with the support of an emperor, and under Bishop Damasus, had had the leisure, one might say, to focus on those who were not Christian. Laws, inspired by bishops, made paganism a crime and allowed the destruction of temples. The question remained: How might an atheist, a disbeliever of Christ, and a potential denier of gods, fit into the Christian structure? For every mind must be defined by an all-inclusive religion. Surely such a man couldn't be accused of worshipping the devil, since he claimed not to believe in the devil, but still, surely he'd be accused of some evil?

"Cornelia, Saturnine," Victorinus said. Cornelia had one purpose, he must have thought: to ruin him. He couldn't grasp why she'd changed or what he'd done to deserve it.

The absurdity of the situation struck Saturnine. Head down, in doubt and confusion, she considered how to tell Kharapan to go, but Lupicinus came forward.

"I'll hear your evidence," Lupicinus said. His look at her held reluctant admiration.

"My Lord Lupicinus," Victorinus said, "this man's a barbarian, known to my wife's maidservant." He gestured at Flavia.

Lupicinus glanced at Flavia, wondering how this creature, blushing painfully, her eyes determinedly averted, knew a man from Hellenica.

"Even so, I'll hear," he said. "Remind me of this day if I ever say your entertainments aren't amusing," he added.

In fact, this man of Chi and Saturnine's challenge powerfully attracted Lupicinus. He felt agitation or excitement. He'd heard of Hellenica, a place known for its libraries, its philosophical schools, and old-style philosophic ways of life. He hadn't entirely believed, or perhaps refused to believe, that the place existed, and if it did exist, he'd allowed himself to believe it was hardly a place at all, barely civilization.

I note that Hellenica was a small country on the edge of Empire. Eight hundred years ago, Alexander, called the Great, ravaged humanity, but expanded Greek civilization to the larger world. After Alexander, philosophy and philosophic schools thrived in Egypt under the Ptolemies. At the time Romans conquered Egypt, about four hundred years ago, in a confusion of boundaries and changing administrations, a man named Labeo convinced Romans that it would benefit them to have a peaceful nation on the southern border of Egypt. A Treaty between Rome and Hellenica formed boundaries and rules, including ease of travel. The people of Hellenica paid an annual tribute to Romans in excess of an amount that would otherwise have been collected as a tax, and Hellenica continued as a prosperous country. Over the years, the way of life, the governments and cultures of Hellenica and Empire diverged. Hellenica became the last outpost, the resting place and heritage of Greek culture, of the philosophy that thrived there.

I don't know why these Hellenes called their country Chi. Perhaps it had something to do with what Plato said: that x symbolizes the soul of the world, the place where two bands cross.

Victorinus gave his manservant a nod. The young servant, scantily clad—even in the cold—took up a heavy chair with a thick red pillow from the wall, and Kharapan sat down. He smiled into the faces around him. His open expression made almost everyone smile. Victorinus was scandalized by how unselfconscious and relaxed this barbarian seemed at a table with those of Rome.

Saturnine sat down. Lupicinus seemed to look kindly and with interest on Kharapan. Victorinus's smoldering anger, his helplessness, made her regret. She felt uncertain: she'd thrown Kharapan out as evidence, but for what prize?

I note. I wonder: how it is that words between men might break open worlds, words exchanged that ring with the sound of discovery, truth.

"I'll tell Kharapan what he's up against," she said softly. "You don't mind if I try to relate our previous conversation?"

Lupicinus bowed his head, waved a hand (graciously) for her to continue.

In a dull voice, feeling a bit mad, Saturnine recounted the conversation, her three reasons for Christianity's rise in the Empire (here she blushed), and Lupicinus's claim that there could be no civilization without religion or superstition, that even the gods of Rome had formed an Empire. Without gods, Lupicinus had claimed, humans would be wild and independent cats in alleyways. Lupicinus, she said, believes that the Orthodox Church will form a great civilization, beyond Empire, for the entire world.

Saturnine noted Kharapan's serious expression. Kharapan's manner gave the moment weight and substance.

"Is my summary fair, my lord?" she said. She gave her husband a hopeful look, but he would not return it.

"Very fair, my dear," Lupicinus said. He leaned forward and studied Kharapan.

"I think, my lord," Kharapan said with a smile, "you, Lupicinus, are the cat."

Lupicinus felt slightly agitated, but not understanding, he waited.

"It would seem that you and Saturnine share a common interest," Kharapan went on. "Saturnine," he said. "You explore how Christianity came to be the core of Empire, that is, the reasons why it might become the Empire's supreme fiction. Lupicinus, you see that Christianity forms the new core, but in your case…" Kharapan paused. "I have to say something about my country's word 'core.' I told you about it once," he said to Saturnine.

"I remember," she said softly.

"I'll describe it for Lupicinus."

Lupicinus smiled inwardly at Kharapan's use of his name. A man of Empire wouldn't use his name without a title such as 'my lord' unless equal and an intimate. He and Kharapan faced each other as men. Lupicinus had the rare virtue of being able to see beyond names, positions, boundaries that society placed on a man: this was Lupicinus's goodness. It amused Lupicinus to notice Victorinus's astonishment at the way he, Lupicinus, listened to a barbarian.

Kharapan explained that a core is in the nature of a supreme fiction. Individuals had a core or essence, a guiding passion. Civilization had a core too: a supreme fiction that drew individuals together. But, he said, the core of a civilization is an abstraction. The core of civilization might be called a myth, and if so, to this extent, Lupicinus might be correct: perhaps rational creatures need a common myth or story in order for society to become a civilization. And yet, that core, that supreme fiction, can be godless, can contain the idea of *agnosis*, of trying to fathom the unknown, which is a different sort of wisdom and knowledge. The grand story doesn't have to be wrapped in religion, Kharapan said.

Lupicinus looked down.

"These questions of civilization remind me of the work of a woman in Hellenica named Metis," Kharapan said. "To her, society with a Christian core, God and Kingdom, is hell on earth; on the other hand, to her, the Great Unknown, with a core of godlessness and respect for the unknown, is the best civilization. She writes—it allows people to follow their individual passions." He paused. "She's your nemesis," he said to Lupicinus.

Lupicinus only smiled.

"For you, Lupicinus," Kharapan continued in a serious, reflective tone. "A primordial idea guides you. However, it's not your core, it's not a passion of body and mind, but of mind alone. The idea leads you in an overpowering way." He leaned forward. "Since it's impossible to have civilization without God, you say, and Christianity forms the best civilization for man, so you believe, you think there's no choice. You join them." He paused, searching Lupicinus's face, which was expressionless. "Your Christianity is based on faith in an idea, the idea of civilization. You think the fiction of the Church is necessary to civilization. You don't believe in their God. Rather, you see Christianity as the supreme fiction. Exactly as a supreme fiction."

"Lord Lupicinus advises the bishop of Rome, the pope!" Victorinus interjected, despite his resolve to remain silent. He was so amazed that Lupicinus listened to the barbarian, that he could hardly pay attention and almost forgot to be angry with his wife.

Kharapan peered with interest at Lupicinus.

Lupicinus hesitated. He'd kept his atheism hidden so long that the need for excessive vigilance hardly amounted to a concern for him. He'd nearly forgotten how once he'd strained with words and had adjusted his face to harmonize with them. Sudden laughter filled him. He put his hand to his lips to hide it but couldn't control himself. He laughed outright. Tears of laughter filled his eyes. He bent forward, shaking with mirth.

Saturnine and Victorinus looked on in surprise and exchanged a questioning glance. Saturnine wondered: was it true? Was Lupicinus an atheist? She was only surprised not to be surprised—but hearing it spoken out loud seemed shocking. It occurred to her for the first time that there were likely many disbelievers at the top of the Christian hierarchy. The Church suddenly seemed to her like a secret society, protecting and preserving its power in the name of God.

"Ah! You amuse me," Lupicinus said.

The delightful relief of laughter. After all of those years, a barbarian saw everything! There was nothing to blind Kharapan. His, Lupicinus's, disbelief must have been obvious all along. Christianity cloaked him in Rome: no one could see or was aware of what they saw. Kharapan, unbound by the strictures of Empire, knowing nothing of Lupicinus, didn't care to appease him and simply saw and acknowledged the truth. Lupicinus felt little danger. Victorinus would never take a barbarian seriously, and Saturnine, although she might understand, was only a woman. Victorinus wouldn't listen to her, and she naturally would doubt her own insights. As for the servants, he'd grown accustomed to thinking of them as sheep: if roused one moment by uncertainty, they were appeased the next by food and warmth.

Lupicinus held up an aristocratic hand to stop Victorinus who seemed about to stand. "You have an interesting theory," he said to Kharapan, "but you haven't convinced me that there can be civilization without God. I am not convinced that Hellenica amounts to civilization. It's not Empire. It's not Rome."

A servant who had been standing behind them for some time, finally interrupted: she bent down to Saturnine and whispered that the meal was ready. Saturnine looked down, and then, looking at Victorinus and then Lupicinus, said, "It's dinner."

Victorinus started to rise.

But Lupicinus remained seated. "I would like to hear what this man has to say," he said, his eyes fixed on Victorinus. "If you don't mind."

Victorinus paused, and then sat down. "Of course," he said.

TEN

KHARAPAN REFLECTED IN the pause. He sensed Lupicinus's interest in him. Something in Lupicinus attracted Kharapan too.

Kharapan had often noted the faces of powerful men: years of moral ambiguity and rationalized shameful acts gave them a look of half-mocking submissiveness to what they perceived as the unavoidable evil through which a man must wade in life. Lupicinus interested Kharapan precisely because he didn't have this half-mocking expression. He lacked that look that came from a life of 'rationalized shameful acts;' instead, Kharapan sensed a bitter honesty in the man, in spite of what must have been a life full of lies. Lupicinus hadn't denied his lack of belief. Kharapan considered that Lupicinus might be capable of speaking the truth. That is, Kharapan thought that Lupicinus, in spite of his lies to others, might struggle to remain true to himself. Nonetheless, he thought, even if Lupicinus tried to face the truth, some truth in his acts and thoughts, his lies would inevitably prevent him from having a deep understanding of himself. Lupicinus did not live his passion, he denied his core, whatever that core might be, and Kharapan believed that passion, this core, was the only path to wisdom.

Compassion moved Kharapan. Ideas make up a man and direct him, but as Kharapan well knew, they can also become a stronghold. An idea's power, its reason, could become a kind of sickness that occluded the lessons of experience, stunted the fullness of life that came when one dwelt in mystery and the unknown. That narrowed vision made overcoming a mistaken idea nearly impossible. The experience of the unknown, of the ineffable, if cultivated, guided a person to a different sort of life. Kharapan sensed in many men of Rome, especially the powerful ones who often seemed to him like the walking dead, that they were incapable of true dialogue. Kharapan had no interest in speaking to those men. But Lupicinus… Kharapan felt a pull toward this man. He felt the twinge of compassion but wondered at the same time if he only imagined this sliver of life, of potential, in Lupicinus. That is, Kharapan doubted too.

Kharapan realized Lupicinus waited for him to speak.

"Our minds tend toward one another," Kharapan said. "The rational animal has a passion for community. Gods are not necessary to bring us together. Certain supreme fictions are more palatable, closer to truth in allowing the nature of fiction to breathe, in allowing each of us more life because we can be true to our own cores, our own supreme fictions. Staying close to what is unknown is a noble act, a most noble kind of act. It has the virtue of humility, along with wisdom and compassion. Saturnine," he added, "You should remember this in your writing."

Saturnine paled but looked at Kharapan with amused eyes—so he knows. She felt Lupicinus's eyes on her. Victorinus also gazed on his wife, full of suspicion and dread, although of exactly what he didn't know.

Kharapan felt uncertain in the tension that followed. He understood that Romans might consider it subversive for a woman to write anything but correspondence. He didn't know the details of Saturnine's life, knew only what Flavia had chosen to share with him over the years. He didn't know that Saturnine had stopped writing after she married. He didn't know how secret she kept it when she did write. He didn't consider what the fact of her writing might mean to Victorinus or to Lupicinus. Still, he could not entirely regret his words.

Lupicinus's eyes moved from Saturnine to the mosaic floor.

Kharapan fumbled inside his worn leather bag. He had never shown Metis's codex, *Kingdoms*, to anyone in Rome. Besides being subversive in Rome—though this was not the reason he never showed it—it was linked to the murder of a Christian monk in Hellenica a long time ago. Kharapan carried the work as a kind of warning, a reminder to be cautious. In this strange moment, however, he had a desire to show *Kingdoms* to Saturnine, to show them that such a codex might exist. He pulled out the worn tied parchment codex and handed it to Saturnine.

"It's in Greek," she said.

It might have been secret writing. Victorinus glanced at

the cover then sat back; he had studied Greek but failed to master it: many men, even great men, knew only Latin—many great, powerful Christians and senators, even emperors.

From a cursory glance, even the first sentence—"Imagine two worlds…"—Saturnine could see that it contained a discourse on two civilizations: one, the Kingdom of God, a place of suffering, and the other, a place called the Great Unknown. She suspected its conclusions. She closed the book, amazed that the codex existed, amazed at such a writer living on the edge of civilization—a woman! She was astonished and deeply impressed by the fact that Kharapan carried such a codex in Rome.

Lupicinus made a subtle gesture for it, and Saturnine handed the codex over to him. Lupicinus examined the beginning and read the last sentences out loud: "The Kingdom of God is a menace. After its fall, humanity will be blemished: the world will be ruled by Christian atheists, not those natural atheists, those beautiful godless creatures, untainted by a nasty doctrine, who will have died out long before." Lupicinus gave a harsh laugh.

There was an uncertain pause. Everyone, including Kharapan, suspected something terrible would follow.

Lupicinus pondered the idea of Christian atheists. He'd been raised pagan, in pagan Rome, an anachronism in the not-too-distant future. He could never be one of Metis's Christian atheists. But he felt Metis was right in this respect: Christians, those raised Christian since birth, would populate the earth. A disbeliever in such a world might be a Christian atheist, and yet Lupicinus didn't believe that the Kingdom of

God would fall. Christian atheists, if any, would undoubtedly be invisible creatures in a Christian world.

Lupicinus handed the codex back. Kharapan put *Kingdoms* in his leather bag.

"It's a mere story, a tale," Kharapan said. "In Chi, we fiercely believe in stories but are never so extreme, never so sure about the truth that we don't laugh. It's in this sense that we use the word 'fiction.' Don't we all have that sense of fiction, that we don't know the truth, the full truth? It's the natural state of the rational animal." He paused. "In this respect," he said, "that we don't kill to prove the truth of our convictions, that we allow others to differ even if they offend us, we're more civilized than Christians."

He broke off. He felt off-balance, and recognizing it, paused and considered his walking stick. Monotheism, he knew, was not the only way of thought that led to fanaticism. A human being was a wild landscape. It was not uncommon to be lost to the power of an idea, any idea. Still, he believed that Empire had institutionalized and encouraged the fanatic in man, while Chi worked to soften it, to warn of it.

Lupicinus held the arms of his chair. "What civilization?" He spoke as a man who had all the strength on his side. "Rome is civilization. You may have something to eat in your so-called country, you may have 'a guiding idea,' but you don't have an empire. You don't have roads, great cities, plumbing and water systems."

"We have roads…," Kharapan said, smiling. It was not roads that Lupicinus struggled against. "We have the schools of philosophy."

It was then that Kharapan leaned in and spoke of what he imagined would be, and was, close to Lupicinus's soul, if one can speak of souls in this context.

"As individuals," Kharapan said, in a voice filled with feeling, "your view and mine, the way we live, reveal more than we ourselves do." He paused. "Our lives, the paths and experiences and events of our lives, reveal the differences between Rome and Chi, how civilization and culture shape a man's life, and the decisions he makes in order to live. To explore whether civilization exists without God, and more, which place is best for the rational creature, we might explore our lives. If you were willing to speak the truth."

Kharapan looked keenly into Lupicinus's eyes to see if Lupicinus understood, and he saw that he did.

Was it a challenge? Did Kharapan view it as a challenge at the time? Lupicinus took it as a challenge. Later, they both used the word, but the nature of the challenge changed in Kharapan's mind. Did Kharapan imply that men were born unformed, at least in part, molded by the world in which they were born and raised? What would Lupicinus's life have been if he had been born in Hellenica? What would Kharapan be if he had been born in Rome? It seems likely to me that in spite of Lupicinus's character, Lupicinus's life, if he had been born and raised in Hellenica, would have been different. I am not sure I can say the same for Kharapan had he been born in Rome. In any event, Kharapan would likely have said that a man has an unalterable core that might be expressed and revealed in different ways depending on external (so to speak) events, circumstances, and challenges. To my mind, although perhaps our ideas are not so far apart, Kharapan didn't give enough weight to character. One might say, I would say, individuals have an immutable character, and we learn about this character over years, from observing ourselves. And yet, perhaps one might live closer to one's true nature. Kharapan encouraged one to live one's core. And perhaps he believed (he wanted to believe, but perhaps had trouble truly believing) that if one lived one's core, in accordance with one's true passion, that person could overcome any character weakness. In any event, he believed that one found moral strength and wisdom by paying attention to and living one's core.

Kharapan suddenly sat back with a different feeling. He didn't know if he wanted to learn the truth of Lupicinus's life. The image of Arminius, his original Stoic master, came to him. Kharapan grasped the wooden walking stick. He realized that it wasn't his place to prove one thing or another, which civilization was best, for example. Instead, he thought, a conversation between a man of Hellenica and a man of Empire could build a friendship, could form a bond that rose above civilization. He considered telling Lupicinus all this, but glancing at Lupicinus almost shyly, he remained silent. A man like Lupicinus would laugh, would, with a cynical hand, likely wave away the idea of friendship with a man like Kharapan.

Lupicinus was sunk in half smiling reflection. Startled, the idea of speaking to Kharapan—a barbarian from Hellenica— drew him. The intensity of desire revealed the extent of his world-weariness. Kharapan, Lupicinus supposed, offered to play the philosopher: one who reveals a man's mistake, and in his case, Kharapan believed, not only a man's mistake but the mistake of Empire. Lupicinus felt enraptured by the audacity of the challenge. He wanted to prove that neither he nor the Orthodox Church, the core of Rome as Kharapan called it, was mistaken—and as Kharapan surmised, his life and the Church's were intimately bound. He wanted to prove it not only to Kharapan but also to himself: prove that he wasn't afraid to speak the truth, prove that his idea held up against any and all challenges. The mere idea of speaking the truth gave him a sense of relief, of release. He had to acknowledge too, in himself, a slight unease, as if he might be mistaken, as if he might in fact have gone wrong, might have failed to see some essential truth in a life of reflection rather than openness. His unease increased the lure of the challenge. It was dangerous to speak the truth. He risked exposure in the world, but he was aware of an even greater risk: should he discover some error, some mistaken idea, he risked his sense of himself, the scaffolding of his life.

Lupicinus looked at Kharapan, his eyes filled with challenge, but he saw that he had to control his thoughts. He felt the glimpse of Rome's eyes. He had to laugh—at his desire to speak the truth, at the man who inspired him, and at how the world peered on them even now: on a rich old Christian man and a dirty impoverished barbarian engaged in impassioned discussion. Besides, he couldn't imagine a place where such a conversation would take place—inviting Kharapan to his domus was unthinkable. Upon further reflection, he remembered what had happened the last time he'd told the truth to someone.

This moment—these words between them—seemed the rare event. But a different part of Lupicinus, one accustomed to Church duty, to the duty demanded by his idea and, so, to himself, had been grappling beneath the flow of words and feeling—grappling with the idea of Kharapan, this man of Hellenica traveling so freely in Rome with the subversive text.

"You're a romantic," Lupicinus said. "You think a philosopher should rule."

Kharapan smiled. He had seen something in Lupicinus's eyes, but it had passed. "No," he said. "No, not even a philosopher should force a way of life. Society must allow people to be evil—it must allow individuals their personal fictions, and it must allow rational creatures to make mistakes about their nature. We are small creatures in the face of vastness. We can hardly bear it. Some bow and can't stop humbling themselves, seeking gods to bow low to. Others refuse to look. A few smile into its face.

"As to evil…." Kharapan gave Lupicinus an intense look. "Suppose a man kills an old woman, an old money lender. Suppose this old woman had a sister that she tortured and abused. She was mean and petty with everyone. Where is the tragedy? In this: not her death, for in a moment she is gone, and she was destined to die as the cat dies. The tragedy is in her life, in her mistakes, her daily acts of meanness. She failed to understand the superior functions of the rational creature. She wasted her life. And the killer, he'll live on. Imagine how he suffers. He suffers in planning to kill her, in the act, and in having to live with the memory of having killed for the rest of his life. He lives forever with this vile act. And if society removes him from its midst, it is besides the fact of the pain he suffers, even if he doesn't understand his own suffering. It might even help the killer if the state punishes him, help him think himself punished by this external being, this supreme fiction. Keeping evil to oneself without punishment is far worse, far worse." His gaze rested on Lupicinus.

"Did you know those people you describe?" Saturnine asked.

"Many like them," Kharapan said. "Don't we all? Mistaken creatures: we can see it in their faces. We might be angry at someone who harms us, but if we look into his face, even a killer's face, or the old woman's face, one who doesn't know he's wrong, we see his wrong view of what it means to be human. We see as evident his wrong notion of what it means to be a rational creature, his sad view of life, the terrible world he lives in. This face might subdue our anger. It nurtures our capacity to forgive. We're moral animals but refuse to believe and make excuses so we can act otherwise. We find only pain and suffering when we go against our nature."

"Yes, we are mistaken," Lupicinus said. "But God guides us toward virtue, to the proper relationship between ourselves and others." He retreated to God's words. He was not free to speak.

Kharapan hesitated. He peered at Lupicinus. "Some men are mistaken due to an idea. They're as evil, that is, as mistaken about their nature as those who don't try to understand their natures at all. These men with an idea are misled by the power of stories. Some of these men have influence and when they do, suffering and death result. If one is overcome by a story, everything falls to it, even lives. That's the danger of losing a sliver of doubt, the sliver of fiction. Then, imagine the vileness this man lives with in his body! He has his idea, but all the evil that resulted from it. He'll never be free. He ruins his life. And yet even this man can face what he's done and live rationally, that is, morally in accord with nature. It's never too late, for it's natural for a man to be noble and virtuous and unnatural not to be these things."

Lupicinus's thin lips drew tight.

Saturnine held her breath. Victorinus rustled. But Lupicinus smiled after a pause, a forced unsmiling smile. "Christ is our savior," he said. "And among other things, Christ gives us civilization. We're in union under God. All men see truth or fail to be saved. They have a choice, but it's limited to salvation." He lowered his eyes.

An awkward silence ensued. Kharapan studied Lupicinus but Lupicinus didn't look up.

"I hope we may proceed to dinner," Victorinus said after a time.

"Of course," Lupicinus said, standing. They all stood.

Victorinus took Saturnine's arm. The cool air, the moment, invigorated Saturnine—and yet she felt a breathless trepidation of something.

Lupicinus went to Kharapan and paused before him, half smiling. They need lies, need them, he wanted to say. He bent his head before Kharapan.

"Forgive us," Kharapan whispered. "Forgive us our painful grappling, our desperate attachment to the idea of God, to the idea of a Being that loves us back, forgive and forget us, and live as you yourself believe, in truth."

Lupicinus was startled. I can't forgive, he thought vehemently, shocked to feel tears stinging his eyes. He hid his eyes and turned away.

Saturnine glanced at Kharapan. In her glance, Kharapan's face became gentle, and Saturnine gave a brief nod. Victorinus, after a half angry glance at the barbarian, escorted his wife into the domus, making sure Flavia followed. Lupicinus followed them in.

BOOK II

ONE

VICTORINUS, ALONE AFTER dinner with Lupicinus, tried to satisfy Lupicinus's questions about Kharapan—the connection to Flavia, if he didn't exactly understand it, how his wife had seen Kharapan once ten years ago, the night Philo had been killed. Unfortunately, Lupicinus remembered Philo. Even in the chaos of Maximin's trials, executing the son of an ex-Prefect of Rome had been noticed. Lupicinus asked if Cornelia wrote about her theories in regard to the Church. Victorinus said that his wife started writing after her father's death, that she wrote harmless feelings, the kind of thing women wrote. And in any case, he said, she promised to stop. She would burn the stuff.

"Why burn harmless words?" Lupicinus said.

Victorinus felt Lupicinus implied a sinister connection between Cornelia and Philo, the boy accused of practicing black magic.

Lupicinus was largely distracted. Kharapan, besides the rest, gave rise to a unique opportunity to define atheism in

Church doctrine. Lupicinus imagined telling Bishop Damasus about the man of Hellenica and the codex he carried. And yet, he worried. He'd learned long ago how little control he had over events, even when he himself put something in motion. What would happen to Kharapan? to Hellenica? to Saturnine (with her own writing), and Victorinus? Would the Church seek to discover and eradicate the disbelievers in Rome, in Empire? A part of him wondered, too, with hesitation and doubt, at the unaccountable feelings he'd felt for Kharapan, that lone man, that man of Hellenica, perhaps for himself in Kharapan's presence.

Forces of individual lives, experiences, natures, gathered in society, social structures, the rare encounter that seemed outside a world—Kharapan's appearance and the discussions, mere words exchanged, reverberated like wind rippling over the sea, gentle at first, building out and beyond to a crescendo, a force crashing ashore.

Lupicinus departed in a mood of silence. Victorinus felt a barbarian stole Lupicinus's attention and perhaps damaged his reputation with the Church's elders. He could not control his wife or even intimate dinners in his own domus.

TWO

VICTORINUS SUMMONED FLAVIA to his office late that night. She had not been asleep. A cold wind blew through Rome, through old trees, ruined palaces and temples. She'd been listening to the wind. He told her to shut the door and directed her to sit in a hard chair.

He took a few steps. A single lamp struggled with shadows. "You haven't told your Mistress about your past, but you'll tell me."

Flavia had seldom spoken to this master. She sat still, her skin translucent and pale.

"If you disobey me or lie, you'll never see Cornelia again, and I'll make sure you're sold to the most vile buyer."

"Yes, my lord," she said softly.

He sat behind a dark desk, in a tall wooden chair that had carved lions at the top. "Tell me about those who owned you before the Flavianus family."

Flavia hesitated. A sense of doom had filled her from the moment Kharapan appeared in the garden. Alone, she had fallen into reverie, a reverie of a life that Kharapan seemed somehow, unaccountably, intimate with.

"I was a free woman," she said in a flat voice. "I served at an inn outside Rome." She did not have the energy or even desire to come up with the old lie that she had always been a slave.

Victorinus gave a start. He knew the type of service a woman gave at those inns. "The Flavianus family must not have known," he said.

"No."

"My wife doesn't know?"

"No," she said quickly, looking at him. As she studied Victorinus, her confidence grew. Her past had been deceitful. He could punish her, but she saw that telling part of the truth gave cover to what she wished to hide. With Saturnine's dark, curly hair, her own translucent pale skin and blond hair, no one guessed mother and child; and yet, they looked alike; they had the same face, same eyes, same height and build. How long the secret of her motherhood would remain hidden now that Kharapan had appeared, checked any real confidence.

"What inspired you to sell yourself into slavery?"

"I thought—better to be a slave than live the life I had," she said. "I knew a legal counselor. I pretended to be his slave, to have raised his children, though he had none. He offered me to the noble Flavianus family, for sale."

She paused and thought too late of the glaring missing fact in her story: she'd gone to the Flavianus's domus as a wet nurse—there was a baby missing in her story. "I devoted my life to being a good maidservant," she said. "I've never failed my Mistress or been remiss in my duties. Duty was all to me."

A silence passed. Victorinus contemplated how a girl in her circumstances might choose to be a slave in a rich domus rather than serve the needs of men at an inn. "Go on," he said.

"I met Kharapan three years later," she said, glancing furtively at him, but he listened passively, twisting his lip at Kharapan's name.

"You know that he saved Miss Saturnine... Cornelia... the night Philo was killed," she said. "I met him years before: the day the monks interrupted our party. I know Miss Cornelia told you about it. She doesn't know I met Kharapan then. She met him the night Philo died and has not seen him since." It was mostly true. Kharapan discovered her, living as Flavia, the day the monks fought in the street.

"Caught in a violent fight between monks of different sects," she said.

"Yes, yes," Victorinus said. Cornelia had told him the story of the violent monks—as a child, she and her mother and their party had been caught in the middle of a brawl. "No lion could hold such rage," she'd said.

Flavia told him how Kharapan had helped her, he'd led her away from the mob. "I agreed to meet him that day, to thank him," she said, fondling the cloth of the high dress at her neck.

Thinking of that first meeting in the ruins of Temple Athena and its contrast to the present, when Kharapan appeared in the garden, caused Flavia's eyes to mist. Over the years, she'd grown used to grappling with her past, and the silences she must keep. Kharapan's appearance in the garden that day marked the inevitable end of that silence, of those secrets, and gave her a new depth of feeling and compassion for herself.

Victorinus waited. The slave's apparent emotion might be due to the memory of battling monks, but he had a growing suspicion of something different.

"At first, I met him out of obligation," Flavia said, "and, after a time, friendship. Of course, a man of his position couldn't befriend the family, or become known to them... but he promised to stay away from the Flavianus domus. It was a matter of luck," she added, "that he happened to be in Rome the night Philo was killed.... I asked him to follow Miss Cornelia. I didn't know what to do." She broke off, afraid that the duty of a maidservant would have been to warn the parents and not to send a barbarian after Saturnine.

Victorinus grimaced. "He helped her, it's true, but I won't allow the connection to continue. If I'd known you were continuing to meet such a man, I wouldn't have allowed it, and as Cornelia herself knew nothing, she can't be blamed."

"No, my Lord," Flavia said.

He scowled; it struck him as odd that Cornelia hadn't insisted that Flavia tell her more, who this man was or how she'd met him. He sensed something strange, something missing but wasn't fully aware, even of his uncertainty. Perhaps Cornelia had met with Kharapan all along... but he couldn't forget how in the midst of Cornelia's emotion that day, she'd said she'd not seen Kharapan since that night ten years before.

He peered at Flavia. "Was he your lover?"

She gasped. "Kharapan? No."

Victorinus gave her a searching look. She might be attractive, if one noticed, but although not so old, she was too reserved for his taste. He couldn't imagine other men with different taste in flesh, even if a barbarian, and her embarrassment and unstudied surprise convinced him that she spoke the truth. Besides, the thought of any female of Empire, even a slave, taking an interest in a barbarian... unless she had no choice... but she'd met him when she'd been the Flavianuses' slave. He stood and walked around the desk, closer to her, leaning back on the desktop.

"Fine," he said. "You've done well to tell me. Listen: I control your fate."

"Yes, my lord," she murmured, thinking that no human controlled the Fates.

"I'll forget your crime, your deceit, if you please me. I need you to please me."

Flavia felt sudden confusion. Sex didn't bother her but a heavier burden: the horror if Victorinus should make love to mother and daughter, and the need to refuse, or the thought of what would happen if she didn't deny him his wish, and what it would mean once everyone learned the truth.

"No, no," Victorinus exclaimed, understanding a part of her thoughts. "This is what I demand..." He paced, turning his face to hide his amusement at the sexual misunderstanding and the depth of horror on her face.

"I want you to meet the barbarian one last time," he said. "Tell him never to come here. Tell him I order him to leave Rome. He has no right to be here, and if he's here legally, he doesn't have the right of a citizen. I don't care if he's tortured or killed. Given the codex he carries and how he speaks, he can be ruined. I will destroy him."

Flavia nodded. And yet she thought that she and Victorinus had as much control over Kharapan as over the fixed stars. His word "order" almost brought a smile to her lips.

"If my eyes catch sight of that barbarian, you'll be lost. Cornelia won't be able to protect you or find you. Of course, once Cornelia learns the truth about you, she won't bother to look."

Flavia gave a small nod. Banishment would be the same as death for her. But who could tell what would happen? All of the possibilities advancing on her almost made her light-headed.

"You've been loyal, and she relies on you. However, if you force me, I'll sell first and explain afterwards." He sat on the edge of his desk. "Do you understand?"

"Yes, my lord," she said.

"In addition," he said, a little hesitantly, ashamed. "I want you to tell me if she writes."

Flavia flushed, her eyes lowered—she was to be a spy. There was too much uncertainty; she wasn't even sure what to hope for. She even felt a little sorry for Victorinus. "Yes, my lord," she said.

Silence filled the space between them. "You may go," he said.

THREE

TWENTY YEARS BEFORE, a woman on the streets of Rome, a city with over a million lives, a woman with a baby, knew that to survive, she and her baby had to enter the Church. No emperor had yet declared Orthodox religion the only lawful guide to the thoughts of rational creatures. But even in the year of Julian's reign, that last great pagan, the Church, with its hierarchies, its Christian emperors—the Church hovered on the precipice of declaring its place in Empire and its dominion over the world. Even then the Church of Rome took in abandoned babies and destitute prostitutes and made them Christians and slaves, and Honora—her name at the time—had no doubt as she stood in the dark on the magnificent church porch: she and baby had to go in, each on her own. The Church would take in abandoned babies and reformed prostitutes, but not mother and child—at least this is what Honora believed.

The mist of darkness dissipated, and morning grew thick with itself. Honora hadn't named the baby. The universe, she thought, the Fates would name her. Moira controlled the fate of both gods and men, but the goddesses, the Fates, took a greater interest in human life. The baby gave a low murmur. Honora's hands pressed the soft blanket, the life underneath. The baby, with dark curls and olive skin, stared out with serious, contemplative eyes as if to accuse and forgive at once. Honora laid down her baby, wrapped in a rust-colored blanket, on the concrete. Weak against a cold pillar, she took an audible breath. Not daring to look back, she moved into the shadows and crossed the grass. She crouched in an alleyway.

Sunlight shimmered on the grass and gilded the church porch but did not warm the day. The great metal doors opened. A girl came out and took up the baby. The church girl stood at the edge of the porch before going inside.

Inside, a wooden Jesus with voluptuous eyes stared down the center of a room as grand as any in Constantine's palaces, as beautiful and ornate as the baths. The church's immensity seemed to prove the validity of its doctrine, as if truth could be forced out of the universe by sheer physical exertion and masterly ability to build. And yet, as someone said, our mightiest projects betray the degree of our insecurity. Our gaze transforms into horror, for we know by instinct that such structures cast the shadow of their own destruction, are even designed with an eye to their later existence as ruins.

Honora had never believed, as some philosophers said, that she could choose a way of life. Destiny unveiled itself in time. She bathed in a river of events, as the philosophers themselves said. But the birth of her daughter forced her to choose, or at least to have the impression that she chose.

Going to Rome rather than returning to the inn after her husband Justin, Saturnine's father, died; refusing to raise her daughter to that life, leaving her baby at the church... for the first time she felt as if she were defying the Fates. It seemed like her first act against the inevitable.

She would offer to serve as wet nurse, tell them that her baby had died, that she hadn't known the father, that she'd found faith in Christ. Honora intended to wait hours, in case they might suspect. She planned to go to Constantine's bath in the women's hours before approaching the church, but terrified of being separated from her baby she hadn't moved. She didn't know how much time had passed. She could hardly pay attention to the world. A monk approached. She wasn't looking at him, but then saw her baby's rust-colored blanket beneath his sleeve, a baby in his arms. He passed by, walking briskly. She stood, hands limp, mouth open.

She followed the monk down the wide street next to the walls of the Circus Maximus, and up the tree lined slope of Aventine Hill, and on a path to a Grand domus. He disappeared inside. Honora pushed through manicured bushes to a small side garden where she could see the front as well and leaned against the bark of an umbrella pine.

How could they want a girl? But her baby was beautiful, and she knew these people would take her in.

It must have seemed a long time. She finally saw the monk walk out the front door, his hands free. Honora flushed, her heart raced, and she hesitated before following him. She could hardly form a thought, could hardly see. She felt choked and followed the vague contour of his gray cloak until the great church took shape and they were almost upon it, and she cried out, and grabbed his sleeve, and when he turned back, she fell in a sob at his feet.

"My girl!" she cried, but when she looked up, his eyes, his sallow expression, made her lower her own eyes, made words other than truth come to her tongue. "Died," she said.

"I'm sorry, accept my blessing." He made a Christian gesture over her.

"I have nowhere… I can serve as wet nurse," she said in a dull tone, standing, trembling.

Her thick blonde hair tangled around her shoulders, but even so, she must have made a good impression. "I'm a free woman," she said, pulling out her papers.

The flutter in her eyes wouldn't stop: she had said her baby died.

"Are you willing to believe, to accept Christ as the one and true God?" the monk said, lowering the papers and appraising her with incurious eyes.

A mad smile came to her lips. "No," she said, looking up, hardly seeing.

"We will not judge your past. You can be baptized, the church will provide for you."

"No," she said softly. "I'll never believe."

"Then why stop me?"

He was annoyed but she had no answer.

The monk's eyes seemed thoughtful. He reached into his purse and took out a card. He said Marinus traded in wet nurses and maidservants. "Tell him Monk Peter sent you," he said. He gave a slight bow and left her.

Honora held the card. She had never been in a big city and yet in some things could not be naïve; this advocate, Marinus, would sell her as a slave in the lowest quarter, and not only to serve as wet nurse. And yet, her hand opened, she peered. At the time, the idea seemed a mere modification to the original. Was it true? she wondered. Had she seen anything at all?

At the free bath, in front of a mirror, she worked her hair, pulling it into a bun. She remembered some of what Justin had told her: Epictetus said, if there's too much smoke in the house, one is free to leave. Socrates took his life with poison.

After the bath, Honora visited an old midwife and begged for poison. Honora promised to return with money, making up a story of a destitute prostitute who had lost her child, who would give her coins when Honora returned with the poison. The new false words gave her an unaccustomed distance from herself, and later, she knew that the feeling had been a sign, a warning. Something in Honora moved the old midwife, or perhaps from what the midwife had witnessed of life, she supported the cause of death, and thus, although the woman did not believe in Honora's friend or that she'd ever see Honora again (and would be surprised when indeed she did see her), she made up a vial that, she told Honora, could kill two large men but would lose its power if not refreshed. Honora made a pouch from her dress fabric and tied the poison around her neck—and from that moment wore that vial, refreshed often, at her neck.

A shabby servant opened Marinus's door and escorted her to his office and told her to wait in a chair with others.

When the inner door opened, she stood ahead of the others, insisting her business was urgent.

Marinus told her to enter, and at first, as she spoke, looked upon her as a prize, first for pleasure and later to sell. But when she told him of the Monk's delivery of a baby to the Grand domus that morning and of her plan for him to sell her to that household as if she were his slave, his aspect became eager. "We must leave at once," she said.

He took her papers, stamped in the myriad ways of Rome. He took a key that hung at his neck and unlocked an old lockbox, placing her papers inside. She would never see those papers again. They left, accompanied by Marinus's guards.

Hours later, the slave Flavia sat in a rocking chair with Saturnine in her arms. Amazement, relief, terror mingled in her.

A night is hourless. At first, her thoughts expanded in the night in relief. But in this vague existence, in silence, she came to understand what had disturbed her when she first entered the domus. A shiver passed through her. As if to protect her child, she stood and checked the locked shutters, and blew out the candle, and sat with Saturnine in the dark.

When an old man, servant of the senator, Theanis Flavianus, admitted Marinus and Honora to the domus, the silence of the marble halls and rich mosaics disturbed Honora, but she didn't understand why. The old manservant opened a door to a library, and she and Marinus stepped inside. The senator—a large man with a not unkindly expression—stood near an empty hearth, his hands behind him. Honora glanced at him and then stared down and could hardly make out

Marinus's words. Against the rhythmic beat of her heart, she heard the sound of the advocate's preening voice. After a time she noticed Marinus backing out, leaving, and thinking the offer had failed, she turned stiffly to follow. But the senator called her back. After some confusion, she understood that he wished to speak to her alone.

Theanis wondered, as if to himself, why Monk Peter sent this lowly advocate, but he understood wet nurses could be hard to find. He told her that he had named the baby Saturnine, and he gave her a heavy look, which she trembled under and could hardly keep her eyes steady under his gaze. Saturnine.

He questioned her. She told him she was resigned to Fate and didn't question the Fates' divine wisdom: she carried out Marinus's orders as if in accord with fate, because in effect, his words directed her just as the Fates directed her. As she spoke, it seemed to her that the flat world turned, that lies became true.

"Do you read?" he said. He had seen her looking at his walls lined with books.

"No," she said.

Theanis opened the door and ordered a stout female slave to bring Saturnine.

The officious slave returned with the baby, her dark curls on embroidered white cloth. The baby reached for her. Honora took up her baby and bent her head into the warm body and fell into an audible sob. He might have thought he understood the cause of her emotion—he believed her baby had died. She managed to control her emotion, fearing that the senator would notice something amiss. But Theanis ordered Honora to test her milk, and then summoned his wife, who seemed to Honora to float into the room. Honora listened, amazed, as the senator described her circumstances as if she'd come from a house of one of the best advocates in Rome. Constance examined Honora as if examining fish in a market stall, silently nodded, and left the room.

Theanis said they'd take her. Honora watched the advocate come in, look pleased, and go away. Theanis changed her name too. Flavia: the name referred to his patronymic and made reference to her blond hair. He said they'd send her back if she didn't suit them. "We'll have the advocate send your things," he added.

"I have nothing."

He paused. He motioned the servant to take her. As they started out, Honora heard his manservant announce an advocate at the door, sent by Monk Peter with a wet nurse. She stopped, but Theanis said, after a pause in which he looked at her, "We'll try the girl we have."

"Impossible!" Honora whispered, rocking in the dark, thinking of events of the day and the position she now held.

The scandal in this domus if a mother, such a mother, a former prostitute, was discovered! To Honora's mind, she and her baby would have entered the church separately, and she as a former prostitute. She would not have had anything to hide except motherhood itself. She had not had a chance to consider how different her life would be in this life, the risk she created for her daughter.

How many men might know her? How many people

from the village where she'd lived with Justin? Would Marinus reveal her papers and prove she'd lied? Would he fail to destroy her papers, and would another find them? Her current position made her entire past an evil, for all that she had been and done would be scandal to this present life. And this new life also made the future an evil, for better to take her own life than risk her daughter's unimaginable chance for a good life, a girl suddenly given a fortunate place in the world.

Saturnine's father had been scornful of status, of social rules, but for Honora... perhaps the poison at her neck poisoned her thoughts. In the darkness, worn out by the treacheries of the day, peering vaguely into an uncertain future, reveling in an onslaught of memories—she came to believe that death could be the only silencer. Each breath was a selfish act that risked discovery and linked Saturnine to deceit and scandal; and should the truth be discovered, it would be far worse for Saturnine to have such a mother—if that mother still lived.

And yet, as Honora felt the calm silence of the room, she thought she discerned a slim chance of life. Even if someone recognized her as a prostitute, she thought, it was possible that no one would know that Saturnine was her baby. Still, in such a case, she would be banished at the least, and to lose her daughter would be the same as death. No, her only chance was this: that both her past and her motherhood remain hidden.

That was it, she thought. This was the Fates' plan. The mirthful Fates—in punishment for imagining she could defy their authority by coming to Rome and leaving her baby at the church, in return for her first lies—decreed that she must live a lie, must lie to live. Truth, if discovered, meant death.

Honora rocked back and forth, listening to her daughter's peaceful breathing.

In the three years that passed from the day Flavia became maidservant to her daughter, no one recognized her as Honora. Although she stayed awake nights fearing discovery, she became more confident. She wore her hair pulled back, out of fashion, dressed meekly and severely. She thought she had hidden the Honora in her.

One day, in the hottest month, the women of the domus, Constance and Saturnine and the slaves, left the domus for Constantine's bathhouse. The Flavianus household had failed to go north for the summer for reasons purportedly connected to Theanis's business in the senate, but everyone knew they had stayed because of his concern over a limping racehorse. The great bathhouse was unusually quiet, and the women enjoyed their hours there, but all good feeling vanished when they stepped outside. Saturnine's old-style carriage had no wheels and was carried by four servants at the end of two wooden poles. It smelled rancid, having been recently painted red and yellow, the colors of the family chariot. Three-year-old Saturnine cried and shook her cage-like box. Her cries became shrieks, and her mother approached in anger, her thin wet hair flat against her head like a cloth. Constance, Saturnine's mother, held up her left hand, displaying the pink silk pearl design of her undergarment, and the group of women paused at a corner of the road. Suddenly, a mob of monks approached from behind, and another, an opposing sect, came down the road in front, holding clubs.

The monks rushed at each other. The servants dropped

Saturnine's carriage, which landed upright in the road. Monks bludgeoned each other with iron clubs. Blood splattered their robes. A man fell next to Saturnine's carriage, writhing in pain, while another hit him on the head, crushing his skull. War raged between Christians over who would name the new bishop of Rome. Only days before, a mob of Catholics, with Damasus as their general, slaughtered men, women, and children with machetes in the Basilica of Julius.

Flavia tried to go to Saturnine. Someone held her arm, but when the man spoke the name "Honora" she felt stunned by a confused pain.

"I have to go to Saturnine!" she said, forgetting to say "to my mistress." But Saturnine had already been pulled to safety.

Flavia faced this tall, dark-skinned man. It seemed to her as if he had materialized out of a dream. She knew him, but not in this life, this city, not on these streets. He was a barbarian, not even a creature of Empire, but it was more than that.

Kharapan. She'd hardly thought to consider him, perhaps because she'd not regarded him with fear. Later she reflected that he was the one man who knew more about her life than any other. The Fates sent him to mock her feelings of security. Kharapan and Justin—Justin her lover, her husband, Saturnine's father—spoke of their 'philosophic bond,' one that surpassed boundaries, apparently even that of death. Kharapan, she would come to reflect, was the only man who could imagine he had a duty to her and Saturnine.

"Let us go," Flavia said, closing her eyes.

"The girl," Kharapan said, thinking of the little girl with

olive skin and dark hair, the one who did not look like her mother. And then he'd found his hand on Honora's arm.

Her expression, even her first words, exposed the truth. Perhaps she would not have been able to hide Saturnine from Kharapan regardless.

"I've searched for you and the girl a long time," he said. "More than three years."

"Listen," she said, leaning in, whispering. "I promise to meet you, alone. At the garden of Temple Athena, at dusk. I will tell you everything."

She left him, feeling his eyes on her.

No one seemed to notice their exchange; circumstances justified her flushed face and breathlessness. She did not look back at him, but knew he watched, probably followed them.

At their domus, Flavia stood outside the library listening. Constance didn't mention the dark-skinned man. The monks' behavior enraged the senator. "Let them send each other to heaven," he said. He said he would consult the Sibyl at the Jupiter Capitolinus.

Near dusk, Flavia told a servant she felt ill, and under the pretense of retiring, she slipped out of a low shuttered window.

The city seemed without substance, as if it might blow away in a slight wind. A yellow mist settled on the hot streets and glowed near flames that burned in terracotta pots; temples and public buildings seemed only half-visible in the light. The shallow clip-clop of horses, allowed in the streets at dusk, echoed in the spirituous night. Smoke of the vestal fire rose in the distance: a virgin awake all night protecting Rome, but shacks grew against corners of buildings, clustered in alleyways.

Kharapan leaned against a fallen marble column on the overgrown grass next to the rounded walls of the ruined Temple Athena. He must be eighteen, Flavia thought, for he was younger than her. He held the long wooden walking stick. He doesn't understand the ways of Rome, she thought.

The small garden glistened with humidity. The ruins of the temple took up a small corner in the center of the city, below the Jupiter Capitolinus on the hill, but in this sylvan scene the overgrown garden and abandoned temple secluded them without walls.

Kharapan's eyes, his presence and body, forced her to become Honora. She couldn't help an embarrassed, surprised smile.

"The girl," he said.

His eyes—no one but Kharapan had looked at her as a mother—the look, the acknowledgement of her motherhood, seemed to give her, in spite of everything that had happened, a self that in coming to be revealed its long absence.

She couldn't help but nod, yes: the girl was hers. Hers and Justin's. In what felt like words impossible to utter, in a low voice, a whisper, she told him how she'd come to Rome and become a slave to her own baby girl. As to Saturnine, she said, and saying her daughter's name a hot flush rose in her face and neck. As to Saturnine, she said, with tears in her eyes and a thickness of voice, Saturnine had a wholly other life and must never find out the truth.

Kharapan shook his head. "Your life, Honora."

"My name is Flavia. Saturnine can't know anything in any event," she added. "She's three years old."

119

Kharapan was silent. "It's true," he said after a pause. He told her how he'd gone to Village G. and found out that Justin had died. "I searched for you. Justin's family is in Rome," he added.

Flavia gave a panicky look. She had never met Justin's family. They'd refused to meet her. "The Jews will never accept her. Promise you won't tell them!" Circumstances had made it impossible for Flavia to find them to tell them that Justin had died.

Kharapan brooded in silence.

"Think of the life she leads and what she's destined for! Think of the consequences if the truth is revealed," she said. "Her father is a senator. Imagine if they discover her true mother, her own slave, a former prostitute! Imagine if they discover her Jewish family in Rome. And you…." She looked at his full Ethiopian mouth and tightly curled hair. "For her sake, for her good life, the truth can never be revealed." She paused. "You do understand?" Her voice rose. At Kharapan's silence she looked away and stared without seeing.

"What is this 'good life'?" he said.

"What are you going to do?" she said after a time, when he remained silent.

His pause felt long. It would be better if he were dead, she thought.

"I'm glad to see you," he said, smiling.

She shook her head. "Listen," she said. She told him she would meet him when he came to Rome; she'd tell him about Saturnine. In return, he must not attempt to see her.

He did not promise. He said he would not bother Saturnine now, just three years old. He would see how things developed and then he would decide what to do.

FOUR

SATURNINE MOVED DOWN a crowded street, a street darkened in shadow, like a haunting spirit. Against walls, inside stores, in alleyways, people sold fruit, vegetables, spices from Egypt and India, souvenir statues of the gods, carpets and clothes. Human sweat, sewage, dust, cinnamon incense blended and rose in rank miasma.

In the first light of day, Saturnine had struggled, wondering how to rise to this life in Rome. But she'd received Victorinus's note from a manservant saying he would be indisposed until late evening, and this gave her a reprieve: she would not be Cornelia for a day. Saturnine noticed Flavia's pale pallor and assumed it related to Kharapan's visit, but she was glad when Flavia said nothing, nothing about Kharapan, no comment about her own plan to go out alone in Flavia's cloak.

Saturnine stopped in the middle of a street, unaware of herself. She laughed. She had to laugh. Barbarians! Savages, she thought. An orange cat paused to stare with yellow eyes. There was a cat that night, Saturnine thought.

In the hours that passed—Saturnine could not have said where she wandered—she came upon a small marble temple amidst the noise and decay of the city and, deep in thought, held out her coins. The attendant hesitated. The poor didn't enter, and he studied her dress but finally held out his hand. She entered the small pink palace. It was an older, free toilet, one that admitted both men and women. The cost ensured that only the wellborn or wealthy entered. Eight people filled nine places of three parts of a square. Two women stopped talking to stare at her. Saturnine lifted her robes and turned a little sideways to sit beside the man who took up part of her narrow seat. The seats had a design of two fish leaping toward each other with unnaturally large heads, teeth displayed, open smiling mouths. The pink marble sparkled. The large man next to her moved, but once she sat down, his leg pressed against hers. The warm seat comforted her. The thought of the existence of Metis's codex *Kingdoms* threatened and excited her. A man read thin sheets of parchment, the two women across wore yellow and aqua silk that blended with the pink room; the women glanced at Saturnine, and Saturnine thought they looked familiar, but she looked away; the women spoke about furniture, one promised to lend the other her decorator. This is what she might aspire to! Saturnine thought. This tide, this fungus. And yet, what else? Even in disguise she couldn't use the cans on public corners. Even in her toilet she had no choice but be wife of a senator, citizen of Rome!

Walking, pausing, the sound of musicians, street-criers, merchants, echoed in narrow streets, but absorbing it all, Saturnine sensed silence: silence in the cobblestones and in the space between mortals and things. But how interpret it? how believe in a space here—in Rome. Memories came, threads forming the fabric of Rome, of Empire.

Maximin's trials ended soon after Philo's death. Emperor Valentinian elevated Maximin to a position that took him away from Rome. The city began to recover. It was a bitter end for Saturnine. For a time, she sunk into a stupor so severe that Flavia found herself encouraging Saturnine to write. Anger gave Saturnine a sense of being all-alive in the world, but as time passed writing became a refuge.

In Saturnine's sixteenth year, Emperor Theodosius proclaimed Orthodox Christianity the Empire's religion, declaring the death penalty for heretics, forbidding divination, outlawing all unorthodox thought—heresies, religions, gods, superstitions, reason, all else in the open, untamed mind. Saturnine pretended to laugh at Flavia's worries, and read out loud from her work, "The zeal of Christians to convert; the promise of miracles, raising us from the dead…" She paused. A strange feeling came over her when she read her work cold.

"No one would guess your mind," Flavia said, fondling the folds at her neck.

"Yes, no one sees me," Saturnine said, making a soundless movement of her fingers. "I'm as camouflaged as the butterfly, a bare *psyche*, with as little effect on the world and barely a part in it."

One night, Saturnine went to the library and made a fire. She pulled out an old scroll of Homer. The relative emptiness of the shelves struck her with what had been, reminding her of the manuscripts they'd burned in the time of Maximin's trials. She sat on the couch with the *Odyssey*, covered with dust. It crackled when she unrolled it. She read, "…when in my heart I have sorrow—as now I have sorrow in my heart." Her father opened the door. Their eyes met. He'd returned from dinner with senators as if burdened. He sat across from her and smiled when he saw Homer.

"Keep your heart close to the old religion," he said.

She bowed her head.

After a time he added, "I hope you are never swayed by Christians." He peered at her.

"I'll never be Christian," she said.

He studied her for a moment.

"Father," she said. "You consulted the Sibyl at the Jupiter Capitolinus about me. Tell me what she said."

He told her it wasn't wise to hear one's own prophecy, but she insisted, and after a time he said that the Sibyl told him the signs revealed that her path was like a cold northern one, indifferent to the battles roiling in Rome. He looked at the fire and said nothing more.

Saturnine thought of her atheism—for it could only be called that, and the word denoted sickness, a disease. Ancient texts and a few modern intellectuals would have found it no shame to question the nature of the gods or to disbelieve.

"You took me from the pope's church," she said.

He gave a wry smile. "Yes," he admitted.

"Then you saved me."

He paused. "Perhaps."

Saturnine had a clash with her mother soon after. She'd

started wrestling at the baths. She beat girls her age and even older, pushed their heads against the ground until they called out "Paetus." Wrestling made her lithe and strong. Some called her Atalanta. Atalanta, abandoned at birth, raised by hunters and consecrated to Diana, defeated Peleus a Thessalian King, father of Achilles, in a wrestling match. One day her mother overheard someone call her Atalanta and in a low voice fumed, "You must stop." It took Saturnine a few moments to understand. She gave up wrestling. Everyone stopped calling her Atalanta. By the middle of her seventeenth year, she was as soft and full as her mother's statue of Venus. And at a party to celebrate a Charioteer, Saturnine met Victorinus.

Saturnine married Victorinus Marcus at seventeen, in the year Emperor Theodosius ordered all bishops to surrender to the Catholic faith as defined by him and Bishop Damasus of Rome.

On the night before her wedding, her father arranged a private dinner. He dressed in a rich green robe, and she lay shyly at the table next to him. He told her that he'd buried coins in the garden and left their domus in his will to her—it was all that was left of a dwindled estate that had once encompassed properties all over the Empire.

"You are good to me," Saturnine said, in bewilderment.

That night, alone in the library, Saturnine burned some of her writing. There was too much to hide. It hurt her to watch the parchment burn. She felt as if she destroyed her own flesh. Still, she vowed to stop writing forever.

For more than two years, as marriage determined her duties, a vague unease filled her, as if she were moving in an unknown element, at a distance from herself. The passion she'd experienced in writing frayed like decayed cloth; her anger became tangled threads of doubt. Victorinus converted to Christianity. He called her Cornelia. Her given name, Saturnine, was a reminder of old gods, he said. Most acquaintances called her Cornelia. It amazed her that the world could change her name.

In the year Saturnine turned nineteen, Saturnine's mother, Constance, grew ill, and Saturnine hardly left her side. They had not been close, but Saturnine did all she could to ease the dying woman's pain. Constance's death devastated Theanis. He wouldn't be consoled. Months later, after Saturnine's twentieth birthday, its day marked by Flavia alone, an old servant came to Saturnine's domus to announce the death of her father. On the day after his funeral, three months before events of this chronicle began, Saturnine returned to the home of her childhood and wandered its silent rooms.

The stillness of death folded around the columns. Outside, wreaths circled the domus to ward off evil spirits. The few servants went about their tasks, their closed expressions adding to the eeriness.

In the library, the sight of the room and her memories felt suffocating at first.

She summoned a passing servant and ordered him to prepare a fire. The slave, an old manservant of her father's, had kind eyes and bowed his head. Flickering flames illuminated random aspects of the room: the top of the wooden desk, a table leg with the carved torso of Mercury, the shelves of scrolls. Heat, smoke, dust filled the room. But it began slowly to warm.

Saturnine took a piece of blank parchment, a bottle of ink, and pen from her father's desk and sat in front of the fire. Her hair fell against her shoulders, tangled and damp from the moisture of the humid air. She wrote: My parents are with the spirits of the dead. I have a duty to worship them in the festivals. It's a small thing to grant them immortality.

Her worship of the spirits of her dead parents would make them immortal, so they would have believed.

She took up a new sheet. She wrote: Laws make my thoughts illegal. What is my duty? Should I convert and pretend to believe?

Silk shawls at the market, exotic scents, gave her a thrill, but they didn't spark the feeling she had when she turned to words, the relief of releasing her unspeakable thoughts. When reflecting or thinking of her writing, face in the sun, Saturnine felt the world become spectacularly amorphous. Leaves shimmered in an invisible breeze. She looked on, trembling as if newly acquainted with God, immersed in an illusion of changelessness and eternity. In spite of anger, in spite of the evils of the world, the sky spread luminously over their city, their earth, indifferent and blank as a new sheet of papyrus.

Saturnine went to her old bedroom and pushed away the small rug and pulled out the floorboards. She found the dusty parchment in which she'd written down Kharapan's words. *The risk of not engaging in your passion is worse than death—the danger of being dead among the living. Years could be wasted, ruined, thrown away. Integrity is a delicate fragile thing.* She sat back and gave a small laugh. The world called her Cornelia, and it seemed right, so lost was she to herself. "But can it be?"

she whispered. Did she have a duty to confront the entire world? To risk everything? All of humanity seemed against her.

She knew the strain that came from writing secretly, knew it would eventually distance her from Victorinus. She feared the consequences of discovery. Who would support her in this way of life? And why worry about truth? No sundial or water clock revealed the same time.

Saturnine reached again through the floorboards, and her hand came upon the small hard thing, the piece of lead Kharapan had given her.

Flavia suddenly stood at the door. Saturnine looked up, the parchment in her lap, the lead in her hand.

"Don't!" Flavia said in a muffled voice.

Saturnine bent her head in a smile. Flavia's doubt sometimes served to encourage her. In the face of Flavia's fear, Saturnine's old rebelliousness rose within her.

"Go, leave me," she said.

Flavia hesitated, and then noting Saturnine's severe expression, bowed out.

Saturnine smiled at herself. In writing a little she'd made a festival to her own dead spirit. She'd been granted a brief return to life, a brief immortality. She could see how dead she'd been.

But the three months which had passed since, seemed merely a last death spasm before all was lost.

Saturnine returned to her domus before dark. She fell into a deep sleep. When she opened her eyes, Victorinus stood over her. She sat up and slid to the edge of the bed.

"What is this?" he said, fingering Flavia's cloak. "You'll convert. I don't care if you don't believe."

Saturnine looked down. "What is philosophy, poetry, but words, Victor?" she said in a low voice. "Why can't I engage in the highest activity of man? I can keep my words secret, at least let me do that."

"What's this? Are you taking back your promise not to write?"

"I'm a woman," she said as if to herself. Sappho wrote, *Although words are only breath, words which I command are immortal,* but Saturnine felt her words as only breath. It was hard to believe in her own words, in the life they forced her to.

"Ask yourself why you're afraid of converting," he said. "You have some fear of faith."

"Is it wrong to be mad?" she said. "Does Christianity have the answer to that as well?" She might let herself go mad, what did it matter? Or, she thought, if I let a child grow inside of me, would I forget words? "I say, let me be mad, if madness has reason in it."

He waved a hand in the air. "You'd go mad from stubbornness."

She stood. "Mad, stubborn... there are others without faith."

"One or two, enough to prove that it's a disease. Or perhaps you have savages in mind."

She flushed and went to the dark window, standing with her back to him.

"Don't tell me that a barbarian has influence over you?"

She gave a small laugh. Kharapan had promised to see her again. But whatever he might tell her, if he could tell her anything—it didn't matter: he was a barbarian! And she a woman of Rome.

"No," she said. "He's nothing to me."

A silence followed.

"What about love?" His voice was thick.

She turned to him. "Can't one love, Victor, and still be fully human? Can't I think as well as love?"

He was momentarily without words. She was animallike, unfathomable; it had aroused him in the past. "You don't know your soul and settle for godlessness."

"And you?" Her voice rose. "I call you Victorinus, but there's no one there. You are They."

His mouth turned into a vicious twist like a smile. She stared at him in challenge.

"You might be barren," he said, as if gently, looking at her.

She paled. She understood him. He would be faultless if he divorced her; he could adopt, but that's not what he meant.

"I'm not barren," she said, staring up at him, chin down.

His understanding came slow. He looked at her; his look turned to disbelief.

She was suddenly afraid. Her fear revealed more than words.

One night, in their second year of marriage, she returned alone and in secret to her domus, rivulets of blood dripping down her thighs. Flavia was astounded. Saturnine couldn't hide the truth. She had taken precautions, but when she found herself pregnant, she went to a midwife for an abortion. It was criminal: the child legally belonged to Victorinus. Saturnine had no hesitation about carrying out this act. She couldn't be Cornelia as a mother, not yet. She couldn't bear to give a child to the Church. A baby had been too real for her to contemplate and forced her to face truths she knew without knowing, would make her hate Victorinus. A father had legal rights to a child, but a first decision by nature was the mother's. In aborting the child, she hadn't resolved the future; she had to have Victorinus's children—marriage demanded it—but she was young and might give herself time. "Do you want to be his wife?" Flavia said, aghast. "I must be his wife. I'll always be his wife. I'll have his children," she'd said.

Victorinus groaned. "You were pregnant? You contrived the death of my child?"

In the pause she lost the chance to lie, or could not lie.

"You don't want to be my wife!"

"*You* threatened to leave me."

"I'd never leave you…. What's this, Cornelia? Tell me, because I'm lost."

Saturnine watched him.

He stared at her as if trying to understand. "Yes, you're right, I see you, I finally see the truth."

She felt a chill and crossed her arms.

He grimaced. "Is everything a lie?" He paced, ready to strike or in hopeless despair, he didn't know.

"I want your children, Victor," she said, but doubted even then.

"You're a criminal." He could barely look at her. "Explain," he whispered. "Explain why." He sat in the small white chair.

Saturnine averted her eyes. Kallirrhoe wanted to kill her baby so that it wouldn't be born a slave, so might Saturnine avoid having a child that would belong to the Church. Some-one had left her at the church, and she'd been saved. She had to speak, and she stumbled over words as she told him: It had happened over a year ago; she'd been mad and didn't know her own mind. "I couldn't be Cornelia as a mother," she said.

He rushed at her, grabbing her wrists, his face close to hers. "Criminal," he whispered. "Deceitful criminal." The shock and shame in her face made him drop her hands and move away.

"I've given you everything," he said.

He turned his back on her, trying to master himself. They stood in silence. A realization came to Victorinus. The abor-tion was a crime, and strange, but a part of him understood. As odd as she was, he understood how she hated that her own child would join the Church. And yet her abortion, her criminal act—instead of being fatal to their marriage, gave him a new power over her. In any event, it pushed him to an ultimatum. He understood it now; he didn't know how he hadn't understood it before.

"I see it now," he said, turning to her. "You must decide if you want to be my wife. If you want to be married to a Roman senator, a Christian senator."

"I want to be your wife."

"Then you will convert. And burn the writing."

"Let silence be my greatest fault. I promise not to write."

"No, Cornelia, Saturnine…" (Saturnine cringed at the sound of her name.) "For God's sake, you murdered my child."

Saturnine closed her eyes.

"Am I so repulsive to you?" he said.

She shook her head. Tears filled her eyes.

"I won't charge you as a criminal," he said, after a time. "I don't want you to stay because you fear it." He shook his head in distaste. "I won't return your dowry; you don't deserve it."

"I don't want a divorce," she said. "I've never wanted that."

He struggled. He sat down. Tears blinded his eyes. "There are times," he said, "when I'm not sure if there's a God."

His words, his aspect, pained her. Saturnine took Victorinus's life for granted. She never talked to him about his purpose, what he might be or strive for. But she felt so unlike him, felt that he fit into Rome in a way that she did not. It didn't occur to her to speak to him about possibilities in life, or possible ways of life. Later, much later, it seemed to her that she had not been a good friend to him.

"Have you made your decision?" he said in a tired voice. "Do you want to be my wife? Will you convert and have my Christian children?" he added with a sardonic smile.

"Yes," she said.

"Tell me tomorrow."

"I don't need to wait," she said. "I've always known I'd have your children."

"Is there anything else?" he said. "Anything more I might learn that would shock me?" He wasn't entirely serious, but her serious expression, her hesitation, made him uneasy.

"No," she said.

"And if you can't have children? if some midwife hurt you?" Saturnine couldn't answer; she only shook her head.

"When will you burn the writing?" he said after a time.

"I'll sleep at my parents' domus on *Saturnus*, and do

it that night," she said. "There aren't many servants left." And I'll wake on *Sol, Kalends of Martius*, the new year, she thought—the day to designate Caesars, the day to honor Rome's first king, the shepherd with shaggy hair dressed in the skin of the cloven-footed animal.

"We'll sell the domus," she added. She'd been unwilling to sell, and they'd argued over it. He had legal power over their wealth, but as she'd inherited the domus, only she could legally sell it. Once sold, he would have no restraints on the use of the money.

"Then we'll go to the church on *Sol*," he said. "Know this. I won't give you another chance." He didn't know what more to say; after an awkward pause he went out.

When he reached his private quarters Victorinus sat for a long time. Their domus would overflow with children, he thought, all devoted to Christ.

He went to her bed late that night. He pulled down her loincloth; his hands rushed to her breasts, to the curve of her hips. The softness of her body, her passive surrender, the slight rise of her body, made him gasp. Saturnine lay still with his body on her, marveling at the intensity of the new disgust she felt at his touch and at her own self-loathing. She put a hand on his arm and in an effort to counter her vile feeling, said, "Go. Let me sleep. I'll be a new being on *Sol*, better able to love you."

FIVE

ON THE MORNING of *Saturnus*, Kharapan stood on the road outside Village G. He'd been drawn to the path he'd taken many years before but having reached the outskirts of the village, he had no desire to enter it. He turned back on the cobblestone road, his thoughts on Rome.

After leaving Saturnine's garden, he'd bathed, had a haircut and shave, and had his clothes cleaned. He'd worked on the Rome-Alexandria run and had money, but Kharapan was a man who somehow always had enough money and rarely felt its lack; he hardly ever went hungry. He smiled to think of how he'd stood in Saturnine's garden, dirty, newly arrived after a long voyage, excited, nervous, how she'd come out to greet him, invited him to join them.

The day after, he'd met with Flavia at Temple Athena at dusk: he told her he would tell Saturnine the truth. "My past will destroy her," Flavia had said. Kharapan blamed the long years of secrets and an overwrought imagination. He said he hated to wait an hour, and she'd gasped, and promised to tell Saturnine herself, asking for two days, until *Saturnus*. He agreed to stay away until *Sol*, said he'd seek out Flavia when he returned to Rome before going to Saturnine. So he'd walked out on the road and found himself outside Village G.

His thoughts, like vines knotting old trees and flowers, wound in and around the past—Saturnine, Lupicinus, *Kingdoms*, which he'd shown in Rome for the first time.

He had a strong feeling, as of an intuition, a reckoning perhaps, some sort of reckoning to come. In his travels, the experience of a moment became intimate as a practice and art. It seemed to him that the world guided him and gave him clues to existence, at least to next steps, interwoven connections inside and out. He honed his ability to see and interpret messages that the world gave him.

The flat gray stones stretched out before him. A yellow morning light illuminated red poppies in fields. He heard someone coming, heard the sound of hooves pounding against stones. Kharapan stopped. Birds grew silent as if in homage to the official messenger, who sleek in clothes that clung to his body in the wind, stood in stirrups, leaning forward to urge the horse to move faster. Dust and small rocks flew up in the air behind them. The road, though straight, inclined up a small hill and disappeared into a blank mist.

Word traveled quickly in Empire. Words, ideas, thoughts spread as if Mercury really existed.

On his first journey into Empire, barely a man, he had gone to Alexandria. The bread maker asked Kharapan if he knew that Miriam was the Mother of God. He said he didn't know Miriam. At the bath, a slave told him that the Son was of like substance but not the same as the Father. Kharapan came to feel as if he himself, his mind and deepest desires, had little existence, as if a phantom in this world. In this large powerful place called Empire, he felt that Chi and the life of philosophy might disappear as a path in a sandstorm.

Alexandria helped Kharapan see himself and his own country with perspective, but understanding increased his painful sense, as if a physical manifestation, of the vulnerability of Chi. He sometimes thought of Metis's fear of the power of Christianity, though she had not yet written *Kingdoms*, her concern over the irrationality of belief, and thought "this is what she senses."

From a woman he stayed with, a prostitute called Aulia Patina, he came to know the kind of love the Epicureans called the sweet and flattering pleasure, and although he understood that Aulia Patina did not provoke in him the violent emotion of love, his desire to repeat the pleasure he felt with her was insatiable, and he felt a danger. He could not stop this life flood. He felt himself drowning, or so it seemed, but he had an intense passion for a philosophical life, to live a kind of integrity.

Aulia Patina told him about the life of the city that involved a story of gods. Kharapan had trouble following. Arians, she said, claimed that Christ was of like substance to the Father (*homoiousios*) and raged a war against homoousions who said Christ was of the same substance, same being. Aulia Patina tried to explain how three consisted in one God, how a man might be God and go to heaven. Aulia Patina called Kharapan a heathen, amazed at his utter lack of knowledge of the gods. She was a homoousian, a follower of Athanasius, a Catholic, but as a lover of mankind, she told Kharapan, she wouldn't fight over words, although Kharapan sensed that she had the passion over her God as others seemed to. These people were quick to anger, and Aulia Patina, too, seemed ready to join a mob, ready to support her beloved Bishop Athanasius.

Arians tried to eliminate non-Arian Christians from the city, as well as those who followed the ancient religions. The Arian emperor Constantius sent his men, including George of Cappadocia, who was appointed bishop of Alexandria. With troops at his command, George acted like a dictator and bribed and threatened pagans into attacking homoousians, followers of the Catholic bishop, Athanasius, who'd fled in fear of his life. George arranged for the cults of Serapis and Dionysus to attack the Great church while homoousians worshipped. But then George turned against pagans too and destroyed temples of civic cults that had existed since the time of Alexander. "Alexandria is in unholy chaos," Aulia Patina told Kharapan. George prohibited sacrifices and ordered the military to sack the precinct of Serapion and tear down the altar of Juno Moneta. And someone under his command, overseeing the construction of a church, cut off the curls of Jewish boys. But more than a year before, George himself had been forced to flee in fear of his life. At first, the followers of Athanasius took possession of the churches, but new troops from Egypt expelled them, and those that survived were exiled. Recently, a notarius named Paul, nicknamed The Chain, arrived from court with an edict to persecute George's opponents. In the bishop's name, backed by an emperor, he called people to trial, and even tortured philosophers on the rack.

"Jesus Christ is the redeemer of humanity," Aulia Patina said. "If He is the same substance as God, then redemption means being taken into the life of God, being made divine. Jesus Christ is salvation. He offers deification."

"We struggle to be a sage, but no man is a sage," Kharapan said.

Aulia Patina shook her head and warned Kharapan that he'd go to hell, but without passion or energy. He was godless, and foreign, an outsider. She, like others, turned their concerns to the fight within their city.

In the life of the foreign city, Kharapan came to understand that every philosophy in Chi, every school or group in Chi, as much as they argued and claimed to be dissimilar, even opposite in nature, had a way of life, if it might be called that, of *agnosis*, of honoring the unknown or mystery, what was unknowable, backing off in homage to honor the unknown even in the midst of the most heated argument. *Agnosis* acted as a limit, a salve to passion. *Philosophia* was, in part, the consciousness of knowing nothing.

Neither Alexandria, nor Empire, nor Aulia Patina tempted Kharapan to believe in God, in the gods, in any god of any man's imagination. To the contrary, the experience strengthened his purpose and mind. He'd practice the stuff of integrity by struggling to stay close to what he didn't know, and in Empire, the task rose to the surface and became clear to him. Alexandria made him intimate with the struggle, and he considered this an improvement, an advance toward his dream of knowing what values and words he would die for.

For him, he told Aulia Patina, a lone creature gazing

over a vast sandy desert might acquire the wisdom of a philosopher. Nature was a force guided by rules but also by an unbearable mystery.

Aulia Patina didn't understand how Chi had come to be so scraped clean of gods.

Kharapan thought about it. In the festivals of Chi, when men covered themselves in ash and women wore dried leaves, and music and dancing filled the village, some said they celebrated spirits, others felt the joy of existence and mystery. "In Chi," he said, "you might find every idea, even of god, except, perhaps not the one-god of Christianity. Some will have gods, some of the godless believe in rebirth, that the essence of ourselves is eternal although the knowing intellect dies. But the difference is this, I think: those of Chi are not so attached to their ideas that they force others to believe. We have our arguments and disagreements, but they do not end in violence, at least not in murder. We have a saying in Chi: a wise creature is one who knows what he doesn't know."

Aulia Patina's laughter tinkled like silver bells.

Kharapan smiled. "You think I'm a fool," he said.

"No. I've heard you say 'I don't know' so often, and now I see the truth: you're the wisest man of your country."

"No," he said in a low voice. "There are wise men..." His lack of knowledge didn't come from a deep understanding of the boundaries of knowledge. His unknowing came from ignorance, a lack of an unworthy kind. Even if he could spout wise words, memorizing sayings was far different from wisdom, and he wouldn't pretend to know, not even nothing.

She peered at him seriously. "But you know you are godless."

"You can call it that if you'd like," he said.

Aulia Patina took the goods he'd brought from Chi and sold them at a significant profit. He let her keep his ten percent. Even with her daily labor, she liked to make love to him. His innocence and long-limbed beauty, she said, was a relief to her.

A slight breeze hinted at a weak sun, hinted that winter had come, hinted that weeks and even months had passed. While Aulia Patina worked, or sold during the day, Kharapan cleaned her apartment and was lured into complacency by his sensual existence and the easy rhythm of the days. But one day, walking down a crowded street to buy bread, he stopped in the road as if his body refused by itself to take another step. People ran into him and yelled at him, but he stood still. A thought struck him, not a new thought. It was this: his life might pass in this way, and he would never attain, would not even move toward, his cherished goal of knowing his core. One could not be a sage, a perfect being, a god, but one could strive to live in and practice the higher functions of man. He'd once imagined being an old man wandering among the schools in Chi, never knowing himself, and he'd once seen himself in the Aristotelian school, never becoming one of the Aristotelians, never going beyond that life. He realized that he might become an old man in this life, this same life. Although he knew himself better, he didn't know his core, his words. He'd become invisible, observing others as he'd observed in Chi, not advancing to manhood.

Standing in the narrow road he had a nagging sensation. He ignored it, at first, even for a long time, and then looked around trying to understand. At the crowded shops he saw a sign, "Arminius Leather." He smiled and laughed out loud. It seemed as if the world approved of his thoughts. He'd passed that place a hundred times and never noticed the sign, the name of his Stoic master, Arminius, until he'd had this insight.

When he told Aulia Patina about his experience and explained that he had to leave Alexandria, she was sad. She tried to diminish his experience. She said he must believe that either the Fates or God guided him with his "signs."

Kharapan shook his head. "I'm not saying that gods control my fate," he said. "Every aspect of life from air to dirt... a person wandering in this midst fits in and is guided. We're intimate with the world. Aspects of the world are relevant to a man beforehand, even based on his past, his nature, his experience, the state of his body."

His ideas coincided with the Stoic notion that Nature was a symphony of connectedness. His only duty was to make assessments of the Nature that appeared, so to speak, and to understand how it guided him.

Kharapan returned to Chi with a significant profit, which convinced the merchant Tyrolian, to Kharapan's abhorrence, that Kharapan had the core of a traveling merchant. Kharapan did not care to explain about Aulia Patina. Zosimus, too, helped fill Kharapan's bag and asked to see the piece of lead. Kharapan pulled out the lead, black and heavy and small. "Not gold!" Zosimus cried. "More work to be done." Of course Zosimus must have known something of his true passion.

Kharapan didn't stay long in Chi. He fell into and could hardly break out of the routine of his early life. He didn't speak his mind. He simply cleaned and helped the philosophers in the Aristotelian, Stoic, and Epicurean schools.

"I think you're beginning to recognize yourself," Arminius said one night, when Kharapan went to the Stoic domus to say goodbye.

Kharapan was too unsure to respond.

"Don't be afraid of losing what you've learned in Chi," he said. "You have Chi inside of you now."

But Kharapan did fear. Arminius touched on that fear, Kharapan's secret Achilles' heel. His strength and his integrity depended on Chi, on its existence and on returning home to it. He felt he would lose himself if he stayed too long in the Empire. He needed to hear lectures and discourses, to witness philosophers' lives. Arminius had too much faith in him, he thought.

"How did you recognize yourself?" Kharapan said to the old master.

"In conversation. I'm respected for conversation as if I'm offering a service, as if they beheld a man of wisdom, but I couldn't exist or be what I am without it. Relationship with others turns me into myself. I know you understand."

Arminius gave him a gift; he held up his walking stick. It was too much, the passing down of a great gift, and Kharapan wasn't a Stoic, not even a philosopher. But Arminius insisted. He said Kharapan had a practical need for the walking stick and added that Kharapan had a unique potential to return as a man.

Kharapan accepted the walking stick, taking it in his hands as if it might break. Arminius said, "Learn the feel and the balance of your body, let your senses and feelings guide you. Think of the walking stick in that way and let it remind you."

Kharapan came to learn what these words meant. He would learn, painfully, what happened when he lost his balance, when he disregarded his feelings and senses and instead fell fully into certain ideas.

He met Justin, Saturnine's father, on his second journey, and they struck that 'philosophic bond' between them. In that journey, Kharapan crossed the middle of the earth, the Mediterranean Sea, for the first time. He worked the Alexandria-Rome run as a seaman, a fine vessel of the Roman merchant fleet. The ship carried a thousand passengers and enough Egyptian grain to feed Rome for months. The stern rose into a gradual curve and at the flat forward, the wide sweep of the prow, a brightly painted figure of Isis strained outward on each side of the ship. Their skippers were the most experienced in the world, but heavy winds forced the vessel on a course to the south coast of Asia Minor, Crete, Malta, and Sicily before reaching Portus, the main port to Rome. When they reached Portus, Kharapan helped unload and pleased the shipmaster so well that Kharapan might have found a profession in the shipping business, but Kharapan sought the larger world and took up his bag.

In Rome, a battle raged between Arian and orthodox Christians, but, unlike Alexandria, in Rome at the time,

Christians, Jews, and pagans generally left each other alone. Pagans had a stronghold in Rome itself, a majority in the senate, a majority in the aristocracy. And a pagan, Julian, had been declared emperor. This emperor had a passion for his gods that equaled the Christian passion for theirs, and a pagan revival flourished in Rome. Kharapan hesitated and then sought out the Jewish section of the city. While sitting in a small courtyard, he saw a young man about his age with dark curls and dark eyes. The man's curious stare made him feel shy.

The young man approached, in anger or suspicion it seemed to Kharapan, and he rested a foot on a low wall, demanding to know where Kharapan was from. He had smiling eyes.

Kharapan was struck by the conversations he'd had—between a man of Chi and those immersed in a world of gods. He'd already learned to seek a particular kind of conversation, one that he thought existed between the boundaries of knowledge, a conversation approaching gaps between worlds, the space that inspired one to speak and where one hoped to discover a common bond or truth. However, so far, he had mostly spoken to men, much older men, and he felt shy with this young man. But he told Justin (that was his name) where he came from, and he tried to explain to him why he traveled. Although he sold things, he said, and might be called a trader, in fact he hoped to discover something far more subtle and important, and it involved his core, his being, his way of life.

Justin had been attracted by Kharapan's exotic appearance, he'd approached the dark stranger in hope of provoking his family who, one or another of them, were always nearby. The more Kharapan spoke, however, the more Justin forgot whoever might be observing. Justin couldn't believe Kharapan had the freedom to go where he wished and the courage to do so without much money, without a secure position in the world, although Kharapan had money even then, and he had his goods of Chi to sell. When Kharapan spoke of his godless-ness in response to Justin's inevitable question about God, Justin paused before saying in a grave voice, "I'm Jewish, but I can't distinguish myself from other mortals. All people are human above all else, regardless of country or religion. All people might love each other." Kharapan, of course, felt it was so, and at the time, even if they didn't fully appreciate the rarity of each other's minds, the two young men felt an immediate bond.

Justin invited him into his home. They climbed the stairs to the third floor of a five-story building, and Justin opened the door to a noisy apartment of brothers, sisters, cousins, and elders. Justin's family looked at Kharapan as if at a stray animal. But they saw that Kharapan was young and harmless, and they took an interest in him. Over the days, Kharapan helped them in the market, and they sold his goods for him. He insisted that they keep the ten percent profit. He and Justin took their bath and exercise together, and Justin showed him the city.

Kharapan's stories about his life at the schools and with an Alexandrian prostitute fascinated and intrigued Justin. Kharapan explained that his experience with the prostitute had given him a lived example of unnecessary pleasure, which proved dangerous. "Our love is pure," he added shyly. Justin grabbed Kharapan's wrist. They made a pact: the friendship between them would be as firm and lasting as that between any two of the greatest of philosophers.

When Kharapan left Rome and returned to his country, more than a year passed before he saw Justin again, although they wrote to each other.

When Kharapan returned to Rome and entered Justin's apartment, he found Justin and his mother arguing. Justin flung himself on Kharapan and wept. Now that his friend had come, everything would be decided, he said. Justin's mother also hung on Kharapan, begging him to bring Justin to reason. Kharapan discerned most of it: Justin's family had chosen a Jewish girl for his wife. The families had come to an agreement. However, on a journey to Milan some three months before, Justin had stopped at a roadside inn, an inn of the lowest sort, according to his mother, and met and apparently fallen in love with a woman, Honora.

"A prostitute!" His mother cried. "An old woman too."

"Mama, she's only twenty."

Justin visited Honora often, perhaps encouraged because of the arguments. But his love for Honora was real, and he told them he would marry her. Justin's father hadn't spoken to him for a fortnight.

Justin took Kharapan's arm, and they went out. In the courtyard, they stood apart to appraise one another. Kharapan had become thick and strong and blacker on the boat. Justin had let his thick, black, curly hair grow long and wild, and he wore loose clothes on his long thin body. They went into the city, hardly aware of where they walked. Justin spoke in a passion of Honora—her skin so pale he could see through to the veins. Her skin showed a vulnerability she herself couldn't reveal, he said. "One whose spirit is pure under those conditions," he said. She'd been surprised when he'd wanted to please her. He couldn't bear to have her at the inn—she wasn't a slave, but the innkeeper treated her like one. "The Innkeeper bought her from her family many years ago, and he told her she could buy her freedom, but he's never paid her. Honora says that she doesn't care for money, and she knows no other life. She doesn't believe me when I say I'll take her away and marry her."

He held Kharapan's arm and fearfully looked into his face. "Tell me what you think."

Kharapan spoke after a time. "A man has no choice but do what he thinks he must. No one can stop another's errors, if they are errors. Errors provide an opportunity to learn."

Justin stood still for a moment. "Then you'll meet her tomorrow," he said.

Two days later they entered a shabby inn. Honora, a modest woman with thick blonde hair, spoke little. Her color rose when Justin entered the inn, but otherwise she showed no emotion. She served wine and bread, and in the middle of the meal, Justin asked her to come away with them.

"You'll be my friend and wife," he said.

Honora, after a long pause, said "I will. I'll go with you."

Not long after, the three of them were on the Roman cobblestone road. The innkeeper refused at first to give them Honora's papers, but with two rugged young men insisting, he gave in. Honora had made him enough money long ago to return what he'd paid for her. She had her papers. She was free. They went north.

Kharapan left them at a farm in Village G. An elder widow gave Justin and Honora room and board in exchange for services. Kharapan gave them the last of his goods as a wedding present for them to profit by and promised to return in a few months. Justin took his arm and with a firm grip, hugged half of Kharapan's body. And keeping hold of Kharapan's hand, took up Honora's and said that the two people he loved most in the world would also be bound in friendship.

When Kharapan returned to Village G. three months later, he found Justin and Honora immersed in their lives. Honora served the widow so well, the woman could hardly bear to part with her. Justin had found work in a neighboring village and hoped to own his own store and make enough money to buy their own domus. Honora would have served Justin more if he'd let her, and she sometimes glanced at her young husband with a half-astonished, half-bewildered look. When Justin saw that look, he reached out his arm to her. Justin had sent a letter to his family, he told Kharapan, asking that they accept Honora—but he'd heard nothing. He told Kharapan something else: Honora was pregnant.

When Kharapan left them, he didn't suspect that he would never see Justin again. He lost track of Honora as well, until he found his arm on hers more than three years later in Rome.

Kharapan left Justin and Honora, and Rome, under auspicious circumstances. A favorable wind carried the ship from

Portus to Alexandria in less than ten days, and he had a calm and easy journey up the Nile. But when he arrived in Hellenica, he found everyone in an uproar. The people discussed and argued over a text written by Metis called *Kingdoms*. They spoke in confusion about Metis's refusal to say whether or not she'd accept an esteemed two-year post at the Study in the Great Village. No one who'd been offered the position had ever refused or even delayed acceptance. Metis had been offered the post at the unusually young age of twenty-two with the support of certain statesmen, the Aristotelians, and perhaps her father. The post offered her time to think and to write, and it pleased and excited her whole family, especially her father. However, for some reason, she hadn't accepted the offer and kept postponing. She avoided her family and got angry if they—her father or brothers—came to bother her with the matter.

Kingdoms confused and delighted the people of Hellenica. Much of the text had been read out loud at the Great Hall to a packed audience. Some said it made unique use of the sliver of fiction. As an imaginary discourse on two Kingdoms (an extreme version of the Empire and of Chi), it turned Chi's idea of the sliver of fiction into an artwork, in spite of the work's ultimately narrow claims. Others argued that Metis had done away with the 'sliver of fiction' entirely and instead propounded what she believed constituted a future threat, a claim of what would come without the slightest doubt. Therefore, they said, the work lacked true wisdom and a balanced view. Metis grinned and refused to expound on her theories, at least not openly, not with everyone. In spite of differing opinions on the meaning of the text, most suspected that it was brilliant. Aristotelians claimed Metis as their own, and said that, like Plato, she illustrated truth with stories.

Metis had a small but passionate clan of young followers sitting at her feet, acting as scribes, hoping to glean insight about what could be done to save the world. Metis awakened them to the immorality and threat of the Church—a threat not only to Chi but also to the unlucky people of Empire and all of humanity. The extent of the evil, she told them, was hardly comprehensible. Metis's intellect and confidence made her impossible to resist. Metis was a force.

Kharapan read *Kingdoms* with urgency. Rage seethed beneath Metis's confident sentences. As with the other young people of Chi, perhaps even more, given his experience in Empire, her insights and words inspired him to a passionate outrage against the Church almost in step with hers. Her Kingdom of God made a rational creature's deviation from Christ, any deviation, a crime. The mistaken and faulty rational creature had to live an impossible ideal and, by definition, was a criminal. People hated themselves. They failed to recognize their natural morality. The Church taught rational creatures that they were naturally bad, immoral, and the state grievously punished them. In the Kingdom of God, thoughts might be traitorous, reason itself was a crime. The Kingdom of God was a decrepit and degraded place. People became informants: children informed on parents, dissatisfied neighbors informed on each other. People found it easy and even pleasurable to implicate fellow beings and watch them burn at the stake. The Kingdom of God aimed to rule the world, and the Church had an insatiable hunger for power. Those who'd been born and grown up in the Kingdom of God had a ragged, immature morality, vulnerable to outside forces, to the sway of the world's right and wrong. They didn't understand the inner struggle. Even those wise Roman philosophers were lost, Metis wrote. People know that one has to be trained in mathematics, Epictetus wrote, but not in morality. Those of the Christian Kingdom failed utterly to cultivate wisdom.

Metis's Great Unknown glorified Chi. The law incorporated that truth, she wrote, that a man or woman had a natural moral nature, and that one enlarged his or her moral nature in the intimate struggle of existence and through discussion. People trusted in dispute resolution because dispute resolvers understood people as moral animals. One was allowed to kill, at least once, for example, if that person, like a dog, say, was lost in passion. One couldn't be angry at a dog for killing, but it might have to be removed from society. For most humans, the pain of having done wrong was itself the punishment. The shame of the act, and the knowledge of one's own evil was adequate punishment. Man was naturally a noble creature and acted against himself in doing evil, for to be mistaken was to stain one's own nobility. But to commit an evil was mostly just that, an evil against oneself, one's own human self.

After reading *Kingdoms*, Kharapan's anger at Christians and fear for Chi had never been more acute. He recognized the truth in much of what Metis wrote. However, after reflection and distance he experienced a familiar feeling of bafflement about Metis. *Kingdoms* gave rise to that confusion that Metis's angry confidence often inspired in him. He was impressed with *Kingdoms*, and with her intelligence, and although one might say she'd written it without irony or humor, without a 'reserve of doubt,' he found the codex hard to fault because it was imaginary—she wrote of imaginary worlds. He convinced himself that as a work of imagination, *Kingdoms* must have more than a 'sliver of fiction.' Metis couldn't believe her Kingdoms actually existed, or feel she knew for sure that they would come to exist. That is, he didn't think she could believe in her Kingdoms without doubt, could fail to understand the messy complexity of life, which would be the actual future. He knew that she'd been working in monasteries in the north, translating and copying texts, had intimate knowledge of Christians and Christianity. Still, he felt the work lacked complexity: perhaps if she'd based it on actual life, on Christians she knew, and not imaginary people and worlds, she would have had to subdue her passion, would have been without such firm notions or theories. Instead, he thought, she would have been left with the contrary complexities of real individuals. In the end, and as usual with things having to do with Metis, he didn't trust his intuition, and was left without an ability to comment. He might have only smiled and shrugged when asked his opinion, but he listened to their arguments.

One day something happened that sunk all of Hellenica in guilt. People saw Metis's work and the author herself as intimately involved, if not directly culpable. Christians had come to Chi in the past, to sell in its markets or journeying through, as other Romans, but not long after *Kingdoms* circulated, a monk came to the largest square in the Great Village and set up a box in the busy marketplace to announce the good news of Jesus Christ. When no one gathered and the people ignored him, he became fierce and called them heathens, savages, barbarians. His attack went on and on. He had the capacity to persist.

Kharapan witnessed everything and later felt at fault for everything. The monk, a man neither young nor old, with a short gray beard and a heavy body, spoke in a low beautiful voice, but frustration broke his tone. As the monk grew angrier, spiteful even, tension grew. Perhaps events had less to do with *Kingdoms* itself than with the essence of Chi: the idea of preaching, of telling people what to believe, was outrageous to their hearts and beliefs. Of course, they argued amongst themselves over ideas, but the monk's mirthless tone, the absolute certainty of his message, and then, of course, the insults that followed, outraged them. But Kharapan blamed the events that ensued, perhaps the failure of the people of Chi to laugh at the monk, on *Kingdoms*, recently circulating among them.

The subdued hue of dusk sent the last boats home. People closed shop and put away goods. The monk continued his sermon against the sound of closing doors and products being loaded back into carts. A few people remained. Kharapan stood steadfast in the shadow. He felt ashamed at the monk's audacity. Of course, as he considered later, he might have at least offered a bit of laughter and that might have saved the evangelist. But he'd just read *Kingdoms*. Perhaps Kharapan sensed something would happen and wasn't sure even then how he would respond. Perhaps he wondered if he himself would make "something happen." At last something did happen. A man named Zeno, Kharapan's age, one of those who sat at Metis's feet, approached the monk with a metal stick in his hand and slapped him in the head. The monk fell and lay barely moving. A man and woman rushed over, and after a moment of indecision, Zeno and another man dragged the monk to an empty room at the edge of the square. Zeno left him. The square grew empty, and at last, only Kharapan remained.

He didn't go immediately to the monk. He would blame himself for this all his life. He stood in the courtyard deep in thought; he had not been less outraged than Zeno. Steeped in the wisdom and dire warning of *Kingdoms*, the monk's appearance seemed an inauspicious omen of the Church's threat thrust before their eyes. However, sometime later, he became aware of himself, as if he didn't know how long he'd been standing there, feeling as if he'd awakened from a dream. He rushed to the barn and found the monk groaning, and he gave him water and went to summon the doctor.

Meanwhile, Zeno and a few others had gathered in Metis's small room. Metis told them that the monk's presence marked the start of a subtle and complex war. The monk's act had been the first aggression. *Kingdoms* warned them. They couldn't remain passive now. Zeno felt uncertain. He'd hit the monk without much forethought. His mother had been at her cart. He couldn't stand for her to be insulted. Metis encouraged and admired him: they'd been outraged, but no one else dared do anything. And like the others, all

155

seventeen or eighteen years old, Zeno said he'd throw himself into Metis's war. One suggested they circulate Metis's book in Empire, provoke the outrage of non-Christians, try to start a war within Empire itself, but Metis said it was too late: a monk lay hurt, possibly dead. They couldn't work openly, and *Kingdoms* might be traced to Hellenica. No, theirs was a small country and would be at risk; they must work secretively. First they had to make sure the monk didn't live to tell the tale, and then they had to hide his body. If Roman Christians discovered what had happened, the people of Hellenica, their country and way of life, would be in imminent danger.

When the young people returned to the barn, they found Kharapan bent over the monk. The doctor had come, bandaged the monk's head, and told Kharapan that whether the monk lived or not depended on whether he survived the night. There was nothing more he could do.

"He's alive," Kharapan said, "but has a fever. We shouldn't move him. He has a lump on his head. The doctor thinks his skull is cracked."

"Move away," Metis commanded.

Kharapan looked at her and at the others. Disbelief filled him. He stood, trembling and shielding the monk. "I would never have believed!" he cried. "It goes against everything Chi is, the reserve clause, the uncertainty—"

"My loyalty extends beyond Chi," Metis said. "We can't let Chi be destroyed, or there'll be no 'reserve clause.' We can't leave others, those outside of Chi, to a miserable destiny. It's our duty as sisters and brothers of humanity."

Kharapan trembled. Invention, art, philosophy, war, all

seemed swept up in this powerful moment, but how could any one of them have enough certainty to kill? How could they stop the weight of history? On the other hand, he felt he would die for Chi.

"What is it to kill this man? How does that rise to these grand words, brothers of humanity? How does it save Chi and humanity—" He broke off. "No," he said. "It would be murder. You'd have to submit to the law, and you might not survive."

He peered at her. When he told her she might not survive the law, he meant that the dispute resolvers might conclude she'd kill again, but he didn't believe it. He was being petulant.

Metis's eyes were unwavering. "The state's purpose is to grant freedom for the passions of the individual."

"Not the passion to kill! Not the freedom to kill!"

"No, not to kill, but in Chi we have the right to explore our humanity. That privilege enables us to see oppression. Having seen and understood, how can we not act? How can we remain passive? We must fight oppression: we must save Chi, and others too. The importance of what we do now has gone beyond Chi."

"You sound like one of them," Kharapan said. "Like one of the most fanatic Christians in Empire." He paused. "It's above the law," he said softly, to himself. In spite of his words, he couldn't believe Metis or the others would go through with their murderous plans once they came to their senses. It must be a strange night to find them, the young people of Chi, arguing in this way over a hurt man.

The monk groaned. They crowded around him.

"His name is John," Kharapan said. He'd looked into his bag. He noticed the faces of those around him soften. Even Zeno stood still. Metis peered at the monk with an intense look.

Kharapan tried to give Monk John water, but it dribbled down his face. The monk suddenly jerked back and forth in a spasm.

"We're all guilty," Kharapan said. Zeno's fearful eyes settled on Kharapan.

Metis motioned to the others to wait, as if they were about to rush forward and smother the monk, as if she held a strange power over them. "Kharapan is right," she said. "If he dies, we're all guilty. If Zeno is named to the Romans, all of Chi is at risk of falling with him. We must stand as a country."

Kharapan gave her an uncertain glance. "The punishment is knowing what we are capable of, that is what we have to live with," he said.

A sound from the monk drew their attention. Foam from the monk's mouth trickled down his face. He made a choking sound, and then his body stiffened as if in surprise. Then he stopped breathing altogether.

No one moved. No one knew what to do. The monk lay still.

"He's dead," Kharapan said after a time.

They stood around the room. Kharapan was motionless over the monk.

"No one could save him," Metis said, breaking the silence. She strode over and covered the dead man's face with his dirty cloak. "We'll cremate him while it's dark and scatter the remains."

"Cover our guilt!" Kharapan said.

"What would you have us do? Send Zeno to the Romans to be slaughtered? Chi would be implicated and in peril from Christian revenge—Zeno will submit to *our* justice."

Kharapan felt an aching sickness in his body, but he submitted. They went to Zosimus's metallurgy shop, where the dark fire in the crematorium burned, and lifted the heavy body and stood back to watch as the monk's body was engulfed in flames. Metis's followers left one after another without speaking. After the last one left, Kharapan and Metis were alone. She gave him a look, one he remembered from long ago, a haughty, insolent look, and then she too went out.

Early in the morning, before first light, Metis swept up the monk's ashes and took them to a western region of the desert and scattered them near a large cactus. They had no choice, she thought. She had a new ache in her body, a new sickness of being. No one could be happy with so much misery in the world.

The next day, many citizens of Chi awoke to guilt and were shocked (and perhaps relieved) to discover that the monk had disappeared. The council called an emergency open meeting. A hundred people crowded the Great Hall. Metis and her devotees sat to one side, close to the front. Kharapan stood where he could watch Metis. When questioned, Metis admitted everything: they returned to the monk, she said, and found Kharapan trying to save him. Once the monk died, they cremated him, and she scattered his ashes. Romans might come, she said, but they wouldn't be able to prove anything. The people of Chi might admit that he'd come, but they must say that the monk continued south or else that they knew nothing. To do otherwise would endanger Chi. Anyone who reported Zeno to the Romans or told about these events would be a traitor, she said.

The complexity of a secret crime against Romans astonished the people in the Great Hall, even if some were privately glad for what Zeno had done. There had been rare legal disputes, civil and criminal, between Empire and Country, but never murder. They felt afraid, especially with Metis's *Kingdoms* circulating among them. Romans might accuse them of being enemies of the Church. The council felt it had no choice: they would try Zeno in Chi, but not report it to Romans. Some whispered that Metis herself was guilty of something, but they weren't sure of what. Word passed of the decision: if the Romans discovered the truth, so be it, but no one would tell. It was a matter of avoiding a threat to Chi itself. It was a matter of survival.

Zeno had a quick trial, and he felt remorse. The dispute resolvers and the council didn't think he'd kill again, but they feared the unease in Chi and so they banished him for a year. They decided that he'd struck the monk out of passion and hadn't intended to kill. Zeno was ordered to report to the council when he returned and explain how he intended to live. They hoped exile would serve as a warning.

No one after these events wanted to talk about *Kingdoms*. No one wanted to speak of Christians. Those who had sat at Metis's feet slipped away from her. Metis, bitter and angry, rejected the post in the Study, and a few months later converted an old hut on the edge of the desert into a rugged permanent residence, refusing to join in the society of her countrymen.

Kharapan left Chi soon after, and during months of travel he contemplated what had taken place. Monk John's death would not be resolved: the monk's family and friends would never find out what happened to him. Kharapan felt deeply dismayed, not only for this but also for many reasons. The terrible knowledge of what he was capable of, hurt Kharapan deeply. Yes, he thought, this equaled him. Knowledge of what it was like to be implicated in a man's murder gave him compassion for those who'd killed. He grappled with a battered view of himself—he'd had little integrity when integrity had mattered so much—but he also found a need to alter his ideas about Chi. Since he'd journeyed to Empire, he'd often reflected on the difference between Empire and Chi, and he, perhaps self-righteously, believed that the people of Chi wouldn't kill to prove the truth of their convictions. The people of Chi fiercely believed in stories but were never so extreme, so fundamentally attached to belief, as to lose the ability to laugh. So he'd believed. Chi recognized the sliver of possibility that they didn't know the truth, and in this sense, used the word 'fiction,' the 'sliver of fiction' that was in all ideas. But Zeno had killed a Christian and implicated the country.

Still, Kharapan felt... convinced himself... that in spite of what happened, the people of Chi differed from Romans. His argument consisted in something of the following: the murder of the monk was a singular event, carried out in passion, not to defend cold ideals, and it taught them a lesson.

It had been a single example of passion, but it was done and would not be repeated. It was done by an individual, by Zeno, without the support of or affiliation to an institution like the Church. If the schools fought among themselves, they did not try to turn another's thoughts through threat of death! No, the idea brought a smile to Kharapan's lips. The principle seemed firmly established in Chi: a man had to come to his own conclusion in his own way, by his own path, even if he belonged to a particular school. From that time, Kharapan carried a copy of Metis's *Kingdoms*; he believed it would remind him of his dark potential and serve as a warning to him.

By the time Kharapan returned to Rome and Village G., his hopes of finding his friends were shattered. The elderly woman whom Justin and Honora had lived with had died. As if to avoid ill omen, no one even admitted knowing Justin or Honora, until a barman finally said that Justin had died from a painful intestinal disorder, and that a month later Honora had given birth to a girl and disappeared. Kharapan sank under a tree and wept. It seemed to him that the world had become an empty, evil place, and that philosophical wisdom and training were useless.

On his way out, the grown daughter of Justin and Honora's last landlord caught up with him and handed him a letter. "It's never been opened," she said. "It arrived after the poor girl left; we tried to help her, but she had no family, and no one had the means to take her in."

The letter was Justin's letter to his family, returned to Justin unopened.

The letter, like other signs but more direct, gave Kharapan knowledge of his destination. He wearily took up his mantle. He would tell them that Justin had died, that they had a grandchild, a girl, and in spite of their pain, he would tell them that their gesture toward Justin and Honora, returning the letter, refusing to take them in, had been based on a failure on their part to understand *agnosis*. He would tell them that they were mistaken in thinking that they knew things they did not, things that no one could know.

In the twenty years of his wanderings since, he carried *Kingdoms* and the terrible secret regarding Monk John's death.

In the late morning of *Saturnus*, sounds behind Kharapan again disturbed him, and he looked back and saw an entourage approaching: horses, a golden carriage, monks following.

He moved to the top of the small dirt hillock on the side of the road. At the front of the procession, a few horses and riders came forward. Rich red velvet robes hung on the men. The horses' hooves struck the stones, the black hair clumped in sweat. A dank, stale smell rose in the cold air. The men struggled to make the animals move slowly. Two white horses pulled a carriage, two men in red robes sat in the carriage seat. The horses snorted, shook their heads, raised their legs as they walked as if tired but proud of the greatness of the man in the carriage. On closer view, Kharapan could see that the white was partially painted on the horses: white sweaty drops splattered on gray stones. The carriage jolted back and forth on uneven stones. Kharapan saw a fat arm, fat fingers holding something, yellow cheese, perhaps. He saw thick, jeweled rings: one round white, another square blue, and a third square red, painfully squeezing swollen fingers. As the carriage passed, he faced the man, the loose jowls, thick, cream-fed skin, white-blue eyes. The blue eyes looked at him, startled, interested, and the carriage passed by. Was it the pope? But no—even Kharapan knew that Damasus, bishop of Rome, was eighty years old and unwell.

Dark clouds gathered and the humidity increased to a breaking point. Rain fell in large drops and then in a downpour. Kharapan took out his wool cloak and crossed the road where puddles were already forming, making his way between drenched monks and donkeys at the end of the train. On the other side of the road he went down a narrow muddy path lined with large stones and into wet solitude, ascending a low grassy hill. Prickly branches broke as he passed and stabbed him, but the muddy smell reminded him of the Nile River. *Natura*, he thought—one had no choice but to live in the ways of the rational creature. He continued down the path and crossed a hill. The valley spread out below. The rain stopped as abruptly as it had come.

SIX

LATE IN THE day, Kharapan heard a low, animal-like groan. He stood still to hear: "He is evil. *He* is evil." There was a pause. "Idol worshipper!" Then silence.

Kharapan turned a bend and saw a boy. He was dressed plainly, neither in monks' clothes or in the rich dress of priests, but with his hair cut in a square at his shoulders in the fashion of the Church. The boy sat on the ground, head down, pulling at a stem of grass, absorbed as if listening to the stem's silent music.

Kharapan coughed.

The boy looked up. He stared at Kharapan. "Are you demon or man?" the boy said in a resigned voice.

"I'm a human being."

"Why would the Devil tell the truth?"

"I can't win this argument. It's hopeless and ridiculous."

The boy paused. "Yes, I agree with you."

"May I join you?"

The boy nodded, and Kharapan sat next to him, leaning

against a large rock. The boy had a softness that Kharapan liked, in spite of his hard words. He was small, his face delicate and round. He had large brown eyes. Dirt besmirched his beige toga, and he smelled like sweat but like something else too, acidic, tart.

The boy suddenly stood in a panic. "I must have left this morning," he said, looking around in confusion and fear. "It was only this morning."

"The road's not far," Kharapan said, "and we're probably just a couple hours from Rome. Water?" It happened often in his travels that he came across people in various states of distress.

The boy grabbed the gourd from his outstretched hand.

"Drink it slowly," Kharapan insisted.

Kharapan pulled out thick white bread and goat cheese that a farmer's wife had given him and tore off some of both for the boy. Kharapan ate too, and, after a time, a pleasant weariness came over him. He asked the boy his name, and told him his own, and after a silence, couldn't help but ruminate out loud. "Well, Thaddeus, in these last days, I've been remembering some part of twenty years, more than twenty years."

Thaddeus watched him with large eyes.

Kharapan told him about the first time he took a boat from Alexandria to Rome, when, in Rome, he'd met a man in the Jewish quarter, idealistic, true. They'd become friends, philosophic friends, he said. A year later, he said, they'd taken this same road outside of Rome to an Inn not far from where they sat now. They'd taken a woman away from the Inn, a woman named Honora. The three of them had traveled to a village, Village G., up the road, where Justin and Honora married and settled as man and wife.

Thaddeus had an odd smile: Kharapan spoke to him like a man, as if he might have an opinion on things. "What happened to them?" he said, after a time, when Kharapan paused.

"They were well matched and expected a child. But, sadly, my friend died before his daughter was born. Honora went to Rome with the baby."

Thaddeus had a blank expression, as if the characters of this story had fallen off into a large amorphous place.

Kharapan asked him about the church party. Thaddeus told him that the bishop sent Monk Lolianus to Milan to visit Bishop Ambrose; the monk hardly ever left Rome, but his work, assisting in the translation of the Bible into Latin, brought him the bishop's favor, and so they'd dressed him in finery and sent him off. "Besides, he talks to himself," he added, "and annoyed the other monks, and so the bishop wanted to send him away for a time. But he is kind."

"The bishop?"

Thaddeus had a sour expression. "No, the monk."

"You seemed disturbed by something when I came," Kharapan said.

Thaddeus shrugged. He felt he could speak to this man; or at least, he found himself doing so naturally. He said that he'd been riding in the carriage with the monk, but after taking a break in the bushes, a guard, Adulianus, grabbed him and said, "You're a sinner, evil. We'll scrape your insides until you're good." Thaddeus's face crumpled as he told Kharapan this. Thaddeus had pulled away from the guard and ran, and had hidden behind a marble gravestone, those gravestones that line the cobblestone road, graves that were denser the closer one got to Rome. He often ran away, he said. He didn't always leave because of a decision or desire to hide; he sometimes went missing, simply wandered off, or stood still and found himself lost in thought. Other times he hid, and everyone assumed he'd show up eventually, as he always did. He always returned, he said.

"Are you Christian?" Thaddeus said, his eyes darting at the distance, at Kharapan, at the ground.

"No." Kharapan paused. "The idea of God is one thing that is at least clear in this respect: I am sure I don't know one way or another."

Thaddeus looked confused. "I was raised in the church," he said. "I must have been abandoned." He hesitated. "You're not Christian, so perhaps it's not wrong of me to say, but…" he lowered his voice "… the monks are so afraid of sin that they punish themselves and think of nothing else, while the priests scheme for power," he glanced at Kharapan.

"Yes, it's sad," Kharapan said after a moment.

"I too was an orphan," Kharapan said when Thaddeus didn't continue. He told Thaddeus he'd grown up in the Aristotelian school as a servant, in his country called Hellenica, and later worked in other philosophical schools. He happened to like thinking about philosophy very much, and he studied the ways in which a rational creature might live.

"When I spoke before of the friend I'd met in Rome, who died, and of how his wife and baby went to Rome,"

Kharapan went on. "The baby, the little girl—Honora left the baby at the pope's church. If the baby hadn't been adopted, you would have known her."

The words took time to become sense in Thaddeus's mind. "The mother left her baby at the church?"

"Yes, she, Honora, the mother, intended to join the Church as a slave, separately, to secretly raise her own baby girl."

Thaddeus didn't speak for a time. "The baby was adopted?" he asked shyly.

"Yes, by a rich family in Rome. And now, after twenty years, she, Saturnine, will find out who her mother is."

Thaddeus listened as if in a dream. "Her mother?"

"Is it *Saturnus*?" Kharapan said. "Yes, she might know already."

Thaddeus seemed confused.

"Yes, today," Kharapan said. "Her mother was to tell her the truth today."

"Her mother! Then her mother—"

"Her mother lived as the maidservant in that same domus, with her own daughter. Ah, it's complicated, Thaddeus. By the ways of Rome."

A silence passed.

"I believe that some meetings occur for a reason," Thaddeus said in a solemn voice.

Kharapan smiled. That's what I would have said, he thought. "You're right, Thaddeus. I believe you're right."

It had grown dark. Kharapan closed his eyes and soon fell asleep. He awoke in the dark. The boy was gone, and he thought he wouldn't see him again, but the bushes rustled and Thaddeus appeared.

"Oh, you're awake," Thaddeus said. "If we start now, we can reach Rome soon."

A large moon lit their way. Kharapan spoke of the nature of friendship, the rare and unique relationship between rational creatures, fellows who battle for character, allies in the moment-to-moment fight. Thaddeus listened, enchanted.

"I met someone from your church," Kharapan said. "Lupicinus."

Thaddeus stopped. "His Lord!"

"We had an interesting discussion."

Thaddeus studied him as if for the first time. "His Lord has great power. He sits beside the bishop." Thaddeus grew silent. "I'm not sure his tongue reflects his thoughts," he said after a time, cringing, likely wondering if he'd uttered some blasphemy, but Kharapan didn't seem to notice.

"I don't know what to say, Thaddeus. I take a man at his word and try to understand him. Even you wondered if I was a demon," he added with a small smile. "There's a sad state of sickness around us." A man refuses to let reason guide him, he went on. But at the same time reason makes him doubt the faith that the Church demands. His reason tells him to doubt, and doubt terrifies him, and so there is a circular path of pain and confusion until a poor man sees demons everywhere. If someone had the talent to show a man his mistake, the man would recognize his own nature, honor his reason and his doubt, and realize that he'd been thrusting himself into a sad state of sickness. But the power to show a mistake is a rare talent, and in our day, perhaps even one with such a talent, even a man such as Socrates, given the difficulty of arguing against a man's notion of demons, would rarely succeed. "Of course," he added, "those without faith are often mistaken, greatly mistaken."

"I didn't really think you were a demon," Thaddeus said.

They approached the massive brick walls and thick tunnel-like gate into Rome. Beyond the dark tunnel the road twisted through a tree-lined bend and disappeared up a hill. Kharapan felt his way through the gate, sliding his hands over the brick, cold in the early morning air. The walls were as thick as the length of two men, more cave than gate. The first walls around Rome formed the sacred circle, blessed by the gods: since the gods made Rome the Ruler of the World, all decisions had to be made inside the sacred boundary. Later, Romans built newer and thicker walls, those that Kharapan and Thaddeus passed through, beyond the sacred boundary, to assuage the growing fear of barbarian attacks and to accommodate a growing city. At the time, there was no imminent threat, and the gates were left open and unguarded.

Kharapan leaned against the archway, laying his hands against the smooth cold marble, and where marble had chipped the brick below. Thaddeus stood next to him.

"Where will you go?" Kharapan said. "You can come with me if you like."

"No," Thaddeus said, blushing and deeply surprised by the offer, perhaps forming a wedge in his soul, a space for a different and wholly new way of life. "I return to the church," he said. "I go to the monk's window. He never questions me."

They stood in the dark under the deep Roman sky and glowing clouds.

"I feel like we'll be friends," Kharapan said.

Thaddeus held out his arm. "I am your friend," he said.

Kharapan held Thaddeus's arm. Thaddeus almost swooned at Kharapan's firm hold, and at the idea of this gentle man being his friend. Kharapan told Thaddeus where he could find him—in the Jewish quarter of Rome, an apartment on the fifth floor, the white balcony decorated with marble faces. He said to ask for a woman as dark as him named Kenyon. He said that if they didn't find each other soon, if he happened to leave Rome, he'd seek out Thaddeus when he returned.

When Thaddeus left Kharapan, he had a new sensation. A strange man, a barbarian, had come to him like a benevolent god: a lone man in the hills and trees had given him food and spoken to him as a friend—spoken mysterious words—when he'd been fleeing another who loomed treacherously in his mind. The story, too, of the woman, Honora, and the girl, Saturnine, seemed an old and magical tale. And yet, as he approached the church, his feelings of wonder dissipated into vague uncertainty. And as he knocked on the monk's thick shutters, all good feeling, thoughts of Kharapan and all they'd said to each other, seemed to vanish as if a dream.

SEVEN

SATURNINE AWOKE IN the dark between *Saturnus* and *Sol* in front of a dying fire. Reading the work before burning it, particularly those pages in Philo's hand, she'd wept. She must have fallen asleep. She sat up and pulled back the damp hair stuck to her forehead and brushed off flecks of black ash that streaked her cotton dress. She gazed into the glowing embers. It was still dark, still night. Not yet *Sol, Kalends of Martius*, the New Year.

She thought she heard a knock at the kitchen door where the servants ate. Is this what woke her? Was someone out there? She stood, put wood on the fire, and, hardly aware of her surroundings, went to the kitchen door. She opened it. Kharapan stood there. He looked at her as if trying to decipher something. At a sudden downpour, she stepped aside and motioned for him to come inside.

She was surprised, abashed (at this strange hour?), but she suddenly understood: Flavia must have sent for him. Saturnine gave a harsh laugh. "Flavia told you to come."

She thought of Flavia's strange mood that morning. Flavia had asked her if she loved Victorinus. Saturnine had looked at her in astonishment, had said, "I don't understand. What choice do I have?" Flavia said women can live alone today. Saturnine cried, "You worry about my strange mind, and now you're sending me off to live alone? No," Saturnine said. "Rich Christian widows live alone, not divorced criminals." She'd laughed sardonically. Saturnine thought Kharapan must have given Flavia these ideas.

But for Flavia that morning, the closeness of truth forced her to see anew. After Saturnine told her that she'd burn her writing that night on *Saturnus* and convert to Christianity on *Sol*, and, moreover, that she'd told Victorinus about the abortion, besides all the rest, the imminent 'break' of her secrets opening long suppressed thought, Flavia understood all at once what she'd known but not dared acknowledge: Saturnine's own desire for security stoked as if a long fire by Flavia, made Saturnine bend to Victorinus's will, and Saturnine couldn't satisfy him without sacrificing her nature. Flavia suddenly understood that acting out of a desire for security was unworthy of Saturnine. Although they'd shared a rare open discussion that morning—Flavia told her she'd met Kharapan, and Saturnine had asked, mortified, whether Kharapan was her lover. Flavia had said "No!" and laughed. Saturnine laughed with her, but Flavia still had not been able to tell Saturnine the truth of her origins. Her daughter looked at her as a maidservant, and Flavia had been unable to break through that barrier. Flavia felt the full weight and force of failure, not only at that moment but in the past. She'd wanted to be a good maidservant, even a friend, to protect and watch over Saturnine, but her aim had been too low. Saturnine, alone in the world—and this, too, Flavia felt, had been her fault—hadn't been strong enough to resist Flavia's own fears, her own desire for Saturnine's secure life. Justin, she thought, would have taught Saturnine to be true to herself, and Kharapan would have been her friend, encouraging her to write. Saturnine might have had a different sort of life. As Flavia rang for the servants that morning, she reflected that she could do one thing for her daughter: she could send a note to Kharapan asking him to come to Saturnine as soon as possible, to Saturnine's old family domus on *Saturnus*. He might stop her from burning her work. He might change her life. She could not tell Saturnine the truth, but he could—and must. Flavia knew in her heart, had always known, the value of what Kharapan offered.

"I found her letter only now," Kharapan said. "I just returned to Rome."

"It's unnecessary," Saturnine said turning away. "You shouldn't have come."

He studied her. Did she know? Did the truth mean so little to her?

Saturnine walked back to the library. She paused, seeing the ash and half-burned parchment and scrolls on the floor. What does it matter? she thought, and went in.

Kharapan followed her. The fire crackled; rain splashed onto the base of the windowpanes. The shadowed room seemed somehow sad and ominous and had the musky odor of ashes. "You're burning your work," he said.

"Yes," she said. "And Philo's." She gave a defiant laugh, in bitter challenge not directed at him in particular. She stood next to the couch watching him, her fingers on the plush material.

"I don't understand."

"Nor should you. It's not for you to understand."

"It won't change your thoughts or who you are," he said.

Saturnine balked. "I'm a matron of Rome. It will clarify that."

"It clarifies nothing." He motioned to the papers. "Burning those is a lack of courage to live as you must, to live in a way that matters to you. Besides, it accomplishes nothing. After all is destroyed, you will find yourself as you are."

Saturnine felt indignant. "You think I'm a ridiculous creature. I know what you're going to say," she added. "I know better than you might believe."

She held up her hands to stop him although he remained silent. "You saved me as a child. You're a friend to Flavia." She stood and walked to the fire, then turned to him. "I'm not that child anymore. You caught me at a strange hour! But if you're truly Flavia's friend, pretend that you are mine and—"

"Saturnine!" He stepped toward her.

She looked at him with fear. In the space of a moment, she felt that something new and strange would happen.

"I am your friend. My friendship with your father, your mother…"

She didn't understand. She thought of her parents. And yet, she took hold of the mantel, her eyes on him.

"Flavia didn't… I see that you don't know." Kharapan paused. "His name was Justin," he said.

Saturnine stared into the fire, her face pale and still.

Kharapan told her how he'd met Justin, how Justin had fallen in love with a woman named Honora who worked at an inn outside of Rome. At the mention of the name Honora, a quiver came to Saturnine's lips, and her glance fell over him, but only for a moment. He went on. He told her how Justin had died, and how he, Kharapan, had lost Honora and the baby but found them three years later in the streets of Rome in the monks' battle.

"I think you understand," he said, after a pause.

She gave the slightest nod.

"Flavia," he said bluntly, as if without compassion for her. "Flavia is Honora. I found my arm on hers before I knew it was she. She is your mother, in all ways."

When Saturnine didn't respond, he went on. He spoke of Flavia's past, her life at the inn, and with Justin, and how she'd become Saturnine's maidservant, about that long day when she had given up her child so that she, Saturnine, might live.

"You probably would never have discovered the truth if I hadn't seen Flavia that day, in the monk's battle. Since then, since the time I found her in Rome—and you too—I met with her over the years. I wanted to tell you the truth even then, but you were only three. Life passed, I don't know, perhaps I've waited too long. The night Philo died, I was deeply taken with you, but you had experienced so much."

The morning following Philo's death, when Saturnine came home in the still, hourless hours, Flavia let out a cry but had grown stiff at Kharapan's name on Saturnine's lips. Flavia eventually understood that he had not told Saturnine the truth, but she had gone to the temple with dread later that day to meet him. Kharapan had spoken with passion. He had thought it through. He said, as much as he wanted to see Saturnine, as much as he had been taken with her—as much as he believed she needed his sort of friendship, and would need it in coming years—in spite of that, still he'd decided that it was wisest not to tell Saturnine the truth then. At his words, Flavia had felt a thickening in her body, a return to life. He'd told her that for him to see Saturnine, to be her friend, without revealing the truth was impossible. Lies would swell, distort words, and deform their friendship. Any attempt at friendship would immerse them in a conspiracy because her Roman parents would never agree to such a connection. No, he said, friendship consisted in speaking openly; only then did a true bond form. And so, Kharapan had decided to wait. After, in the years that passed, perhaps Kharapan decided against it each time he came to Rome, aided by what Flavia said or chose to tell him; and then, years passed before he returned to Rome.

At Kharapan's mention of Philo and that night, Saturnine glanced at him and sat on the couch. Kharapan sat in a chair facing her. She watched the fire.

He told her how he couldn't see her, not while he wasn't free to speak, and so he had decided not to see her at all. But he had been there all along, looking forward to this moment, this moment of truth. He laughed, and said, as if to himself, "I found myself in Rome on the day ten years had passed, and I walked up the hill. It was enough."

Saturnine looked at him as if at a man she had not seen

before but took an interest in, a man who had been, ghostlike, a part of her life. Flavia, her mother! Wonder, shame, sadness mixed in her. A few moments were enough to take in and imagine what Kharapan had told her—Flavia's life, her life at an inn, the man who loved her and took her away (her Jewish father), and the life she'd had as Saturnine's maidservant. Her thoughts lingered over their life together: Flavia serving her, Flavia's reserve, her silences, Flavia caring for her when she was sick, serving her needs and keeping her secrets. Flavia had meekly bowed to every capricious desire of Saturnine's while her own daughter lived as one of the wealthy of Rome. Flavia pushed her to fit in, to appreciate this life, to be careful and not risk so much. Saturnine had believed Flavia feared for Saturnine's mind, but it was not that. It had never been that.

Her thoughts turned to the present and future: how would it be when she looked on Flavia as her mother? What would happen when the world found out? How would Victorinus react?

The thought of Victorinus made her put a hand to her mouth to cover a gasp and a shocked burst of laughter: poor man! He thought he'd discovered all of her secrets.

Kharapan watched Saturnine.

Thinking of Victorinus made Saturnine sure of one thing: she would make amends to Flavia. She would stand firm against the world's scorn, even if divorce was inevitable. She would raise Flavia to her rightful position. There'd been something strange between them. She understood it now. But all secrets would end.

Still she regretted in part. Her mother had been a prostitute! A slave! Flavia made them both strange by becoming her maidservant. Saturnine's father had been a poor Jew. She would not, should not have lived this life among the upper echelons of Rome. Perhaps she would not live this life now. It was not hers. But this was not yet clear to her. Saturnine feared scandal still, feared what her life would be if Victorinus abandoned her. All of Rome would talk about them, of *this*, with a barbarian thrown in as salt. She and Flavia might live in her parents' domus, but what life would they have, outcasts, ridiculous, alone? She felt terrified, in part—*Sol* was indeed a new life—but Saturnine was resolved to live with the truth.

But one idea, one thought in particular, made her cry out. She stood and paced the room.

She turned and looked at Kharapan with a shocked expression, without seeing him,.

"I didn't let her tell me," she said. "I was afraid. I selfishly wanted this life, wanted nothing to stain it. I grasped at security. That's my character. I see myself clearly now. Look," she flailed an arm toward the burnt rolls and parchment. She had never before felt she knew herself so well. She wanted to burst into tears. She did not deserve the luxury of tears.

"Yours is not the main fault in this," Kharapan said. "I don't believe there's a way you could have made Flavia tell the truth—and surely, you never guessed. Even I bent to her desire for secrecy, and I should have known better."

"I don't know," she said, thinking of all of those times when she'd come close to Flavia's secrets but had turned away. She'd done it recently, when Flavia spoke of seeing Kharapan. And why had she, Saturnine, never demanded to know more about Kharapan? Even the night before, when Flavia had stood over her in the dark—she hadn't let her speak.

"I didn't let her tell me," she said quietly.

"Flavia knew my mind the moment she saw me in your garden," Kharapan said. "She was cornered by me, by your husband."

Saturnine gave him a questioning look.

He told her how Victorinus had threatened Flavia. "You need to know, it seems the last secret I can think of. I can't count on Flavia to mention it."

Saturnine went to the fire. It angered her that Victorinus had threatened Flavia, but she couldn't blame him. Their world, his world, didn't admit barbarians, and he looked on Flavia as a slave.

"There's so much more I want to tell you, of course," Kharapan said. "Since we met, I felt that it would be easy and natural for us to be friends."

"You can't trust me," she said. "I'm not strong. My name's not even Saturnine."

Kharapan smirked, picking up his walking stick. A silence passed. "Tell me what you've heard about barbarians," he said after a time.

She gave an embarrassed smile. She thought she understood him, but her biases didn't matter. It was the world's that mattered, and the world was Rome. Still, she looked at him with shy, embarrassed eyes. His simple dress and walking stick reminded her of a shepherd. Romulus had lived on Palatine Hill in a hut, but though a model of his hut still honored him, Rome had palaces and no longer cared about shepherds. She thought of senators and emperors, of Victorinus and Lupicinus.

"Tell me," he said.

The light that would bring the new day seemed far away. The shadowed room seemed to represent a past life. Wearily, Saturnine sat on the couch and leaned forward, resting her arms on her thighs. "I read that barbarians in the north," she said, "where it's cold, absorb the moisture and therefore are large, have deep voices, pale-white skin, blond or red hair, blue eyes and full blood. Their full blood makes them brave warriors, but the cold makes them dimwitted, so that their courage in battle ends in foolhardiness." She paused, but Kharapan waited and so she continued.

"In the south, people have dark complexions from the sun, are of short stature, have high voices, curly hair, black eyes and deficiency of blood. The Ethiopian is intelligent, but his blood deficiency makes him a coward and a poor warrior."

Kharapan laughed. "We are poor warriors."

A soft breeze from the open window enveloped them. A full silence followed.

"I thought you'd be my friend a long time ago," she said; "I was a brave child, so sure... You saved my life," she said. "I hardly thought of that; it was what you said—I wrote it down—the nobility of exploring one's mind. No one spoke to me like that; no one spoke those words. I fell in love..." she paused, blushing, "with the idea of it, I suppose."

Saturnine grew quiet and rubbed her face and nose in her soot-besmirched tunic. "I know so little about you; and yet I feel like I've known you all of my life. It's strange."

"And now we have time. We will be able to say everything to each other. Forgive me," Kharapan said. "I must speak while I have the chance."

She smiled, remembering similar words, similar intensity that night ten years before.

"Our bodies touch the world of men," Kharapan said, "what the inner self might not care about. That outside world tests us. If not prepared, you could commit some horrible act." Saturnine narrowed her eyebrows as if angry. "The circumstances of any moment can threaten our integrity. And, if we conform to the world, we suffocate and we become the walking dead." He paused.

Saturnine smiled. Again, it felt to her as if they were reliving that night long ago, when Kharapan's words, his strange faith and passion inspired a girl. But now she was an adult, a woman of Rome. At least, she had this life and the city of Rome to contend with. So she thought.

"Saturnine—The moment is here: you've been granted the chance to make a choice. If you choose well, you'll become stronger and learn how to be guided through difficulty. Life will test you at the level of your strength. But if you make a mistake, you do not advance, and after a long habit, you risk being unable to advance at all. You destroy yourself. You learn to ignore your true self, rather than practice integrity. I've seen it in many, the dead eyes, the tough cast of face. I thought I would see it in Lupicinus. I could be wrong, but I thought I saw something else there, too, something rare."

Saturnine studied him.

"Strange," he added, "why it's so. Why there's a right

decision, why we have to encounter choices, why it wouldn't just happen that we are ourselves, that we live our cores. Human crisis is not about whether to believe in Christ, but the moment-to-moment choices we make, the decision you have about whether to write, for instance, regardless of consequence. The ongoing, moment-to-moment tests of integrity form the essence of life."

"But why?" she said. "I'd be killed or exiled. I'd have to live alone and in shame."

"If you continued the struggle to know yourself, you'd build courage as you strengthened your integrity. If you follow your core, you learn how to be guided, you become stronger. You would find joy!" Kharapan stood and moved two steps closer to where she sat, leaning on his walking stick with both hands, his voice taking on a greater intensity. "And why does it matter? Individual passion moves society toward freedom. By living our cores in the face of opposition, society will, must, adjust its laws to allow us the freedom to carry out our passions. Your personal fight helps others. You push against rules and give others freedom. You have a duty to yourself and others, and that duty is shaped by and placed within Rome."

She went to the window. The soft light of first morning—the new day! Time didn't pause. Flavia would come. Saturnine hadn't finished burning her work.

"I've said enough," Kharapan said.

Saturnine turned to him with a tired smile. "It's hard to believe I have such a duty to the world, or that it matters so much what I do. But I like to listen to you."

No one had so bluntly criticized her. He'd seen her weaknesses, and it occurred to her that a man who loved her would understand her faults. He would tell her what to do, and she would trust him to know that he guided her in the right way, she would feel the rightness of what he said because it was right. She felt Kharapan was right, but she feared and wondered and felt she could not satisfy him or his aspirations for her. She thought of Philo. Her eyes grew misty. Looking out into the gray rain she saw the world through Victorinus's eyes. Rome fit him like a well-crafted glove. It was a mere trick of the Fates that she wasn't crafted in that manner, and she couldn't blame Victorinus that he was born for a particular sort of life. She was married to him. Love and marriage could ruin a person, she could see that now. But she had one duty she would not turn from: Flavia would be seen and accepted as her mother.

"Saturnine," Kharapan said in a thick voice. "Come to Chi. You'll find others like you. I'll take you there; you'll discover another world, a whole new world."

She heard his seriousness. "No," she said, blushing. "I've thought of it. Perhaps one day."

Kharapan took *Kingdoms* from his bag and handed it to her. Her hands moved toward the codex and took hold of it. "But it's important that I explain," he said. "I must tell you—"

But they heard a sound. Flavia stood at the door.

Saturnine put *Kingdoms* on the floor and went to Flavia, and without being able to utter a word, stood close to her, head bent. Flavia's eyes welled up with tears. Saturnine looked at her as a mother.

"I wouldn't let you tell me the truth," Saturnine said.

Flavia shook her head, as if unbelieving, and then went

past her and sank onto the couch. Flavia wanted to tell Saturnine that she must be brave enough to live alone if she had to, that she couldn't let fear guide her. But she was too full of emotion to speak.

"I'll go," Kharapan said.

Both looked at him. He told Saturnine where he stayed in Rome. He said he'd wait to hear from her.

But they heard approaching footsteps. Saturnine saw that day had come.

They were still, as if statues of themselves. Victorinus appeared at the door. He looked at them in astonishment—Kharapan standing with his walking stick, Flavia sitting on the couch. He thought his wife deceived him: she stayed in her parents' domus on *Saturnus* to meet Kharapan, to plot something, who knew. And yet, he had a surprise for her and self-possession enough to order her out of the room.

"Cornelia, I need to speak with you. Come out at once."

"No, there's something you need to know," she said.

"Come out!" he said. "What I have to tell you will pale in comparison."

Saturnine doubted it. She went out with a heavy heart, determined to speak. What he told her, however, shocked and pained her beyond expectation.

On Lupicinus's order, churchmen and guards had arrived at their domus in the first hour of *Sol*. They said they had orders to find Kharapan and to take Flavia to the church to question her. Victorinus, reluctant but with no choice, had led them here. The churchmen were at the door, and Victorinus had thought to send Flavia out, but now thought otherwise.

Victorinus ordered his servant to direct the churchmen to the library, and to tell them that Kharapan, the barbarian, was here.

Saturnine cried out, but it was too late. Perhaps in the moment Victorinus forgot to think of the half-burnt papyri and parchment. Perhaps he'd not noticed it, or perhaps, in the back of his thoughts, he knew but no longer cared. There is a destructive tendency in some men. They might attempt anything to protect themselves, engage in fierce and often unnecessary battles of self-preservation, but upon some event they cross a line that has been there all along and simply shrug and give up.

In a moment, Monk Lolianus came in, the monk Kharapan had seen on the road, followed by several men, including the redheaded guard, Adulianus, the one who tyrannized Thaddeus. Victorinus pointed to the library. Lolianus hesitated, but Adulianus rushed in, followed by others, and through the open door Saturnine saw them take hold of Kharapan. The walking stick fell to the floor. She moved to go to him, but Victorinus gripped her arm, hurting her.

Kharapan faced Monk Lolianus. The two men recognized each other. The Monk felt startled and disturbed. It was hard to mistake the singular man he'd seen on the road the day before. During the Monk's audience with the bishop in the first light of morning to report on his meeting at the church in Milan, the bishop had made a small request, as he described it: the bishop asked that he lead a small number of church guards to a domus in Rome, to request the servant, Flavia, and bring her to the church. The bishop said that they wished to question her about a dark-skinned barbarian named Kharapan whom Lupicinus had met and about whom he felt some concern. They hoped to find Kharapan. But Monk Lolianus hadn't known that the dark man was the same one he'd seen on the road, and he didn't know what either he or the woman were accused of. He wasn't expecting to find the man himself.

Adulianus passed them, Kharapan at his side making no attempt to resist. Monk Lolianus bowed toward Victorinus and Saturnine, and started to leave, but Victorinus stopped him. "You've forgotten the slave," he said.

"Flavia?" Saturnine gasped.

"There are things you don't know, Cornelia. She's kept secrets from us."

"Then you know she's my mother," Saturnine said. Events were unstoppable. Truth would have its way.

Victorinus's mouth opened but no words came out. "Impossible!" he finally cried. "You're saying this to keep her here."

"No, I learned the truth this morning. Kharapan knew she was my mother. He knew my true father. Flavia's my mother, and she'll be raised to her rightful position. Tell them," she added to the monk.

Monk Lolianus stared at the floor, his face pale and sweaty.

Victorinus looked from the monk to his wife, as if the monk might have something to add, some new knowledge or insight—God's thoughts perhaps. "You don't know what you're saying," Victorinus said. "She was a prostitute. She sold herself into slavery."

"Yes," Saturnine said, "and she's my mother." Her voice was clear, defiant.

Victorinus tried to tie this knowledge to what Flavia had told him that night in his office, but could not, although he had vague thoughts of Kharapan being intimately involved. It was all confusion and deceit.

Flavia remained still, standing near the sofa in the library, her expression calm, absent.

"This monk has orders," Victorinus said. "Flavia's a slave until there's a legal change."

Monk Lolianus avoided Saturnine's eyes. It was true, he thought, he had his orders. Circumstances made things strange, but he couldn't find an excuse for failing to bring the slave or mother. Here he was, out in the world, finding himself thrown in the cold waters of an unforeseen moment for which he felt ill-prepared. But a man is never alone: the monk had a bishop, a Church of Rome, churches across an Empire, God Himself in his thoughts and in his orders.

"I'll take her," he said. "If she's done nothing wrong, then no one need worry." But he doubted and felt ashamed that he doubted.

Saturnine rushed to Flavia, holding her, breaking into a sob. "Don't take her," she said.

Victorinus went to Saturnine and took her arm, bending down to whisper that she, too, could be in danger. As the monk came for Flavia, who put up no resistance, he seemed not to notice the papyri and parchment on the floor. Saturnine realized that she might be able to help Flavia and Kharapan only if she were free herself, and she relented.

Flavia stepped around Saturnine and Victorinus and went quietly with the monk.

Flavia's blue eyes startled Victorinus. Perhaps from some curse, he thought he saw Saturnine in them. Saturnine too looked into Flavia's eyes and saw something unusual but would understand too late.

They went out.

Saturnine went to the library window to watch Flavia and Kharapan go down the road with the men. Something odd occurred. Flavia swooned. A churchman grabbed her, tried to hold her up, but she crumpled to the ground. Saturnine ran out.

Rain and mud spattered Flavia's tunic. Saturnine grasped her mother's arms, her chest; she groaned over her. Kharapan, held by the guards, stood wordlessly near.

Saturnine noticed Flavia's dress open at her neck, saw the leather pouch, and found a little empty vial in her hand.

Flavia looked at Saturnine and said, "You are free at last."

"I don't want to be free!" Saturnine cried, but Flavia was beyond caring for the world.

Flavia had experienced a new clarity in the end. Standing in the library after the churchmen had come—the Church! it almost made her laugh, the beauty and simplicity of the Fates' plan, the circle, the perfect circle—she realized how she'd anchored Saturnine to this life. Her death would not have the consequences Flavia had imagined. Her death would not allow Saturnine to live in Roman society, married to Victorinus. The truth, her death—for these two things were unalterably linked in her mind—would free Saturnine to be who she must be. She herself had tied her daughter to this life.

Flavia's own life had been a thread that wove the appearance of a world of Rome for Saturnine. Opening the vial, drinking the poison, made her an actor in a drama directed by another. Circumstances turned suicide into the shining will of destiny. Flavia had one last surprise in the end: she had become Honora, the woman who loved and was loved, at last, by a daughter. It was a fine end, confirming the infinite wisdom of the Fates.

BOOK III

ONE

I FEEL I am submerged, have been submerged, in the second book of my chronicle as I was those days after meeting Kharapan. In the third hour of *Sol, Kalends of Martius*, Monk Lolianus and a small church party arrived at Lupicinus's domus. They were escorted to a large office where they found Lupicinus and Quintillius Pius, a tall thin man who engaged, at the time, in services of a sensitive nature for the top echelons of Rome. The monk, uncertain of Lupicinus and distressed to see Pius, managed to give an account of the morning's events: Kharapan captured, the maidservant's suicide, a confession or rumor (he wasn't sure which) that the deceased maidservant was Lady Cornelia's mother.

Lupicinus barely showed expression as he listened to the monk's recital of the morning's events, but his chest was full, his breath short.

For days, since *Mars*, since meeting Kharapan, he'd reveled in the idea of Kharapan's challenge. He wasn't sure if he would speak to the bishop or forget Kharapan, forget the codex *Kingdoms*. The idea of the challenge allured him, perhaps because, as the philosopher said, one must never stop sculpting one's own statue. A man is like the sea god, Glaucus, covered in barnacles, seaweed, and pebbles; he must scrape away what is superfluous in order to reach a pure state. Lupicinus sculpted, and although the statue, in his case, might not have been what the philosopher had in mind, his life made its own art, might be the highest form of art of modern man. So he believed at the time. Society too, even Empire, might be scraped clean to reveal its essence. Lupicinus wanted to explain to Kharapan that what Kharapan might call civilization's core involved God in its essence, even if godlessness remained to haunt and challenge the order of things. He knew Kharapan would disagree. He even imagined he knew what Kharapan would say. And yet, he wanted to speak of these things, of his life and of what he knew, and why he knew them and the insights he'd had. But he finally made himself accept once and for all that a conversation, or rather a long engagement, with such a man as Kharapan was impossible.

He'd gone to the bishop on *Saturnus*. A barbarian and barbarian land gave rise to a unique opportunity, to clarify atheism in Church doctrine, and there was no one better than he, Lupicinus, to define the crime. Besides the rest, Lupicinus believed that a man like Kharapan, a codex like *Kingdoms*, weakened the minds of men and undermined civilization.

In an hour of *Saturnus*, he'd explained his thoughts to the bishop. He told the bishop that heretics were the secret agents of Satan. They claimed to be Christians but taught an abyss of madness and blasphemy to lure people to the Devil. Moreover, pagans were under the influence of demons they called gods. But who is this among us, an atheist in the pure sense of the word, a godless man? Would Satan distort the truth in a man so that the man didn't believe in Satan himself? Is this man infested with demons or merely a diseased man? The Devil is up to his most subtle trick. Atheism is the threat of the future, a greater threat than any the Orthodox Church had known.

Damasus—the High Priest, the bishop of Rome, the Papa or pope, the supreme head on earth of a universal church— was eighty years old. He considered himself the savior of Orthodoxy, the one who resolved the question of the true doctrine in his lifetime, but Lupicinus told him that the next battle was for a larger world, not only heretics and pagans, but barbarians and atheists. It surprised Damasus to consider godlessness and foreign lands. He doubted. But Lupicinus told him about the codex that Kharapan carried: how it described the Kingdom of God as hell on earth and exhorted people to be disbelievers. Who knew how many copies had infiltrated Empire, and with what effect? "Barbarians of Hellenica are more dangerous than the fiercest barbarians who threaten the walls of Rome. They walk into the Empire and live among us, and talk to us," he said. Damasus asked how he had met such a man. Lupicinus gave an account of Victorinus's dinner. Damasus might not have understood entirely, but he nodded and sighed. He said there was no end to the war on discordant thought.

As Lupicinus spoke to the bishop, he'd felt a vague confusion and felt he'd lacked his usual sense of clarity. And now the Church held Kharapan in prison, and the maidservant had suffered a strange death by her own hand. Was she Saturnine's mother? Lupicinus had less certain reflections, in the background of which might have been the circumstances of his own mother's death. He suddenly felt a sense of urgency, but about what exactly? He could not have said. He had to go to the church to see Kharapan.

The monk waited in silence. Lupicinus asked the monk whether they had the codex *Kingdoms*. Monk Lolianus said they had taken Kharapan without bags or things. However, he described the state of the room: scrolls, half-burnt parchments, the hearth filled with ash. Lupicinus ordered the monk to return to the domus immediately with a church party to search for a codex called *Kingdoms* and to take any and all other texts, to search the library and Saturnine's bedroom in her old family domus for texts, as well as her husband's domus.

The monk nodded, bowed to Lupicinus and to Pius, and went out.

"Perhaps I'll be even more useful now," Pius said to Lupicinus with a stiff bow.

As they set off for the church, Lupicinus was absorbed in thought. A man with an institution behind him, justifying his acts, might accomplish almost anything. Stoics say that God put things in motion and then helplessly watched nature evolve as it would. Lupicinus, like a Stoic god, might watch, might be forced to watch events unfold.

TWO

SATURNINE, IN A white peasant dress streaked with burnt charcoal, dark hair falling in disorder down her back, seemed a waif of the spirit world, her long arms naked and limp at her sides as she bent over Flavia's inert body on the couch.

"A mother," she whispered and grew silent again.

Victorinus, standing behind her, wasn't sure if she spoke to him. "And your father?"

She glanced back at him. "A Jew."

"A Jew!" He took a few steps back. "A Roman Jew?"

"Yes." She heard relief in his voice: at least Kharapan or some other barbarian wasn't her father.

"It's not your fault that these creatures claim you," he said, events having sapped him of anger. "You're of the Flavianus clan, you were adopted. Cornelia," he cried. She'd turned back to Flavia. "You need to hide the parchments; you can't burn them. Hide them for now. The churchmen might return. You were here with this barbarian, and they'll wonder at Flavia's suicide. They'll remember the state of the library, the scrolls and parchments on the floor."

Saturnine, weak, turned to him. He was right. She hated his lack of concern for Flavia and Kharapan, and she wondered if he would turn her in if it came to that, but she saw that what he said was true. She needed to leave and find Kharapan's friend in Rome before the Church's agents returned. She couldn't help Kharapan if the Church imprisoned her. But she was in shock. Saturnine had plunged through the night and arrived in this new morning a different creature. She'd imagined she'd change after this night, but her prior worries now struck her as monstrously self-absorbed. She bent her head. Shame filled her. She had been afraid of living alone in Rome. She wished she could have that life now. Her chest burned with the night, the life, so close.

Saturnine raised her hand to keep Victorinus from approaching or touching her. "I told you," she said in a low voice, "the Church…." In self-loathing, she could hardly arouse anger. She was sick with the world and herself and felt she could not understand anything.

Victorinus was absorbed. "What did she try to hide by killing herself?"

A low moan escaped Saturnine. Flavia's death seemed the fatal end of a series of events that began with her own invitation to Kharapan to join Lupicinus. In all of it, in every act and thought, Saturnine felt she'd been concerned only with herself, oblivious to others. She had failed to be cautious with Lupicinus, with him in particular, how? why had it been so? Perhaps this fatal end had been decreed by events much earlier. Even as a child, Saturnine thought, she'd put Flavia at risk when she wrote. She couldn't think far enough back to remember a time when Flavia might have felt safe. Saturnine had believed that secrets kept her safe, but all of these secrets led to tragedy, a latent tragedy waiting for a slight wind to set it into motion.

She gave her husband a heavy wondering glance.

Victorinus couldn't meet her eyes, and he turned away as if to pace. If he forsook her, he would destroy her, but if he failed to defend her, he might implicate himself as well. He'd found out about his wife's subversive writing and the baby she'd killed, and he'd forgiven even that. But deceit rooted in her past, even if not her fault, and burst out like fresh ruin with its dark life.

"Leave me," she said. "I'll hide all of this. Go to Lupicinus—try to find out what is happening." She noticed his uncertainty. She didn't trust him and didn't believe he had any power to help, but the Church's emissaries hadn't taken Metis's codex, and they'd return for it. She had to leave and find Kenyon, Kharapan's friend.

"We can explain," Victorinus said, a little guiltily for imagining forsaking her. "Lupicinus was there when Kharapan came. That'll prove that your connection with him is innocent."

"Go," she said. She could hardly gather the strength to protect herself or him from his words that threatened to sever any remaining thread that might bound them.

"I'll go," he said after a time.

Saturnine went to the window to watch her husband and

his attendants walk away. She couldn't hesitate now. Besides fearing the return of the churchmen, Victorinus might send his servants to spy on her. But she was numb and in spite of rising panic, she could hardly move. She took up *Kingdoms* and scrolls and parchment and went to her bedroom, quickly discovering that it was too much to hide. She hid some of it under the floor and put the codex and a few pieces of parchment of her own and of Philo's in a bag, found Flavia's thick cloak and wrapped it around her, and then returned to the library and looked down at Flavia. The gentle features of her maidservant, her mother, seemed so peaceful, as if she were relieved of the weight of the need to deceive. It was unfathomable to Saturnine—all of the air, the sound, the motion, and then nothing.

She noticed Kharapan's walking stick on the floor, and taking it up, she covered her head with the hood of her mother's thick cloak and went out.

She went down the street, the cloak's hood covering her. Pausing in the Jewish section, in a courtyard where people made preparations to celebrate the New Year, she removed the hood. She saw the gray building with pink carved faces at its corners, a white balcony, and white flowers. Elaborate decoration masked the shabby interiors of the poor. She climbed shadowed steps to the fifth floor and knocked the door with her foot.

A heavy woman, two scrawny children in rags, and an old crooked-limbed man looked at her. These people might be Saturnine's family. Her a face wracked by sorrow, her dress streaked with ash, Saturnine asked for Kenyon just as a dark-skinned person opened the door of an interior room and said, "I am Kenyon."

Saturnine stared. It wasn't only Kenyon's appearance. Saturnine looked at a woman who had known Kharapan and spoken freely with him all of her life. Kenyon had large bones and thick arms. She dressed poorly, like the coarsest street urchin, and had lumps of hair gathered with strings, a series of dark potato-like balls on her head, and yet she held herself with ease and confidence.

"You are Saturnine," she said. "Come."

Saturnine went past her into the small interior room. The room was narrow but neat, with pillows on the floor. Kenyon shut the door.

"Please," Kenyon said, motioning to the pillows.

Saturnine sunk onto the floor. Her cloak fell off of a shoulder. She couldn't speak for a time.

Kenyon sat across from her, knees up. The walking stick lay between them. Saturnine spoke, barely coherent. The church had Kharapan. He'd come to her last night. He'd told her about her parents. She had no idea of time. They'd taken her mother... she'd watched her die... she'd taken poison. She fell into tears and covered her face. Kenyon remained silent.

"I came while I had a chance. We must try to save him."

"I told him to tell you the truth."

"That doesn't matter now," Saturnine said.

Kenyon shrugged.

"None of this would have happened—it's my fault," Saturnine said, more to herself.

"Don't imagine different worlds. It changes nothing," Kenyon said.

Saturnine felt as if Kenyon spoke to her as a child, although she suspected that Kenyon was only a few years older than her.

Saturnine was silent. This stranger knew more about her than she herself had known until last night. Saturnine spoke as if to an intimate but it was a ghostly acquaintance.

"Flavia made the choice to live as she did," Kenyon said. "You must leave a person to her fate. It's the respect you can give, to leave someone to fate, even if it seems harsh. I mean that for Kharapan as well."

Kenyon's hard manner dried Saturnine's tears.

Kenyon went on. "He won't want us to interfere, even if we could do something to help."

Saturnine stared incredulously. She didn't say more, afraid that words or argument might weaken her own untrustworthy resolve.

"What have I done?" Saturnine whispered to herself after a time. "Even my memories must change."

"Yes," Kenyon said, thinking down a different line. "They demonize Jews, heretics, anyone with a different mind."

Kenyon had to warn her Jewish friends about Kharapan's trouble with the pope's church. What a strange mixture of happiness, fear, regret if they found out who Saturnine was! to find Saturnine, but to fear for Kharapan, Saturnine, and themselves, and to have lost forever the chance of meeting Flavia. So many years ago, after they'd found out about Justin's death and his child, they'd wanted to find Honora and the girl, wanted to take them into their home. It was too late. At the time Kharapan hadn't known himself where they were, but three years later, when he found Flavia and Saturnine in the streets of Rome, once he had decided to abide by Flavia's desire not to tell Saturnine the truth, he could not tell the girl's family. Secrets expanded. Kenyon thought that the Church might force Kharapan to reveal his connections, where he stayed in Rome; the Christians might 'see' the Jews who, when seen, often became objects of suspicion or hatred. Christians considered them demons and Christian gospels excoriated them even though Jesus and the Church fathers had been Jewish, even though the gospels were Jewish texts. The battle had turned into one *against* the Jews. The Empire had become a Jewish world where Jews were hated, so it seemed to Kenyon.

The cold sun entering the window bathed half of Saturnine's body in light. Saturnine stared at Kenyon as if Kenyon kept hidden information from her. Who was this creature, this barbarian of Chi? What sort of life gave her such confidence?

"I brought this," Saturnine said. She took out *Kingdoms*. "Kharapan gave it to me."

Kenyon took the codex. "Metis's book?"

Just then they heard a cry and the sound of scrambling; a hard knock followed. Saturnine sat as if paralyzed. Kenyon opened the door. The old man held a church boy by his robes.

Saturnine gasped and jumped up and grabbed the boy by his robes. "You followed me!" she cried.

"I'm a friend; I'm Kharapan's friend!"

"Let him speak," Saturnine said, letting go. The old man bowed, and Kenyon shut the door.

"Speak," she commanded. He seemed barely sentient. "Speak!"

Thaddeus peered at her. But he spoke to Kenyon, who had dark skin like Kharapan. He'd met Kharapan by rocks and trees and had returned to the church in the dark. He sometimes disappeared but didn't go anywhere in particular, but when he disappeared today, he'd had a particular place in mind, though he didn't know where it was.

"Slow," Saturnine said gently.

Thaddeus spoke slowly, glancing at Saturnine who wasn't looking at him. He'd slept in the monk's cell, and in the morning had accompanied the monk to question a maidservant about Kharapan.

"Did you tell him about Kharapan?" Saturnine said.

"No. Kharapan's my friend," he said, pained.

He went on. When the monk's party arrived at the second domus, he hid outside, and after a time he saw Kharapan come out. Soon after he saw guards and a servant, but the servant fell. He paused briefly. He went on. He had stayed hidden, not knowing what to do, and then he saw a man leave, and then he'd seen "her"—Saturnine—but he didn't know it was her. "You had Kharapan's walking stick," he said. "I knew where Kharapan stayed in Rome; Kharapan told me." He was afraid to come in, but this old man found him on the steps.

He grew silent; he had crunched eyes and an anguished face.

"How can I believe you?" Saturnine said, studying him.

He faced her. "Kharapan said a girl was left at the church but was later adopted. He said she would find her mother, that her mother would tell her the truth after twenty years."

"I see," she whispered. "What does the Church accuse him of?" she said.

Thaddeus didn't know. "You're Kharapan's friend," he said.

Saturnine closed her eyes. The word friend pained her. She'd been weak when Kharapan had offered friendship, and this sliver of a church boy understood friendship. She might never have a chance to tell Kharapan... to thank him. Tears stung her eyes. She stared at Thaddeus without seeing. "Did Lupicinus mention a codex called *Kingdoms*?"

"I don't know." Her skin had the softness of eggs, he thought, and she had a kind, open face, in spite of the strain, the pain and exhaustion that marked it. Thaddeus felt sorry, even deeply pained, about her mother, for he assumed it was her mother he had seen fall. He wanted to ask her about it but was afraid.

Saturnine was silent for a time, but something occurred to her. In this apartment, she'd found this other world, another possible life, but this boy represented yet another possibility. "You were left at the church?" she said.

"Yes."

"What's your name?"

"Thaddeus."

"Thaddeus, we would have been brother and sister," she said. He blushed but was pleased. "Will you be my friend, as you are Kharapan's?"

His eyes moved strangely, but his voice was firm. "Yes, miss," he said.

"Call me Saturnine, only Saturnine," she said. "Can you return to the church? Can you come to me this evening with news? Will you see Kharapan?"

He nodded. "I think so."

"But even if you don't learn anything or see him, will you come?"

"I'll come," Thaddeus said, "to the domus, the one you were at this morning?"

"No, don't go there: meet me at the Temple Minerva, after dark has fallen." She glanced at Kenyon, but seeing only a distant gaze, looked back at Thaddeus.

"I'll come," he said. "I can't say when…" He hesitated at the uncertainty of night, the time when the monks or guards might claim one of the boys. "I'll find you," he said.

She was a little worried. This boy held her hope, and if he betrayed her, or could not help her or Kharapan, what life or choice did she have?

"Go to the church!" she said but took his hands and looked at him.

Thaddeus turned deep red at her touch. When she let him go, he moved for the door with the quickness of a rabbit, but Kenyon called out "boy" and he stopped. "If you give him this… but no, it might be dangerous," she said, holding Kharapan's walking stick. "It means a lot to him."

"I can take it," he said. The stick was long and looked ridiculous in his hand, but he thought he could hide it somehow and give it to Kharapan at night.

"If you speak to him… well, he knows how we feel. Find out if he wants to be saved and tell Saturnine what he says."

He looked at the dark woman, nodded and went out.

Saturnine felt she should go. There was nothing more to accomplish here. Kenyon was absorbed, and when she looked up had a smirk on her thick lips.

"I'll take you to Hellenica," Kenyon said. "Kharapan said you would go one day."

Saturnine was surprised. "Why? Why would you bother?" She spoke from curiosity not from any thought that she'd go.

Kenyon shrugged. "There are reasons. You're in danger," she said. "You don't have to come, but my friends will likely think it wise for me to go, for my sake and theirs, at least for a time. The Jews are never safe. A friction, another's trouble, can amount to a death sentence for them. They'll care for your welfare, you know, once they learn who you are, but now is not the time to stay." She paused. "You're thinking of fighting the Church."

Saturnine hid her eyes.

"It's stupid. Kharapan's life is a training in how to speak the truth, how to confront difficulty and test the strength of his character. That is how he thinks of it. He won't want your help. And you don't have that understanding in any event. There's nothing you can do but get into a lot of worthless trouble."

Saturnine snorted, but silently acknowledged the truth.

"I'll wait until the end of tomorrow, *Luna*," Kenyon said. "Tell me by then if you'll come with me to Chi or not."

Saturnine leaned against the chipped cement wall. It was

almost enough to go with this woman, to follow this barbarian blindly. The irrational power of Rome had its gaze on her, but besides that, she wanted to escape the chaos of her mind, the chaos of her world—what did she have in Rome? who was she?

Kenyon saw Saturnine's hesitation. No one could control another life, and she didn't care to try.

"Are they my... family?" Saturnine whispered, nodding toward the door.

"Yes—the old man is your grandfather; he's absolute in his ideas, but once you know him, he's likable enough. The little ones would be your cousins, I suppose."

Saturnine took this in. "Are you going to tell them who I am?"

"I don't know. You can tell them."

"Tell them if you want but wait until I go." She moved to go.

"Kharapan stayed away from you," Kenyon said, "because he couldn't bear to keep secrets from you. In any event," she said, "leave word about your plans by the end of tomorrow."

"There's no need to wait."

Kenyon gave a half smirk. "I'll wait," she said.

Saturnine felt that Kenyon cared very little whether she, Saturnine, stayed or went, or about Kharapan's fate. And yet, perhaps the people of Chi were strange, the most fortunate of strange creatures, perhaps Kenyon's shrug was a legitimate response to a world.

THREE

DARKNESS PERVADED KHARAPAN'S senses as if it had penetrated his skin. A man in a pitch-black cell haunts a place
between dreaming and death—and it seemed to Kharapan
that his life, the tests of integrity, even in his 'philosophy
as a way of life,' led to this darkness under a church. And it
seemed to him, too, that Metis had a hand in his being here,
entangled in his life as she was, had always been.

He had grown up in the Aristotelian school, the wealthiest
of philosophic schools in Hellenica, with about fifty scholars,
more students, and numerous staff. Illustrious masters and
private sources funded the school. His father had been on
the cleaning staff, and Kharapan, orphaned at five years old,
moved to a closet at the end of a hall. He took over his father's
duties. He swept halls and cleaned scholar's rooms, ran to the
Great Village for fish or supplies, and was as busy from early
morning to late at night as the most industrious scholar. Until
he was twelve, the idea that he might live as a philosopher
was so remote it didn't even occur to him. In the Aristotelian

school, he listened to scholars, watched them studying and writing in the Great Library, and melted inward, in awe of their knowledge and powers of mind.

Natural curiosity led him to the back of lecture rooms where he listened to discourses ranging from the nature of plants to the nature of the stars. The Aristotelian scholars gathered data—about history, politics, biology, zoology, astronomy. They classified and trusted in their observations, and as one philosopher said, had "an almost religious passion for reality in all of its aspects." Kharapan sometimes pursued a subject, but if he checked out a book from the Great Library, some vague inner thought pulled him from the text. After a time, he'd raise his eyes and notice the book in his hands and be disappointed at his inability to pay attention to the world.

As a boy, he attended early-life school in the Great Village, and it was there, when he was twelve years old, that certain ideas formed of knot of wonderment in him, made him realize with his whole being that he wanted to live as a philosopher. For a long time his passion remained in him as an unexpressed idea and not a real possibility.

Kharapan sat on the dusty floor in the back of the classroom, a small room of the abandoned temple with high ceilings and white walls, wearing the blue baggy clothes of the Aristotelians, those near-rags passed down to him. As his teacher Quinta spoke, he had the unique sensation of his inner thoughts merging with outside ideas that came together without struggle, naturally and wholly.

Quinta, a squat woman, poised on a thick walking stick, said that to the ancients, philosophia meant an interest one took in the art of life, an interest that engaged one's whole being. How much one knew, how well one recited the work of other philosophers, what theories one proposed—all these were secondary, supportive, or entirely irrelevant to the philosophic way of life. What mattered, she said, what truly defined a philosopher, was the unique shape of his moral life.

About twenty children gathered in the open space, sprawled in various positions on the floor or on chairs. The vast ceilings and thick walls held the heat at bay.

"For the ancients," she said, "and even for Aristotle himself, knowledge was never purely theoretical but rather a transformation of being. 'Geometry engaged the entire soul,' Plato said. As you'll read in Isadora, the purpose of the earliest philosophic schools was to train human beings in the conduct of life." She quoted Seneca from a parchment codex: "'In the schools, the living word and life in common benefit one, more than written discourse: one can see a good man's life, penetrate his secret thoughts, and observe firsthand whether that good man lives in conformity with his own rule of life.'"

At night, Kharapan read Isadora with an urgency that equaled the pull of his inner thoughts. Isadora, a historian of Hellenica who'd lived two hundred years before, traced Hellenica's history to those creatures who first proposed a rational explanation of the world—such as Heraclitus—and to those who struggled to determine the best way to live—such as Parmenides and Pythagoras. For her, however, it was Socrates, whose practice in wisdom entailed both a rational gesture of the mind and a way of life, that epitomized the ideal of the philosopher and the core of Hellenica itself. Isadora wrote that Hellenica's core involved a love for and cultivation of mystery. Its core was Socrates.

Quinta told the story, repeated through the centuries, one that everyone loved and even Kharapan had heard: a friend of Socrates asked the Delphic oracle if anyone was wiser than Socrates. The oracle answered that no one was wiser than Socrates. The answer confounded Socrates, but then he noticed that all of the people he questioned, politicians, poets, artisans, thought they knew what they didn't know, and he concluded that if he was the wisest person, it was because he didn't think he knew what he didn't know.

"The Delphic oracle," Quinta said, "might say that no core is wiser than Chi's. Many of us practice very hard to learn what we don't know."

The children laughed, but Kharapan felt uneasy. He didn't know his core or whether he had one, and many, even his own age, knew their cores. The Aristotelians of his day were scholars, interested in knowledge for knowledge's own sake, in theories and data, rather than in honing a way of life. Some of them may have believed that the best life was the life of the mind, but they did not speak of the way of life, as if it would be embarrassing to do so. The way of life of a human being didn't matter to truth in the world, to pure scholarship.

"Being aware of one's lack of knowing invokes a mood," Quinta said. "Those who admit and cultivate an awareness of what they don't know, can't take themselves or others entirely seriously. They understand that everything human, and even philosophy, is highly uncertain." She said that the humor of antiquity, a kind of humor that existed in Chi, fertilized

Socrates' philosophic life and freed him from one-sided seriousness. Laughter purified one from intolerance.

The idea of Socratic laughter enchanted Kharapan. Even
in the Aristotelian school he found an absence of laughter, of
lightness. He didn't know enough of the other philosophic
schools in Hellenica. The Aristotelians spoke of the other
schools with disdain, and given Kharapan's great respect for
the Aristotelians he had hardly dared even to think of the
other schools.

Through Quinta and Isadora, and through the primary
works themselves, Kharapan's thoughts became entangled
with the lives of those philosophers who lived philosophy
as a way of life, including the ancients and Romans of long
ago. He read Epicurus, an ancient Greek, who withdrew from
society and lived a life in common with others, shared posses-
sions, and believed friendship was the highest good. He read
Epictetus, the stoic, who'd lived in Rome hundreds of years
before, who'd been a slave, and, once freed, lived a simple life
teaching students. Perhaps Kharapan felt most sympathetic
with the Stoics. I think so, even if he refused to call himself
a Stoic (he would say that none of the words, or perhaps
all of the words, of the philosophic schools or philosophies
defined him).

Each night, alone in his candlelit closet, Kharapan read
and was lost in thought; he seemed to feel in his body an
expansive and expanding mystery. Scratching his knee, he felt
the bones and thought a little fearfully, "This is me. I exist in
the world."

He wanted to be like Socrates. He didn't know how to go

about it. He didn't know his core, and even his questions were all confusion to him. But he had one thing: he knew what he wanted. Socrates claimed to be wise because he knew he knew nothing, as he said. But Socrates had certain knowledge: he knew the value of moral intent. His lived life revealed what he valued. A value was absolute when a person would die for that value, and Kharapan wanted to know the words and values that mattered enough to him to die for. He wanted an integrity that would defy even death.

"Not everyone in Chi practices wisdom," Quinta told them; "not even everyone in the schools, but the wisdom of *agnosis*—of the unknown and potentially unknowable—is alive in Chi. Here, a rational creature can live philosophy as a way of life in community with others."

In the north, she told her students, the philosophic schools—Aristotelianism, Stoicism, Epicureanism, Academicism, Skepticism, Cynicism—had become largely extinct. In the north, she said, the Christian Church dominated, and philosophy was a topic for academics to expound on in secondary authority, to discuss and memorize, rather than live as a way of life. In Chi, theories and ideas became increasingly secular. "In the north," she said, "they have absolute knowledge of God and know what happens after they die, and in Chi, we only discover what we don't know."

The children laughed, but Kharapan could not. A new inner desire and new fear made him serious. He worried that he failed even to be inspired to Socratic laughter. His thoughts consisted of something like this: The farmers of Hellenica produced the whitest flour and best oils, and its metallurgists and craftspeople enjoyed renown in all the world. The people of Hellenica had talent in language and, being on the edge of several worlds, many could speak Greek, Egyptian dialects, and Latin: cities as distant as Alexandria summoned them to translate texts, and many Hellenes learned Coptic to work in monasteries that populated the Nile Valley to the north. Still, Kharapan thought, the Empire had power, weapons, and armies. Hellenica's vulnerability pierced him and became what he viewed as his own vulnerability. If he lost Chi, if he did not have Chi to return to, he would not have integrity, he would fail to be the man he both wanted and needed to be. I don't believe he ever lost this suspicion or fear. I think he had it even at the very end.

After early-life school ended, one day Kharapan had a perplexing interaction with a student named Metis. She was the only daughter of one of the richest farmers in Chi. Metis's father, who wasn't a member of the school, had once written a well-received analysis of how the minds of men were superior to women, but that was before he had a daughter, one who was beginning to prove that the powers of her mind and her intellectual ambitions surpassed her brothers. Metis, it was said, found this text about the superiority of the male mind and never forgave her father for it. She attended Aristotelian lectures and engaged boldly in discussion, and her confidence, especially her anger, sometimes staggered Kharapan. She was quick to fury, even with masters. Masters and students dismissed her anger, excusing it as an eccentricity of genius.

Kharapan began to suspect that Metis took a peculiar interest in him. He couldn't understand. He offered her his services as he did others: he could clean her cell or run for supplies in the Great Village. She stared at him and wouldn't answer, asking for nothing. For days and weeks, she never spoke to him, but sometimes gave him a look so filled with wrath his skin tingled. He, in turn, couldn't stop watching her, trying to be near her. Her words in classrooms or halls, her moods or angers, gave him a sensation… as if he couldn't breath… and yet he felt there was something to discover, not only in her words but also in the sound of her voice. Sometimes she seemed to guess his confusion and gave him a haughty look as if she considered him ridiculous, even laughing loudly when he passed.

One day he found himself alone with her. She'd come into the library where he was dusting. She stiffened when she saw him but walked to a shelf and pretended to search for a book. Kharapan tried to keep busy, but when he felt her stillness, glanced up and saw her staring at him. He blushed but didn't turn away.

"Why do you hate me?" he said, smilingly.

"Because you're ignorant and stupid," she said.

He blinked at the harsh words but didn't disagree. "It's true," he said. "I don't know anything… I can't seem to know things."

She stiffened, as if in the suspension of a wild cat, and then, as if bursting, she swept an arm over a shelf, knocking all the codices to the floor, and walked out.

Kharapan would never believe that it was he who made her feel unworthy, made her feel something lacking in herself. For her, although she tried to laugh at him, even his gentleness, his lack of knowing, his honesty, and the way the masters and students loved the young custodian (although Kharapan himself was unaware of it), all this aggravated Metis. She saw, or rather sensed, how he, the boy, had the potential to be a true philosophic master. Kharapan possessed a natural unassuming, unconscious humility. Unlike Kharapan, Metis was not ignorant of the other philosophic schools, and she understood enough to resent him and even to feel competitive with him. She would never achieve what Kharapan did so simply, but she had the powers of mind that many thought highly of, even if some, those in other schools, might believe hers the lesser talent. The Aristotelians loved her. She was the one who could know.

"You're blinder than I am," Roshua yelled one day as Kharapan tried to sneak past.

Roshua, a large, loud blind woman, showed up at the school only to sit in a dark corner. He helped her, bringing her water, wine, food, guiding her to her room in a domus by the river. She could distinguish his steps, perhaps his aura. She spoke to herself and often had a terrible odor.

She held onto his blue sleeve. She told him that he was just as alive as the other creatures wandering the halls. Kharapan pulled away and pretended he didn't understand, but that night he took out the box from under his bed. Since he'd begun work at five years old, he'd put his small wages in the box. The next day at dusk, he went out through the narrow winding alleyways of the Great Village, past white walls, soft against the vast yellow sky, and through the center square where the last merchants were closing shop or putting goods into carts. He walked on, along winding paths to the open desert and the simple domus nestled between sand dunes and cacti where the Stoics lived and practiced living.

The Stoic school, like other philosophic schools, didn't have standing under the law. The Stoic head owned the property of the school, and it was open to the public for a small daily fee. The teachers taught without salary. A woman in green would take their coins and let them into an open courtyard. The thickness of dusk cut the harshness of sun, but the area was also shaded by a brush overhang. Kharapan sat on the floor against a back wall, behind rows of chairs, where he could watch and see the master when he came out, but where he, Kharapan, could remain slightly hidden.

One master and a few teachers lived at the Stoic domus but they had a large membership: farmers, merchants, politicians, dispute resolvers, rich and poor. The Stoics practiced their art in daily life. When Arminius, the Stoic master, came out in his green cloak carrying a worn parchment codex and holding onto a long wooden walking stick, everyone grew quiet. He sat in a cushioned chair and stretched out his legs with a sigh. After a silence, he spoke of what, he said, seemed the tragic situation of human beings.

"It's not up to us," he said, "to be healthy or rich, or to escape illness and suffering."

Moments, he continued, depended on causes external to rational creatures. Some sought to acquire things they couldn't obtain and to escape inevitable evils, and in so doing were unhappy. There is only one thing that depends on us, he said: the will to do good, to act in conformity with reason.

All else but the will to do good is indifferent, neither good nor bad.

He spoke of how a rational creature might live a good life, and Kharapan began to see how far he was from that good life that was also a moral one.

Arminius admonished them: one must accept, even love fate whether it consisted of illness or theft or loss of one's mother. The Stoic's ideal image of a sage was a rational creature so aware of himself that no event alters his peace of mind.

He held up the parchment codex and gave an example based on *Epictetus's Discourses.*

A man on a ship hears thunder and feels the winds of a storm begin to rise. His senses are the result of an interwoven network of causes arising from a rational universe that is nature. What is his inner discourse? If he should note to himself nothing else but that nature confronts him with a storm, his inner discourse corresponds to the objective perception and reflects truth. However, if in his terror he says to himself, "I'm wretched; the boat is sure to founder; I'm going to die," he'll be in error as a Stoic. The correct moral response is to recognize that the storm and even death are indifferent. Neither the storm nor death itself are morally good or evil. To act in accordance with nature is to recognize nature as nature and to will whatever happens. To be a Stoic is the bold and even happy confrontation of all storms.

Arminius paused.

"Every person can construct a fortress within himself. In correct assessments we find freedom, independence, invulnerability. Our correct assessments, the reason of the inner discourse, becomes the cliff against which waves crash without effect, leaving us in peace."

He concluded by reading from *Epictetus's Discourses*. "'When Emperor Vespasian told Priscus not to come into the senate, Priscus answered, 'You can forbid me to be a senator; but as long as I am senator, I must come in.'

"'Come in then,' the emperor says, 'and be silent.'

"'Question me not and I will be silent.'

"'But I am bound to question you.'

"'And I am bound to say what seems right to me.'

"'But, if you say it, I shall kill you.'

"'When did I tell you that I was immortal? You will do your part, and I mine. It is yours to kill, mine to die without quailing: yours to banish, mine to go into exile without groaning.'"

Arminius paused. "What good did Priscus do, being but one? What good does the purple do to the garment? Just this, that being purple gives distinction and stands out as a fine example to the rest."

Arminius closed the parchment book and looked out on the assembled listeners.

No one moved or spoke.

Kharapan's thoughts came like a sharp breath: he sensed how a man might have integrity. He recognized fault in pining after his father, his regret that he could not be an Aristotelian, his possible envy of Metis, and many other things.

"We train ourselves to deal with impressions," Arminius said. "Existing in nature one must practice to arrive at correct impressions and so avoid error. 'The son of our friend is dead'—Answer: that is beyond the will, not an evil. 'His father disinherited him.' It is outside the will, not an evil. 'Something made him grieve.' That is an act of will and evil. 'He had endured nobly.' That is an act of will and good. 'The son dies.' Nothing more? Nothing."

The dry wind accentuated the harshness of the words.

Everyone except Kharapan stood. Some engaged in discussion, others wandered out, but Kharapan remained very still. After a time, he stood and walked on the path to the Aristotelian school.

In months that followed, Kharapan attended Stoic discourses, studied Stoic texts and practiced Stoic exercises, and when he could, took up the same duties at the Stoic school as those he carried out at the Aristotelian school. But he existed as if in the background and never faced or spoke to Arminius.

One day, when Kharapan was about fourteen, Arminius entered the Stoic library. Kharapan practiced an *askesis*, a Stoic exercise in wisdom, and as he swept, he practiced an inner discourse: he tried to determine whether his assessments were good or bad or indifferent. Busy monitoring his own thoughts, he didn't see Arminius come into the library. When Kharapan glanced up he was surprised. Arminius watched him with a quizzical expression. Kharapan held still, trembling.

Arminius gave a small nod. "Kharapan," he said, and paused as if waiting for Kharapan to ask a question.

Kharapan flushed; Arminius knew his name! But his mind went blank as if swept clean by the whitest sandstorm.

When Kharapan didn't speak, Arminius bowed his head and went out.

Kharapan felt stunned. He'd failed some test. It seemed to him impossible to struggle out a question from the confusion of his soul, and besides, he couldn't speak from shame. He had to face the truth: after months of Stoic practice, he still didn't know his core, or if he'd ever have one, and in his sand-scrubbed thoughts he had to acknowledge that he had no wisdom of his own. He could spout many Stoic sayings, but he had no experience, no direct knowledge of the real meaning of those sayings. He had no words of his own.

He didn't have the perspicacity to recognize (at the time) his own qualities and talent—and perhaps this was the real aspect of Kharapan's ignorance. He didn't appreciate the power he had to know what he didn't know, the strength and capacity to face what he didn't know. He would one day understand the value of this, but also its dangers.

After the incident with Arminius, Kharapan was filled with foreboding.

One day, he turned off the path that led to the Stoic' domus and instead of going to the Stoic school, he headed toward the river.

The Stoics called Epicureans hedonists. Epictetus himself wrote that Epicureans would destroy civilization by withdrawing from society and living in retreat, but Kharapan entered the Epicurean Garden amazed that whole other worlds existed so near the one he'd lived in all of his life. People, many in red cloaks, lounged in a green, flower filled garden that stretched down to the Nile River. The head of the Epicurean school, a tall woman, strong and not pretty but with something in her stride, eyes and face that emanated energy and intelligence, came up to Kharapan and welcomed him. She happened to be present when he arrived, and besides, although he could not have known it, she had heard of him. She led him to an intimate place where they could talk. He felt as if she'd been expecting him. He'd seen her in the Great Village, in her rich red cloak, and knew her as the head of the Epicurean school, and the fact that she approached him so simply and kindly impressed him deeply.

She called herself Philodemia. They sat in chairs under the shade of a many-branched tree, and in that first hour, Kharapan confided in her what he hadn't told anyone, hadn't been able to tell anyone—his struggle, his lack of knowing, his desire for wisdom and integrity.

Philodemia was silent for a time when Kharapan had finished. She asked him about his daily life, his hours. She told him that his open manner, especially as he wasn't practiced in speaking to others, impressed her. She liked his simple life and hopes. He hadn't practiced the art of Epicureanism and yet took pleasure in a simple life. And yet, she went on, he seemed not to understand himself, as if he hadn't found his place or path to wisdom. She cautioned that the desire for integrity could be like a desire for wealth—it could amount to a hunger for power or a desire to be immortalized.

She didn't know if he would be an Epicurean but felt that their way of life would benefit him.

He agreed, although he said he couldn't be faithful to any school. He loved the Stoics and had a deep respect for the Aristotelians.

Philodemia laughed at his serious manner. "Here is an *askesis* you need right away...." The fundamental exercise consisted in relaxation, serenity and the art of enjoying the stable pleasures of the body. Whatever other exercises he did, he had to do them in this peaceful state.

She instructed him on the three pleasures. The flesh, the body, was the basic experience of existence; the only genuine pleasure was that of existing, and—simply—one felt this pleasure when one wasn't hungry, thirsty, or cold. Thus, the three pleasures were: the natural ones, to be free of hunger, thirst, and cold; the natural but unnecessary pleasures, such as desire for sumptuous foods or sexual gratification; and the pleasures neither natural or necessary, produced by empty opinions, such as desire for glory and immortality. By being free of unnecessary pleasures, and finding satisfaction in natural pleasures alone, one could know real pleasure, that of simply existing.

Before he left, Philodemia gave him a scroll with sayings that she told him to memorize. But, she warned, he must practice while relaxed, and so it was good to be in the Garden while he worked. Furthermore, he had to practice friendship for that was the means of transforming himself.

Kharapan immersed himself in Epicureanism with relief. Already at fourteen, he felt tired of knowledge and the pressure to gain knowledge. He wanted to be like a fish, even if this wasn't exactly what the Epicureans taught: he wanted to look out in wonder at being alive and not question what things or universes were made of, to sink in this water which he swam. For a time, it seemed that the simple natural Epicurean pleasures were a danger because, to him, they seemed too luxurious. He sat in the Garden, without thought of what he wore, in blue or green, or the Epicurean red, or a mixture of colors, and his favorite discussions were with Philodemia. He memorized sayings such as: "if gods exist they have nothing to do with human beings;" "death is not to be dreaded;" "what is good is easy to acquire;" and "what is bad is easy to bear." He meditated on death, an exercise intended to awaken gratitude for existence, since the Epicureans considered life a pure chance that was lived only once, irreplaceably and uniquely.

Kharapan meditated on death, but sometimes forgot if he intended a Stoic or Epicurean exercise. The Stoics, in preparing for the harshness of nature, did an *askesis* to accept death with serenity, while the Epicureans meditated on death to understand the pleasure of existence, the singular enigma of life. The Epicurean Sage reclined without hunger, cold, or thirst, in utter peace and happiness, and without concern. The Stoic Sage was the rational creature so aware of himself that no harsh event altered his peace of mind. In neither school could a human being become a sage, but one could pursue sage-hood. All humans would drown, all were beneath a great sea and would drown, but one might struggle to drown in the light at the surface rather than in the utter darkness at the bottom of the sea.

Kharapan grew confused—not only with the different ways of life but also with opposing physics. Epicureans said that one had no need to fear death if one understood the truth. The universe, they said, was composed of atoms and a void in which those atoms moved, and within the infinite void an infinite number of worlds formed. Everything happened by chance. Death was nothing, the end of flesh and soul that disintegrated back into atoms; if gods existed, they too were formed by chance and atoms, and hadn't created the world and were utterly indifferent to rational creatures. The Stoics taught that the one universe repeated itself endlessly. For them, the universe was rational and everything in the world was related to and needed everything else. This kind of universe was the only one reason could produce, and the slightest event implied the entire series of causes, all preceding events, and the whole universe itself. Human freedom of choice was possible only in judgments and discourses about reality that gave meaning to the events that nature rationally imposed.

And the good life for the Aristotelians was a life of the mind.

Kharapan felt farther than ever from wisdom. It occurred to him that it might be worse to study more than one philosophy if one wanted to know oneself. Even in the Garden he felt he might not be suited for a life of simple pleasures, for he yearned for the challenge of himself, yearned to strengthen his integrity, to speak his mind even in the face of death.

In passing months, Kharapan lived in the midst of the three schools and at times felt anguished—he had yet to explore the Academy, or those philosophers, Skeptics and Cynics, who engaged in a lived *askesis* without a school. He didn't want to be a master at a school, and he was unaware of what others might think of him. He only wanted to recognize himself.

One night, months before he turned fifteen, a conversation with Arminius changed Kharapan's life. He'd expected some encounter with the Stoic master, perhaps dreaded it, but he hadn't expected that this conversation, so important to his life, would involve Metis too.

He attended a discussion in the Great Hall, what had been a white temple before the Greeks came to Egypt. The people of Chi held discussions and debates there as a kind of entertainment. These discussion and debates served as a forum where the philosophers of different schools came together. Kharapan often went to the Great Hall. The night's event consisted of a discussion led by a farmer named Puda, a Stoic Friend—one who attended lectures but was not an official member of the school. The high ceilings and huge room gave Kharapan, in an old red cloak and baggy blue pants, a feeling of wonder. Torches lit the room and emanated the thick smell of burning oil. Kharapan saw Metis at the front and was surprised because he'd never seen her at a discussion. She'd left the Aristotelian school, saying she refused to be a part of the passive elite, and she'd gone to live with the poorest farmers who worked for her father to live with them in poverty and hardship. Recently, he'd heard, she'd begun to do some work translating Coptic texts for monasteries in the north.

Puda spoke about how corn changed over seasons, how it turned yellow and died, ordinary words that held fascination because of his enthusiasm and way of making corn symbolize life. He spoke about what they didn't know about corn, where it came from, the yellowness of it, its growth and death, how the stalks sunk into earth and returned to the dirt. In the silence between words, in the pauses, Kharapan felt space hinting at a vast unknown. Language gave them an illusion of the quotidian. "So in the fields, especially there, I'm immersed in mystery," Puda said.

"What about what we *know*?" Metis blurted, interrupting. The large echoing hall seemed to emphasize her words. Her angry eyes encompassed them all. "Feelings have no truth. They don't exist out here." She waved a hand in the air. "We're too passive. We speak of Nothingness."

Kharapan knew vaguely of Metis's concern with what she saw as the danger and oppression in the north, the rise of the Christian Church.

In a monastery in the north, Metis infiltrated their world. She made observations and amassed data. She had Aristotelian principles to guide her: seeking knowledge, seeking to know. A person who devoted herself to the activity of the mind depended only on herself. The closer one was to a sage, the more one could be alone.

One of the philosophers, an Academician, said, "Feelings are as real as corn. One should be careful to understand that pain serves as a guide to life."

Metis waved her hand dismissively. "We're in danger," she said. "None of you see—with your eyes, your mind. Your so-called wisdom blinds you. No one in Chi can see the truth, not only the philosophers, but even our politicians, our merchants—no one notices the growth of a Christian Empire, dangerous to the existence of Chi itself, to our way of life, to our very thoughts and beliefs."

"We are a small country," someone said. "Romans don't consider us a threat."

Metis laughed a strange laugh, and she strode out with an angry confident gait. Some heard her whisper, "It's child's play to them" as she left.

Her words broke the impetus for discussion, and in any event, the discussion ended.

Kharapan went out. As usual, Metis gave him a vague unease, but he also had wary respect for her. Some Aristotelians looked forward to her study on Christianity and suspected it would be a masterwork. Kharapan wondered: should the people of Chi take heed? But what exactly was it that they, the people of Chi, should do? Didn't some have jobs that consisted of contemplating that sort of thing, the larger world—politicians, dispute resolvers, the merchants who mixed with Romans? He didn't trust his own thoughts. He feared for Chi but suspected the vulnerability in himself that made him fear.

He went into the dark night. Someone put a hand on his shoulder, and he turned and was struck: Arminius. The great man asked him to take a walk. As they walked out alone under a black-blue sky on the path to the Nile, the young man had never before been so fully present.

Arminius moved slowly, leaning on his long wooden walking stick. He didn't speak until they reached the black expanse of water. The bland, familiar smell of mud filled the cool night air.

"I've never heard you speak," Arminius said with a hard look but also a slight smile. "I don't remember ever having heard you say a word."

Kharapan, abashed, couldn't manage a word then.

Arminius looked at the river. "I sometimes watch you," he said.

Kharapan flushed with wonder.

"Tonight, for instance. I think you know Metis from the Aristotelian school? I think you could have said something in response to what she said." He paused. "Tell me what you think of her or of what she said."

Kharapan struggled, but the mention of Metis bewildered him. Arminius waited. Kharapan finally said, "She seems to love human creatures, perhaps too much." He paused. "She wants more from us than…. She's angry. People, worlds, nothing meets her expectations. There's something… dangerous in her."

"She'll need great humility to overcome the powers of her mind, and she has little. But she's young," he added. "You don't speak!" he cried. "You think she won't listen, but you might speak of humility, you might even have a power over her because, unlike Metis, I think that great humility resides in you."

Kharapan felt a thrill, and guilt too. He hadn't spoken! He couldn't believe that Metis would listen to him or that he would have any power over her.

"It is a rare thing, humility," Arminius continued. "But you have to speak, to find the words that define you. You've lived among the schools and practiced the ways…." He paused. "I assume you want to develop as a man."

A long-suppressed anguish welled up in Kharapan. For a time, he couldn't begin. He spoke solemnly. He wanted to be wise more than anything, to live as a philosopher, but he wasn't wise and failed at the art. He couldn't choose between the schools and didn't know the best way of life and wasn't particularly drawn to any way of life. He didn't know himself, didn't have a core. He didn't live in the moment, didn't love fate, though he accepted it mindlessly. And in spite of his lack of natural ability, he lived well, and didn't mind not belonging to a particular school.

Arminius had a quizzical smile, and his sharp, intelligent eyes peered at Kharapan. When Kharapan finished speaking, Arminius turned to the dark water.

"What you describe may be true, but only in part," he said at last. "You may not know yourself, but the problem isn't so large as to preclude all natural ability. You're aware of yourself, in a way. You speak honestly. And I think you have the gift of being able to listen, to take in words, and the feeling and import of what's being said. You have substantial humility, and that's a moral quality that will define you. But you must find the words that make you a man. A man may fail to develop, you know. You fall within and among us and even disappear in what seems to you to be the greater abilities of others. You think Metis's abilities are superior to yours, so you don't dare to speak to her."

Kharapan was silent. He knew what the old man said was so.

"Difficulties define us," he went on. "In your case, it's possible, even likely, that you'll live as a philosopher. But in your case, Kharapan, you must court difficulty! See it as an opportunity to test yourself and to find the words that define you. You're so gentle, you might sink into oblivion. Better difficulty than oblivion, don't you think?"

Kharapan couldn't believe Arminius had such confidence in his abilities or such fear for his failure as a man. He looked carefully into Arminius's face.

"I, too," Arminius said, "was like you, unaware of any particular talent, feeling the worthlessness of my abilities." He smiled at Kharapan's astonished look. The old man held his wooden stick at an angle and leaned his cheek against his hand that gripped the top. "I could listen, see into people. I know you understand this. But I didn't know it had value. Now, I'm old. But one should always test oneself because it's better to know the extent of one's powers. If you continue as you are, safe and unchallenged, you may never know." He paused. "Don't you think it's so?"

Kharapan paused only a moment. "I do," he said, and had never felt so certain of his words.

"You have to leave Hellenica," Arminius said.

Kharapan felt a jolt.

"You're too close to us. Proximity takes away your ability to see. I'm afraid for you. Go into the world, have experiences that test you. Our country isn't large enough to throw you into the severest kind of opposition." Arminius laughed gently, as if to himself.

Arminius held up a hand, fingers splayed in the dark as if to look through them. "Few men develop into adulthood," he said. Although events and feelings might penetrate such a man, he let feelings go. An adult moves with calmness clear to those around him, though he himself is unaware of it.

"I haven't tried the Academy," Kharapan said after a long silence. He heard doubt in his own voice, although his notion didn't completely lack a rational basis. Academicians went from school to school. They distinguished themselves from what they called the dogmatic philosophers, Stoics and Epicureans, and said that rational creatures had an innate desire for the good and a natural tendency to act in a way that was good. They used all philosophies to choose the attitude they judged best in the moment, in life, in the practice that was their art of living. But Kharapan knew he did not have the experience to know even what they knew, even if it was nothing.

Faced with Arminius's silence, Kharapan thought of other philosophic lives he might explore—the Skeptics who realized their philosophical work by renouncing philosophy itself, suspending judgment, and living, eventually, after the philosophical work, like everyone else, adhering to custom and norms of society, or the Cynics who lived in nature, abandoning society to live and model the good life in a practice of public poverty.

Arminius stared into the water and seemed to forget Kharapan. After a while he spoke. "The water seems the same when we watch it, the same shape over rocks; it is different water than before but also the same."

The old man smiled at Kharapan and, nodding his goodbye, turned and walked away.

Kharapan stayed by the water. By the first light of morning, he'd decided to leave Chi. The idea of oblivion, of never knowing himself, was worse than anything, and the idea of finding himself, of knowing his core, greater. He didn't love fate, a part of him blamed Metis—if he'd confronted her, he might not have to go—but he knew he had to leave.

Two days later he was on his way. It seemed as if he only needed to make a decision before the world eased his way. He had savings, and a long friendship with a merchant, Tyrolian, and the Alchemist, Zosimus, each who gave him goods—toys and dyed cloth and metalwork—to sell in the Empire. Both told Kharapan to keep ten percent of the profits. Zosimus placed a piece of lead in Kharapan's hand. "Come back to us with gold," he said.

Kharapan boarded a flatboat heading up river with all that he owned in one bag and the goods of Chi in another: this is what he had become, a trader. He was filled with sorrow. Yet, as the barge drifted past the invisible boundary of his country, a calm fell over him. Perhaps he was like Solon, for whom wisdom's goal was to discover new lands. If not Solon, Kharapan would find that the world flowing past, always new and yet the same, gave him an understanding of himself. From its mysterious source, the Nile River carried him to the center of the earth, to the world of known gods.

In the years that passed, confronting Rome, he had been able to *see* himself in outline against what he was not. He encountered difficulties in Rome, but in Hellenica too. He never lost his longing to stay in Hellenica; he returned often but found himself wandering among schools as if lost to himself, failing to live 'philosophy as a way of life,' and so he left. He had been there when *Kingdoms* circulated, and the monk was killed, and although he carried *Kingdoms* from that time (before giving it to Saturnine), he had never managed to 'break through' to Metis, always felt uneasy around her.

Now, on the hard prison floor, Kharapan fell asleep. He

dreamt of holes: below, a hole to a raging sewer, so large men could ride boats in it; above, a hole that opened onto a vast starry sky. The sewer sounded like the sloshing muddy Nile, until a different sound sent a shiver through him: a rhythmic munching. Something was with him on the earthen floor. He felt along the floor until his hand touched something sticky. It was the smooth end of a bone and the soft mush of rotting skin: his own leg being eaten by maggots. He awoke shaken and felt as if the ground wouldn't hold him. But only his own familiar smell filled the cell, and the ground was hard. Later, when he contemplated the dream, it filled him with a profound sense of peace.

FOUR

THADDEUS WASN'T ABLE to go to Kharapan for hours because of his duties on *Sol*—cleaning church floors, servant quarters, monks' cells. Late in the day, Thaddeus opened the thick door and, taking an oil lamp from the wall with one hand, holding a pitcher of water with a cup attached with the other, he closed the door behind him and descended.

Kharapan shielded his eyes. When he could tolerate the light, the sight of Thaddeus gladdened him. "Thaddeus," he said.

Thaddeus placed the lamp on the wall and put the jug of water on a small, dirty table. He poured Kharapan a drink. Kharapan drank thirstily. He was in one of the many small cement cells, all empty, higher than the floor, sloping slightly toward thick metal bars. Kharapan couldn't stand up straight if he stood.

"How long have I been here?"

"It's still *Sol*. It's not yet dusk." Thaddeus paused. "I met Saturnine."

"Where?" He worried that the Church had Saturnine but before Thaddeus could explain, the door opened above. Thaddeus moved to the water jug and pretended to be busy cleaning something.

Lupicinus appeared. He looked down at Kharapan and the boy in the cell and stepped in, closing the door behind him. He descended the stairs. He noticed Thaddeus but disregarded him and then forgot about him. A slave was a part of the church's foundation, as silent and necessary to the structure as stone but invisible to those who reigned above. Lupicinus stood in front of Kharapan with an abstracted expression.

"Saturnine's disappeared," Lupicinus said, "and the codex, *Kingdoms*. We found some of her work hidden under the floor of her old bedroom, but I suppose she has *Kingdoms*."

Even a rank cell could not degrade Kharapan's natural dignity, Lupicinus thought. Kharapan sat upright, his legs crossed, looking at Lupicinus with a curious intent, open expression.

Lupicinus's day had been filled with frustration. After he'd arrived at the church, after speaking with the bishop, he learned that Monk Lolianus and the churchmen who'd returned to Saturnine's domus, as instructed, had found both master and mistress missing, and although they'd returned with codices and rolled papyri from their library, they didn't have *Kingdoms*. Later, Lupicinus had gone to the domus himself, with Pius and others, and found Victorinus, but not Saturnine. The churchmen searched her parents' domus and Victorinus's and found Saturnine's writings but not *Kingdoms*. Victorinus claimed he didn't know where Cornelia was. He was distraught. He told them Cornelia was innocent in the deception of her maidservant, and uninvolved in Kharapan's evil, whatever it might be. "What are you going to accuse her of?" he asked. Pius responded as if in commiseration, "No one is prepared." They'd left guards with instructions to confine Saturnine to her room if she returned. Pius suggested that he question Kharapan himself.

"She must have *Kingdoms*," Kharapan said.

Lupicinus smiled at his openness but felt alarmed; he didn't want Kharapan to be naïve. "I informed the Church that you are a great threat." He paused. "I am your fate, and the fate of your Country," he said.

Kharapan nodded. His eyes were bright, but he had a gentle expression. "We have a special fate between us," he said. "We'll make each other better men."

Lupicinus studied Kharapan. Kharapan's eyes, his serious tone and manner, gave Lupicinus the sensation of that unaccountable and incomprehensible bond between them. The feeling humbled him, as if there were something meaningful yet secret between them. He didn't speak for a time.

Kharapan, in the dark of his cell, besides the rest—his past, Saturnine, Flavia's eyes before her last act on earth—had contemplated his situation. The Church would accuse him of sorcery or something he had little hope of disputing. The Church might also, depending on the pull of hours, the weight of history, or nothing at all, implicate Hellenica. It might claim Kharapan represented the common Hellene, that the people of Chi had dangerous ideas, worshipped the devil or demons. And yet, Kharapan's thoughts in the darkness kept returning to Lupicinus and the challenge he posed. Even before the Church imprisoned him, Kharapan imagined in Lupicinus some test of his own character, and now that test or challenge seemed better defined. Lupicinus might spin the story of him, of Hellenica, to the Church. He might call Hellenica a world full of demons, or he might simply set him free. Kharapan couldn't quite believe it, but he wondered if this itself was the challenge: to reveal to Lupicinus his errors, as well as his own, and those of Hellenica, and enter into a friendship with him. Kharapan would only embark on such a journey if he believed in that sliver of integrity in Lupicinus, and then perhaps he, Kharapan, might not only save himself, but Hellenica also. And yet, how strange and horrible to imagine this sort of challenge! befriending such a man, an enemy, with the absolute power of the Church, the one who ordered his capture, who might destroy Hellenica and philosophy as a way of life itself. And if this was the challenge, then any false note, any self-serving desire for his own safety or that of Chi would prevent a true bond, perhaps destroying them all. In Kharapan's experience he knew that only a true connection, along with an open mood and willingness to speak, led to friendship. But such a challenge with this man seemed impossible. And yet Lupicinus's first words about fate seemed to confirm Kharapan's thoughts. It wasn't the Church with its irrational charges that Kharapan had to be concerned about, but rather the peculiar and particular challenge that the man Lupicinus posed.

Here is a challenge, he thought: to love and forgive a man who might kill me, who might destroy my country. But what choice did he have? He sat behind bars with Lupicinus in front of him.

"I risk being a fool," Lupicinus said with a slight smile.

"The fool tells the truth," Kharapan said. "I hope you risk being a fool."

Lupicinus smiled. His hesitation to believe in the moment came from an age-worn doubt that anything interesting could happen. Although life was perhaps inexplicable, it was the same day to day. No elephant materialized out of the air, although sometimes in boredom he searched for elephants. His firm belief that life was meaningless, at his highest something to be structured and ordered, left him, perhaps, in a parched mood. Those of Chi say that the godless of Chi are the happiest of creatures, that despair belongs to a man of Empire, a man raised on an all-knowing, all-powerful God. For when he loses his faith as, they say, a reasonable man must, that man alone understands and regrets the loss of that God and that world. And yet, the loss of the illusions of Empire isn't the only path to despair. Lupicinus had never had a god. Rather, to his mind, given that human beings were limited, incapable of discovering or knowing truth, given that morality was a "human thing" with no measure or worth beyond the human himself and so without essential meaning, then despair was the only legitimate mood, the only legitimate way of life.

"I thought we'd meet again," Kharapan said.

Lupicinus wouldn't admit or deny fate but Kharapan's words pleased him.

"Although I didn't imagine I'd be locked up," Kharapan said, smiling.

Lupicinus found himself unaccountably charmed. This man seemed an anachronism, a gentle creature from some distant Greek past.

Kharapan went on. "When we met, I said we should share our lives and in that way discover our worlds, Chi and Empire, and which civilization is best. But I've had time to reflect, and I've come to believe that the reason for that discussion is not to compare civilizations, or to prove that civilization exists without god, or to prove one place is better than the other. No, the reason to share our lives is that we hope to rise above civilization and form a bond as men, as friends."

Lupicinus squelched his desire to laugh. He held back, wanting Kharapan to believe in him, perhaps—in the moment, just for a moment. The words beckoned him to a strange land.

"I thought of it when we first met, friendship. I didn't mention it; I didn't tell you then. I didn't give you a chance. I thought you'd consider friendship nonsense, between someone like you and someone like me. I waved the idea away myself, imagining you incapable of such a conversation, incapable of friendship, which is a philosophical act. But here we are, and I have no choice but speak my mind and express my thought, so it seems."

"You seek to gain my love and affection so that I can't bear to hurt you, so I set you free," Lupicinus said.

"What exists between us exists in spite of and irrelevant to the Church. We can have a meaningful exchange regardless of events up there, in the world, regardless of what has to take place."

Lupicinus said nothing.

"And yet, to have the sort of conversation I describe, you have to be alive," Kharapan said. "That is, there'd have to be some chance of integrity in you. The stakes involve more than my death, the death of a mortal body; they involve your death, too, that of your spirit, for it is worse to be dead in spirit and yet continue to live. The stakes involve your integrity, the slim chance, perhaps, of your integrity. But if there's no chance, there's no reason to speak. One only wastes one's breath over a closed, dead man, and in such case, I have no desire to speak to you."

Lupicinus smiled slightly. That light burning in Lupicinus even then, apparently, must have been bare, a low flicker. It seems a slim chance, to me, looking back, that Kharapan saw what he did in Lupicinus. A man might remain lost to himself by a mere chance.

"I don't know how to understand what's between us," Kharapan said, "or how to judge the potential in either of us, except by speaking. Should we engage in conversation, we might arrive at a place we can't go further; and then, if you're responsible for my fate, if I'm to be tortured and killed for being a demon, then it'd be better to get on with it than continue an empty conversation."

Thaddeus breathed in, shocked at Kharapan's words and at the way Lupicinus listened attentively. The boy didn't make a sound, but he felt himself in a quandary. He shouldn't be standing there listening, but at first couldn't leave and then he was stuck, trying to blend into the wall. Certainly, the longer he stayed, the more conspicuous it would be for him to leave.

"You speak courageously," Lupicinus said. "But you have yet to experience torture: you'll admit to sorcery and playing with devils, and you'll destroy your own country."

"Yes," Kharapan said in a soft voice. "But admitting nonsense in torture, nonsense in pain is nonsense, and everyone knows it themselves."

Lupicinus looked around for a chair and spotted Thaddeus. "You're still here, are you?"

Thaddeus jumped and scrambled up the stairs.

The surprise Lupicinus felt on seeing Thaddeus made him sense that what had passed between Kharapan and him was strange, perhaps revealing, although he couldn't quite remember what had been said that was revealing. He found an old wooden chair and placed it in front of Kharapan. He didn't speak for a time. Thick walls, cold cave-like prison—what a place! In Victorinus's garden, when he'd imagined engaging in a conversation with Kharapan, he hadn't been able to imagine the place. Here—what better place to speak words never to be uttered in a world above?

"Truth," Lupicinus said, "is a dangerous game."

Kharapan agreed. "A man risks self-knowledge when another learns the truth of his life, and even if that man never saw that other again, even if the other is killed or went to live on the fixed stars losing all contact with earth, the words would have been uttered, the experience had."

Lupicinus laughed, his shoulders shook. "You amuse me very much."

"You're right to say it's dangerous. You're right to fear."

Lupicinus stiffened.

Kharapan went on. "You suspect you'll make a mistake. You fear that when you understand, when truth is spoken, you won't be able to excuse yourself."

"There's no such thing as truth," Lupicinus said. "An empire is based on images of gods. Rome was born of a boy raised by a she-wolf. We humans make our truth." He paused. "I don't make this claim lightly." He spat on the floor, looking around as if expecting a servant to rush over and wipe it up. "Men such as you, atheists, are invisible, hardly perceived as a threat. I have intimate knowledge of the danger," he said in a harsh whisper. "What you saw in me is true. I don't believe in God. I uphold the Church as a devout Christian, nonetheless. The Orthodox Church is the chance, the fight against chaos. The Empire is threatened all around—wild men, barbarians, breaking in. But I know that man's rejection of divinity is the evil that waits, the Church's true and greatest challenge. It is that truth—godlessness—that will not die like the litter of false gods. Stories and falsehoods make up the foundation of our civilization and uphold the civilized state of man. Either this God is victor and we have a civilized world, or your godlessness destroys Him and we are left only with an animal existence. And chaos."

He took a breath, leaning back. "I didn't believe the Church would recognize the threat of atheism in my lifetime, but here you are," he said. "Here's our chance to define the crime."

Kharapan laughed—with real mirth. "The energy your Christian civilization takes!" Kharapan said. "It's exhausting even to imagine. What strain! If you don't live your life as a lie, all of civilization will fall!" He laughed heartily. Lupicinus looked on with a half smile.

"There's far less strain in Chi," Kharapan went on, "less strain with a core that leaves room for individual stories and truth. You might let go, simply let the Church go and find out what happens and have far less strain and a good life too."

Kharapan shook his head, laughed, and then fell into reflection. Neither spoke for a time.

Kharapan grappled. All of his life he'd felt that his own life, its vulnerable body and pneuma—his spirit and breath— depended on the breath of Chi; he hadn't considered it the other way, that Chi's breath could depend on his own. And yet, Kharapan thought, he had to follow his inner guide, the only guide he had, that told him to speak as he must, to proceed in a way he understood. To engage with Lupicinus would take all of him, the experience of his life, all of his life's practice and work. If he made the wrong decision, spoke the wrong words, he endangered Hellenica, but the wrong decision might be to lack faith in his way of life. Only intimacy, a sharing of one's soul with another, formed a bond between men.

He spoke after a time.

"I'm not like you," he said. "I'm not the disbeliever you think I am. In Hellenica, we have those who call themselves Stoics, Epicureans, Aristotelians, and other names. I court mystery, have discovered in it the foundation for a fullness of feeling, a better knowledge. And when I close myself to mystery, I feel occlusion, narrowness. I learned, after time, to take the narrow feeling as a warning, for a fall from mystery is a fall from truth, a fall into error and sickness. But at times, I too have fallen into sickness."

"You think I am sick. Of course," Lupicinus said, waving his hand. "Our work to define atheism merely furthers the Grand Story, the grand fantasy. The Grand Design is not based on reality, on the truth of individual difference. It doesn't matter what you think, or what any other person thinks: the world will proceed. The Church will have its Kingdom."

"Yes, but we might try to speak of what's real down here."

Lupicinus acknowledged with a half-shrug.

"Here's another difference between us," Kharapan said. "You deny life, the fullness of your own life, in the hope of an inevitable future, even if you only pretend, even to yourself, that this is the reason you act the way you do. I would explain why I say 'pretend,' why I think you fool yourself, but it would take time, a longer conversation." He paused, searching for the right words. "For me, I want a life of integrity, and my own life is all. That's happiness! But try to harness people and control their thoughts and it's an unhappy thing that's not even possible. In fact, one must simply live: there's nowhere to get to."

"The Church will have its Kingdom," Lupicinus said. "I can't help what I see."

They paused. The lamp flickered on the dull, musty walls.

Kharapan thought that Saturnine also felt a burden beyond herself, heavy with the Roman Empire and the idea of challenging such a world. Lupicinus considered opposition to the Church futile. Kharapan acknowledged it: disbelievers in the Empire faced a heavy burden. Lupicinus with his intelligence and insight might have helped others who struggled to find their own mind and way in such a world. Lupicinus might have been a model—his life a model—even if he were killed in the end.

At the time, Lupicinus breathed a cold air, as if the two men were embarking upon a wild, open landscape, a dangerous journey full of fresh life. It was a feeling he'd forgotten or perhaps had never known. He cautioned himself, thinking how he'd admitted his atheism to Kharapan as if it were nothing to him. He'd admitted it to someone only once before, with disastrous consequences. Surely the more he spoke with Kharapan the more he risked. He knew well that a man who drew too close to 'a demon' (in a world upside down) risked being tainted himself. In a worldly way, it was mad to speak to a barbarian accused by the Church. A churchman's duty in this world—he saw it distinctly—was to define atheism as a crime against God, to make Kharapan the blood sacrifice to atone for that crime, and possibly to make a show by destroying Hellenica itself, or at least invading it with Roman legions. He believed that these events would likely take place whether he spoke to Kharapan or not.

"You're immersed in Empire," Kharapan said. "You think too highly of your insight about the Church. If you'd lived in Chi, you'd have other, opposing, insights. But as a man, you can rise above worlds and cultures."

Some unusual feeling or idea took hold of Lupicinus. He felt as if falling. He felt he caught sight of a glimmer, as if peering through a window, only a window, of relief. It was the possibility of release, of relaxing his shoulders, if only for a little while. He knew it wasn't real, this moment, speaking to Kharapan, but for a moment in the space down there, in the underground, he felt he might briefly take his ease.

"One must pause," Kharapan was saying. He leaned forward and said softly, "You fear you might love Chi and its godless people."

Lupicinus stood as if stung.

Silence hung in the stale space. Gaps in conversation are a wild precipice, a chasm that compels a man to speak and so come to know himself.

Lupicinus bowed his head and smiled to himself. They played out a menippea, he thought, exactly a menippea. He, a powerful man, descended into a netherworld to engage in a fantastic situation, to explore and test an idea, the idea of civilization and the place of godlessness in civilization, with a ragged man from another world. It was a story with a known ending: the process would be the story, the discovery, the menippea itself.

Lupicinus was wrong in one respect: he didn't expect then what this encounter with Kharapan and events of the months I relate in this chronicle would mean, how they would change him—if I can dare say, but perhaps cannot go so far—in years to follow, too late perhaps, far too late.

Kharapan watched Lupicinus intently.

Lupicinus straightened his robes and paused, eyeing Kharapan with a curious expression. "I suppose you wouldn't leave if I left the bars open?"

"No," he said, after a time. "There's no need to lock the door, except for appearance, I suppose."

Lupicinus smiled and then gave a low bow, like an actor in a theater, except that it was done with feeling, and then he slowly mounted the stairs.

Later, Lupicinus realized that he hadn't asked Kharapan if he knew where to find Saturnine or about where he stayed in Rome. In any event, if she showed up at her domus, they'd arrest her. And if she didn't return at all, she'd lose Rome itself.

FIVE

THADDEUS RETURNED TO Kharapan's cell after Lupicinus left and found him absorbed in thought.

"I must confront this possibility in Lupicinus," Kharapan said after a time.

At times Kharapan believed, like Lupicinus, that the world moved inevitably toward the jealous God, and that philosophy as a way of life, the ways of life of his country, would be lost to the world. But he also told himself that human nature was drawn to philosophy as a way of life, and so the philosophical way would always exist in some form.

"The key's here—they don't suspect," Thaddeus said. "I can come at night and let you out. You can leave Rome and go to your country, with Saturnine."

"Tell me what you know about Saturnine," he said.

Thaddeus told him that he had spoken with Saturnine at Kenyon's. Thaddeus said he was glad when he heard Lupicinus say he hadn't found Saturnine, because except for their plan to meet that night, he didn't know where she was and thought she might have returned to her domus.

Kharapan reached through the bars and gently took hold of Thaddeus's wrist. "Thaddeus, leave me to my life. Tell Saturnine to leave me to my life. You have your lives. Tell her to go to Chi with Kenyon. Kenyon will take her there. And you too—you might go with them." He let go of Thaddeus.

"But the danger," Thaddeus said, marveling at Kharapan's words. "There's danger in getting close to an evil man."

"Life isn't what we imagine," Kharapan said. "Here is my life. Trouble is an opportunity to test oneself. So this is a gift, a strange gift."

Kharapan fell into reflection. Rousing himself, he said, "The world is intimate in our encounters, we are intimate with it, and everything tells me to stay: the challenge to my integrity, the signs—not only leading me here but being captured!—meeting Lupicinus in Saturnine's garden. Nothing tells me to escape this situation. If I go, I risk my integrity. I risk the life of Chi itself." He paused. "I can live with myself if I believe I did what I thought best, even if I don't succeed." Thaddeus watched Kharapan carefully, puzzled by his words.

"It's not only signs that tell me to stay, but something that happened a long time ago," Kharapan said.

Kharapan suddenly laughed. His bright eyes scared Thaddeus. "The Fates wanted the contest to be even. My body's lack of freedom is the one thing that might unsettle me," he said. "It's true that an evil man poses a danger, but what's so terrifying?" He stared intently at Thaddeus. "It's this: that he'll convince me that life is meaningless, that integrity means nothing, a more fearsome threat than death, for our bodies are not ours, not within our control, and must die. The pain is also," he said, as if to himself, "the threat to Hellenica, the defenselessness of Chi."

"So, you think you're supposed to be imprisoned in a damp cell beneath the pope's church?" Thaddeus said after a time, his voice timid and unsure

Kharapan laughed, but his answer was serious. "I do," he said.

Thaddeus blushed. He'd lost his way in the tangle of thought. Unexpressed words inside of him were a rich bog.

"I'm smiling because I like you, Thaddeus. You surprise me. I think you understand what life consists of more deeply, surely more deeply, than Lupicinus."

The idea astounded Thaddeus.

The door scraped against the ground. Thaddeus quickly turned and picked up the cask of water and rushed upstairs. A slave came in with porridge, as Thaddeus had instructed (saying that it was by order of Monk Lolianus and Lupicinus himself), and Thaddeus showed him the cask of water as he passed and went out.

Thaddeus returned to the servants' quarters. He had to scrub the floors after the service. They had given him six slaps on his hand with a stick for having gone missing, and it still stung him. He would try to find Saturnine at the temple that night but worried that someone would come for him. He would tell his friend, the kind mad Claudia, to go to Kharapan with clean clothes and bedding and to clean his cell, telling anyone who asked that Monk Lolianus wanted him cleaned up for questioning. These and other thoughts occupied Thaddeus. However, before he returned to his quarters, he slipped into an empty cell and sat in a dark corner. There, he let anguish fill him, as if the future had already happened, as if Kharapan were dead, and even he, Thaddeus were gone, but everything at the church continued as it always had. His thoughts made him dizzy, and he wondered at the purpose of moving at all.

SIX

LATE AT NIGHT, Saturnine stood in the shadows near the bushes outside Victorinus's domus. It seemed like someone else's house. She could hardly believe she'd been there only yesterday, on *Sol*, embodying that role, that life. She didn't see anyone.

The day before, after leaving Kenyon, Saturnine walked into the city, her thin ash-streaked tunic and Flavia's old cloak no longer seeming like a disguise.

At a fountain, holding the chained metal cup that the poor used to drink from, she saw the senator, Symmachus, followed by a coterie of servants. In her poor garb she didn't fear he'd recognize her. When a church party passed, she bowed her head but didn't hide her face or her burning eyes. One might fall a long way and become a mere ruin in a city. But better a ruin, she thought, than a being cloaked in lies.

Darkness alerted her that it was time to go to Temple Minerva. Once there, she waited, shrouded in shadows. The darkness grew deep in the thick of night. A small figure appeared and moved furtively as if looking for something.

"Thaddeus," she whispered.

He knelt in front of her, opening his mouth as if to speak.

"Shhh," Saturnine said, holding up a warning finger.

"You didn't go home," he said.

"No."

"Guards are waiting for you."

"I…." She paused. After leaving the apartment where Kenyon lived, standing in the courtyard, her old life had seemed to fall from her like a heavy cloak that had once shielded her entire body. Flavia said she'd freed her—Saturnine felt she'd lost her entire world and all connections to it.

"You returned to the church," she prompted.

"Yes," he said. To Thaddeus, too, this day, *Sol*, seemed the long year of the gods. He pulled out a hard piece of bread and found her hand, placing the morsel into it. She tried to eat but had no appetite and her mouth was dry.

The darkness soothed him and coaxed out words. He told her what he could: the men from the church went to her domus and found her writing. Guards waited there to find her. Kharapan believed he belonged in the prison beneath the church, and he planned to speak to Lupicinus, even if tortured and killed. Lupicinus said he controlled Kharapan's fate as well as the fate of Hellenica.

"Kharapan said we must leave him to his fate," Thaddeus said, and added that he had the means to free him, but Kharapan said he didn't want to be freed.

Saturnine reflected. Kharapan's fate and the fate of Hellenica, she thought, lay in the hands of an uncertain character, a man wielding power, or even in a power beyond Lupicinus, the Church. Kharapan wouldn't leave the church's prison, and she herself seemed outside of all of this, irrelevant. Besides, what could she do? Yet, she had her own needs. If nothing else, her selfish needs attached her to the world.

"You have to take me to Kharapan," she said.

"Impossible," he gasped.

"You said you could help free Kharapan. Then you can save me by bringing me to him. It would be the safest place in the world! No one would imagine I'd try to get into the prison or even be able to."

He could feel her hot face close to his. After a pause, he whispered that he would try.

"But first," she said. Saturnine took hold of the young slave's arm and led him through the dark city. In the streets, they passed the silent statues of men and women, reproductions of humanity, nor did night wanderers bother them. They went along buildings dimly lit by fires in urns, walked between apartments where dung and waste made a rank miasma and cockroaches swarmed and rats scurried around corners, and down a narrow passageway. Saturnine stopped in front of a red door lit by a single bare lamp. Perhaps Flavia had come to this door. Saturnine adjusted Thaddeus's robes so that only his eyes could be seen, and she knocked. At last, through a dirty window, they saw a light moving through the shadowed darkness. A woman opened the door a crack and peered out. Thaddeus peeked out from his cloak and saw that the woman wore a dark shawl.

"I heard you'd lived," the woman said in a nasal voice, an unearthly voice, but from the world of men.

The air in the room was damp and musty, smelling of a strong substance of some kind. It was too dark to see the room's periphery. Saturnine asked for poison. Thaddeus felt his chest fall inward but he didn't make a sound.

"Enough to kill two men," Saturnine said, but then looking at Thaddeus, she said, "No, for three. I don't have money, but if you refuse…"

Her eyes didn't waver. The old woman might hold something over her for engaging in an illegal act, but Saturnine could also destroy her for her role in killing Victorinus's baby. Perhaps a resolve in Saturnine's eyes made the woman turn toward the stairs. She disappeared into the recesses of the building, leaving them in darkness.

When she returned, she carried three vials. "If you use strong wine," she said. "They won't taste their deaths."

Saturnine bowed her head. When she looked up she saw the woman watching her carefully. "You'll never see me again," Saturnine said, hoping it would reassure her, but the old woman only thought Saturnine meant to kill herself. The scandal made her curious, but she didn't intend to interfere. Good business flowed from the bowels of secrecy.

Saturnine and Thaddeus went out. The young slave moved in silence next to her. The massive church came into view, and they stopped in an alleyway near the grass. Flames in urns on the church portico made a gloomy mask of the edifice. Saturnine noticed that Thaddeus's face had lost all expression, as if he were in a trance or lost to existence.

"Do you remember how my mother fell?" she said, her hair falling softly at the sides of her face.

He nodded.

"Some great men, philosophers, decide to take their own lives. I begin to understand it—the willingness, the readiness to die, the desire to make death one's own." She nodded toward the church. "Kharapan is as noble as the ancients. I'll wear poison. I'll try to understand and in the meantime, remember." She paused. "And you—you're not like me."

She took one of the vials of poison and put it in the boy's hand. He had a severe expression, as if maturity were falling like a veil over his young face.

"Yes," she said, "you're alive and have every right to manage your own death. So you're going to take me to see Kharapan, and you've been a friend to us both even though you had to risk the vengeance of such a powerful enemy. You understand friendship. You, Thaddeus, are better than I am."

He started to deny it, but Saturnine stopped him with a gesture of her hand.

He closed his fingers on the vial of poison.

She sunk against the wall. "Go now," she said. Saturnine eyed him. "Go," she said with greater urgency, grabbing his sleeve. "Go."

He hesitated only slightly and then ran across the grass toward the church.

She watched his shadow. "And if I live?" she whispered.

Everything was silent. The night rested on silence—how good the silence, how right to be out in the darkness and dangers of night. A rustle nearby disturbed her. A ragged man came toward her down the narrow street. He came close, his dirty, bearded face peering into hers. She could see his dull brown eyes, and then he continued on.

After what seemed a long time, she saw a small dark form racing toward her. When Thaddeus reached her, he bent down, panting. As he looked at her expectant face, an inexplicable knowledge came to him. He wouldn't leave her. He didn't fully understand or know why, but she gave him knowledge of himself, a sense of a boundary and shape to a previously amorphous life.

"I'll take you in," he said.

Kharapan had been startled and not pleased when he found that Saturnine insisted on seeing him, but when she came down and went to the bars, he grasped her hands. "Saturnine," he said.

"No," she said pulling away. "I'm not here to convince you to come away, to let us save you...." Her voice broke.

She paused. His pale appearance shocked her. She had the image of the man of the garden, filthy, smelling of the sea, a creature of the earth... and when was it? Days ago, but it seemed like a long time ago.

"I felt your presence after Philo died, even in all of the years of silence," she said. "And when you came that night, I was burning my writing—when was it?—I rejected your friendship. I should have expressed only joy. I should have known how important the friendship of a man such as you, what you offered. I felt too sure of myself: I was sure you'd never be absent from my life no matter what I said or did."

She put her hand into the dark one that reached for hers,

but then pulled away. "But since…" She paused to control her emotion. "I know it's not true now."

"No," Kharapan said, "it's true. I'd be there regardless of what you said or did."

"No," she said, correcting him. "I understand that you might not be in my life, that something could happen…"

Her forehead fell against the cold bar and she wept, her hand over her mouth. She hadn't wanted to cry. Kharapan laid his hand on her head. He wished he could take her to Chi. But life, he knew, was contradictory and strange: if he were free, it was possible she would not want to go.

Thaddeus, who stood behind them, shuffled nervously from foot to foot, and glanced up the stairs. "Shhh," he whispered.

At his direction, Saturnine secreted herself into a dark corner under the staircase. After a time, she looked around, at the sloping gray ceiling, the thick metal bars of the small cells. It smelled musty and of urine. When no one came she returned to face Kharapan.

"Each time I see you is a memory that burns into my soul," she said, smiling a little.

After a pause, Kharapan said, "Epictetus asks whether a wrestler wants to wrestle a weak man. He says no, the wrestler yearns for the challenge that proves his strength."

"And yet this is not a game," she said.

"No, it's not play. It is what we are meant to do here."

Kharapan told her that for her, as in his case, the surface of things disguised the real difficulty. For each person, he said, it seemed that life consisted of a rising moral challenge. The

Christian word "pilgrim" touched on what he meant. Mystery cults believed that they rose through spheres as they advanced in wisdom. But in Chi, they didn't have a word for it, only they knew that each person had a journey, one of the spirit.

For Saturnine, he said, even losing Flavia was like a strange gift. For what Saturnine did in the hours to come would be steps of a journey. She'd encountered pitfalls—the lure of luxury and safety, and of love—but there were other dangers she would face.

"No," Saturnine said, "you are mistaken. I'm not strong. It's a matter of chance that I no longer have that safe life. Without Flavia... nothing matters."

"Take into account what you are up against—the Empire! For some reason you have the chance to choose now. Not everyone has that chance. For me," he said. "Even at an early age, working to strengthen my integrity was all to me, but difficulties and challenges make up the substance of life for everyone, and these are neither good nor bad. They're more like tests, like... opportunities."

Saturnine took his hand and placed a vial of poison in it, closing his fingers around it and holding onto his hand.

"Understand me," she said. "You may not use this poison, but even if not, it's a reminder of... my mother and me. I have my own vial."

"I understand," he said. "But now it' s your duty to live, Saturnine. Go. Meet your challenge. Go with Kenyon to Chi."

She looked surprised.

They heard a sound, but it was Thaddeus, coming in with Kharapan's walking stick.

"Go," Kharapan said. He grasped her hand.

He meant her to leave his cell and Rome. She had a sense of bewildered awe. A world, a journey. But she felt bitter. She understood only vague contours of Kharapan's mind and couldn't believe in what he'd decided to do. The clash between the Church and his convictions seemed a mad conflagration, one that could only result in violence and destruction. But perhaps it wouldn't help for him to leave this awful place. It seemed to her that nothing could be done.

"I've loved you a long time," she said, tears streaming down her face.

"I love you too," he said.

She released his hand and rushed up the stairs.

Thaddeus pushed Kharapan's walking stick through the bars. Kharapan held the soft wood. He stuck his hand out and touched Thaddeus's arm. Thaddeus gave a little smile, but he was distracted. He took bare leave of Kharapan.

In the morning, on *Luna*, fog seeped over hills and rain fell on and off in torrents. Saturnine and Thaddeus sat under the portico of a Basilica. Saturnine leaned against a pillar, her head down as she dozed. Thaddeus stared out, unseeing, trembling but not from cold.

Saturnine awoke and looked out, watching people pass in rain cloth, some holding wooden or fabric parasols, moving through the acts of a day.

The rain stopped and Saturnine, after a quick glance at Thaddeus, stood and wandered. Thaddeus followed. Guards passed and they lowered their heads, but the guards continued on, unaware of them.

"This life suits me," she said, sitting on the fountain steps. "I don't care for the comforts of a body."

"We can take baths," he said. "They're free. But we'll have to go in separately."

"No," she said, "I might be recognized, naked."

"Some people, I've heard, in the country, don't take baths but once a year, so we have months before we have to worry."

She looked at Thaddeus as if amazed. "No," she said. "There's nowhere for me but on the street."

Someone threw a coin at her. "See, Thaddeus! We're on our way."

She turned to him with an intense look. "At first you seemed like an animal to me, but now… you're more natural in the world than I am."

Thaddeus's heart pounded, and he looked away.

They walked for a time, slipped through an opening to a wall, and faced the huge old Pantheon.

The crumbling temple exposed a Rome abandoned by emperors, a city where the imperial offices of works—the sanitation and public services—ceased to function. The sun played off the bronze sculptured gods in the pediment of the triangular roof. Gray and red Egyptian columns held up two hundred tons of ancient bronze. The words, M AGRIPPA L F COS TERTIVM FECIT, inscribed along the base of the triangle proclaimed, "Marcus Agrippa the son of Lucius three times consul built this"—but even this was a lie. Hadrian had built it one hundred and fifty years after Agrippa, just two hundred years ago. The mist made the massive building elusive, as if one could walk through it. The perfume of pomegranate filled the air from the oils of the baths of Agrippa and Nero that bordered the courtyard's granite walls. The Pantheon's backside bulged as if it held a thing beyond itself, but marble bits broke off, revealing the tile brick underneath, stamped with names of brickyards and consuls in office two hundred years ago. Thaddeus stood next to Saturnine in wonder: he too might look on beauty, even an ancient pagan temple, might have that right and privilege.

They ascended to the Temple's portico and Saturnine grazed her hand over a column. "Egyptian," she murmured. All of Empire went into the material of the place. The massive bronze-sheeted door creaked when she pushed the flowered handle. The large circular space was cool and empty, and she went to the puddle of rainwater in the center and stood in a circle of white marble. White, yellow, blue granite and red porphyry, circles and squares, patterned the floor. The walls had circles and squares, too, and way up above the repeating patterns in the bronze roof, windowless windows, made a great circle toward a square *compluvium* that was open to sky and gods.

Thaddeus stood hesitantly at the great door of the pagan temple.

A ray of sunlight fell on an ancient yellow marble column from Numidia and on the white marble moon goddess, Diana. Saturnine went out, passing Thaddeus, and sat on the Pantheon portico. Thaddeus sat next to her. She told him she would go to Chi with Kenyon. She had no desire, she said, to go any place in particular. She might as well go into exile, or rather, follow Kenyon.

Thaddeus stiffened and could barely look at her.

"What?" she said gently.

"I'll go with you," he said, not daring to face her.

"Yes!" she said. It was simple and good to her. "Come."

But he was overcome and couldn't believe. He felt faint; the ground seemed to move. He knew it was impossible. "No," he uttered. "I can't go."

He had never been away from the church for so long, and if he returned they'd lock him up and perhaps he'd never see Saturnine, or even Kharapan, again. But if he returned to the church, he might never dare leave it again. Still, he'd believed his whole life that he'd never leave the church and the thought now, his first, of defying the Church seemed impossible. Being saved terrified him as much as being destroyed, and he wasn't sure which turn of events had what meaning. He had a heavy look in his large round eyes.

"Look," she said taking hold of his bony shoulder and peering into his face. "I would have been as you, a slave of the Church. Encountering each other—we're fated to be together. I won't say that we'll die together," for the thought was at her lips. A life is a fragile transient thing. "Regardless," she groped for words.

"They own me, Saturnine." It was the first time he'd said her name. "I might promise to stay with you, but..." He squinted and his next words made a terrible sound that chilled her. "The power," he hissed.

"Thaddeus, look, there's nothing around us."

He didn't answer, and a part of her understood. She felt shaken too.

"They own you," she said, after a time, as if it were only that, a relationship of master and slave. "And nevertheless, we'll leave. It's an act against the laws of our city. Are we immoral? Perhaps we are or perhaps the laws of the city are." The boy was motionless, listening.

"I killed my husband's baby," she said. "It was an illegal act. I would have given into my husband's demands and converted to Christianity," she said. She looked at Thaddeus. "When Kharapan came that night, he found me burning my writing; he criticized me for failing to be brave." Thaddeus said nothing.

"Forgive our weaknesses!" she said in a low voice to no one in particular.

Thaddeus's face changed and slowly assumed a healthier glow.

"I don't know anything," she said. Tears filled her eyes.

"You know what you need to do," he said.

"No!" she cried. "What's happened, what's happening is all due to events outside of me. I'm weak, and I'll go."

"I'll go with you," he said.

She put her arm in his.

They stood and went to Kenyon's.

At Kenyon's apartment, they watched people come and go. Kenyon had not told them who Saturnine was, didn't feel it was her place to do so. They knew only that Saturnine and Thaddeus were Kharapan's friends, embroiled in his trouble because they were friends, and so these people fed them and treated them with dignity and honor. Kenyon inquired about a ship. It was off-season. The office of the Rome-Alexandria run in Rome didn't know of any ship going out. It could take three months to get around the sea if they couldn't find a direct route to Alexandria, but they still planned to go to Portus the next night. Late that night, Saturnine told Kenyon she was going to see Victorinus. Kenyon shrugged and didn't say anything. Earlier, when Kenyon found out Thaddeus would come with them, she had said it was better to have the boy come along. The Church would be looking for Saturnine, an unaccompanied woman, but not for a woman and a boy. Saturnine and Thaddeus would take the papers of the children, Miriam and Jacob, and would travel as brother and sister.

Pausing before leaving for Victorinus's domus, Saturnine said to Thaddeus, "Wait for me." He didn't want her to go, but Saturnine insisted. She couldn't leave Rome with such ambiguity between Victorinus and her. Thaddeus said he too wanted to say goodbye to Kharapan and others at the church, but Saturnine refused to allow him to return, hinting at the forces there, and she assured him that Kharapan would know he had gone with her. Thaddeus was relieved, but a sense of sadness filled him. He didn't know if he'd ever see Kharapan again, or those he'd grown up with, and he reflected with regret on the distracted way he'd left Kharapan. Saturnine hadn't bothered telling him to go away with Kenyon without her if she didn't return. What could she say? If the Church captured her, perhaps Thaddeus would save her, and she wouldn't send him away.

Saturnine went to Victorinus's dark domus and slipped through the curiously unlocked door, finding the same white marble floors, the same walls and pictures and statues inside that she knew so well and that now seemed so strange to her.

Passing the library, she felt him before she saw him. She put a hand against the wall, her heart pounding. When she stood in the doorway he moved to the edge of his chair and stared as if at an apparition.

"Cornelia? Saturnine," he said softly. "You've come back."

She took a few steps into the room.

He stood. His clothes were crumpled, and he had a pale ghostly look. One low lamp burned. He moved toward her, but she stepped back. He stopped. "How did you get past the guards?" His voice had cooled.

"I didn't see them."

"They searched the domus. They found your writings. I couldn't stop them," he said, returning to his chair and sitting down with a weary sigh.

He spoke pensively. "I didn't know Flavia was your mother. When you told me... under the circumstances, I didn't believe... but I'm sorry now. I'm sorry for sending her with them."

She bent her head. The mention of her mother's name brought her back to this life more than anything.

He told her that Flavia had been cremated. They'd had to do it quickly. Saturnine nodded. She understood and didn't blame him.

Victorinus was silent for a time. In the hours after Saturnine had disappeared, with the possibility that he'd never see her again, he realized that he loved her. He softened toward her and felt he understood all that had occurred. To his mind, nothing had changed between them, except that now he'd decided to be with her even if it ruined his career.

"They may not charge you with anything," he said. "Can they call you a criminal for your thoughts? Perhaps. But we'll survive. One day we'll look back on this time as mere passing trouble. It's best if you convert, but I won't force you. We'll fight the Church."

His love, his willingness to stand by her, pained her. She said she didn't know if she'd write, but she couldn't stay with him, she didn't understand it in full herself. Regardless, she couldn't fight the Church or defend herself. His idea that she convert was the only way to save themselves, but that was impossible. "But this is all irrelevant now," she said. "I am leaving Rome. I don't know for how long, perhaps forever. I don't feel like I'm running away but rather as if….The strangeness of myself in the city, the strangeness…."

While she talked he had looked at her with astonishment and disbelief. She didn't expect him to understand, but she paused. It was this house, this man who seemed strange to her now.

"But you love me," he said. "You're speaking out of grief. You'll return to your senses…."

Saturnine shut her eyes. If he loves, it's only this skin on bones, she thought, but tears came to her eyes.

He stood and paced. "Stay at an inn. No one will find you. This trouble will pass."

She shook her head. "It's over," she said, forcing herself to look into his eyes. She couldn't feel love, couldn't feel anything at all.

He was stunned.

"I can't be your wife," she said. "I don't want to be your wife."

"I don't believe it," he said.

"It doesn't matter if you believe."

He looked at her with incredulity and mortification. "When did you stop loving me?"

She didn't answer, couldn't answer.

He felt suddenly weary. The depth and mystery of love had made him large somehow, and Saturnine's declaration, her seeming indifference stripped him bare.

"That barbarian turned you against me," he said.

She felt sick. She'd once believed that his words revealed the inevitable. She'd never seen him so vulnerable. His manner, her guilt, her uncertain love, all made her bow her head.

A silence passed.

"I need money," she said. "I may return to my parents' domus one day. I know that if you sell it, you'll at least hold the money for me."

He gave her a spiteful look.

"I know you'll prosper," she added softly. "I can't say what my life will be."

He went out, moving past her without touching her. The air between them was thick. He was gone a long time, and she began to fear he would call the guards, but he returned with a pouch stuffed with money and jewels. He was generous. Perhaps, in her leaving, in this decision, he felt the return of his life in Rome.

Saturnine bowed to him. They stood silently together.

Victorinus didn't ask where she was going. She smiled at him, suddenly embarrassed, awkward. They hugged and wished each other good luck, good days and years. Tears filled their eyes.

Outside in the dark, she moved slowly. It seemed as treacherous as murder to lose love, to declare it's death. In leaving this old life she felt as if she were abandoning Flavia too. But as she neared Kenyon's courtyard, Saturnine's thoughts turned from her old life to the unknown one opening out before her; she pulled Flavia's worn old cloak close around her body, feeling its warmth.

Book IV

ONE

LEAVING ROME IN hourless night, Saturnine felt in a vague expanse, as lost to herself as time lost to night. In Portus, they walked through the gate of the great walls, and Kenyon led them past inns marked by creaking lamps over doors—The Elephant, The Wheel, the Pig and Crucible—to a narrow alley, a dilapidated wooden building leaning toward the sea. Gusts of wind rattled a flickering lamp over the sign, The Cock. Inside, a dirty notice on the wall read, "The Innkeeper takes no gold, silver, or jewels. You take your own risk." For safety, Saturnine had given her money to Kenyon to carry, but she had jewels tied around her waist beneath her tunic. Thaddeus carried nothing. Three long wooden tables filled the barroom where a few men, soldiers, sprawled with bar servants amidst the stench of beer and scraps of food. Ancient grime half hid a mural depicting a fantastic orgy.

The innkeeper, a robust woman, looked as though she spent years at sea. Kenyon inquired about a room, and noticing the innkeeper eye Saturnine, told the old woman that Saturnine was dumb, unable to speak. The innkeeper said she had one room on the third floor with a large bed. They climbed rickety steps and found a room with a small dirty window, a candle that struggled against the shadows, and a rusty chamber pot; the walls were covered in obscene scribbles.

Closing the door, and making sure the innkeeper had gone, Kenyon spoke in a low voice. "You, Saturnine." She studied her disapprovingly. "You have to stand less straight. Your voice would reveal too much. Everything about you is class and distinction. No baths. That should help. But you must slouch. Do not gaze at people so directly. You must be one of us."

Saturnine put her sack on the floor. It contained what she had left of Philo's scrolls, her own work, *Kingdoms*. She lay down on the bed, too weary to worry about its cleanliness.

"The soldiers are a good sign," Kenyon said. "They might be waiting for a ship."

Saturnine felt it was just as well for her to be deaf and dumb, to not even try to form words around a vague and uncertain life.

They slept clothed, Thaddeus in the middle. Saturnine woke early and listened to the street noise—the screech of the sausage man, the cry of the cake seller, the Innkeepers luring those who passed by to come and take their pleasure.

When the old innkeeper, the *copa*, came over while they ate gruel and dried meat downstairs and told Kenyon she'd pay good money for Saturnine, Kenyon looked Saturnine over, tempted to haggle; she made a brisk shake of her head and told her that Saturnine wasn't a slave—she had papers, and a litigious family in Rome. The *copa* left them.

Kenyon recognized other dangers. In choosing this place, she'd wanted to minimize risk: no one would search for Saturnine here. But no respectable woman would stay here, and she couldn't help but notice a bearded man who leered at Saturnine and spoke about her loudly with his friends. Thaddeus stiffened, his eyes widening with each new potential encounter. But Kenyon wasn't unprepared to kill.

Outside, a small army camped on one side of the dock. Tents sprawled haphazardly, small fires blazed. As they walked toward the ship's offices, three guards passed, and Saturnine and Thaddeus lowered their eyes. Kenyon passed without more than a glance. Kenyon told Saturnine and Thaddeus to wait while she inquired at the office of the Alexandria-Rome run, and when she returned, she told them she hoped they'd be on that ship: a huge dark shape rocked on the sea in the distance.

Still, empty days passed. Kenyon feared that one day following another in this way must lead to disaster, but at last the dock became busy with activity and the air full of motion. The magnificent ship came close to shore. The wide prow bore a brightly painted figure of Isis on each side. The ship had come to Rome with a cargo of spice, silk, and non-perishable goods and docked for winter but would return to Egypt. It would leave with the right wind and good omens. It would carry troops to Alexandria where the soldiers would continue to Carthage. But Kenyon returned in a few hours from the office of the Rome-Alexandria run with bad news:

the officious man wouldn't grant Kenyon's request for passage, even if he didn't suspect that Kenyon traveled with a woman wanted by the pope's church and a runaway slave.

Kenyon had to secure passage with the shipmaster, instead, and obtain exit passes. She showed the shipmaster, a slight man who managed ship's business, their papers, and was careful to haggle: fugitives were willing to pay triple. She knew the cost, but would allow an increase for off-season, and for letting them ride with soldiers. He said it was impossible. Two women couldn't travel with soldiers. Kenyon was forced to find the sailing master and risked revealing that she and the others were friends of Kharapan's. The sailing masters of the Rome-Alexandria run loved Kharapan. The sailing master told the shipmaster that as friends of the line, the three could take their own risk and ride.

Kenyon, Saturnine, and Thaddeus gathered supplies using one of the carts on the dock: pots and pans, rolled mattresses and a tent, livestock—chickens, pigeons (goats were prohibited, as they presaged storms)—sacks of grain, barrels of wine, and a chamber pot. Water was the only amenity provided on board. The shipmaster allowed them to set up camp on deck before the soldiers boarded. Saturnine and Thaddeus huddled between their supplies. Kenyon paced the wide-open deck.

One morning they heard the cry of the herald announcing the departure of the vessel. The army broke camp and with surprising swiftness loaded the boat, corralled the horses and mules in a corner of the deck, and crowded on board. Rumor circulated of the sailing master's auspicious dream of flying. It was *Mars, V ides of Martius.* The winds were favorable,

aturnine

the date not unlucky, and nothing inauspicious reported—a sneeze on the gangplank, a crow squawking in the hull, a dream of turbid waters, keys or anchors. No seaman reported an owl or night bird, which presaged storm or pirate attack. Gulls and other sea birds meant danger but not death. The sailing master shouted out rules and inauspicious signs to sullen and fearful passengers: in good weather no one was allowed to cut hair or nails, speak blasphemies, even in a letter, and no dancing was permitted.

On *Mars*, the ship set sail. Saturnine watched the men. Sailors labored and shouted, working a pump or raising a sail. Soldiers stood like statues, tall and still on the deck as if unable to know themselves as human or alive, as if they couldn't fathom being on a wooden vessel in the middle of the sea. As the plunging of the ship grew familiar, the ship's deck came alive, and patterns were set. Saturnine and Thaddeus remained huddled together. Kenyon sat in the open deck, surrounded by soldiers. Saturnine overheard them. Since cursing was forbidden, their voices sounded hesitant, almost prayerful in tone. Soldiers! They stood or sat in a circle facing Kenyon, their faces open, alive and admiring, and after a time, Saturnine sensed an extraordinary intimacy between Kenyon and the soldiers.

It would take ten days to three weeks to reach Alexandria, depending on the winds. No one thought of return trips. The ship carried the burden of life. Existence resided in the moment, in the thrill of movement. Rome slipped farther behind than distance or days, and they faced a vast inscrutable sea.

Two

THE OLD BISHOP lay thin and wasted on his silk couch in his private chamber. A lush tapestry of St. John covered a wall. The massive Bible next to him had a thick gold Christ figure down the middle surrounded by rough gems—emeralds, sapphires, rubies. Damasus's weak hand lay on the naked Jesus, a little licentiously to Lupicinus's mind. Damasus wouldn't live out the year. If Damasus truly believed in Christ, he must have been afraid, tottering on the brink of the final act, the plunge into heaven or hell. Damasus must have realized he hadn't lived without great sin. Pius stood behind Lupicinus's couch.

Damasus gave a nod that meant Lupicinus should proceed: he should question the barbarian himself. If Lupicinus saw something in Damasus's eyes—uncertainty? distrust?—he told himself that forty years of forging a reputation would withstand one week of speaking to Kharapan.

Lupicinus rose. He told Damasus he'd report back in one week, on *Sol.* Pius gave a deep bow.

Lupicinus hesitated in the dark church hallway. He suddenly felt tired. He continued down the hall and went out into the bright day. He returned to his domus. In spite of having only seven days to speak to Kharapan, two of those days passed. During those hours he didn't know if he would speak with Kharapan or see him again. Perhaps he doubted: a part of him understood that he should let Kharapan be interrogated, tortured, even killed. It was how he proceeded in matters of the Church, leaving the work to others once he provided the story. He could hone the idea of atheism with words, without Kharapan himself. But at least in the hour—it seemed a mood of the hour, fleeting, temporary—he had lost interest in the Church and, with it, in godlessness. He felt exhausted by ideas, even those that once made him quick to passion. And then... he didn't think it was so, but it seemed like a suggestion... he wondered at the reason for his hesitation, whether it might be fear that revealing the truth of his life to Kharapan would reveal a mistake. Perhaps he also waited in order to savor the rare sense of embarking on something all his own. In the end he decided that he would go to Kharapan, but he didn't know what would happen or whether anything that mattered would be revealed, about himself or the man of Hellenica.

Early *Mercurius*, Lupicinus opened the metal door to Kharapan's cell, took up a lamp, and pressed into darkness. When Lupicinus saw him, he felt taken aback. Kharapan was pale and sickly and pitifully shielded his eyes from the lamplight with his arms. Lupicinus put the hard chair in front of Kharapan's cell and sat down but then stood abruptly.

"I'll report to the bishop, that is, I will decide your fate by *Sol*," Lupicinus said.

Kharapan crossed his legs stiffly; his pale face had lines from where he'd lain on the ground, and he looked confused. He couldn't stand in the cell and so he had stretched on the hard floor. The floor was cold, and a chill had seeped into his body. The smell of cleaning fluid, vinegar and water, pervaded the air. The old woman Claudia, a friend of Thaddeus's, took as much care of Kharapan as she could.

Lupicinus had named a day, but Kharapan had no idea what day it was or how many days had passed.

"What are you thinking?" Lupicinus said, as if accusing him of something.

Kharapan thought he understood something of Lupicinus's mood: he'd challenged Lupicinus to speak, to engage in an essential act, and now the man of Chi hardly seemed capable of taking an interest in him. The nearness of death and long hours in the dark turned Kharapan's thoughts inward. At times, he felt as if he didn't know himself, as if he'd lost his identity, even the words that defined him. At other times he felt like a stone that soaked up the darkness, or as if he looked down on life from a high place, and he felt a subdued joy, felt that nothing mattered, felt that he was equally willing for Lupicinus to speak or not, and that it didn't matter what the Church chose to do. He and Lupicinus would die, and the Church would carry on. But something else, too, a certain philosophical realization pertaining to Lupicinus, as it were, added to Kharapan's sense of distance from the challenge he'd made to Lupicinus.

"One speaks of 'ways of life' in the open air," Kharapan said, pausing. "In the dark... words fail one..." he faltered. "But you are here.

"I may have implied something in error when we last spoke," Kharapan went on. "I need to pay attention to what is my own. I have nothing else in my power." His eyes now accustomed to the lamplight, he looked intently at Lupicinus. "It's not my place to challenge you to act in any way. You act for yourself as you think fit. It's not my place to wish to live, for living and dying are not in my power. It's not my place to avoid fate or to wish for what is not in my power to get, but only to master myself, to protect my integrity, to try to make correct judgments of life as it passes." He paused. "My duty is to be a man, that's challenge enough. I've practiced. I've struggled. I have no other duty. Whether I become sick, or am killed, or even if Hellenica is destroyed, these are not mine. They are outside of my power."

Lupicinus listened in silence to these strange harsh words the Stoic called wisdom. But an idea in the background of Lupicinus's thoughts, an idea of a different kind, disturbed him.

"It doesn't change anything," Kharapan said. "My purpose for being here may be to engage in discussion with you, if you are able, but I must remember what concerns me and what does not. The extent of my powers, of my being, is limited and small."

Lupicinus gestured to Kharapan to be silent, and Lupicinus stood and paced.

Kharapan had intuited only a part of Lupicinus's feeling. It was true, Kharapan's pale looks and confusion disappointed Lupicinus, as if he worried that Kharapan might no longer be capable of taking an interest in him or the challenge between them. But something else disturbed Lupicinus, too, had bothered him since he'd entered. After a time, he stopped in front of Kharapan and looked at Kharapan, cross-legged on the hard floor.

"The Church could turn you into a Christian and set you free as one of the faithful," he said, in monotone, as if he were stating a fact or truth.

"Impossible!" Kharapan said.

"Quiet, let me think."

Lupicinus's thoughts came quickly. Kharapan in a cell beneath the church, pale, sickly—even a man such as he knew Kharapan to be—gave Lupicinus a terrible knowledge.

Lupicinus's thoughts consisted in something of the following. Kharapan had engaged in life, as he said, in a certain practice, speaking his mind, devoting himself to *agnosis*, to the unknown and fathoming all that might be unknown. But even so, even if he might be the strongest of men in character, Lupicinus understood the weakness and vulnerability of a man. Even a whole life of practice and devotion wouldn't save Kharapan from the power of the Church, an institution of Empire. What he understood seemed strange and new to him. Kharapan, weak and pale before him, made the idea take on mythical proportions. It made him fear for man. The Church could force Kharapan to believe, even Kharapan, and let him live, set him free rather than kill him. It could destroy Kharapan's philosophic way of life rather than his body. It was an astonishing conclusion, a power beyond imagination, but Lupicinus trusted his intuition, his ability to understand the world. It might take hours to turn a man's thoughts, his private thoughts, perhaps months, but it wasn't impossible for an institution with endless money, men, and time. Even darkness wore Kharapan down. They could break the man in a man and make all men Christian. It was the pure way to destroy atheism.

Lupicinus had to admit that although he wanted the Church to build its Kingdom, he hadn't wanted it to be at such a cost. He had never wanted the Church to destroy man. It seemed there was a tentative balance, a risk he hadn't fully considered or appreciated. He'd been more secure in his dream of civilization than he should have been. If the Church tortured and killed atheists, those who refused to hide disbelief, men like Kharapan, then Lupicinus, a part of him, wanted those men to at least die holding on to their ways of life and notions of character and integrity. In fact, he'd imagined that atheists in a Christian Empire would thrive. They'd remain silent, masking their thoughts, but they would thrive without the emotional burden of faith. The thought that atheists, disbelievers, non-Orthodox Christians—those who refused to remain silent, refused to lie—might not die but instead have their minds altered by torture, cast a chill on his dream that even death had not. It postulated a city populated by Christian ghosts, devoid of reason, more truly Christian than any other rational creature. Kharapan as a devoted and obedient Christian, knowing God.

Of course, this was a large claim, and likely not something he would witness in his lifetime. And yet, the possibility shook Lupicinus. The idea shed a dim question on his life, his past. He might have doubted, if briefly, might have wondered whether, if he had understood the stakes, these stakes, he would have made a different choice. And yet, the moment passed. No, he didn't believe his life would have been different even if he had understood as a boy what he understood now. In any event, the Church would have its Kingdom regardless of his life decisions, his small life.

Lupicinus explained his revelation to Kharapan, but nothing, not Kharapan's vulnerability or the absolute power of the Church, convinced Kharapan that anyone could make him believe in the Christian God and live as a Christian.

Kharapan laughed out loud. "No," he said, "You have an imagination...." A man's moral assessments are secure, Kharapan said, an impenetrable fortress. If integrity couldn't defy torture, a man would kill himself and thus defy torture's result. Torture could produce any words, but once a man recovered, he'd return to his natural ideas. A tree might be worked into an unnatural shape, he said, but it would produce the same fruit.

But in the silence that followed, their thoughts converged. Even as he protested, Kharapan felt a shudder. Lupicinus's hypothesis echoed his own fear, that he could not, in fact, be the man he was without Chi, weak even in the Empire, even without any potential forced conversion by a Church. Lupicinus felt the weight of thoughts because he faced Kharapan, a man, yes—an idea of man—but also a man whom he might love, yes love! Lupicinus felt the threat to a man whom he might love, and his feelings and insights of that hour worked in him in a way that he didn't realize then would leave a wound.

Lupicinus felt a need to leave the cell. He gave a brisk bow to Kharapan and went up the stairs and out the heavy door to the church hallway. The door to the cell shut as if closing off another world. He ordered a servant to bring Kharapan more blankets and then went outside.

Lupicinus had been outside only moments when Monk Lolianus called out to him and approached in his awkward heavy slowness.

"My Lord," the monk said, breathing hard.

Lupicinus waited for the man to speak.

The monk told him about Saturnine's writing, besides the rest. "It's clear she doesn't believe... in the sacredness of our texts...."

The monk told him that Bishop Damasus asked certain scholars to advise the Church on the threat of godlessness. The monk's tone was accusatory: he'd witnessed Maximin's trials, and many battles between Christian sects, and here, he thought, was something new that would lead to violence and destruction. He had no doubt Saturnine, for instance, was mistaken, that she'd be saved by conversion and faith, but she didn't strike him as such a threat to the Church.

Lupicinus felt himself scowl. Instead of satisfaction at what he himself desired—he would have a hand in the Church's proclamation against godlessness—he had the sense of having turned the world against himself. The Church and its so-called scholars would analyze Lupicinus's soul and pronounce it diseased. It would be nonsense, but a nonsense that he himself would never be able to overcome even if he wanted to. It would be a proclamation for all time, as if God Himself had ordained it. He had a sudden desire to free Kharapan and retreat to his domus for the rest of his life.

Lupicinus felt off-balance. He felt too much himself "out here," too intimate with his own intimacy in a world where private truth, he'd long recognized, had no place. In any event, he told himself, regardless, regardless of the menippea, as if traveling an unknown land, an underworld, with Kharapan, this odd mood would not last. He would be the good churchman in the world above, preparing to advise the new pope of Rome.

Lupicinus noticed the monk waiting. "Let the scholars analyze," Lupicinus said. "When I report on *Sol*, should the scholars be ready, we can confer.

"Is that all?" he said when the monk made no answer.

"Yes, my Lord."

Lupicinus went to a solitary bench next to the great wall and sank down. The wall of Rome behind him and the imposing church in front cast deep shadows.

THREE

THAT DAY AND in the days that followed, Lupicinus returned to Kharapan's cell often, sometimes several times, day or night. He stayed for hours or left after moments. At times he studied Kharapan with an abstracted expression as if he beheld the last mortal of a lost and ancient world. The underground of the cell, cold and uncomfortable, seemed to him an oasis of solitude and unworldly time, their words making a web between them. In spite of the finite hours, they spoke extensively and without haste.

Kharapan spoke about the Aristotelian school and the time he had spent in other schools. He told how he came to leave Chi: the conversation he'd had with his Stoic master, Arminius, which involved Metis as well (he cringed inwardly at his mention of Metis, reminding Lupicinus of *Kingdoms*). He spoke of his travels and of how he felt a man intimate to the world might follow signs. But he left out certain formative experiences, those connected with *Kingdoms* and Metis, the death of Monk John, and those related to Saturnine. This gap made a questionable space in his narrative that, to his mind, might corrupt true intimacy between Lupicinus and himself. He believed that a bond between them was a link to Lupicinus's "sliver of possibility," to what some might call soul, and to the chance of life for both of them. And yet, to speak of Metis, or Monk John's death seemed, contrarily, ironically, to implicate Hellenica, to increase the risk of its destruction, and the thought of mentioning Saturnine (or her real parents) made him fear for her somehow. As Lupicinus listened, he was oblivious of Kharapan's inner struggle. Lupicinus himself had yet to reveal his life, if he told benign tales of his life, his family or of the world, but he revealed more than he suspected. He sometimes grew quiet, as if on the verge of speaking.

Lupicinus told Kharapan once that they were engaging in a Menippean satire. He explained that the Menippean satire explored fantastic situations in order to test an idea, a philosophic idea: the plot forced characters to the question that pounded in their hearts. Characters descended into the netherworld, wandered through fantastic lands or situations, in order to expose some truth. Diogenes sold himself into slavery in the marketplace in order to experience and answer a question. The double man, the two Marcuses, a man and his conscience, carried out a fantastic dialogue about good and evil.

"Look at me," Lupicinus exclaimed while sitting on the hard chair in front of Kharapan's cell in his luxurious robes, lights flickering around him on the stained cement walls. "I descend into a dank prison, an underground, for the purpose of discovering, with a barbarian (excuse the word), whether civilization exists without God and what kind of civilization might be best for the human creature."

"Is that what you believe? That we're acting out some fantastic story?" Kharapan said. He stood (although bent) and would have moved, but he had little space and sat down again, crossed his legs, his walking stick at his side. Lupicinus noticed the walking stick long before and might have wondered.

"You have a narrow view of life, of what is possible in the world as it is," Kharapan said.

Lupicinus waved at Kharapan, at the air. "You pretend the world isn't what it is or simply refuse to see," Lupicinus said. "Our... relationship is fantastic, not part of the world above. I am Rome, at the height of the world. And down here, it's fantastic. I may play the fool. Fool I might be down here, but not in the real world." He spat on the floor.

"You're here, however," Kharapan said, smilingly.

Lupicinus said nothing, trying to hide an echoing smile.

"The Christian world will forget the philosophic ways of life," Lupicinus said.

"Your Bible is a menippea, however," Kharapan said, thinking down a different line.

Lupicinus acknowledged the comment with a nod of his head. He had more than a casual interest in the menippea. He considered himself an expert in the literary nature of the Bible and he contemplated how much to reveal to Kharapan.

Kharapan went on: Written words had great weight. In the oral tradition, people understood the boundaries of myth—they knew the ancient myths as wisdom tales and not literally true. Pausanias admitted that wise Greeks spoke their sayings in the form of riddles, as wisdom tales, and didn't believe the legends. But once those myths were written down, men believed that the acts of which they spoke had actually happened. A man needs willpower and support of a community to withstand the power of words, to remember the nature of a story.

"At least your menippea announces itself as fiction," Kharapan said. "But the Bible is a menippea that claims to be God's words, claims to be true. The Christian Bible is an outrageously hubristic text. It isn't even beautiful. A godless man will see Jesus as a man, overcome by ideas that he couldn't know, demanding every human to believe or else be destroyed. Fanaticism is the ordinary result of a man taken too much with an idea." He paused. "Jesus has been your model," he added with a smile.

Lupicinus nodded, also with a smile.

"When a man says he's a sage or a god," Kharapan said, "it's time to look after his goods." He referred to the practice of protecting the insane.

"You forget the good acts of the Church. It cares for the poor and offers the kindness to neighbors and strangers. Christianity subdues human evil."

"The Church must instigate so much violence with its aspiration to domination. It's not in its core, in its beliefs and doctrines, to be a mere cult. It must own every mind."

Lupicinus had an inner smile. He couldn't help speaking. About ten years ago, he told Kharapan, after Maximin's trials, he took on a Church project to discover and list those books, documents, and texts that were considered harmful or dangerous to the Orthodox mind. During the trials, thousands of scrolls had been burned in Rome, but there was still much work to be done for the Church. At the time, he said, he needed a distraction, something that immersed him completely, and so he'd been glad to take over the work, but he found it more interesting than he could have imagined. Several decades before, after the Council of Nicea, copies of false gospels, and writings concerning those gospels, were destroyed, and over the years the true gospels had been narrowed and defined. Many ancient works were destroyed, so that in recent years only those works that supported the Orthodox position could be found. "At first I searched for the usual materials, heretical works, but my search expanded, and even I was surprised by what I found."

He told Kharapan that he discovered he could prove the true nature of the gospels as fiction. Of course, he'd known, but he'd traced the literary threads that made up the Bible; that is, he discovered enough material to prove the fictional nature of the gospels. What's more, he'd discovered to his surprise that there was no evidence that Jesus Christ had lived at all. Jesus Christ himself was myth. He traced the Christian gospels to Jewish, Roman, Greek, Persian, Egyptian influences—to sun gods and pagan superstitions, the stories of a son of God, and those that contained a trial, conviction and crucifixion, and resurrection. The Bible, he said, warming with enthusiasm, was a grand Menippean satire (in the secular sense), pulling together myth and literary strands from the entire Hellenistic world. It was amazing, in its way: as if the Bible, from all of those strands, was the natural story meant to be thrust into the world, into the future, the syncretic story that pulled together elements of a syncretic world, with god-names and god-natures mingling so as to unite them into one, single all powerful God. "I had my hands sunk in the origins of myth," he said.

Kharapan remained silent, watching Lupicinus.

"My work was all out in the open," he went on. When he'd started, he'd traveled to the libraries of the world. "I found texts that constituted a greater danger to Christianity than could be imagined: for if I could trace the history of the Bible in such a way, others might too—and they have. The early Church fathers must have known about the origins of these tales."

He paused before continuing.

The gospels had been written decades after Jesus was supposed to have lived. The writings of Paul showed that he didn't even know Jesus was a real man; he'd assumed that Jesus was of a spiritual nature like other savior gods. Over a hundred years ago, some Church father must have realized the lack of historical evidence, the complete lack of mention of this famous Jesus Christ even by historians living at the same time in the same city Jesus was supposed to have lived. In particular, there was an extensive history, several books, written by a Jewish historian, Flavius Josephus, living at the time of Jesus Christ. One paragraph in Josephus mentions Jesus but it was awkwardly inserted, clearly false, so poorly done as to mention the tribe of Christians even though they had no such name at the time.

"The insertion," Lupicinus said, "reveals the concern of Church fathers." He paused. "I searched for an original Josephus," he went on. "Forgetting the purpose of my work, I wanted to find that original text, to prove that no historian, not even the historian of the Jews in the time and place of Jesus, knew of such a man."

Kharapan watched Lupicinus with a half-smile.

"And so, you see, I discovered ideas that opposed Orthodoxy, and you might guess that even to explain why a particular work posed a danger would itself be dangerous—for the explanation, what turned into ten years of work, proves the falsity of the story, of the Bible and of the One God. I have extensive notes, a detailed text, but I have yet to give it to anyone. They reveal the Bible as fantasy, an invention that captures the stories and myths of our world and adds something original too: either by imaginative genius or by mistake, the story, our Christian story, makes Jesus Christ a man, a real man. Of course, I will pass on this work one day to a trustworthy person. Someone must take care to protect the Church."

Lupicinus smiled slyly. "I will pass it on to another atheist Christian like myself who understands as I do, for there are many of us."

Kharapan's solemn expression made Lupicinus smile. He thought Kharapan wondered at how the Church mystified the entire relevant part of the world, but the source of Kharapan's thoughts were different.

"I understand now," Kharapan said. "This work is your sliver of integrity. It ties you to what is good, to what you love and to the truth, in spite of yourself. This is the core that I sensed in you, the sliver of integrity that led to our discussions, to everything."

Kharapan laughed to himself. Lupicinus's work was likely more dangerous to Christian minds than *Kingdoms*, but he didn't mention *Kingdoms*.

"You look into material that might be dangerous to the Church and discover the nonexistence of Christ himself and the source of Christian myth… and this document of yours turns out to be more damaging, harmful, possibly the most destructive document to the Church ever written. The care you must have taken to build your proof and document your findings! It's the ambiguity that's remarkable: you yourself aren't even aware whether you will help the Church or try to destroy it." Kharapan laughed. "Ambiguity defines your life, in spite of yourself, an ambiguity that allows for a sliver, a mere sliver of possibility."

Lupicinus looked down; he couldn't immediately respond. "Perhaps," Lupicinus said, after a time. "The work I did, the insight I had could not have been arrived at by a believer. I do not agree, however. I do not hope to destroy the Church. Some Church father changed the Jewish historian's work. Who was it? He saw the need to hide the truth. And it would have taken a concerted effort: the destruction of originals, the creation of the new version…"

"You want the truth, in spite of yourself," Kharapan said.

"I admit, those who believe see with different eyes," Lupicinus went on, ignoring Kharapan. "The gospels are beautiful if one believes that God speaks, but not if read with a secular mind." He quoted: "'But a woman whose little daughter had an unclean spirit, immediately heard about Him. She came and fell down at his feet...', a tale worthy of Lucian, except for its utter lack of humor. And any believers who read my work, if ever read, would understand as believers: they would not read of mythic stories, but instead of 'false texts' that had to be destroyed."

Lupicinus grew distant. "Damasus ordered the translation of the gospels into Latin. I opposed him, fearing it would turn people from the Church... but," he added, "Damasus is a great man. Make no doubt about it. He has a genius for uniting the Church and making Rome its head. He understands how people read the Bible as if it is true, as if God existed. And what I've discovered is practically lost to the world, the old myths and true stories. The ancient memory is submerged and people, even those who remember, pretend that Christmas and Easter and other Christian holidays have their origins in Christ. It reveals the nature of humanity, and its need for God, even if it knows the stories are lies, even if it has evidence and knowledge. Even if I sent my work out in the world, it would have little effect. No one wants the truth." His voice had grown bitter. He looked at Kharapan with a mocking smile. "And you, the Church invests you with power. You have the force of the Devil! There's more than mere mortal in you."

Kharapan dropped his eyes and his cheeks grew dark.

"What?" Lupicinus asked roughly. He thought Kharapan was ashamed for him and for the Church.

Kharapan didn't answer him. Sometimes the world, confrontation with the world, took his breath away. Lupicinus searched for truth with passion, but this did not change Lupicinus's mind about the Church, and yet, Kharapan thought, perhaps Lupicinus was right, because myth, illusion, and story were the threads and fabric of civilization. Kharapan could see the way the world leaned. Sometimes in Empire he couldn't help but think that his mind, his thoughts and ideas, were but airy illusion. The illusion was this: he refused to care or see, as Lupicinus said, that people wanted to believe that a man, Jesus Christ, was God, even if he were an obsessive, dominating figure. If Kharapan looked, if he saw the world as Lupicinus did, how could he live? The God-filled world seemed extensive. He could sense his desire to turn inward and not say another word. This doubt, this sense of exhaustion, was something he sometimes felt in Empire. It was the feeling that always had alerted him to the need to return home. But, at the moment, that was impossible. He had his slim faith (as he sometimes thought of it). He had his walking stick, which he held. Speaking required faith, was grasping in the dark, being led by vague, obscure questions, believing that good might be teased out of darkness. He felt a failure of faith, for if he said too much, he could implicate his country and give justification to Empire to destroy them.

"Some views make me dizzy," he said finally. "I feel off-balance, swaying on so-called solid ground as if after a sea voyage. It's the only way I can describe it."

Lupicinus felt disheartened. "You think I'm struggling for some light or truth in my work, my project... you think it might save me or build integrity. You might be right. The work saved me at the time, at least distracted me from a terrible darkness... You don't understand..."

Lupicinus stood up abruptly and turned away. After a pause, he mounted the stairs slowly without turning to look at Kharapan.

FOUR

LUPICINUS'S DARK MOOD disturbed Kharapan. Alone in the silent darkness of his cell, Kharapan tried to find certainty. Lupicinus was intimate with the kinds of events that affected future men, that might be taken up in history, so to speak. Lupicinus also had a secret inner life—speaking now might influence projects Lupicinus would undertake in secret or in public. Besides, Kharapan had to believe that the need for truth was inherent in the species, regardless of what or who ruled the earth. And then, he thought, if everyone wants to believe in stories, to treat them as absolute truth, if everyone wanted to hide his eyes from the pain and uncertainty of *agnosis*, the vast unknown, he wanted a different sort of life. He had a sense of himself in the cultivation of *agnosis*. It was what he wanted, even if he was carried away by illusions of a different kind.

When Lupicinus returned he announced that it was the morning of *Saturnus*. They had one day before Lupicinus had to report back to the bishop and end this menippea between them. They both paused in reflection.

"We have extensive libraries in Chi," Kharapan said. "You would likely find that work you thought destroyed."

Lupicinus's eyes narrowed, but Kharapan was thinking of something else.

"Tell me," Kharapan said, "is it better to have money, influence over people, even power over an Empire, name, position—all of these things—than to speak your true mind?"

Lupicinus crossed his arms and sat back. "No, it's not better to have those things you mention. It's far worse to lie, but it's best not to be blind about the way the world is."

"Even if the Church rules the earth, should I conform and change my life?"

Lupicinus paused. "You're blind, whether by choice or nature or experience. Once the Church permeates every aspect of life, as it surely will, no rational creature will be free of its influence. All will be born and raised Christian."

"A man knows a lie. If I say the sun shines in this cell, you know I'm lying."

"Yes."

"A man finds the truth beautiful, and he can't do otherwise. If I told lies, it would bore you and we would stop speaking, and if I sensed you were lying, I would stop speaking to you."

"Yes, it's so."

"Is friendship important to a man's life and necessary to guide him and keep him from harm—that is, keep him from harming himself?"

"Perhaps."

"One says it's day when one knows it is night. How can you know what is best for my life or for the life of any other rational creature?"

"Not you, not you, perhaps, but I know for others, for Roman humanity. We are the world, the civilized world, and I take part in leading them."

Kharapan shook his head. "I'm not sure." He paused. "Certain philosophers say that a man acts and can only act (there is no other possibility, they say) in a way he believes is best for himself. A thief steals because he believes it benefits him because he obtains certain goods. And yet, the act of stealing is harmful to him and stains the good man in him. If another can show the thief his mistake, he will understand himself and never steal again." He paused. "If it's true, what the philosophers say, then you must be mistaken when you say that you act 'for the good of humanity' or because of 'the way the world is.' These are lies to yourself, lies you're unaware of or won't admit. The truth is, you must believe falsely, like the thief, that it benefits you to lie and pretend to have faith in the Christian God. You mistake what's best for you. Speaking the truth, even if difficult and full of struggle, guides you to a good life, to integrity and honor and friendship. Speaking lies, you have pain and ugliness. A reason for your mistake must be that you fail to understand what you don't know: you have a keen ability to understand the ways of the world, but you go too far when you say you know what's good for humanity or Empire. You fail to have an equal talent in *agnosis*, in understanding mystery and honing the lack of knowledge that is every man's real fortune."

Lupicinus's face was dark. "I lead an Empire," he said. "I'm not like you, wandering the streets with only myself and my good acts to care about. Some men are leaders of the world and are so close to power they must decide what is good for others, for civilization itself. These men have to form and hold firm the myth for the masses, the myth that binds an Empire and keeps it and civilization from crumbling. Rome is in danger. Its borders aren't secure. The people doubt pagan gods who once favored and protected Empire, and so a new myth is required, one that encompasses every human creature, extends beyond our borders to the world." He paused. "Nothing else has given the rational animal more purpose. Nothing else binds people across territories so readily, and invests so much power, authority, and responsibility in the small numbers who hold and formulate the word of God. The Church will save human civilization from destruction. It will keep humanity from destroying itself with wars and chaos." He paused again. Kharapan watched him. "As a leader I have no choice but struggle for what is good for others. I have to put aside and sacrifice my own happiness. My life is ugly, you say? I don't disagree. But a great duty comes to one with his hands against the fire of that power that is God, God's own words. I have that duty. If I'm not making decisions for humanity, someone else will."

"Leave rational creatures to themselves," Kharapan said. "They'll find their own passions, subtle and filled with joy, and you'll have your Empire too. And if Empire must fall, then let it fall. You mistake the lower faculties of the rational creature for the greater ones. Houses and nests are not great things. Let them be destroyed."

Kharapan held up his hand. Lupicinus let him continue.

Kharapan said something like this. If by nature, as the philosophers say, a man can only act in a way he thinks is good for himself, and if he mistakes the good as power and wealth or even some other vague amorphous thing, rather than integrity, friendship, truth—if this man mistakes for himself, how can he lead others? Instead, he mistakes what is good for others. He sacrifices his happiness, and in doing so loses the wisdom to preserve and protect the happiness of others. Time will judge him, not as honorable and noble, but as evil and base. And he himself lives a miserable existence. "That is the empty end and means of all your sacrifice."

"So you're changing your mind; you believe a philosopher should rule," Lupicinus said with a sly smile.

"I speak to you, as an individual. I care for your life." He paused. Lupicinus felt an ache in his chest.

"A leader of men might be a model, his life," Kharapan went on. "This is where goodness in ruling might reside: in the knowledge of oneself, and its application to principles of government. But due to the great danger power presents for every human creature, a government must regulate itself through laws that limit power. In Chi, there are layers of disbanded authority. Seven council members regulate and oversee matters of state. Then there are the dispute resolvers, who act from their core, their love of this particular duty, and they listen to trials and decide disputes, but still submit difficult questions put before them to members of the community who discuss and write up reports. The philosophic schools are outside of the state's authority and regulate themselves. No, better not leave power to any one man, for he's too weak a creature. A man's life is a model," he went on, "and so it might be for government. Beauty lies not in conquering and force, but in a model of a good life, and in good rule of just law and just application. Such a model will inspire other lands and distant nations. Justice and goodness are the pride and glory of a nation."

Lupicinus clapped ostentatiously. "Very well," he said. "Very good for this great power you speak of. I'm sure they'll go far in the annals of history." Truth was in the world above: a powerful Christian Roman Empire. Truth was visible and not some ideal floating around in a man's mind, so Lupicinus thought—even in spite of the small country of Hellenica.

Kharapan only smiled. He grew thoughtful. A silence passed between them.

"I'm about to take a risk I don't know how to avoid. Strange," Kharapan said, "that the very things that are the most intimate and sensitive to my life, that have not yet been spoken between us, are those things that seem most relevant, that matter most."

Lupicinus sensed a change in Kharapan and remained silent.

Kharapan had been contemplating and concluded that he must reveal the secret that had burdened him for twenty years. He believed it was this revelation, and only this, that might save him and Chi.

"What you're capable of, so am I," Kharapan said. "I'm guilty of murder."

"You mock me!" Lupicinus said. "You think you're guilty because we're both men."

"No," Kharapan said. "And yet, that's true. But no, I'm guilty of my own crimes, potentially guilty of everything that can be a crime."

Kharapan straightened his leg on the cold cement; his hands rested on the walking stick. He told Lupicinus about the time he'd found everyone arguing over Metis's *Kingdoms* when he'd returned to Chi from Rome.

Lupicinus's body tightened, but he gave only a slight nod. He understood but only in part, at first, what Kharapan risked.

Kharapan described how he'd been overcome when he'd read *Kingdoms*, how the passionate work, as well as his own experience, had roused him so that he'd hated and feared the Church as much as Metis. He went on to tell what happened when Monk John came to Chi: the monk's preaching, subsequent death, how Zeno was tried and punished but Hellenica hid the truth from Rome. He told Lupicinus that he hadn't immediately gone to Monk John that night, and later was disturbed at how *Kingdoms* had affected him. As he read *Kingdoms* his body passed into something, as if into a sickness. He passed into a way of being that blocked the fullness of the world. Anger took hold of him. In that state—which he now considered diseased—knowledge impressed itself upon him, and he felt sure that he knew absolutely that what Metis wrote was true. He knew he'd been wrong, ignorant of or had simply ignored the threat of Christianity, and he knew that the only moral duty—yes, the only right moral act—was to fight the Church, even if it meant murder, destroying its messengers if necessary. He knew it was necessary.

There are layers of sickness, Kharapan said. Only looking back could he see that the feeling of knowing absolutely, was sickness. But even when he felt he knew, when he felt he had to work to destroy the Church, he felt sick with the burden, with the horrible acts he knew he would have to perform.

And then Monk John had come and perhaps what had happened had saved Kharapan, because he had not actually killed the monk and instead had been offered the chance to understand what he was capable of. But he'd learned something about states of mind and body, as he thought of it, which served as a guide. The feelings he'd described when he'd read *Kingdoms*, he said, returned from time to time, not only in relation to the Church but to other things as well, usually events that inspired his anger because of some act of ignorance or cruelty. However, after that first time, after the experience of reading *Kingdoms*, he knew to be cautious. He was alert to the feeling of crossing over, to that sickness that threatened to subsume him, that made him righteous and feel he was absolutely correct. His mind said it knew. His body was sick with what the mind directed it to do.

"I choose to follow the lead of my body," he said. "It feels sickness when my mind doesn't. I don't murder anyone, so far. Eventually, the feeling of knowing passes, and I feel the influx of *agnosis* and mystery like a healthy wind. I can breathe. My mind conforms and helps to cultivate *agnosis*, and I realize I don't know the truth, or I fail to acknowledge complexity.

Kingdoms is fantastic and unreal, for if it dealt with real life, it would wallow in complexity and lose its power." He held up his walking stick. "A wise man told me to listen to the body's sense of feeling as much as ideas, to use this stick as balance. I came to have intimate experience of what he meant. I admit it is a luxury I live, a luxury of the body, a kind of natural happiness I allow myself in the world, and perhaps it's wrong... depending on the circumstances."

Kharapan gazed at Lupicinus gently. "I wonder," he said to him, "whether you feel this sickness? Whether the idea of civilization consumes you.... And yet, I think, how can you be aware of the feeling of sickness if you've been submerged in it for so long."

Lupicinus answered immediately. "Yes, the truth in the world consumes and conquers me, but unlike you, I believe it's true, regardless of how bad it makes me feel. I feel pain." He went on. "Pain from what I've done and what I see, but I've never been guided by pain. The phenomenal world is true to me. The feelings I have are merely an aspect of facing the truth of the world. There is no place for happiness, and there are more important things than happiness or pain. Feelings are irrelevant and have no particular connection to truth."

Kharapan shook his head. "My guide has been an inner sense, the bodily feeling and mental practices that help me make decisions." He went on. He could be wrong, and at times he admitted that he acted as if he didn't believe or refused to believe in the reality of the external world. He chose happiness. He selfishly courted happiness and allowed himself to believe that this kind of selfishness was philosophically a good way of life. He left evil to thrive as it might. He chose not to kill or engage in violence. But everything he'd learned, the philosophic practices, made him know how difficult it was to have correct judgments, and so he had to follow his inner sense.

As Kharapan spoke, Lupicinus dwelled, in part, in a wish that life could be simple, that he too could follow and be guided by a physical wellbeing and happiness.

They were silent.

Kharapan reflected. Metis had turned her back on Chi and had never produced another work, as far as Kharapan knew. In the twenty years that had passed since she'd written *Kingdoms*, since Monk John's death, she had lived for most of that time in a shack on the edge of the desert. Kharapan visited her when he returned to Chi, and if he found her there, he returned every day, even if she would hardly speak to him. When he asked her to join a debate or meeting, she would refuse, and if he tried to get her to speak about life or ideas, she remained silent. He'd carried *Kingdoms* for more than twenty years. Metis smiled when he told her about his experience with *Kingdoms* and the role it played in his life, a queer smile that disturbed him.

Kharapan thought of Metis's work in monasteries to the north of Hellenica as a translator of Christian texts, and he didn't mention the rumors of murders in those monasteries that reached them in Chi. He had to speak to Lupicinus about the experiences that formed him, but rumors of Metis had little to do with that, he thought. He felt disturbed but couldn't, had never been able to believe Metis would intentionally murder someone. He knew she had declared a secret war on Christians after Monk John's death, but the young people who had sat at her feet had slipped away and he had assumed, as everyone had, that she had given up those ideas. But now he wondered if it was his bias about his country that made him unable to see the truth—his bias that the people of Chi wouldn't kill over ideas, that the idea of *agnosis* and mystery would prevail over such violence. Perhaps he feared his own guilt, his guilt in leaving Metis too much on her own for so many years. He'd never managed to do what Arminius his Stoic master had suggested: to speak to Metis in a way that she would heed. He had no power over her. No, he couldn't believe Metis would kill, but he thought then that if he lived, if he left this place and could return to Chi, he would surely confront her and make her tell him what she knew.

Lupicinus watched Kharapan with an absent expression. Who was this but a poor barbarian in rags? And yet, neither he himself nor Empire viewed Kharapan as simply a poor barbarian. The lived life could be an art form. He, Lupicinus, might sculpt the statue of his own life, but it was mere craftwork, not art, more interesting than exquisite. Even if he were ordained a saint by history, his life would never achieve the true art of Kharapan's life. The beautiful life. He himself could only achieve the kind of life that existed in fantasy—if he were able to achieve even that—the banal sentimental story of a saint and his miracles.

Kharapan, though, had a natural genius. Lupicinus thought he knew what Kharapan was made of: his noble principles, his struggle to stand up to his idea of morality against all obstacles, living with *agnosis*, his willingness to die to remain true to his way of life, and living and dying as an example to others, even if no one took note. Truth didn't matter, Lupicinus thought; it didn't matter if Kharapan's principles were true or not. It didn't matter if Kharapan actually found anything that was true in the world, nor did it matter if he died mistakenly for what he believed. What mattered was the exquisite life, more beautiful than ancient poetry. Beauty existed in lived morality and its expression. The beauty of Kharapan's life jumped over and was free of mere truth. Kharapan had achieved a dream, even if no one knew about it but Lupicinus. The beauty existed, here in this dark cell, even if no one knew.

"People can be lost," Kharapan said as if to himself. "They ignore the sick feeling in their bodies, sometimes becoming stuck in that state of madness from which no one, no other man, can pull them back."

"But at times you judge yourself wrong, you used the word 'selfish.' You say you're selfish to choose happiness."

"Yes," Kharapan said. He paused and looked at Lupicinus. "Is it right for me to reveal Chi's crime to you? Do I betray my country? Am I evil? Tell me, how do we know, how can we learn to distinguish between right and wrong? I've never told a Roman—how could I? But now you know another reason why I stay at the church in this cell. The monk's death served as a lifelong caution to me, and I carried Metis's *Kingdoms* as a reminder of my flaws. But it wasn't enough. It isn't enough. I'm obliged to be here, to speak. I speak truth, as is my duty as a man. I follow my guiding principle and it's all I can do."

He paused and studied Lupicinus. "I've disappointed you," Kharapan said. "You wanted to think me good."

"No, I understand," he said. "But is it all? You were a bystander. You might live and be happy."

"Yes, you might say it was one event, but it was more because it showed, like a view down a long corridor, the possibility within me to engage in acts of violence. I felt the possibility in me. Besides, I've betrayed my country, not only revealed my capacity for murder." He paused. "The knowledge of myself, of what I might do, is painful to me. And yet, it's also true that it's not the greater part of me, for I struggle toward joy, and there are times I find it."

"You wear the burden of being a good man. No one said it's an easy life."

Kharapan peered at Lupicinus. "Leave Rome. Come with me to Chi. Epictetus asks, what wars, deaths of men, destruction of cities and other great matters do you have to attend to? No, we might both attend to the higher functions of man. You can continue your work on the origins of the Bible. In this life, we either gather memories that brighten our lives or ones that stain them irrevocably. You might still engage in the higher functions of man."

Lupicinus felt tears and lightheaded. He might recognize Kharapan's nobility, but it was a dream to believe that human beings in general were nobler than he, Lupicinus, knew them to be. He was stuck in a practical reality. He failed to value the individual—that is, himself as a single unique individual. It was far, far too late, he thought. "Confess my sins and be forgiven," he said with a bitter laugh.

"You, more than I, have been deluded about the greatest matters, deceived by your intelligence and powers of mind. You have let those powers mislead you, and you know it yourself. But you can still forgive yourself, for doing so is a natural act." He paused. "I'll only be killed," Kharapan went on, "but you'll have a more painful end. You'll live a life of emptiness and lies. Death closes a life of pain as well as it does one well lived, but it's life that matters. You might still live well."

Lupicinus stood, aching, his head throbbing. "I'm tired," he said. "The details of my life are ugly, and ultimately unimportant, but when I return, nothing will be left unsaid between us. You think I'm afraid to reveal my life. I am not. All will be told, and then we'll be finished with all of this." He gestured vaguely and paused. "I'll tell them to come now with your meal." He bowed his head and turned, then slowly climbed the stairs.

FIVE

LUPICINUS RETURNED LATE on *Sol*. He'd ignored urgent messages from the church, avoided everyone, and refused to speak if he happened to see anyone. He had insisted he would respond on *Sol*, but *Sol* was almost over.

In the cell, he opened a leather bag he'd brought with him, and he took out a bottle of wine and good cheese and bread. He prepared portions for Kharapan and himself, passing it through the bars. Why he didn't open the bars and sit with Kharapan is unclear—perhaps he feared someone above might discover the intimacy of it. I think he might have been afraid of something else, but of what? I'm not sure. Of Kharapan? Perhaps he was concerned that changing the nature of the boundaries between them might alter the conversation.

"My life has not been beautiful," Lupicinus said, settling back, an elegant silver wine goblet in his hand. His voice sounded strange even to himself, emerging as if musty, as if unused to speaking the truth.

"Its moments are ugly," he went on. "You know enough

about the violence of the Church. Everything you suspect is true. If I wasn't in the street with a club or machete, I directed violence and murder in the name of the Church alongside the general Damasus—in the pursuit of my idea of civilization, as you say." He paused, taking a sip of wine.

He thought to start at the beginning. He told Kharapan about his conversion at thirteen, how he'd risen in the Church, how he'd been behind Church battles, directing soldiers, inciting violence when necessary, in what amounted to war, Church war.

As he spoke, at times he grew carried away with talk of battles, advice to bishops, his role in affairs, speaking with excitement and pride, glorying in the power he had wielded. But he noticed his own pride and cringed, cringed inside himself, adjusted his tone, and moved on. He paused after a time, thinking of Achaleus. "I killed with my own hand, and it had little to do with the Church," he said.

Kharapan listened, his eyes on Lupicinus.

Lupicinus said that it seemed to him that his life consisted of a series of events in a scheme of destiny that, one might say, led to his young lover's murder: his early love of truth before his conversion at thirteen, the first lie, his part in the violence of the Church, the trials in Rome, his rise in the Church hierarchy. Vanity and pride, along with false security and overconfidence led to the murder of Achaleus and also to his mother's death, which he admitted might as well have been by his own hand.

The details fell out as if Lupicinus couldn't stop or control them, running like grain out of a hole in a sack. At times

Lupicinus was overcome by emotion and had to pause. At other times he spoke in a dull monotone as if he were reading a list and not speaking of real events from a life.

It was then, he said, after his mother's death, that he took on the project of looking into texts considered dangerous to the Orthodox Church. For a long time he worked without interest or passion, but then what he found began to revive him and give him a sense of purpose. He spoke about the last ten years, his role in the Church, in the world—it went on almost unchanged—and about his work and his times of chosen self-isolation. He spoke of the pain of living with memories of the dead and of his deeds.

It was night when he finished, but neither man could mark time in the torch lit darkness of the dungeon. A silence settled between them and spread like a pool of water. Lupicinus felt exhausted but also filled with a strange empty feeling, something like relief. He expected nothing—nothing would change—but he felt a kind of deliverance, even joy, as if the moment were more real than other moments he had lived, as if these last hours, these last days, had woven his life into a sharper pattern. He stood, uncomfortable with this new sensation, as if trying to force himself into a former self, a former way of being. He swayed in front of Kharapan's cell, brushing crumbs from his vestments and feeling slightly dizzy, perhaps from the wine.

"You think," Lupicinus said, "you think the experience of our lives, the comparison, proves that Hellenica is a better civilization, but you're wrong. Our lives prove nothing about the world, especially not yours. For you, men such as you, will be extinct soon enough, regardless of what either of us might say or how either of us chooses to live."

Kharapan, who had been silent while the other talked, a goblet of wine untouched on the floor before him, saw Lupicinus's growing agitation. He smiled. "When a man reveals the details of his life there's a warmth, a high. But then there's the drop, the fall, the shame. All of us have felt it in Chi." It was so; perhaps the depth of shame was hardly different for any particular shame, but he suspected Lupicinus would have a heavy fall, a heavy shame to manage now that he'd revealed the truth. This was the real danger. They'd come to it.

Lupicinus's face flushed.

"You want to kill me," Kharapan said. "If not now, you will. I am a witness."

"You underestimate me," Lupicinus whispered. He gave a low bow and took up the torch, leaving the leather bag and goblets. He mounted the stairs slowly, and quietly closed the door above, leaving Kharapan in darkness.

Lupicinus walked down the dark hall, pushed open the heavy church door, and walked into the cool night air. It was a dark night, without moonlight. He walked across the long open grass sward and turned into a narrow alley, into deeper shadow.

His vision grew blurry, and he stopped and put a hand against a cold, moldy wall. He didn't understand what was happening within him. A howl escaped his throat. He bent his head. He was crying. He had not cried in years. He couldn't control himself and he sobbed. It felt good to cry, his head empty of rationality or reason, plans or ideas. After a time he grew silent, and he noticed the silence around him. He listened, his head down, his breath emerging from him warm in the cold air. It struck him as strange to imagine stepping over the threshold of his domus. Lupicinus pushed away from the wall, adjusted his robes, and walked home.

Lupicinus didn't return to the church the following day, *Luna*, but sent a single urgent message to Bishop Damasus: he needed one more day with Kharapan. Otherwise, he refused to be disturbed. He did not want to see one note from the world and gave his manservant leave to invent whatever excuse he liked.

At first he felt flushed with health, as if life mattered and had meaning, and he could see how dry and parched he'd been, how he'd forgotten what purpose felt like. He didn't remember when he'd last felt as if life had meaning. In the past, he'd felt a sense of relief when he closed himself off to the world: he retreated and let the world go on as it might, and read—satire, philosophy. But he hadn't done that in a long time. On the following day, *Mars*, two weeks from the day he'd met Kharapan, he woke with the same feeling, and in spite of hints of urgent business from the manservant who had served him for years, he would not be disturbed. However, later in the day, how the world might see him began to seep back in. He began to feel a little astounded at the week's events, at allowing himself to be so taken with Kharapan. He returned to the church at midday. He went directly to Kharapan. The circumstances of the cell, the intimacy between them, struck him with new force and strangeness.

"You think I have a chance to live, to change my ways and

live. But," he paused, settling the torch into a wall sconce, "I look at the world, at the Church, and see. I still see." He looked at the barbarian and was struck that he seemed not to have moved since Lupicinus had last seen him.

"You've forgotten your desire," Kharapan said with strange joy. "You left it at thirteen. It's this that guides us, the rest, the world around, falls into place of its own accord. You used your love toward a lesser form, and you could not love those words, God's words. You're hurt and can't help being gouged. Without a return to desire and living it fully and openly, you'll never find your way. Your ideal man is full of faults and weaknesses. In Chi, the sage, a god-like being, is the model of the ideal man, even if we don't believe one can ever really become a sage. The model, the ideal, leads us on the path toward perfection, knowing all along we'll never reach the destination. Since your ideal is sick, you are sick. You don't aspire to health."

Lupicinus didn't respond. Kharapan's words refreshed him even then, as if quenching a thirst.

"You should have let pain guide you," Kharapan said. "What each of us controls is narrow and doesn't even include our own bodies, health or sickness, status or power, or how we affect others. It doesn't include what we love—we are helpless in the face of it. You can't know what's best for civilization. You're not sacrificing for others, but acting for yourself, as a man does, but you should have acted in a way that wouldn't cause you pain. It's not too late. You can struggle for nobility even now."

Lupicinus said nothing, sitting now in the hard chair just outside the bars of the cell, his head bent, aware of the silence and the shadows that enveloped the recesses of the room. Kharapan sat straight as usual, legs crossed. He leaned toward Lupicinus and held the bars. Lupicinus peered at him. "Come with me," Kharapan said. "Come live in Chi."

Lupicinus smiled, a cynical, sad, angry smile. His life of suffering and the suffering and deaths of others had meaning only in the light of the idea of civilization. He and others had sacrificed a great deal, but—there was a "but"—there was still the world and the truth of that world. He simply recognized that truth and engaged in it so to speak. The idea of stepping aside, a mere man, naked, free, leaving the world… It was too much for him. He owed his life to Rome, as painful and dark a life as it might be. He owed a painful life to those who'd suffered and died. A part of him feared the vague destiny that was before him if he left Rome. A part of him understood that if his idea of civilization and what had had to be done in the name of civilization changed, it threatened to change his entire view, turning him into simply an evil man. If he lost his faith, to any extent, he would fall into doubt, would have to look back over his life, cast in a new light, with different insight. This was what Kharapan wanted, of course. This is what Kharapan said he must fear: learning his mistake. But Lupicinus still believed, he told himself (even then), still saw and believed in the necessary Kingdom, the inevitable civilization in the world of man.

Still, Lupicinus was aware of a change in his old self—not a failure of faith, exactly, but a crack in his feeling about the world. He believed at the time that the feeling would pass, that he would return to the life he knew, for he was old even then and had lived a long life. What he felt at the time seemed to be a slight recklessness, like fresh life within him. He didn't recognize it for what it was: a crack in his attachment to the idea itself. He didn't allow himself to ponder it at the time, but the mysterious substance, the feeling, those first feelings, had been born and lived in him like organic matter. Feeling would wedge open a space from which his true character, perhaps his core, would emerge, perhaps a brief space, a brief light. His core lived in him, if not ever free, but still as if that self upon being offered a brief space to exist, a brief moment of light, would no longer be enslaved, regardless of the consequences. Perhaps, if the process had been faster in Lupicinus—for the ideas and feelings of this time took some years to settle in him—certain terrible events might not have happened. And yet, events and the mysterious process that worked in Lupicinus might be said to have led to something, some life out of rubbish and ruin, some light, if late and dim and undeserved. Was Lupicinus a ruined man? In later life, it is true, he became reclusive, kept silences with others, backed away from decisions, lost power in the world. It is true: people spoke of Lupicinus as a ruined man. In any event, he had no right to be saved. But at the time he spoke with Kharapan, and for a long time after, as I've mentioned, nothing was clear to him, if he struggled with himself while pretending to himself and others that nothing had changed.

Lupicinus stood. "Don't you care to know your fate?"

Kharapan paused. "Only one's own immorality is unbearable," he said.

Lupicinus smiled, his head lowered. After a time, he left.

When Lupicinus arrived in the bishop's chambers, he wasn't surprised to learn of God's opinion: the atheist was a criminal. He would hone that doctrine himself when he had the chance.

The stone has been cast, Lupicinus thought. No one was innocent in the conspiracy of God's word.

Lupicinus told the bishop that although what the scholars proclaimed was true, he advised caution. There could come a time when atheism threatened the fabric of the Church, but at the moment, it was almost unknown in Rome.

"As for the barbarian," he said, pausing.

Lupicinus must always have been acting, and yet he'd never been so aware of it as in that moment. It seemed to him that there was a different air up here. He felt surprised he could breathe. He studied those around him. He looked into their eyes, but no one seemed changed or to notice a change in him.

The barbarian, he said, might be burned at the stake.

"The death of a barbarian will raise a stir but would be lost in the greater crimes of those of Rome. This is, I think, how it must be. I recommend we advise authorities, in any event," he said.

The bishop nodded after a time. The Church operated its own court for Church and secular matters, which could not be said to be impartial.

"As to Chi, as to Hellenica," Lupicinus said. He looked down. When he raised his head, he said he'd go to Alexandria himself in *Mauis*, in two months, at the start of shipping season, to meet with the bishop, those who knew the administration and the land. He might as well, he said, continue to Hellenica with churchmen, even soldiers, to observe and question the people of Hellenica, to discover the extent of the threat, if any. He didn't recommend emergency vessels. He didn't believe the threat so urgent that they should travel in dangerous weather, or rush into war, if one could indeed engage in war with such a small country that had, as far as they knew, no armies.

In fact, all this—his plan to go to Alexandra and Hellenica—came as something of a surprise to Lupicinus. He realized as he spoke that he wanted to go to Chi, just once while he could.

The bishop and his men found no fault with the plan. Lupicinus told him he'd prepare a missive to the emperor's Court describing 'the case on immoral dangers' and requesting an introduction to General Kastor in Alexandria. Everyone in the room understood the formality. The Church had great power and could accomplish what it willed.

Damasus said let it be so.

As to the barbarian, Lupicinus said, he'd summon the advocates. Pius could question him and document his deeds in the morning.

"One more day will be nothing to us," the bishop said.

"No, one more day is nothing to us," Lupicinus said.

Lupicinus paused, alone in the cool corridor of the church. The rest, what would happen in Chi, he likely had a glimmer of even then, but what he had to do and would have to prepare for, was too painful to contemplate. He put it out of mind.

Lupicinus went to the church late that night on *Mars*. He walked purposefully, unhurried, bundled in a rich dark material. At the small side door, he felt around for the latch in the dark and then opened the door with his own key. Inside, he walked down the cool corridor, barely lit by torches. When he came to the prison door, he took a torch from the wall, and cracked open the groaning green metal door. The torch spread limited light as he pressed into the darkness, down the cold stairway. He didn't see Kharapan or hear him breathing and had a moment's fear that something had happened, that he was too late. But Kharapan rustled. Lupicinus paused at the bottom of the stairs. He could see Kharapan's shadow, darkness blending with darkness, and knew that he himself was bathed in light, a man on stage.

Lupicinus hung the torch in the wall and picked up the key. He unlocked the heavy chain around Kharapan's bars.

"Will you go?" he said.

Kharapan struggled out with his walking stick and stood outside the cell. He was large and strong next to the small older man.

"I'll go," he said after a time. "If you and I are done, if you want to release me. I'll go."

Kharapan felt a change. He'd been prepared to die and now had to ready himself for life. He understood that there might be worse things to face than death. He couldn't be sure of Lupicinus. His purpose changed into an urgent need to get to Chi, so he went to the stairs, hardly taking note of Lupicinus.

"You'll need this," Lupicinus said, calling him back. Kharapan stopped and turned.

Lupicinus took off his thick cloak and went to Kharapan. Kharapan let him fumble with placing the cloak around his shoulders. It was a kind of embrace. The rich cloak would make him conspicuous, but Lupicinus was right, he'd need it. It would be cold crossing the sea. Lupicinus took Kharapan's right hand with both of his and put a sack of coins in it. He peered mischievously into Kharapan's eyes.

"Don't you think that perhaps the moral act is to kill me?" Lupicinus said.

Kharapan paused. A silence passed, Lupicinus holding his hand. "I am so long in the habit of selfishly choosing happiness, even, as now, evil might be prevented if I kill you, when I have the chance. And yet, I can't be sure that killing you will change events, as circumstances exist. I can't be sure what is best. It might be worse to kill you."

Lupicinus smiled. Kharapan took his hand away, and moving toward the stairs, turned to give Lupicinus a last silent nod. He paused only briefly at the door above before going out.

Silence descended on Lupicinus. He looked around, surprised to find that the underground cell, empty of Kharapan, seemed a mere dank cold and ugly place.

The next day word spread that the barbarian had mysteriously disappeared. For a time, a rumor circulated that demons had infested the Church's foundation.

Kharapan arrived at the harbor of Portus in the dark of *Mercurius* and learned from an innkeeper that a ship—the Rome-Alexandria run—had left for Alexandria the day before. In the first light of day, the office man of the Rome-Alexandria run, who recognized Kharapan and eyed his cloak, told him that a friend of his, Kenyon, and two Jews were on that ship. He added that they expected a storm. Kharapan regretted. He grappled with plans, needs. A man engaged in the world loses the joyful view above, the grave reflection. Urgent, intimate life filled him. Problems had to be solved, movements of various kinds made. Late that day Kharapan convinced a fisherman to take him out on the sea in a small craft. They headed out in the early morning and rowed like bandits through the mist. Kharapan felt enlivened to be on the open sea, in the middle of the earth, wrapped in a thick cloak, though the vessel that bore him was tossed about like a reed on the ocean waves.

Six

THE RHYTHMIC SOUND of waves lapping the ship's hull, gray fog and a gray sea turned their thoughts inward.

"This colorless world is a reflection of myself," Saturnine said to Thaddeus.

She heard Kenyon's voice. Kenyon seemed unconcerned about the rumor that they were lost at sea. Thaddeus, too, seemed at ease on the boat. An old seaman, Heron, who cooked for the sailors, had befriended him. Heron pitied the boy when he was seasick and told him to fill his stomach with bread, and when Thaddeus recovered, he hovered near the cook, a loaf always at his side, and learned about chickens and spices. The soldiers had their own cook who had designated times to use the kitchen. Kenyon had negotiated with the soldier's cook to prepare food for the three of them in exchange for supplies, but the sailor's cook also gave food to Thaddeus.

"We might stay here forever," Thaddeus said. "On a ship, surrounded by sea."

"Yes," Saturnine said, "land is ruined. One can't breathe on land."

They sat on the wooden deck, knees bent, close together, and spoke in low voices like children in the night.

Thaddeus absently fingered the pouch on his neck. Saturnine watched him: in Thaddeus, she sometimes caught bits of herself. "We'll make our own world, Thaddeus, wherever we go."

"Yes, our own world. But," he added hesitantly, "we would buy food from people, and come to know them, and we'd have to go to the baths, and they have schedules. And then, we'd have to pay rent."

"Yes," she whispered, "but no gods. No gods in our house. Once we close the door. We'll have a rule: 'no one enter who believes in God.'"

"We won't have many visitors then," Thaddeus said after a time.

"No! No one will come to our domus."

They laughed intimately.

Kenyon approached. "You two are pleasant together."

Saturnine felt rebuked. Thaddeus looked down.

"Let thoughts come but then let them go," Kenyon said. "Isn't life wonderful?"

Kenyon must have seen the flash of anger in Saturnine's face—Saturnine wondered if Kenyon mocked her—and apparently this greatly amused Kenyon. She sniffed in laughter, then her large body shook.

Saturnine looked at her, but suddenly, for some reason, sensed Kenyon's concern for her and tears stung Saturnine's eyes and she looked away.

Once when an old sailor leaned against the rails not far from Saturnine, rubbing his weathered hands and looking out over the sea, Saturnine stood next to him. He looked at her with kind, watery brown eyes, but only bowed his head and left the silence, which pleased her at first. Fog and sea seemed indistinct from each other. She didn't know the hour, the day, or how long they had been at sea. The infinite expanse of water changed the pattern of one's thoughts, and this sort of watery meditation lured one to the end of the rails and made one forget, or remember. But after a time, as she stood next to this man, a realization gave her a shock. What could she say—to this man, to anyone? Words gave substance to a life, and what could she say to anyone other than to Thaddeus or Kenyon? How to describe her life? Her past was an illusion, and not only that, but she'd discovered she had little understanding about herself, let alone how to be herself in the world. What did it mean to be herself? She wasn't armed or prepared for the world, and she'd followed a stranger to a barbarian land. To what end?

That night Saturnine lay wrapped in Flavia's old cloak, trembling. Unfathomable waters pushed against the boat, making the board of the hull creak, and in her imagination, cold sea blended with the air that entered her chest. The infernal cold rooted in her was not a breath of spirit but mere inanimate cold. Her body, this nakedness, this skin, her breathless staring. This was all she was, a body on a mattress with cold penetrating it.

"Kenyon?" she gasped. Kenyon rustled then lay still, listening. "Why am I on this ship?"

Thaddeus breathed heavily, waiting.

"Perhaps you're fated to be on this ship," Kenyon said after a time.

"How? Random events led me here." Saturnine waved a hand through the darkness. "Kharapan happened to have a connection to a man who fathered me. And the rest—all outside of me. No, if left on my own, I would be a Christian wife to a Roman man."

"Rational creatures are connected in ways we aren't aware of or don't imagine, those alive at the same time experiencing existence together." Kenyon paused. "We are not so alone, not always allowed to fall into error on our own."

Saturnine closed her eyes. "Even now I follow blindly."

"I'd rather you didn't. I'm not keen to lead someone blindly."

Saturnine didn't respond.

Kenyon continued. "They say that the peeling away of external identity is a necessary step to knowing your core. One's core is one's spiritual breath, one's pneuma. Your peeling is a quick one."

"My breath is only cold air," Saturnine said. Grasping at a slim opportunity, she added, "You don't give me a chance to speak." She pause and grappled for words in the silence. "If I'm inexperienced... regardless, I don't know who I am. I don't know what to say." Her tears made her glad for darkness, but fear for herself sent her hand toward Kenyon—she put herself into the hands of this creature, into the strong hands of this barbarian, large, dark, sure, from another world.

Kenyon took hold of her hand.

Saturnine was unable to speak for a time, but after a while, she told Kenyon how even her dreams mocked her. She'd dreamt she had to keep secrets, hide her identity, though she longed to reveal herself, but when she tried to reveal herself, she found the terror of not knowing what to reveal, found that secrets from the world were secrets even from herself. When she paused, Kenyon said, "I'm listening."

Saturnine pulled her hand free. The tent cloth flapped and shuddered in the cold wind, and she closed her eyes.

"Saturnine," Kenyon said.

Thaddeus breathed loudly, as if unaware he could be heard.

"Have you read Metis's work?" Kenyon's voice had irony in it. "She won't think any Roman fully human; you'll strike her as uncivilized."

"Uncivilized?"

The childlike uncertainty in Saturnine's voice made Kenyon laugh. "I'm telling the truth," she said. "If you read her work, it could go some way in soothing the creature."

Saturnine had a severe look. She'd forgotten Metis, forgotten *Kingdoms*, forgotten (or perhaps was afraid) to think of Chi. Saturnine realized that Kenyon tried to make her remember herself, her passion, her core, as the people of Chi said. "I want to read it, regardless if it soothes your creatures or not," she said after a time.

Kenyon laughed. "Saturnine," she said. "I think I can like you."

Saturnine smiled to herself at this faint praise.

"Travel by ship is good in a way." Kenyon went on in a storytelling voice. "We see ourselves at a distance and talk about our lives unanchored by earthly attachment...."

As Kenyon spoke, Saturnine sensed words as if they gathered people and vague ideas in designs, as if they made sense of people and the world. She thought: this place on the deck of a ship with a barbarian she'd started to listen to is as good a place as any to be alive.

Late that night Saturnine stood at the rails. The sea raged. Saturnine clasped the wooden railing in the cold. Violent waves and gusts of rain menaced the vessel, but the beauty! She felt a thrill. They could die. But this beauty! This majesty! In the wind and the splash of rain and sea she felt joyful, her thoughts flying over everything. The mystery of her mother's secret life and her suicidal death. The mystery of Kharapan and his gentle philosophic nature, willingness to die, and his long involvement in her life. The mystery of civilization itself, of Rome, the Church, layers of ancient life, pagan temples, and emperor's castles in the ruins of her city. The mystery of what her life had been, her marriage to a senator of Rome. The mystery of Thaddeus and Kenyon, slave and barbarian, unconventional friends aboard this wooden vessel. And within this landscape, the mystery of herself, a creature, clinging to a narrow wooden rail in the wind, drenched by a sea that was indifferent to her joy or torment. At the other end of the deck, the soldiers' horses rustled and snorted nervously, uneasy with the pitching of the vessel and the waves that burst over them.

Saturnine became absorbed in *Kingdoms*. She told Thaddeus: "It forms me." Metis demanded a moral imperative: one had to stop the destructive force of the Church.

"I know why I'm here," she said. "I know where I am headed and why."

Saturnine soaked in Metis's words of outrage. Morality exists in rational creatures. Law must be free of moral judgment. But in Christian Kingdom, sin is punished, ordinary human behavior is a crime—disbelief, any deviance of thought from that imposed by the Church is a crime. No one can be Christ and so everyone is a criminal. People live in fear of the Church, of immorality. People spy and inform on each other. While the Christian world appeared orderly and unmarred by apparent vulgarity or ugliness, nevertheless a seething evil existed underneath. Such a place came out of a man's fevered imagination, creating a fantastical perfect creature with a charismatic power. And with the force of armies, the Church made an impossible ideal the core of society.

When Saturnine read the codex to Thaddeus, he alternated between giggles and gravity. Saturnine hardly paid attention to him.

"I feel as if in a dream," she said to the sea winds.

Thoughts of Kharapan failed to moderate Saturnine's passion for Metis and *Kingdoms*. Kharapan admired the text, he carried it with him. He'd shown it to her and given it to her that night. And yet, he didn't seem to think about the Church as Metis did. Imprisoned there, he chose to stay and speak to Lupicinus. He acknowledged the threat, the threat to himself and to Hellenica (he wasn't naïve), and yet.... Saturnine didn't understand, or felt confused, as if she were lacking a part of an intricate design.

In any event, Saturnine told herself she didn't care what

Kharapan might think. She was angry that he had stayed at the Church and thought him mad to speak to Lupicinus. Saturnine had been weak, had chosen the relative safety of secrecy over truth, but she still had information that Metis did not: she had lived in Rome, the center of Christian authority, and she knew the imminent threat to Chi. She had to warn Metis.

Saturnine peered at Thaddeus, his skin red from the sun, his long hair tied back with a strip of leather. "Tell me about cooking," she said.

"A pinch of salt," he said, showing her the quantity with his fingers, "thrown into the water expands the substance of it and soaks into the matter of the vegetables."

Saturnine laughed. But when he blushed, she said in a serious tone, "We both have our devilish inspirations." They grew silent.

The three ate porridge and chicken out of tin bowls that steamed in the cold air and warmed their hands. They hardly noticed anymore the rhythmic waves, the salt water splashing on them, the dampness that permeated everything. Kenyon noticed a change in Saturnine, but Saturnine didn't like to speak of Metis or *Kingdoms* with Kenyon.

"The Church of Rome won't feel threatened by a small, friendly barbarian country, one without armies, even weapons," Kenyon said, taking up a conversation as if they had been speaking of it.

Saturnine looked at her with burning eyes but said nothing. Kenyon's lack of belief confirmed the truth to Saturnine's mind: the people of Chi must be naïve, unaware of danger.

Saturnine knew that Lupicinus had only to lift his hand to destroy Chi. He would speak to the bishop about demons, sorcery, black magic—it didn't matter what threat he conjured up—obtain an assent from an emperor, send out a messenger to an army base near Hellenica, and there would be war, or rather, pure destruction.

Sleepless in the long nights, Saturnine paced the deck. Some said the earth's shadow projected an illusion of darkness in the sky. One might glide from fixed star to fixed star on waves of light, sailing upon depths as blue as the Mediterranean Sea if one had a vessel that could navigate the balmy sky. But one might travel too far. A more ancient night lay beyond the dome of the heavens, beyond the universe. Chaos and primal matter waited to plunge all into darkness.

BOOK V

ONE

WORD CIRCULATED ABOUT a light in the sea—the lighthouse of Alexandria—and, at last, the huge vessel entered the working harbor, Eunostos, the harbor of happy return. The ship anchored on *Jupiter, six Kalends before Aprilis.*

Those on board took up their place on land. Kenyon, Saturnine, and Thaddeus left behind what they couldn't carry and walked down the plank through the crowded dock. They entered Alexandria through the Gate of the Moon on via Canopica, one of the most magnificent avenues in the world. Four chariots could race side by side. Street criers sold goods. The air was redolent of dung, sweat, perfumes, bread, and spices.

Kenyon pulled Saturnine into a quiet narrow alleyway and said that she could leave them in Alexandria. Saturnine swayed as if with the sea moving beneath her—so she would feel, so her life remain, floating in vague waters, cast upon a stormy sea, wave upon wave, until she returned to Alexandria to take up her true mantle, her unique individual life at last.

She said she would go to Chi. "I must, whether you guide us or not." Kenyon shrugged and guided them to an expensive inn, and left Saturnine and Thaddeus, saying she'd return the next morning.

"One is completely on one's own with her," Saturnine said to Thaddeus. And yet, something in Saturnine liked this way of Kenyon's.

The inside of the inn had an ancient majesty, red-velvet chairs, high-ceilinged walls trimmed in gold paint. The inn-keeper, an old and regal woman, gave the travelers suspicious looks. Saturnine felt disconcerted by the contrast between her interior life, *Kingdoms* in her bag, and the luxury of the inn, but with a commanding voice said that she and Thaddeus, her brother, had made the journey from Rome. She said that they would stay one night before continuing on to acquaintances of the family in Cairo, where they had letters of introduction.

The innkeeper noted Saturnine's exquisite Greek and saw her money but asked to see their papers. Saturnine took out her original ones—those that named her as Saturnine of Rome and noted her senatorial connections. The woman looked at Thaddeus, who hadn't said a word—in fact, he didn't know Greek—but she bowed obsequiously to Saturnine. The innkeeper likely assumed that Saturnine was a runaway, prob-ably not from the law, but from family. Perhaps she was a rebellious Christian who intended to give away her riches in order to lead a simple life in the desert. Others like her had passed through.

She escorted them to a large room on the second floor with two beds and a window that overlooked the city, and with eyes moving over Saturnine, she noted that it was still the women's hour for a bath. She pointed out the map of the city that had information, including hours of the public buildings.

Saturnine stared out the window at red rooftops and church spires after the innkeeper left, noting Thaddeus's expression, one she'd seen before, as if his features lost clarity. "What is it?" she said.

"I've been baptized," he said, his eyes darting at her and then away.

She sensed it too. Here, on land, the Church permeated everything.

"We won't be in this city for long. We should go out," she said. But the thought of bathing dismayed her and seemed unnecessary given the problems in the world, given all that did matter.

She washed her face in the bowl of water. She took up the map, and they went out.

To Saturnine's mind, the city seethed with zealots. The irrational religious, she imagined, seeing only what they hated: Christians, Jews, Hellenes. Saturnine felt lured to one place in particular. Alexandria had once held the greatest library in the world, with over 400,000 books. Its museum once pampered scholars, writers, poets, scientists, appointing them for life, providing them a salary, food and lodging, and tax exemption so that they could devote themselves to intellectual pursuit. Tools of scholarship were invented and developed: the authoritative text editions, the commentary, the glossary, the grammar. But at the time, the Museum gave membership to men in government service rather than to those of learning, and tax exemption went to the Church and its officials. Alexandria still had the best collection of Greek books in the world, a library, the Serapeum, with over forty thousand books and a staff of sorters, clerks, copyists, repairers, scribes.

After buying street food and eating on the hard steps of a temple, they found their way to the library. They found a hushed silence in the open space of the interior. The staff looked at Saturnine and Thaddeus with concern, and one went over to them, but Saturnine explained in Greek that they were visiting, and she gave the woman a gold coin, and the staff relaxed when the two unwashed sat quietly in a corner. The library had books in small open rooms marked by subject matter, and rolls on several shelves marked by tabs on their ends. Saturnine took in the smell of learning, the high ceiling, the hush, the homage to words. Men in thick, beige scholarly robes read at tables in a connected room, scribes copied, and an officious clerk searched for a book. Saturnine didn't notice the man watching her. After a time, a clerk announced in a firm whisper to no one in particular, that the library was closing.

Outside, the bright sun seemed as if it would never set.

A man stopped them in the street. "I noticed you in the library," he said. "You're not what you appear."

Saturnine, startled, stared at him.

"Your dress would suggest you're a servant. To be honest, forgive me, but at first I feared you might be mad, with the dirt, the angry look." He smiled mischievously. "But the way you move, your skin, your coins, your voice, the Greek. You're beautiful, of course." He looked uncertainly at Thaddeus but received no word or explanation. The man introduced himself as Alypius and said he studied mathematical episteme, the scientific knowledge.

"You're not from Alexandria," Alypius said.

"No," she said, "Rome."

"Is he your slave?" he said, in a lowered tone.

"My brother."

He changed the conversation. "Ah, I love Rome, the Pantheon! I wish it were a church."

"God forbid!"

"You're not one of us."

She didn't answer.

"It was a long time before I converted to Christianity," he said. "It's a long story, a Homeric one. Sit with me. I'll tell you."

She hesitated. It amused her, given circumstances, *Kingdoms* in her bag, that this man might think he could convert her. They followed him to the porch steps of a basilica. "How does a man who claims to study true knowledge think he knows the truth about God? You called it a Homeric tale," she added. "Summarize."

He smiled and paused.

He told her that he loved to learn as a child, to study philosophy. As a young man, he'd traveled to different schools and sat at the feet of philosophers. "I wasn't Christian. Some years ago, I fell in love with one of my teachers, a young philosopher. I still work with her father, a mathematician. One evening, after a lecture, I expressed my love to her. She threw up her hand, cut me short, and walked off. The next day in front of others she threw a black and red stained cloth at me. It was blood—her monthly fluids. 'This is what you love,' she said. 'The smell and retch of the body.'" Alypius was silent for a time. "I never returned."

"Hypatia," Saturnine said.

"You've heard of her. It's too bad for me. I don't tell anyone this story, and here, I'm telling a stranger. But you intrigue me, and the situation demanded an amusing story."

"Strangers grant us surprising freedom."

"She did me a favor. She was right. Doubt made my passion rise above everything: doubt made me weak to the body's desire, willing to forget my soul. When life is empty, we're quick to fill it with the basest passions. Before conversion, I couldn't cope with the indignity of death, with the idea that the gods that had no interest in human life. The agony of doubt left when I became Christian. There's only emptiness and despair without God." He paused at her doubting smile. "What?" he said. He thought she was amused by the interest he still obviously showed in passion.

"Your 'emptiness and despair' is a Christian invention," she said.

"What do you mean invention?"

"If gods, assuming they exist, have no interest in human life, it doesn't mean life is meaningless. The curiosity of the unknown is enough to thrill us." She paused. "No," she added, "despair and emptiness are irrelevant to the question of faith in Christ. Christians don't own meaning. It's one of their lies to increase membership."

"You're hard on us," he said, but Saturnine hardly paid attention. She sunk into reflection.

Saturnine scorned the idea of Hypatia, bound to old gods and old ways. If Hypatia recognized the danger of the Church, she didn't fight them. Saturnine thought of how her own destiny lay in a foreign land. Saturnine felt, or realized, that she might be a traitor to Rome, this new Christian Rome. The thought was new and made her tingle, and sit up as if at attention, straining to hear.

She noticed Alypius studying her. "Enough!" she said. She stood and motioned to Thaddeus.

Alypius walked with them. "We don't have to talk about God. Did you know, the inside of the Pantheon is a perfect circle, the radius from floor to ceiling and the hemispherical base are equal?"

"Yes," she said. "Required study for children of Rome."

"Join me for a drink. No one will suspect your mind. They'll think you're my servant."

She laughed but felt alarmed. "No."

"Meet me tomorrow."

"I'm leaving the city."

He took out his card. "Then you'll remember me when you return."

After they left him, Saturnine gave a sarcastic laugh, and railed to Thaddeus against the ignorance of a man who sadly seemed intelligent but must be mentally feeble.

In the room at the inn, they lay side by side. The wonder of the journey occupied Saturnine.

Thaddeus's worried voice interrupted her thoughts. "We

can stay in Alexandria," he said. "We can live here, the two of us."

"You changed your mind. You're afraid of something, something even worse," she said, staring at the ceiling, not looking at him. "You're afraid of Chi, or of…" She glanced at him. Thaddeus reddened. Saturnine looked at him as if seeing something that she'd missed before.

"I can't stay," she said after a time. "I have to go, to find out…" But it suddenly seemed uncertain what she had to find out. "You'll come?" she said.

"Yes," he said.

They pulled down the soft woolen sheets. Saturnine unhooked a cloth and covered the window and returned in shadowy darkness.

"Thaddeus," she said. "You won't leave me? As strange as I might seem, as I might one day seem to you, you won't leave me?"

"I'll never leave you," he said.

In the morning, Kenyon found Saturnine and Thaddeus waiting. "You didn't bathe," she said with a quizzical look. She herself was clean and wore a new simple tunic.

Kenyon led them to the sea. They boarded a small vessel that took them on the Schedia canal, around the city, to the Nile River. On the Nile they found passage on a flat barge and traveled south against the current. The Nile River flows to the Mediterranean Sea, the water's source unknown. Saturnine felt that they moved away from the known world, from the world itself. The warm wind whipped at her hair and clothes, and the cloudless sky spread over the land.

The barge stopped in several small Roman cities. At Hermopolis, they disembarked on a dock that had huge storehouses and walked on a street lined with colonnades that led to small temples of Hadrian and Antinoos and a central marketplace with fountains, a gymnasium, baths and offices of imperial officials. Off the main street, they discovered a more ancient world: twisting narrow streets overshadowed by a monstrous Egyptian palace of worship to the god, Thoth. In the square, Saturnine bathed and bought light woolen pants and a top that came down in flaps over the pants in front and back. Her hair bounced above her shoulders in thick waves. Thaddeus's light skin, sunburned on the ship, had turned brown, and his light blond hair hung around his shoulders when he didn't tie it in a loose knot at the back of his head.

Vessels crowded the River—the painted vessels of the rich, flat barges, a myriad of small boats. They sat at the edge of the barge, their feet in water. Kenyon conveyed her love of the place. The Nile's rhythm mirrored Fate (*moira*), she told them, the ancient idea that controlled both gods and men, and that held the seeds of both godless philosophy and theism. The river made three relentless seasons: inundation, when the river rose and covered the land leaving nutrient-rich silt for planting crops; germination or winter, lasting until late *Martius*, when harvest began (the third season). The river gathered the forces to labor; people monitored it like their diviner.

They slept under a cold sky and woke to a hot sun. Shrubs lined the river and marked a boundary between brush and sand. Beyond the brush it seemed as if nothing definite could be discerned. Life itself was fluid in the visible waves of heat, as if no earthly matter was solid. The wide, flat, muddy Nile slithered through the dry barrier of desert, under a musty, colorless sky. They'd reached the Nile at the beginning of harvest and in passing days journeyed into true harvest that came earlier farther up the Nile. Docks swarmed with activity: people harvested wheat, then flax. In a few days, Kenyon said, the river would be thick with barges loaded with grain. The sun grew hotter, the air dryer, and Kenyon moved slowly as if Ethiopia were within her.

At some point in their journey, they spent days at a village without finding passage. Boats headed down river with the harvest. Kenyon suggested they walk to the next village, a two-day journey. On the empty road, they met four men with two oxen that pulled a heavy cart. The men traded Rome's goods for gold, ivory, and pottery in Africa. Night came. The men made a fire and told crude stories, laughing through rotting or missing teeth, and although Kenyon joined them at the fire, she hardly said a word and was uncharacteristically solemn.

None of them slept, not Saturnine, Kenyon nor Thaddeus, but morning came and walking at a fast pace they distanced themselves from the traders.

That night, next to their small fire, Saturnine sat in silent reflection, exhausted after sleepless hours of the night and exertion of the day. Not noticing Kenyon's agitation, she fell into a deep sleep.

A hand over Saturnine's mouth woke her. Her body was dragged over the ground. She stared incomprehensibly before struggling against the man pulling her. He dragged her into bushes next to the bank of the River, tore her cloth wrap, and she felt the weight of his body on her. Kenyon appeared out of the dark, pulled the man's head up, and cut his throat. He made a soft gasp. Warm blood spurted over Saturnine. She rolled to the side. Kenyon motioned with her arm to be still. They heard a rustle of leaves, and turning, saw a rugged trader holding Thaddeus with a knife to his throat.

Saturnine cried out, but Kenyon motioned for her to be still.

The trader told Kenyon to drop the knife. Her arm went limp, but she held onto the wooden end of the knife.

The bushes at Kenyon's side rustled and with an abrupt motion, her arm swung quickly back. A man groaned. Her knife had sunk into his belly. At the instant the man came out of the bushes, the trader who had Thaddeus pushed him aside and rushed at Kenyon. She turned with a fluid motion and managed to stick her knife in his throat. Kenyon turned back to finish the injured man behind her, but Saturnine made a low groan and struggled over to the shapeless rags on the ground.

Blood covered Thaddeus's neck, and his eyes were closed, his breath a rattle. Saturnine let out a howl.

It was some time before she became aware of the dark shadow of Kenyon over her.

"We can make a grave near the river," Kenyon said. "There'll be one more trader out there, but he's taking care of oxen and won't be able to fight us. Still, we don't want to linger."

Saturnine looked up at her. She couldn't fathom her dry tone.

After a time, they went to the river but could not dig much of a hole. They carried Thaddeus's body to the moist dirt, and before they covered him, Saturnine put her hand on his face and took the small bag of poison that hung on his neck. They worked at a large stone and pushed it to mark Thaddeus's grave. As Saturnine stood forlornly over the dirt, Kenyon left to hide the men under bushes.

When Kenyon returned, she found Saturnine by Thaddeus's grave, staring into the slow-moving Nile River. The water had slivers of light in it.

"Whatever happens doesn't matter now," Saturnine said.

"I was fond of him," Kenyon said after a time. "There's nothing Thaddeus wants or needs from us or the world now."

Saturnine sat for a long time in silence. She felt a reluctant admiration of Kenyon, not only at her resolve to live but also for her ability to kill. Saturnine took up her sack and walked toward the road. Kenyon followed. Saturnine was weak, as if her muscles couldn't hold her. She stopped, her head fell, and she cried into her hands, but after a moment her legs moved again. They continued this way through the night. Movement dulled pain. Saturnine, glancing at Kenyon, was overtaken by Kenyon's inexplicable existence, her stoic look, and slow walk. The early morning light revealed them drenched in grime and blood and they stopped to wash in the river, removing their clothes. Afterward, they sat naked on the bank, drying in the sun.

The trader's attack, Thaddeus's death, seemed to Saturnine

like the desert: ungraspable, an illusion, out of focus. There was no meaning, no lesson. Saturnine turned to the side and threw up, hacking dryly. When she raised herself, she had no tears, only a parched sensation in her throat and something like a sandbag weighing down her chest. Some time later she awoke with her face pinned to the side of Kenyon's stomach, her body sore, her neck aching. The thought came to her that she would die in this arid land, absolutely alone. The knowledge felt stunning in its clarity.

"If I hadn't suspected," Kenyon said, "I would have been dead by morning, which is a better fate than yours would have been. I hoped to stop them before anything happened." She paused. "Thaddeus felt little pain."

Saturnine tried to remember her last image of Thaddeus but had hardly seen him in the dark. It seemed to her he wasn't afraid, perhaps not even surprised at what was happening to him. She shuddered, and then, to her surprise, felt hungry. Kenyon wrapped herself in a tunic and left to go to the village to buy clothes and supplies.

Saturnine, alone and naked, like a primordial being, was not afraid. Without even Thaddeus to anchor her, she sunk into a state she would describe, looking back, as a dream, nothing but waves of heat forming illusions.

Two

THEY ENTERED THE outskirts of Hellenica in a windstorm. Saturnine told Kenyon to warn the people of Chi. Kenyon said she'd inform officials, "but best not tell anyone else about the Church of Rome or Kharapan's troubles for now." Saturnine said she would not tell anyone with one exception.

"Tell Metis. No one will believe her," Kenyon said, walking on.

They passed low dwellings shuttered against the wind. They entered winding narrow streets, walkways of the place called the Great Village, and came to a courtyard. The village in a dust storm struck Saturnine as terminal: the edge of the world. But she thought: here is that place, Hellenica, that she had wondered about since meeting Kharapan as a girl. Here is the place where Kharapan grew up, which formed him.

"Here it is," Kenyon shouted as if encountering something sacred. "It's quiet, with this wind."

Saturnine felt uneasy, and glancing at a man in rags, his

long hair tangled, saw him stand and, as if waiting for her to look, pull down his pants and urinate into the wind.

"A Cynic," Kenyon said, following Saturnine's gaze. "Cynics live in a state of nature. *Phusis*, nature, they think, is superior to convention, *nomos*, civilization. He seeks peace of mind."

"Peace of mind!"

Kenyon chuckled. "His point," she said more quietly now as they walked into the courtyard, "is to inspire others to reflect on the errors of convention." Kenyon went around, shaking hands, hugging some, pausing to speak in confidential whispers. She motioned to Saturnine to follow her down a narrow path between two buildings. They went to the Study, a structure like a growth or disease on the back of a two-storied building. It might have fit Saturnine's imagination of a barbarian habitat. It was surprisingly large, one's eyes lost sight of its boundaries. In design, it was a series of connected circles of mud, like a playhouse made by a child. And yet, it was a shelter that might fit man as well as a nest accommodates a bird. I have been there myself.

They entered the door, a waste-high leather flap that one wiggles through, and found themselves in a gray, circular interior, the howling of the wind muted. Sunlight shone through a cross-thatched roof in the open center, making geometric patterns. A large woman, Nubia, a caretaker of the place, welcomed Saturnine. Nubia, barefoot, moving with a slow heavy step, spoke fluent but heavily accented Latin, and said Saturnine could stay in the Study. It was available.

Saturnine offered Nubia money, but Nubia told her they had the support of government funds.

Kenyon told Saturnine: "Metis may be in Chi. If so, it's hard to say how long. I will return at dusk, after you've settled, unless you're not ready to meet her."

"I'm ready," Saturnine said.

Kenyon gave a brisk nod and went out.

Nubia led Saturnine to a kitchen. Neatly arranged utensils, pots, and pans hung on the walls. Nubia took out bread from the fire. They sat at stools and ate bread and cheese, nuts, fruit. "We have the whitest flour," Nubia said, putting a glass of fruit water in front of her. Saturnine's small room had bedding in one corner, a writing table, and wooden chair. Nubia helped her bathe in a tiny room where water fell from a gourd, gathering at the soft mound at her feet, draining through a gap at the bottom of the wall.

"Romans like their baths and oily lotions and stink of perfume, but you'll grow used to our ways," Nubia said.

Saturnine struggled to pull a comb through her hair. Looking in the mirror, she saw that her face had grown dark, and her brown eyes seemed wider and clearer than she remembered. She felt as thin and strong as she'd been at sixteen before she stopped wrestling. Nubia gave her a clean cotton garment and after Saturnine dressed, said, "Come."

Saturnine stepped into a cooler air and, barefoot, followed Nubia down cold stone steps to a large underground room lit by torches. It smelled of leather and papyrus. It had a long thick rectangular wooden table in the center of one part of the room, and aisles of wood shelves on the other. Scrolls, books, bound papers were piled on shelves and on the floor. Nubia pointed out blank Nile parchment and said Saturnine could use as much as she wanted.

The library astonished Saturnine.

Nubia, walking down long rows of scrolls and codices and piles of loose parchment, pointed out topics, laying her large hand on books: Latin, Greek, Coptic, Demotic; studies of mythology, ancient history, Roman history, the history of Hellenica; books on philosophy—Socratic, Platonic, Aristotelian, Cynic, Cyrenaic, Euclides, Epicurean, Stoic, Skeptic. There was a section on the supernatural—mysticism, alchemists, Christianity. There were studies of animals, rhetoric, mathematics, farming, and building. Then a collection of the tools of scholarship—analysis, grammar, commentaries.

Saturnine wanted to ask: where is *Kingdoms*? But she suspected, she didn't know why, that she would not find it here.

Nubia led Saturnine back to her room and left her.

At dusk, Kenyon returned and led Saturnine down white walled paths and out into the desert to a lone dilapidated hut. The wind had died. They stood in the quiet at the door. The place felt deserted. At last the door opened. Metis stood in the doorway in the dim light. Saturnine saw her angry, suspicious expression. Saturnine blushed, disconcerted by Metis's look, by her thin, wispy form—perhaps by the contrast of Metis herself to the rage-filled words.

Kenyon, speaking in Latin, told Metis that the Church of Rome held Kharapan in prison. Saturnine, she said, had been implicated and had come with her to Chi. Metis came out, closed the door behind her and walked past them, and sat on a pillow half-buried in the sand. Kenyon and Saturnine found pillows and sat near Metis. They made a rough circle under the wide Egyptian sky. The shadow of early night colored the world gray.

Metis motioned with a small movement of her head for Kenyon to continue and held her bony knees, meditative while Kenyon spoke. Kenyon recounted in a brisk manner the details about Kharapan's trouble in Rome, that he'd met Lupicinus and had shown him *Kingdoms*, and was imprisoned at the church. Metis glanced at her with a smirk, then looked away. Thaddeus, she said, had offered to free Kharapan—but he'd refused, believed he had to stay to speak to Lupicinus.

Saturnine hardly took her eyes from Metis. The woman had a long narrow face, protruding high, bony cheekbones, and a square forehead. She could have been forty or fifty years old. Her eyes, dark brown, large, and oval, moved from Kenyon to Saturnine, as if seeking the resolution to some unsettled thought. Her graying black hair, hastily pulled back, trailed in wisps around her face. Several of her teeth were missing, made visible by an overbite. Her wrinkled, colorful clothes gave the disorderly sense of the meeting of earth and sky at twilight. Saturnine chose to see her like a winter twig: on the outside it seemed one might break her, but from the power of *Kingdoms* Metis must be green and resilient inside, impossible to break.

Kenyon told Metis she thought the Church would free Kharapan. The Church wouldn't care about a barbarian, even if it thought him demon-infested. After all, the Church had the burden of converting the non-orthodox minds of its own citizens.

"The Church wants all minds, even insignificant ones," Metis said, speaking for the first time. Her bold, raspy, confident voice—the voice of *Kingdoms*—made Saturnine smile.

Kenyon gave an annoyed glance to Saturnine, one eyebrow raised.

"There's nothing I can do for him," Metis said. "There's no point informing me. It's far from new to me that the Church pretends that any unorthodox mind is demon-infested."

She smiled strangely and peered into Kenyon's eyes and then into Saturnine's. She seemed about to say more but looked away.

"I read *Kingdoms*," Saturnine said. "Kharapan gave me his copy."

Metis's fierce intelligent eyes seemed to look at her with disdain, but Saturnine thought she detected curiosity too.

"I, too, wrote about the Church," Saturnine said. "I wondered how the Church's one God became so powerful in an empire of gods." She paused. "I didn't have your courage or insight—to let others read it...." She broke off.

Metis had a mocking smile. "And what of the monk, the one Kharapan is so fond of remembering?"

"The monk?" Saturnine said.

Metis looked away. Kenyon had a grave expression.

Silence weighed on Saturnine. She had the heavy duty to tell Metis of the true threat of Lupicinus, of the Church of Rome itself, but she felt out of balance, hazy, uncertain. This strange cool night seemed a heavy frost that blocked out the real world, as if the Church, Rome, and her former life were all imaginary.

"I need to speak to you alone," Saturnine said finally. "I need to tell you something."

Metis laughed. "What could you tell me?" But she grew thoughtful and leaned close. Saturnine could smell the pungent body, the bad breath. "Come in the morning," she said, as if in command.

Saturnine bowed her head.

"You may go," Metis said. In an abrupt motion, she stood and went inside and closed the door.

Kenyon stood and brushed off sand. As they walked away, she said, "There's your esteemed woman."

They entered the pathway between low white walls which glowed an eerie luminescent blue.

Kenyon remained silent, but when they reached the shadowed mud Study, she paused and said in a low voice, "Kharapan didn't tell you about Monk John? About why he carried *Kingdoms*?"

"No," Saturnine said, part of her afraid.

"*Kingdoms* led to murder," Kenyon said in a dry tone.

The word 'murder' hung on the still air. Saturnine waited, her body rigid. It didn't surprise her, that word. It felt oddly intimate.

Kenyon went on. Almost twenty years ago after Metis distributed copies of the work, Zeno, one of the young men who sat at Metis's feet at the time, killed a monk after reading *Kingdoms*. Kharapan witnessed the monk's murder and blamed himself, in part, for the monk's death. After all, the rage of *Kingdoms* had taken hold of him too. After the monk's death he carried the codex as a reminder, a caution against rage. Not because he honored the text, she said, but as a caution. She herself had been too young to remember the events. Metis, the idea of her, she said, seemed to burden Kharapan. He never failed to visit her when he returned to Chi. He seemed to have some sort of obsession with her and with *Kingdoms*, something he felt he needed to work out in regard to Metis.

Saturnine struggled. It seemed to her that Kharapan had spoken highly of Metis and of *Kingdoms* that evening in her garden. He'd shown her *Kingdoms* as a way to say that she, too, might write. But she couldn't help but remember that he'd wanted to tell her something about *Kingdoms* the night he'd given her the codex. Flavia had come in; she'd faced Flavia as a mother. The rest had happened so quickly. She'd seen Kharapan in the church prison but neither of them had thought of Metis's codex.

Kenyon watched her.

"What happened to Zeno?" Saturnine said.

Kenyon told her that Chi tried Zeno and sent him into exile for a year. He'd returned, no longer interested in either Christians or Metis. As for Metis, people lost interest in *Kingdoms*, or were afraid, afraid it would implicate them with the Romans. Metis was angry and disappointed in the people of Chi, but she had a tendency to anger, Kenyon said. She had considered Monk John's appearance a declaration of war and his death unavoidable. After the murder and the implicit idea that *Kingdoms* was at fault, Metis withdrew from the life of the city. She continued her work with monasteries in the north, where she lived for several months of the year. When she was in Chi, she kept to herself, never attended debates or lectures, hardly bathed, and didn't like visitors. No one knew whether she'd continued to write or not.

"Strange," Kenyon added, as if to herself, "those who've seen her up north in the monasteries say she's different... baths, talks to those around her... even seems happy."

Kenyon hesitated. She, like Kharapan, had heard rumors of murders in the monasteries over the years. She couldn't believe Metis had anything to do with it. No one in Hellenica could believe such a thing. Metis had a brilliant mind and had never carried out any violent act as far as anyone knew. And besides, reports of her in the monasteries—friendly, social—seemed to contradict such an image of her. Still, the thought came to mind. Kenyon wondered if she should say more, warn of some vague danger, but she wasn't Kharapan, and looking at Saturnine's solemn face, she thought she'd said enough.

"I'll be off," she said abruptly. She gave Saturnine a long look, smiled softly, nodded, and left.

Saturnine climbed inside the Study and went down the dark hall to her room, glad for silence. She unhooked the thick cloth over the door and took up a rolled mattress and began to lay it out but stopped and went to the inner window and looked through thick glass onto the courtyard. She didn't see the darker shadow of a face in the glass opposite to hers. A thick exhaustion filled her. Even if Kharapan would warn her against rage, as she thought he might, all of them faced a violent evil. The Church oppressed an empire, and what was one monk's death to what might be a murderous rampage against the citizens of Chi? Metis hadn't been wrong to understand the monk's appearance and preaching as the start of a war, a war involving a battle over minds, the right to believe or not. Although she felt a vague fear, an inner disturbance, she couldn't wholly sympathize with the guilty feelings that made Kharapan carry Metis's codex for twenty years, if he did indeed carry *Kingdoms* simply out of guilt. It was fateful that he'd given her the codex when so shortly thereafter she'd found herself traveling to Chi, to Metis, to a fate beyond Kharapan.

She pulled the drape across the window and prepared her bed. Kenyon, like others in Chi, she thought, was willfully blind to the danger. Metis had no choice but turn her back when everyone ignored her. Events in Chi could prove ignoring Metis to be a fatal error.

When Saturnine finished making her bed and lay down, she could not rid herself of an uneasy feeling. She struggled with some thought; some question needed to be answered or resolved, but she couldn't grasp what it was. Thaddeus's troubled eyes came to her. She returned that imagined look with her own determination. Thaddeus might have saved her, she thought, although she wasn't sure how. She didn't want to be saved.

Saturnine fell into a restless sleep. She dreamt that she was under an ocean. She could breathe, and a woman's warm hand held hers and led her forward, revealing an exotic oceanic world. Excitement and happiness flooded Saturnine, and safety and warmth were transmitted to her through the woman's hand. They laughed and smiled and swam around colorful objects. Then they swam to the surface, still holding hands, and walked down a long beach and then down a road, into Rome. There, they dropped hands. Saturnine tried to show her the city, but everything was dead, gray, and old. She grew confused and unhappy, knowing the woman didn't belong there, knowing the woman would die in this atmosphere and was dying at that very instant. Saturnine had changed too. She was out of place. She despaired. The woman began to fade away. She was dying before Saturnine's eyes. Then the woman changed, offered no emotion, no thought of anything that could or should be different. She laughed at Saturnine.

Saturnine awoke terrified. The sun was full in the sky.

Dressing, she thought of Flavia—in every act she'd accepted her mother's service and kindness without thought. It was more than this. Saturnine had never been on her own; and in a foreign land, it might have been as if the world was on its side so to speak.

She found Nubia in the kitchen and silently ate the eggs and bread Nubia offered her. Saturnine felt groggy, as if she could not wake or free herself of the dream. Nubia asked where she would go, and Saturnine tried to smile and hide her eyes. Nubia told her not to miss the murder trial in the open-air court next to the Nile: a woman had killed her lover but had not killed before and wasn't known to be violent. Two dispute resolvers would decide her fate. The trial would last several days. Saturnine said she'd try to go and indeed was curious. According to *Kingdoms*, people were allowed to kill at least once in the Great Unknown.

THREE

SATURNINE WENT OUT into the bright sunlight. She hardly glanced at the busy village square, at the people who looked at her curiously. She hardly noticed the philosophers in blue, green, or red cloaks. She left the Great Village, and walking in the desert, came to Metis's hut. Black cloth or ragged paper blocked the windows, but Metis sat outside in a low chair facing the desert, her thin legs stretched out in front of her, her eyes closed. She had unwashed tangled hair and wore dirty rags.

Metis opened her eyes, gave Saturnine a disinterested look, and closed them again. Saturnine sat in the warm sand, bending her knees, and looking out at a vast colorless land. Saturnine again felt a dreamy distance, a vague confusion, as if thoughts were spread out like sunlight over desert. Metis's apparent lack of concern, however, forced Saturnine to speak. "I'll say it directly. The Church might come to Chi. That is, Rome might come, with armies."

Metis did not react.

"Kenyon warned officials," Saturnine went on, "but I had to tell you." She paused. "After reading *Kingdoms* I knew you'd understand, perhaps you're the only one…"

Metis sat up, interlaced her long fingers, and looked at Saturnine. Again it seemed to Saturnine that Metis looked into her soul, judging her harshly, but Metis said nothing and waited.

Reflecting on events in Rome, it seemed to Saturnine that 'it all' began that day when Victorinus caught her writing, when Lupicinus first came to their domus. Or did it begin long ago, even before she was born.

She told Metis about Lupicinus's first visit and their discussion, her three reasons for the Church's rise in power and Lupicinus's doubt over whether culture could exist without God. She said her husband caught her writing, and after Lupicinus's visit, she'd promised to stop, she might even have converted, she said, blushing.

"The next time Lupicinus came to dinner, a few days later, Kharapan appeared," she said after a time.

Saturnine told how she'd met Kharapan ten years before. She'd not seen Kharapan since that night, until he came to her garden on the anniversary of Philo's death. Metis gazed at Saturnine without blinking and then turned to stare out at the desert again.

Speaking deliberately, she told Metis how Kharapan had joined them. He'd met Lupicinus. She described the conversation between Kharapan and Lupicinus and the odd connection the two men seemed to have shared, as if there was some challenge between them. Metis glared at her for a moment. Saturnine went on. As you know, Kharapan showed them *Kingdoms*.

"Perhaps it was that, the fact that Lupicinus had seen *Kingdoms*, that made him send the guards."

She told Metis about the night she burned her work and how Kharapan had come. He had given her *Kingdoms*, and he'd told her about her parents, but they hadn't had much time to talk. The churchmen came and took him to the pope's church. She paused, unwilling to speak of Flavia, her mother, under Metis's cold angry eyes.

"I visited Kharapan in prison," Saturnine said. She told how Kharapan believed Lupicinus was responsible for his fate: Kharapan believed he might save his life by saving Lupicinus, by engaging in a challenge that played out in his discussions with Lupicinus. "I don't know," she said, shaking her head. "It's as if to save Lupicinus—spiritually, in spirit—Kharapan thinks he, too, will be saved. It's why he refused to escape when Thaddeus offered to free him. Thaddeus," she said, "a church boy, a friend, killed at the hands of a trader on our journey here."

Metis shook her head. "Kharapan's naïve," she said in that raspy, dry voice. "He's dead. And if not, there's nothing I can do for him. His troubles are nothing to me."

Saturnine felt pained. But she had to speak. Her voice was soft and dull. "Lupicinus looks to Hellenica, not only Kharapan." In Kharapan's mind, she said, pausing, the challenge he engaged in with Lupicinus—it involved his life and Lupicinus's life, but also the fate of Chi, the fate of the country. "If Kharapan saves Lupicinus," she said, "he believes he will save Chi."

Metis glared out at the desert. Saturnine suddenly felt afraid.

Metis stood and walked out into the desert. She suddenly laughed in anger and agitation. She turned and raised a hand toward Saturnine, the long outstretched fingers spread like a bony palm frond, and said, "So, the Church will destroy us at last!" She dropped her hand.

Metis seemed a vision, bathed in sunlight, making a prophecy of doom. Saturnine noticed excitement in Metis's voice, as if Metis felt vindication but not regret (she would later think, reflecting back).

"They should have listened!" Metis said. "But it's too late. I saw and understood early on."

Saturnine thought she understood her, but the look on Metis's face seemed too much like joy. "What're you thinking?" Saturnine said in a low voice.

Metis returned, and sitting, she interrogated Saturnine, calculating days: Saturnine had left Rome over a month before. It was now *Maius*. Shipping season, the yearly winds, began around *Maius*, which meant the Alexandria-Rome run started in-season travel—ten days to cross the middle sea in fine weather. If they came in season, they might arrive at the end of *Maius*. Of course, the Church might arrive any day at all. Metis grew silent and seemed to forget Saturnine.

"I came to you," Saturnine said. "I recognized the danger of the Church, of such a powerful institution that wants to control our very thoughts. I was alone, but when I read *Kingdoms* on the ship," she paused, "I'd found the air that moved me." She shook her head to herself. "You're braver than I! I longed to know you, to have your courage. I knew you'd know what to do, even now. I want that power to face truth. I thought… I thought you might guide me."

Metis did not look at Saturnine when she spoke. "I once thought I would find others, others who understood as I did. But those who joined me after I circulated *Kingdoms*… they were weak and cared more for their luxurious lives. You… Roman," she said glancing at Saturnine, "you have lived a luxurious life."

"It's true," Saturnine said.

"All is written," Metis said, gesturing with her fingers at the dilapidated domus behind her.

"I know about the monk," Saturnine said. "I, too, wrote against the Church…," she said, "In any event, I have no one and no future to worry about losing. I have nothing." She fingered the pouches at her neck. "I wear poison," she said.

Metis gave Saturnine an interested look. Metis scowled. "Bah!" she cried. "Only one thing can be done, and only by me. It's too late."

"What is that one thing?" Saturnine said.

Metis hesitated. "I will send my work out into the world at last."

"*Kingdoms*?"

"No, my new work." Metis had a slight strange smile.

"Is it enough?" Saturnine said.

Metis laughed, angry. "It is enough." She stood. "In any event, it is all that can be done." She paused. "Tell them. Inform the people of Chi that I'll send out my work, that I'll break my silence. I will speak to my Countrymen."

"About the Church's threat?"

"No," she said. "Don't speak about the Church. No need to tell them about the Church!" She would tell them herself, she said.

Saturnine felt bewildered. Metis bowed and went into her darkened shack and closed the door without glancing back.

Saturnine got to her feet. In the hot sun, other worlds seemed far away, unreal. She felt tired and wanted to sleep. Yes, she thought, Metis lived out of the ordinary, but that had been necessary. She had led a life of the mind, and this is what it looked like. Metis, a thin and dirty creature, filled with rage and courage, stood in the face of truth, and this must be beautiful.

Saturnine paused at the edge of the courtyard of the Great Village. Dust swirled as if in excitement about news from underground. People and animals wandered among carts of vegetables and cloth and metal work. She noticed those wearing blue or red or green cloaks and knew they must be of philosophic schools. She walked into the courtyard and passed a shop with a sign, "Smoke Loves Smoke." An old man called out to her. She hesitated.

"Come, walk over the threshold where nature overcomes natures," the old man said. He had soft folds of brown skin in the lines of his face.

Vessels and instruments and apparatuses filled a workroom. A heavy young woman worked at something in the back. Here is another world, Saturnine thought. She peered at a picture of a three-legged hermaphrodite wrapped in the wings of a monstrous blue eagle with its human and bird legs disappearing into a pile of dead blue eagles. Another showed a man bloodily dismembered by a sword, his arms and legs separated at his side. The man told her the pictures represented recipes and processes, dreams, alchemical poems, and symbols.

He introduced himself as Zosimus and said he'd heard about her. He asked about Kharapan and told her that Kharapan had taken goods from the shop to sell the first time he left Chi as a boy. He chuckled to himself.

The mention of Kharapan pained Saturnine. On a whim she asked for a piece of lead. The old man paused, smiled, and nodded, and went to look around his shop. She looked at the picture of a form, man and woman combined, stepping on dead blue birds.

Zosimus returned with a black chip, and she removed the thick string that held Thaddeus's sack and dropped the lead into it.

Zosimus tucked his hands into his large sleeves. "In Chi," he said, "we strive to transmute the material body into the body of light, of spirit. Alchemists have died, poisoning themselves. Of course, we also make things to sell." He gestured at a toy with creatures swinging between sticks, and flower holders. "That one, there," he motioned to a young woman bent over a boiling vessel, "we call the Obscure." The Obscure looked at Saturnine with an absent expression and Zosimus excused himself to join her. Saturnine watched them for a time until she started, as if remembering herself, and left the shop.

Saturnine found herself on a dirt path, and then at the

wide Nile River. She faced north. Her thin green cloth blew up around her legs, and the soft wind rippled the water as if trying to uncover hidden depths. In the distance, Thaddeus melded with the earth. In the farther distance was the World, and perhaps Kharapan too. Tears came to her eyes. But even the river seemed a bare phantom in the heat. Bending her head and turning away, she walked south, into a deeper wilderness before returning to the Study.

FOUR

IN THE DAYS that passed, Saturnine lay in bed or paced the small room, events of her life passing before her, everything in the past, and in the future, vague and uncertain. Several days had passed since she'd spoken to Metis. Metis wouldn't respond to her knock or wasn't there. Saturnine didn't go out, other than to take the path to Metis's hut, and return, oblivious of the Great Village, of Chi. If it hadn't been for Nubia, she would not have eaten.

On *Mercurius*, four days after they arrived, Kenyon found Saturnine in the library of the Study, sitting at the long wooden table with old parchment around her.

"You've made yourself at home," Kenyon said.

Saturnine gave her a sardonic glance. She'd discovered many versions of the Christian story. "It's an illusion," Saturnine said. "My life is all illusion, but Rome is the supreme master, narrowing its versions of the story and then calling it gospel."

Kenyon noted Saturnine's strange mood.

"So, you've warned the officials of Kharapan's predicament and the danger to Chi," Saturnine said.

"Yes. They've sent a messenger north. So far there's no news." She paused. "I'll return to Rome soon. I'll try to find out what I can. But perhaps Kharapan himself will come."

Kenyon studied her. Saturnine felt her stare but kept her eyes on the manuscript.

"So you've told her," Kenyon said.

"Yes," she said. "I haven't seen her since. I've gone, but… she's not there or won't open the door to me." Saturnine thought of the work Metis told her to "tell them" about.

"That sounds right," Kenyon said. "Forget Metis. Go to the schools. There are open lectures." She paused. "But I have a feeling that nothing I say matters."

Saturnine looked at her. "What if you get your news? What if the Church and its armies are coming?"

"What are we to do? We have no armies. There's nothing we can do."

Saturnine gave a sarcastic half-smile: Kenyon held so firm a belief in this 'nothing,' she would leave them to be destroyed and wouldn't even suggest that Saturnine return to the empire with her.

Kenyon rose. "I'll say goodbye before I leave."

At dusk, Saturnine went again to Metis's domus. The meticulously blocked up windows made it impossible to be sure if lamps or candles burned inside. The door shook with her knock. "I need to speak to you," she said. But she wasn't sure what she needed to say.

Metis opened the door and beckoned her in. Saturnine hesitated and entered with trepidation. Metis looked outside suspiciously and then closed the door behind Saturnine. The room was well ordered. Books and manuscripts filled a wall of shelves, except for one long empty shelf; a part of another wall had various tools neatly hung. A narrow wooden desk held a pile of blank parchment, and a neatly rolled up mattress lay against the wall. A pale-yellow glow spread from the small lamp on the floor.

Metis sat on pillows against a desk leg, her knees bent, and beckoned to Saturnine to sit on the pillows opposite.

"'Grim Religion is a menace that must be trampled underfoot and by this victory we might reach the stars,'" Metis said, as if chanting. She smiled, a long slow smile. "Words of one of your own. You are not all ruined, not all ignorant; and yet, he lived hundreds of years ago. It is too late now for people of Empire."

Saturnine watched her, waiting. The air was hot and stale. They sat in the shadows of lamplight.

"I ask myself," Metis said, "can there be beautiful atheists in Empire? No, there cannot. But I discovered another kind of disbeliever, one who is not beautiful…." She leaned toward Saturnine. "My essence allows me to see. I have not been deranged by Chi's unknown."

Here's the voice that lured me, Saturnine thought.

"Judath," Metis said, with angry glee, "wasn't sent to university and didn't learn the classic texts, so Judath read Christian texts at home, the only codices they had. And because she was intelligent and good, she questioned their veracity. Judath had to admit it: she didn't believe. She compared the fantastic tales with the world, one without miracles, and doubted. She never dared call herself atheist. She never uttered that word. For Judath to reason, to doubt, or even to question, was evil. Reason meant, to her mind, that she'd suffer eternal punishment. Judath had been raised Christian and lived in a Christian Empire."

Metis went on. Judath knew her doubt was blasphemous, heretical. Even as a child she hid her questions and learned to be silent. She had a gloomy, taciturn air that others took for a general disposition. Her mother boasted that Judath was bound for the monastery. "In fact, intelligent atheists are severe and excessively moral. They would have been philosophers but only know themselves as criminals full of questions and doubt."

Metis crossed her thin legs and sat straight, her dark eyes fierce. The world forced Judath to pretend, she said: at the baths, in the markets, at home. Christians gave little signs as if to test her, as if to uncover a false faith. At church, she agonized, but pretended. With her Egyptian skin and long black hair, no one suspected her mind. Beauty chained her to convention. Her advantages made her weigh what the world offered against the life she would have if she revealed her mind. To admit doubt would be pain in every way, and it would make her an outcast. She would either kill herself or live on the outskirts of a village, feared and mocked as demon infested and diseased. She herself thinks of her doubt as a disease. She is immersed in Christian learning. Christians, she knows, are moral creatures: atheists, disbelievers, are thrust from God, naturally immoral in their faithlessness.

"'He gave us impossible goals, an impossible goal in Christ,' Judath says. In spite of her doubt, she believes in their God, thinks his so-called words are true because everyone around her says it's so, and because they've inflicted their lies on her since she was a vulnerable child. She will never be free of doubt and sickness of spirit and mind. She marries a Christian. She is now skilled at hiding her thoughts and she knows her duty. But she's worn down by pretending. She can never know herself. Even her children are Christian. Eventually, her contrary instincts weaken her health, her sanity... You have something to say?" Metis suddenly cried in a strange fury.

Saturnine was startled; she had narrowed her eyes, perhaps furrowed her brow, perhaps she looked angry. She had been wondering if Judath was real, someone Metis had known, or whether it was a story, like *Kingdoms*.

"Her life is like my own," Saturnine said.

Metis studied her. "Disbelievers of Empire are all alike," she said. "There is a sickness in Empire that spreads, like a feeble light, infecting all minds. There are diseases of two kinds, depending on whether one is a disbeliever or believer." She paused.

"And there's Christian suffering," Metis went on angrily. "'We suffer because our ancestors ate the apple,' Judath says, some nonsense like this. She doesn't believe but can't get their nonsense out of her mind. You're human, I tell her. Your feelings are human, and suffering is part of animal nature. To Judath, God must be to blame for suffering. A human eating an apple is the cause of suffering, not nature itself. She's angry and filled with spite, for she can't love a vengeful

God who loves only those who rise to the impossible being of Christ. It's exquisitely large and dramatic. They say—Christ gave his innocent blood—but what did he do? Die and go to heaven. Where is the sacrifice? Death is nothing and part of nature. And then, he went to heaven!" Metis clapped her hands sharply, startling Saturnine. "You see," she said, "I am an intimate of their doctrines. It was necessary that I study them in order to fight them, to engage in war."

"War?" Saturnine said.

"She doesn't listen to me," Metis went on as if she hadn't heard Saturnine. "I tell Judath it's absurd to be angry at death or at what Christians call 'suffering.'" Metis laughed angrily. "Who're they angry at? At God, of course, but in fact, there's only nature, and it's absurd to be angry at nature. Judath cries out—'Look at the innocent child slave who's raped and beaten, and what crime did he commit?'" She paused. "A person is capable of suffering. I know."

Saturnine lowered her head but couldn't help watching in fascination, in fear. The idea of atheism, the word atheism, surprised Saturnine but mesmerized her too. How ordinary and normal Metis made it seem to doubt, to question. Metis revealed Christianity as a power, a force, but also a kind of nonsense.

"A child understands," Metis said, as if coiled with anger. She spoke as if she had been waiting a long time to speak. "A child who's beaten looks at his torturer and loves him. The little boy understands the pain of the torturer and how mistakes add to the master's pain. For his own part, the boy suffers bodily pain. Later, it's true, when he becomes an adult and lacks moral training, he'll think his master ruined him, and if he's Christian, he'll blame God.

"I had to slap her," Metis said. "I had to slap Judath. I told her, I said to her, 'You see nothing and are ignorant, all the while thinking you're good and worthy because of your anger over suffering.'"

Saturnine felt laughter within her but hid it.

"Christians touch each other's lives with confusion and misery, they touch each other and propagate madness. And now, as it is, their madness is the core of Empire. The net captures us all. Christians will have their Kingdom. Kharapan is right, at least about that. I've devoted my life to trying to save what's dear, but it's a hopeless battle. I've let the people of Chi spend their lives in happy ignorance, in the practice of life. I let them struggle to obtain that infallible judgment, let them think they provide a window on the correct practice of life. That is what I hoped to save!" she said. "This is what I try to save," she said.

Saturnine didn't understand, but guessed at Metis's sacrifices, her good work and intent.

"There is little hope for the future," Metis said. "Chi will be lost. Nothing can be done."

"Nothing?"

"The wake of the Christian world will leave battlegrounds and destruction, will leave humanity with a ruined spirit…"

Metis went on, as if she knew the truth of existence—I pause to admit that I, too, speak this way. Metis told Saturnine that the death of religion and gods was grounded in historical movement. The Egyptians provided a not too distant example: to the Egyptian mind the land survived while gods were worshipped. The identity of Egyptian worship and the stability of the physical universe were one. With the demise of Egyptian worship, the kingdom of Egypt crumbled. Although the Christian God vanquished pagan gods and claimed an Empire, in order to survive, Christianity needed what was more subtle and difficult to obtain: the faith of every mind, and not only outward worship. Christianity had to convert every mind, for that was the hope for a Christian Kingdom. But this made Christianity vulnerable. Even one godless mind threatened their world. "Indeed, as I have written, *agnosis* has a firmer foundation. Christianity will fail to convert every mind. More and more people will lose faith until the religion itself dies and the Christian Kingdom crumbles."

And yet, Metis said, the fall of the Christian Kingdom would leave a plague. Christian atheists would populate the earth and infect institutions. Morality would be lost in a people alienated long ago from their natural moral nature. Christian atheists would believe morality rested in Christianity and died with the Church. They would doubt morality itself. Nothing would be considered good or bad. Evil would strike them as inevitable, and these ideas would infiltrate the highest institutions—educational, government. In the best Christian atheists there would be an uneasy uncertainty over morality. The post Christian world, flooded by Christian thought, would think it understood the truth: that there was no meaning to life, to feelings or emotions. The concept of mystery and *agnosis*, of core and of human beings as moral creatures, would be lost. The way of life of philosophy would be lost with the destruction of Chi, and thus it would fail to save humanity. Metis sat up very straight, her eyes bright. She rocked rhythmically back and forth.

Saturnine wondered at this terrible vision, this prophecy of doom.

I, too, wonder about this prophecy of doom, at the force of Metis herself. I too must pause at the questions rising in me.

FIVE

METIS AND SATURNINE sat in silence for a time. "Sometimes," Metis said, "I think Chi is the squat desert frog." She looked at Saturnine with a sweet smile. Saturnine saw something entirely new in Metis.

"When the rain disappears and the lake dries, the frog buries itself in the damp lake bed," Metis said. "A thick desert crust dries over him, as hard as stone. He waits. Who can tell how he survives. Years pass. But when the rain comes, the lake again fills with water. The earth shakes with the movement of his body, and he appears, a comical, ugly thing. One laughs to see him. He rises to partake of water." She paused. "That will be what happens to our doubting philosophers of Chi. They will rise again. After the flood.

"Enough," Metis said, scowling. "One story will come to conclusion."

She narrowed her eyes and studied Saturnine. "Saturnine of Rome, who are you? Are you willing to die to fight them?" She grinned, baring the gaps in her teeth.

"If Rome knew my thoughts they would have killed me," Saturnine said. "And yet, I wrote. Atheist is the same as traitor in Rome."

"Yes, but you kept it secret. You, like others, love life too much," Metis said. "You'll have your life rather than protect Chi. You'll have today rather than fight to ensure a future. Even Kharapan is the same, paying attention to his moments, his inner feeling." She laughed angrily.

"You don't know what I'd risk," Saturnine said, holding the poison at her neck.

"Bah!" Metis cried. "You don't know what it means to live in the face of death."

"No, but I have no one and cannot choose an 'easy life' anymore even if I wanted to. I hope to learn from you."

Metis seemed to study her. "We fight for the freedom of humankind, against slavery and oppression. Our weapon is secret revolt."

Saturnine heard a change in Metis's voice.

"The hugeness of what's at stake changes how we must live. I wake in the morning with awe. They don't understand. They say we act above the law, and it's so, but we're in the right. What of this supreme fiction? This 'unknown' that's our model, our guiding god. Fine, but we can't let it debilitate us. We must try to save ourselves, to protect the freedom of our kind. Chi's arguments and words will change when Christians come to destroy us, but it'll be too late."

Saturnine was still, transfixed, afraid.

"We should have fought them long ago. We should have

lived among them and talked to them. We have come late and have no choice now in what we must do."

"Listen," Saturnine said, as if to stop the flow of words. "Kenyon told the officials. They've sent a messenger, but there's no news."

"Bah!" Metis spat in a jar and stood. "If you're willing to do what's necessary then stay, but if not, go."

Saturnine's heart pounded. "I'll stay," she said.

Metis hesitated and then squat down, leaning forward. "Our aim is to overthrow the Roman Empire, what makes it what it is—Christianity."

Saturnine let out a small laugh but a part of her felt she was falling into an abyss.

"You think I'm mad," Metis said, "but as weak as we are, Christians are vulnerable. Irrationality and rage—whether or not we do anything—irrationality and rage will destroy them eventually, along with the failure to convert every mind. They will break apart and dissolve, but in the meantime, we might help them along." She looked intensely at Saturnine. "We'll go to Rome." She paused. "We'll meet there. Killing a pope will start an internal war among them."

"The pope!" Saturnine said in a low voice.

"The bishop of Rome," Metis said. "You yourself went to the church to see Kharapan, even when they were look-ing for you. They are vulnerable and weak even when they seem strong. We kill the bishop. Rumor will spread that an unorthodox Christian sect killed the orthodox bishop. All of Empire will battle with itself." She looked away, lost in thought.

Saturnine couldn't speak. A part of it made terrible sense. She had lived among fighting Christian factions. One might turn the Church's mind from Chi to something more urgent to them, an internal battle. But something else kept her speechless, something primitive, evolving.... Besides, she noted, Metis had used the word "we."

"Are there others that join you in this?" Saturnine said.

Metis had a disgusted look. "The people of Chi want their freedom and love their easy life. But you," she said. "You lived among them."

"Yes," Saturnine said.

It once would have pleased her that Metis recognized their fated lives. Now, with a weight, Saturnine sensed a fate she had not expected nor dared to know. She nodded and said she would go to Rome with Metis or meet Metis there; she would fight them. She would join Metis's secret war. Her decision seemed a dream, as if she acted a part in a play. But if it were a dream, it seemed her destiny. Her life would reach its natural conclusion: fighting the Church, the terrible power, in any way she could.

"Bishop Damasus, the pope, is very old, and I heard he's ill," Saturnine said. "It's likely he'll not live out the year."

Metis fell back with a satisfied smile. "We'll focus on the pope that succeeds him."

"Damasus's natural death may distract the Church, cause internal fighting. Perhaps they will be too busy to consider Chi."

"Bah!" Metis cried. "They've killed Kharapan," she said. "Without a thought, they've cut his throat. And with just as little thought they'll eliminate a people and destroy philosophy itself. It's only a matter of time, of when."

Saturnine was quiet. Her heart pounded, and she turned toward the blocked-up window, finding it hard to breath; when she turned back, her face was pale. "I'll help you," she said.

Metis gave a little smile.

Saturnine felt a new angry resolve. It moved her and gave breath to a future unveiling before her. Yes, she could see through the haze, she thought. She would return to Rome and kill a bishop. Her life had meaning and purpose. Rome. If it wanted to kill her, she might as well give it something to charge her with.

Metis pulled back her dark curly hair. It was dirty, oily, and streaked with gray. She had an absent expression, as if they spoke of everyday things. The light flickered on walls and floor. The blackened windows made it permanent night.

"We will discover the strength of your decision," Metis said. "You'll be tested. I'll know whether to trust you, and then we'll make a plan to meet in Rome."

"What will make you trust me?" Saturnine said.

Metis leaned in. "On *Mars*, in six days, there'll be a debate. I'll speak on the 'Moral Genius,' given the state of the world, given what is at stake. How you act that night will decide everything."

"Tell me more."

Metis opened the door, and Saturnine thought Metis would ask her to leave, but Metis said, "Come."

They went into the dark. The earth glowed a soft yellow. Metis hummed and stopped at an isolated spot. "Here," she said in a low voice. "Here is where we lay the dead, the altar of our peace."

The sky outlined the dark shape of a huge cactus. Saturnine suddenly imagined murdered Christians buried here. Can it be? she thought and felt a chill in spite of the warm night.

Metis turned back. Saturnine followed. At her door Metis said, "The future of humanity depends on us." She shut the door.

Saturnine stood in the dark for a time. She turned and headed toward the village but continued through the courtyard, silent and mysterious in the night, and went down the dirt path that led to the Nile. Upon reaching the dark expanse of water, she bent in the mud, trembling and holding herself. She didn't notice the sound of the river or see the wide night sky.

So her life had passed before her. In the last days she'd contemplated her past and it seemed as if her history and her contemplation of it had all been in preparation for this moment, this question in the air—Would she kill? Would she engage in any act necessary to defend what she believed? The question had been in the background of her life, and now she had her answer too. The answer was out in the open. Metis made the question direct and anchored both question and answer in her soul. Saturnine had not wanted to see, had not wanted to know herself so well. She had been too weak to face the question, or the answer she would give. She'd been able to pretend but had been naïve: the strain over whether to give up writing or not, submitting to Victorinus or not! Her early life was superficial nonsense to her now. She'd been a ridiculous creature, caring only for herself in a narrow world. No, there'd been a more urgent question. If one believed there was a seething, growing evil, one had a moral duty to stop it, she thought, to do what was necessary, to do anything one could, to try to stop it.

Nothing Metis said was new. Nothing came as a surprise.

Flavia wouldn't understand, but no matter. They were different creatures, she and her mother. And Kharapan! Saturnine suddenly laughed—he said to be true to herself. And this is it, she thought. This is my true self. This is taking things to their natural conclusion.

The burden of the world was great.

"We're capable of suffering," she whispered, repeating it from somewhere. Someone had said it. Yes, she was capable of suffering. How much can one suffer? Perhaps that was the question, the ultimate challenge to a life. But a part of her felt a weight, a good and strong weight, and for the first time in a long time, perhaps the very first time in her life, Saturnine saw the future clearly before her. She knew what had to be done and what she would do. She had no doubt.

SIX

LUPICINUS LAY ON his bed in the ship's cabin, stroking the shaft of the knife that had been his father's. The churchmen of Rome traveled to Alexandria for a reason that once would have been all alive in Lupicinus: to gather at the powerful Alexandrian church and convene a conclave on who might be the next bishop of Rome, the next pope. The Christian world waited for pope Damasus's demise. Christians of various sects filled roads and seaways, meeting and planning, preparing the theater, or rather the stage, for the next chapter of Christian authority and power.

Some in the Church's inner circle suspected Lupicinus let Kharapan escape. Rumors spread that he'd been tainted by a demon. Lupicinus paid them no heed. The emperor's court had granted his request to go to Hellenica, directing Lupicinus to a General Kastor on the outskirts of Alexandria. Lupicinus, feeling as if there were a strange whisper in his ear, hadn't made a firm decision about Hellenica and what to do once they arrived in Alexandria. With the imminence of Damasus's demise, the Church forgot about the barbarian and the country on the outskirts of their southern border. Lupicinus could throw his missive into the sea.

In spite of this, however, Lupicinus still believed events— the menippea he imagined—would reach their natural conclusion. After Kharapan left the cell, Lupicinus first heard that whisper in his ear. He couldn't decipher the words, and felt disturbed, as if some menace hovered over everything. On the ship, he kept to his cabin. He rarely spoke to others. He contemplated things alone. Should he go to General Kastor, should an army march to Hellenica, He imagined Kharapan would understand what had to happen. Moreover, Lupicinus imagined that Kharapan had given him, Lupicinus, permission—to carry out the final act, so to speak. Lupicinus understood: Kharapan did not want to live without Hellenica, had no place in the world without Chi. In Lupicinus's waking dream in the ship cabin, Kharapan acknowledged all of this and specifically chose to die at Lupicinus's hands. Lupicinus had brought his own knife out of duty and love, yes love.

Lupicinus imagined the look in Kharapan's eyes, perhaps he imagined it even then, the look reflecting Kharapan's understanding of their fates: Lupicinus would live until some act of God or man killed him. To commit murder is to inflict an incurable life-long wound on oneself. To use Kharapan's words, Lupicinus would be the living dead, but Kharapan would be granted a better fate: Kharapan had lived well, and in the last part of his life had reached that dream of his (although I only discovered this later).

Still, at the time on board the ship, Lupicinus felt he could not count on himself so well. Perhaps it was this that increased the intensity of his feeling, made him unable to stop thinking. He did not feel firm in himself, in his idea, the idea that had guided him for more than forty years. There was a crack, a weakness, a wedge between his feeling (only feeling—not mind, not ideas) and his idea: feeling, once so close to idea, so enraptured and enlivened by idea, now fell away from his long held idea as if without interest. At times he would rather cast off 'idea,' the idea of civilization, a Christian Kingdom, even if true and inevitable, and live in what was to his mind a completely wrongheaded manner. But it was too late. The idea made the path clear, had always made it clear, and Lupicinus had always followed the path. But here, nevertheless, was the wedge, and besides other painful thoughts and feelings, he had the painful and uncertain whispering in his ear. Kharapan likely knew or suspected his feelings, his battered self. Kharapan would claim he'd been right, had known what would break when Lupicinus revealed his life. Kharapan would say this meant Lupicinus had that sliver of integrity, that chance for happiness. Bah! Lupicinus cried to himself.

And yet, as he touched his knife he felt dramatic excess, as if life failed him in not being up to the drama of his imagination, a drama that included a Christian Kingdom. It suddenly seemed to him that all along, for all of his life, he had been guided by an illusion of his own, had felt certain when nothing was certain. He had never before experienced a deeper sense of uncertainty with such clarity, and yet at the same time suspected that his uncertainty, a form of knowledge itself, would not stop him. His uncertainty would not change events or the inevitable claims of history.

SEVEN

THE PEOPLE OF Chi heard of the woman of Rome in the Study, Kharapan's friend. They wondered about her solemn, absent expression, spoke of how she visited Metis, kept to herself, hardly bathed. They knew she'd lost a friend on the journey, had lost a home. They didn't know specifics and wondered why Kharapan had not come with her. They made an effort to be kind, but Saturnine was hardly aware of them and would later describe her time in Chi like a dream, as if she'd been in a dream and could not see. Still, Chi enveloped her and showed itself in ways she was hardly aware of until much later when she reflected.

It is a strange land. We have lost the known world, or so I feel myself.

Saturnine, walking alone along the Nile River, heard a strange noise and thought it was a groaning animal at first, until she could make out the low murmur of voices. After a bend in the river, she came upon a group standing in front of a hastily built platform. A man and woman sat on the platform, as if on stage. At the moment Saturnine joined in back of the crowd, everyone spoke at once. Saturnine was about to turn away, but the crowd seemed to part, perhaps looking at her, curious even in the midst of their excitement. Saturnine caught sight of a thick woman kneeling on the ground in front of the platform, head down, bent. The murderer, Saturnine thought. The word pierced her. She stood still with a firm angry expression.

The woman on stage stood. Everyone grew silent. She was tall, thin, and old. She walked back and forth and paused before she began to speak. The strange Egyptian sounds, smooth and repetitive, seemed to Saturnine like a salve or evil chanting, she couldn't be sure which. The kneeling woman groaned softly. After the old woman sat down, the man on the platform stood and walked to the edge. His ribs seemed to strain free of his chest, but his voice was surprisingly loud and deep. He spoke in Greek. "Kafar, take this experience as *agnosis* and seek wisdom. When you've discovered what the experience, this violent murder, means to you, your life, come and tell me. I'll expect to understand your reasoning. When you know what it is, you'll know to tell me."

He nodded and the trial apparently ended. Everyone spoke at once, a little girl screamed, her voice barely discernible over the sound of the crowd.

The woman, Kafar, rose, and everyone moved aside to let her pass. Saturnine watched her as she went by: the haggard face seemed to glow as if with some unnatural light. Kafar walked down a dirt path without looking back.

"There's nothing like the pleasure of a murder trial," a

young woman said, coming to stand next to Saturnine. Saturnine gave a curt nod and started to walk away but the woman followed.

"You are Saturnine of Rome," she said. "I am Alexis."

Alexis, wiry and young, beautiful in a way, a freckled face, her skin a mixture of light and dark. She wore a white dress, beads around her arms, wrists, and neck, and she studied Saturnine with a curious and mirthful expression.

"I'm not sure I can still be said to be of Rome," Saturnine said.

Alexis laughed, a curious tingling laugh. "Come," she said. "I think we need to talk. I am ordered to be your guide."

"By whom?" Saturnine said, concerned.

"By Chi, by the gods." She smiled at Saturnine's suspicious expression.

"What do we need to talk about?"

Alexis paused. "The trial. I will tell you about the trial."

Saturnine studied her as if to discover some hidden meaning.

Alexis led her to a narrow path in the desert, talking as they walked.

"Kafar hadn't killed before. Nor loved before." Alexis smiled at Saturnine. "Have you loved?" Saturnine smiled but said nothing. "Perhaps she understands better than many of us what it means to be human. Besides, everyone knows her and knows what she's done."

They looked out onto the vast desert.

"I've seen a trial end with a slit throat, but only once." She paused. "Kafar told them she's afraid of herself, and who wouldn't be? Afraid of ourselves."

Saturnine suddenly felt faint and moved toward the shade of a tree, but Alexis stopped her, saying ticks leapt out from trees in a swarm at passing animals. Saturnine sunk to the ground under the sun. Sweat beaded her body, and the green gauze Nubia had given her to wear molded to her skin.

"Here," Alexis said, taking out cloth from a pocket. Saturnine wiped her face. Alexis sat on bent legs, studying Saturnine; she picked up a stick and drew in the sand.

"Go on," Saturnine said.

"The victim's family want her punished," Alexis said, "but it's painful. Life is full of pain and not fair, and they know this, and they respect the law. They might forgive Kafar or come to think of her like a daughter. I've seen it happen. We're a small country and involved in discussion and debate. Forgiveness comes when one becomes intimate with another's pain. Some never forgive, and some don't feel or acknowledge their own pain." She paused. "Beautiful, isn't it?"

Saturnine looked at her. Alexis stared out at empty land, at the huge sky. Saturnine looked, too, but the vastness, the lack of boundaries, the way the heat made the land shimmer, all seemed to mock her thoughts and threaten her, as if nothing could ever be clear, nothing solid grasped. A gentle wind made a low sound in the bushes.

Alexis suddenly ran into the desert. "I used to play that I was master of these bushes." She swung and stabbed as if at a throng of hostile guests. The strangeness of the environment and of this free speaking woman unnerved Saturnine, but for a moment, that stark land struck Saturnine as beautiful: a bare white tree trunk, Alexis's agile form dancing in waves of heat, the bright sun on pale yellow brittle bushes. The sun behind Alexis revealed her thin dark body and made her seem a shadow in this vast land.

Saturnine agreed to go with Alexis to her domus, which turned out to be a room attached to a small domus. Sitting inside, then lying back on a bed in shadows that grew deeper with the passing day, Alexis told Saturnine about her life. Her parents disappeared in Empire when she was eight, and she moved from home to home until she was eleven, and then to the room she lived in now, next to a house where three others lived. She worked in the fields, and surprised Saturnine when she defiantly claimed to have no core. "I don't want anything controlling my life, a passion that drives me." She told Saturnine it was better to live for the sun, music, and certain mild pleasures of the mind. She gave Saturnine a history of her love, which even then included a number of men.

Saturnine would come to believe that Alexis had an attachment to entanglement, not love, that she was entangled with entanglements. Alexis's loves, so to speak, each one, were passionate and ended violently. In fact, Saturnine would come to think that Alexis's core, or passion, if she did not follow it, involved dispute resolution, but I am not so sure. I think Alexis might have been concerned about murdering someone herself, and for that reason watched trials with interest. Alexis would be one of the people of Chi who came to live with Saturnine after events I may or may not describe. Alexis would live in Alexandria for the rest of her life. Such a character! superficial, wasted as much time as possible, often with the help of substances and whatever it was she referred to with the word love. Saturnine defended her, but I think Alexis wore Saturnine out; of course, one might say (and Saturnine most certainly would say) that Alexis had lost her world; she was not a creature of Empire. Alexis had no chance in Alexandria; she tried to survive, breathing (as one could) through the days.

I do not mean to imply in what I say, that Saturnine and I met often in later years, or that we were intimate or friends. We were not. We had encounters over the years. We often sat in silence. We wrote a couple of letters, drawn to each other in some odd, perhaps even sick, way. She suspected, I believe, something of the love between Kharapan and me, yes love. She suspected, too, something about what happened in my last meeting with Kharapan. I did not bother to reveal my mind, in spite of her questions. In short, something about me unsettled her and interested her, too, but she never managed to pierce the veil of my silence or perhaps didn't care to.

That early evening, Saturnine told Alexis that her own core, or passion, had been her life. "My core led me to Chi. Yes," she said, as if to herself, "fate led me here."

Saturnine had never spoken this way. If she'd been born in Chi, she might have pursued her passion openly. She could hardly imagine such a life. Perhaps her life, her core itself, if there is such a thing, perhaps it consisted in the stuff of danger, of limitation. Perhaps she would not have had the same passion if she had been born in Chi, for her passion also involved the heavy responsibility and burden of Empire. Perhaps Saturnine might thank Rome after all, providing her, like a gift, the urgency and necessity of her passion. But this is just the voice of an old man, who cares less, after all, for that external world above, for what happens there or what it is, Kingdom or no Kingdom. I have the luxury, of course, to be alone, mostly alone, while the world proceeds as it might. In writing this, I feel myself weaken, afraid of chronicling events to come, perhaps trying to forestall the event with words.

Alexis laughed at Saturnine's sober attachment to her core. "I'll convince you." She would show Saturnine the pleasures of life, she said, and not in a dry, Epicurean way. They'd attend a philosophical lecture—it was what one did in Chi—and then they'd go dancing in the sky.

"Dancing in the sky?"

"The festival of spring."

Alexis said she would come for Saturnine the next day. Saturnine hesitated and was about to refuse but said nothing. She had no place to be, in particular, until Metis's debate.

Saturnine told Alexis something of her life, and even if guarded, if she avoided speaking of Kharapan, she revealed more than she'd been accustomed to. In expanding darkness, Saturnine told Alexis about her early friendship with Philo, and how he'd been killed. She told of how, after his death, she started to write and how she'd written in secret for most of her life. And she told about her marriage to Victorinus, the man of Rome. Saturnine's one man amused Alexis, hardly love at all.

Saturnine suddenly grew quiet and sat up abruptly. What? she wondered. Her body ached. What will test me? She was ready. She would do what she must.

"What will test you?" Alexis said.

Saturnine stared. Had she spoken out loud? She shook her head.

After a silence, Saturnine was about to say she had to leave, when Alexis asked about Kharapan. She wanted Saturnine to tell her about Kharapan's role in her life.

Saturnine looked into the darkness and then at Alexis, and after a long pause lay back and told Alexis how Kharapan saved her the night Philo died. He'd met with Flavia, her mother, her maidservant that had been her mother, over the years. Cautiously, Saturnine told of events that brought her to Chi. After a pause, she said that she and Kharapan had befriended a church boy, Thaddeus, who might have saved Kharapan, but Kharapan refused his help. She didn't tell about Kharapan's idea of "challenge." She didn't say anything about the threat to Chi and left out everything related to Metis, including the fact that Saturnine had read *Kingdoms*. She didn't mention Metis's name. Saturnine didn't understand her reluctance to speak of Metis to the people of Chi. She would reflect on it later. It seemed to her that she'd wanted to protect her own idea of Metis, as if silence were an armor around it. After a time, Saturnine told Alexis about losing Thaddeus on the journey. Silence followed. Alexis waited in darkness.

Saturnine stared into shadow, musing on the hours, at this intimate conversation with a stranger in growing darkness. It struck her as wonderful and strange. She felt as if these hours with Alexis filled up a part of her empty body, leaving a fuller self. But there were things Saturnine could not share.

"We are a people of words, of endless talking and words," Alexis said. "You kept secrets; you hardly spoke to anyone.

You are not in the habit of words, but we are always telling stories. You probably don't even know about Nubia." She raised her head to look at Saturnine and Saturnine shook her head, no. Alexis told a surprisingly detailed story of Nubia's love for another woman. It involved a long friendship, a torturous unexpressed love on each side, followed by outbursts of frustrated anger over nothing, everyone but them knowing and seeing the truth, and how Nubia and her love were never apart. Finally the two of them managed to speak to each other of their love, made physical love, and soon after, parted and became distant friends.

Saturnine was astonished.

"We saw, but at one discussion they told us the whole story themselves. We have storytelling sessions. Most of us speak openly. We're painfully aware of the particulars of our disgrace."

The idea of speaking in this manner might have made Saturnine cringe. She might have believed that this conversation between her and Alexis had been the rare event. What she told Alexis would be known by all of Chi, she thought. She gave herself an inner warning. She couldn't remember anything she'd said that she cared to hide but warned herself to be cautious.

"I should go," Saturnine said.

"I'll take you back," Alexis said, getting up.

They went out in silence. The night air felt cool.

After a time, Alexis spoke of the trial. She said that everyone trusted Khandra Deo and Khandra Onus. "Dispute resolution is his or her core, and thus, his or her life." She paused. "In addition to the Khandras, philosophers, farmers, alchemists, and merchants discussed Kafar's case and gave their reports. Metis participated in groups like that at one time," she added.

Alexis paused, oddly it seemed, and Saturnine thought that Alexis must know she'd been meeting with Metis. The Great Village had eyes on her, watching her as they watched Nubia, as they watched everyone.

"What do you think of Metis?" Saturnine asked.

"She's brilliant, keeps to herself. She's a rare expert in Coptic but wrote a passionate study against Christians. If the monasteries only knew her mind! But I hear she has friends. She hardly joins in the life of Chi these days, although given her talents, she might have been at the center of things. She was for a time, when she was young. She rarely attends a discussion or debate, although she was once reputed to be an expert in debate."

Saturnine thought of the debate to come on *Mars* and for some reason said nothing.

"She never lets anyone into that shack of hers," Alexis said. "Kharapan visits her when he's in Chi."

I have been in Metis's shack, she mused. In Rome, they had a great city, but sorcery trials. Philo was burned alive. In Rome, senators lived off bribes. In Rome, Victorinus strived to conform to churches and senators. In Chi, they lived in a vast desert and had the small square of the Great Village but had philosophers and complex organizational systems. But Saturnine felt angry at what she felt was the naiveté and ignorance of the people of Chi. She worried they wouldn't listen to Metis.

Alexis suddenly raised her arms and turned in circles, jumping and laughing. She skipped ahead in long strides, then returned at a run, laughing.

"I just love to move," Alexis said. "It's the plunge of a body into the world, don't you think?"

Saturnine only stared, hardly paying attention to her.

Eight

Saturnine, groaning awake, turned groggily. She pushed away the glass of water that Alexis thrust at her and closed her eyes.

"Come," Alexis said. "We have to go to the Academy. Or are you a Cynic? Failing to bathe and wandering at night."

As they walked, Saturnine armed herself against philosophers and their moral wisdoms, those who didn't look out into the world, who refused to see. She marched arm in arm with Alexis.

"We'll have a dash of intellectual spirit before our 'dance in the sky,'" Alexis said; "Throw ourselves in a cold plunge before the warm waters." She begged Saturnine to go to the festival—they were leaving in a few hours and would immerse themselves in bodily sensations.

Saturnine wouldn't agree to go. She felt confused but thought that, after all, it didn't matter what she did until *Mars*.

Alexis pointed out the Aristotelians in blue cloaks, the Stoics in green, and the Epicureans in red. She told her that the Socratics, or the Academy, practiced knowing nothing, but not like Skeptics who rejected certainty about reality, living philosophically by renouncing philosophy itself. The Skeptics had their wisdom too, she added. "There's nothing to grieve over, the Skeptics say.

"The Skeptic says, 'Perhaps.' The Skeptic says, 'This is no better than that'…. In my case," Alexis said, 'I don't have time for peace of mind."

"Nor do I. Peace of mind is a luxury!" Saturnine said.

They approached the stone-white school on the edge of the Great Village. About fifteen people of mixed age waited outside, some in orange cloaks. The door opened. They went inside, handing a coin to an orange-clad woman with bright red hair. Alexis paid for Saturnine and muttered that those who took coins were beginners, but Saturnine wasn't listening. With a pale face, Saturnine paused, and then went to the back of the room.

It was cool inside. The room had cement benches arranged in the shape of an amphitheater around a half-circle floor. Those in orange cloaks sat on front seats, others in the second or third rows, and Saturnine in the sixth or seventh row, obscured in shadow. No one lit a lamp or torch. Their minds and voices were the elements in the room. Alexis glanced up at Saturnine, who was leaning forward, her head resting on a clenched fist, staring intently.

Galeria, the teacher, wore an orange cloak. She was small with a thick torso, thick arms, and cropped black hair. She came out, moving with grace and purpose, pacing back and forth in front of them. The room grew quiet.

"Every error implies conflict," Galeria said, facing them. "One who errs doesn't wish to go wrong but to go right, and so he's not doing what he wishes. The rational creature can only do what he thinks is right. What of logic? Is training in logic necessary?"

She waited. The silence was a pressure.

"I don't always understand logic's purpose," the young woman with red hair admitted.

"Should I demonstrate?" Galeria asked.

The woman nodded.

"And in order to demonstrate logics' usefulness, must I not use a demonstrative argument?"

The woman nodded her assent.

"How then shall you know if I impose on you?"

She had no answer.

"You see, you admit that logic is necessary, if without it you aren't even able to learn this much: whether or not logic is necessary."

There was a ripple of laughter.

"One must develop critical ability, and in support of thinking, engage in problems of logic. At the same time, there are such things as mistakes. One mistakes an act as useful when instead it's harmful. One engages in behavior because she thinks it useful, but she might be mistaken, and for that reason, we must train in order to reduce mistakes, to improve our capacity for judgment. For what purpose? Because, as I said, and what I meant, is that a rational creature can only act on what he thinks is right; he goes wrong because he mistakes what is right. Therefore, one must try to avoid mistake. The task of logic is to distinguish between right and wrong, to reason through life's questions, to be as moral a creature as it is natural for us to be."

Galeria turned to a chalkboard and wrote down an exercise in logic. While she spoke, the Socratic Friends took notes. She said that Aristotle asserted that deductive reasoning was syllogistic: thus the words, "if all men are mortal, and Socrates is a man, then Socrates is mortal"—could be made into variables: "if all Xs are Y, and A is an X, then A is a Y." The students worked on Galeria's syllogism. After a time, Galeria discussed premises on the nature of the hypothetical. Saturnine could hardly keep up, but at one point the discussion drew her in. Galeria found that the red-haired woman had made a mistake, but the woman persisted in her way of seeing and wasn't concerned about the mistake.

Galeria grew agitated. "You think we merely pass time, but an error is no light matter."

"I haven't hurt anyone," the young woman muttered.

Galeria lowered her head and clasped her small, thick hands. There was quiet in the room. She raised her head after a time and spoke in a low voice. "Hipparchia, you haven't hurt or killed, but as Epictetus said, 'Here is no father for you to kill'! You failed in the one task before you. Epictetus failed to find the missing step in a syllogism when he was a student, and he told his teacher, Rufus, 'I suppose I have not burnt the Capitol down…' Rufus told him: 'Slave! the missing step here is the Capitol.' Like him, Hipparchia, you have committed the one error possible."

Saturnine absently let out a low murmur. Galeria looked

up. There was an expectant silence. Everyone looked back at Saturnine.

"Do you have a question?" Galeria said to Saturnine in a gentle voice. "Speak child, what question is brimming in you?" Her compassionate look and kind voice brought tears to Saturnine's eyes.

"Can it be?" Saturnine said. The room had become a blur. "Can it be that mistakes are equal, that to kill one's father is the same as failing to find a missing step in a syllogism? That these moral waves are all of the same weight? It leads either to great evil or perfect morality...."

Galeria smiled and crossed her arms. "How 'great evil'?"

"A man may shrug off killing his father, saying it's the same as failing to find the missing step in a syllogism."

"Or 'perfect morality' you said."

"Perfect morality because if one addressed every question on its own, a syllogism, or murder, and chose the right way, as you say, one might be perfectly moral. One would need to take great care in every moment, to approach every act, each question, with attention. It's impossible."

"So it is: to pay attention to each moment, every question, will more likely lead to a correct decision, correct act, and less likely lead to evil. I agree, perfect morality is impossible. That's why we need to learn, to practice logic and learn how to approach questions. Our aim is to understand how the good creature may respond to each question that arises."

"And yet," Saturnine continued, grave, "some questions are like crashing waves, others ripples, and the nature of what is at stake is far different in each case. Far different."

There was a low laugh. Saturnine looked around as if startled.

Galeria paused for a time. "There are two reasons why questions, your moral waves, have the same weight." She continued in a low gentle voice. "Let's expand your notion of waves. Do you agree that it seems as if they don't come one at a time? Isn't it so? One faces the problem of finding the missing step in the syllogism when sitting in this room, in this moment, but at the same time, other waves crash in our thoughts, and we swim in dangerous waters. Do you agree?"

"Yes," Saturnine said.

"My first point is this: even if waves crash around us, one faces them one at a time. One wave, then another. In the practice of life, it doesn't matter whether a wave is small or large—one confronts each wave with her whole person, using all her faculties and training. The moment of addressing a question or problem is full and whole. In this sense, each moral wave is equal. The rational creature can learn to address questions one at a time, even if separated by moments. This is a training: to stay within a moment and see and understand what it is that confronts one at that moment, for one's thoughts are fluttering and disorganized. One imagines waves crashing about at once and fails to see the question actually facing one and in issue at that moment, but one must attend. It is only necessary to give one's full attention to the question at issue, and with an aim for the good. This attention, this practice, will aid one's correct response to the next wave, and the good is the only correct aim for the rational creature."

She paused. "We practice contemplation and meditation to

help us engage in the moment. There are exercises, *askesis*, which help us. For example, we practice what we call the 'view from above.' You imagine you stand on a mountain and view creatures below; in one version of this exercise, you stand with Death who's ready to take you to the next world. 'Why is that man, that politician, running across the city in a panic,' Death asks, laughing, 'when I'll be helping him into my boat this very night? And why does that woman amass jewels, when she's coming with me in a fortnight?' In any event," she said. "I'll continue to my second reason why moral waves have the same importance."

Galeria's second reason was as follows: it was the nature of the rational creature to desire what was good in each case, and the creature chose based on his thinking, his assessment of what was good or not good. One chose incorrectly because one was mistaken. A thief thinks it serves him to steal, but he's mistaken; an adulterer thinks it serves him to make love to his friend's wife, but he, too, is mistaken. In each case, these men think they act for their own good, but in each case, they are mistaken and go wrong, and in making mistakes hurt themselves and others. One needs training to understand the right act, the way that is taken for one's own good—for what is done for one's own good necessarily involves the good of the city and community. Thus, while one is in a classroom, addressing a problem of logic, one trains, one puts oneself wholly to the task. One attempts to go right here; one practices right thinking so that when one goes out that door she is prepared. In either case, she is engaged in the conduct of life. Whatever task is before her, the same question applies: how would the good creature respond?

She stopped and waited.

"But if one hasn't trained," Saturnine said in a small voice, "and is faced with a force, a monstrous wave...? He doesn't have time to...." She broke off.

"One must engage those who've trained," Galeria said. "Engage and trust one whose conduct in life taught him or her how to make correct decisions. One whose life itself, the practice of the art, is admirable. Assess the person's way of life, not his words. This takes time, a life in common." She paused. "And then, one must train; one must practice in right conduct to be prepared for any question that might arise. Your inner will, the trust you have in your ability of assessment, will become the cliff that waves crash against. One day, waves will lose their power at the cliff's base. Your judgment might be an inner citadel."

Galeria waited. Saturnine struggled against thoughts: Metis's isolation, her blocked windows, and dirty hair and careless appearance. She crossed her arms, thinking about standing with Metis in front of the huge cactus in the desert. However, she thought: someone of great intelligence or insight might see what others do not and must live in unusual circumstances, must act when others will not.

"What does it mean to be human?" Galeria said, breaking the silence, addressing Saturnine.

Saturnine faltered. "I don't know...."

"So it is. A good 'I don't know.' Contemplate it. Take it in and let *agnosis*, the unknown, unknowing, inform and form you. Please feel free to speak to me after session."

Saturnine didn't say anything, and Galeria continued

with the problem of logic. After, they all went out into a blinding sun.

Saturnine felt her mind expanding without focus as the sun over flat earth.

Galeria came outside and smiled at Saturnine. "Are you going to speak to her?" Alexis said.

"Impossible."

They walked off in silence.

This 'way of life' Galeria spoke of, Saturnine thought, where one addressed each wave, must not be possible in times of war. It must be that one had to forego peace of mind. In any event, she couldn't ask for guidance. Even if she had to admit, as she'd admitted before, that she didn't have training, that she could fall into mistake, the mistakes were her own, and she had no choice. One died alone, and in the isolation of being, faced moral questions alone. Galeria didn't know the threat. She refused to see what faced Chi. One who was blind couldn't be a guide for her.

Alexis begged her to come on the journey, the celebration of earth and sky, promising they'd return on *Mars*. Saturnine said she'd go.

Kenyon entered Saturnine's room in the Study. "I came to say goodbye," she said.

Saturnine, still dirty, gave a strange laugh.

"I don't know if I should leave you," Kenyon said, studying her.

"Stay for me? There's no reason. Go. I may see you shortly myself." Again, she gave an odd laugh, but cautioned herself.

"Are you going? I'm tired. I didn't sleep. I'm going to a festival, a dance in the sky with Alexis."

"Are you?" Kenyon seemed surprised. "Did you find Metis?" she said after a time.

"Yes...."

"Well," Kenyon said, and paused. "Saturnine, do you want to come with me? I thought you wouldn't leave, but if I'm wrong.... Come, perhaps it's better. There's nothing you can do, and in case something happens...."

"Nothing?" Saturnine said. "No, I'll stay."

She saw Kenyon's hesitation. Saturnine took hold of Kenyon's wrist, and the movement reminded them both of that night on the ship. "You once said that the greatest respect one can show is to leave a person to her fate. Do it for me now. Leave me to my fate."

"Is it what you want?"

"Yes."

"I'll go," Kenyon said, after hesitating. "We'll meet again."

"Do you think so!"

"I feel it in my heart."

Kenyon gave a bow and went out.

Saturnine saw with surprise, and a not just a little embarrassment, that Alexis and the others had transformed themselves. Alexis, with barely any clothes, had painted her body in blue stripes, as if for an ancient rite, and wore a bow and sack of arrows over a shoulder. Others too, some thirty people, young and old waiting near the river, had painted themselves and looked exotic. They fit Saturnine's image of savages. They carried baskets of food, cooking supplies, musical instruments. Everyone laughed and talked, and as they head out, they started to sing.

The group walked at an easy pace through the light of day and stopped at dusk at an unremarkable spot and spread out rugs and blankets, where they would sleep. They ate a feast of cold porridge, fruit, dried fish, and wine, and then music started. Many jumped in wild flirtatious dancing, pulling each other back and forth. The cask of wine circulated. Men moved slowly and mysteriously to the music, and the women jumped in with a thumping beat. Alexis tried to pull Saturnine up, but Saturnine refused. Saturnine sat, staring in fascination. Alexis threw her hands in the air and moved her hips forward and back and circled the sand. They wailed as they danced, and the dancing and music went on into the night, into the dark shadows. Saturnine thought she heard Alexis's laugh.

The next day they woke late and walked for hours, circling rocks, and tramping along flat plains. Toward midday Saturnine thought she saw a shadow of trees, hundreds of trees, an ocean of forest, but the shadow kept moving further away.

"We celebrate the luminousness of earth and sky and loosen ourselves from society," Alexis said, coming to walk next to her. "You, especially, have work to do. Imagine! Having to rid yourself of Rome." She let out a long indulgent laugh.

At last, they came to a wide, flat sweep of desert where a low circular wall marked out a camping space. They built tents, marked territory. Most of the men and a few women went off to hunt. Alexis joined them. Saturnine sat on the ground and listened to the women and men and the river raging softly nearby. The hunters returned at nightfall with one rabbit and wide smiles. Fires burned and everyone gathered. They drank wine and another liquid, what Alexis called a purifier. People wore fewer clothes, some were naked. Some of the men covered themselves in white ash and looked like spirits in the night. The exotic dark skin, the strange lives, the music, made Saturnine feel angry and wildly free.

In the morning, Alexis woke Saturnine and led her through the thick brush to a clearing, a quiet pond, an offshoot of the river. Alexis took off her wrap and loincloth, and Saturnine undressed, and they faced the glossy water. Alexis climbed a rock and curling her legs beneath her jumped into the deep pool. Saturnine made a slow attempt at descending along the steep bank and slid in the mud until she was immersed in the depths of the warm milky water. The water covered them in its velvety moistness, and they were silent and absorbed, floating and gazing into the sky. They climbed out of the river by grabbing onto a branch, and they lay on their clothes drying in a bath of sun, Alexis thin and muscular, her skin smooth and soft, Saturnine thin but more full-bodied. Naked, they wandered upriver and found a spot with lush green grass near water trapped by rocks that formed a small waterfall. Alexis laid her clothes on the mossy undergrowth and took out hard dried meat from her sack.

Saturnine laid back. "These men," she said. Alexis, she suspected, had been making love to one or more man each night.

"It's a part of the purification and the luminosity."

Saturnine felt heavy. The world slipped away for a time.

That night, Saturnine drank the liquid, and smoked, and joined the dance. She lifted her arms and let her body be swept into the rhythm. She was alive to darkness, she made love to it. Tears streamed down her face. Someone came from the outside world. She heard gasps and happy exclamations, but it didn't concern her, and she didn't look up. The music stopped. She raised her head. Kharapan stood at the edge of the circle, a hand on his walking stick. She stared. She approached him, leaning oddly to one side. She grasped his hand and fell sobbing at his feet.

BOOK VI

ONE

WE ARRIVE AT my last book—which will end in and with Hellenica. There is no need to go on, back to Rome, where all is recorded as history by the conquerors. I put down my own words, but words possibly only for myself, to mark time, to pass time. In any event, I can no longer put off the rest, the end so to speak.

Kharapan had arrived in Hellenica on *Venus*, the day before he saw Saturnine. In speaking to the officials of Hellenica, Kharapan reflected on how natural and easy it felt to speak to the people of Chi, his countrymen. He told of the 'challenge' and how Lupicinus freed him. He did not need to explain what he meant. They did not think him mad. He didn't know what that outcome amounted to and had to admit that he'd never met anyone so tenaciously attached to an idea. Kharapan said the Church might come. He couldn't be sure of Lupicinus or how their conversation affected the man. Still, he found it hard to imagine the energy they'd have to exert to come to Chi, gathering forces and traveling—and yet, all Lupicinus had to do was give the word. Soldiers needed activity. He didn't like it, he wished it weren't so. He couldn't say more one way or another. The officials looking into it had heard nothing so far.

Kharapan learned of Thaddeus's death. Besides being pained, he imagined how alone Saturnine must feel. He was anxious to go to her. He heard other things—how she'd met with Metis, about her idea of "waves," and her friendship with Alexis. The villagers seemed to take a keen interest in Saturnine. Some said they thought she grappled with a terrible question. Others who'd seen her wandering at night thought she struggled with a heavy sorrow.

Saturnine surprised him, nearly naked, partly covered in ash, moving with the heavy beat in a kind of agony, due, he had no doubt, at least in part, to wine and opium. In her sobs at his feet, she had repeated Metis's name. Alexis had guided her to her tent, and when Kharapan looked in, she had been asleep.

Saturnine awoke confused, disoriented, happy—Kharapan, she thought she'd dreamt of him. But when she looked out of her tent, she saw him sitting by the fire. She approached and sat down next to him. Their eyes met. They struggled to speak and were glad.

"So the Church will not come," Saturnine said after a time. "You won your challenge."

"I don't know," he said. "I'll tell you what I can."

Kharapan asked if she'd return to the Great Village with him. As Saturnine prepared to go, she reflected on her discussions with Metis and her decision. Even if the Church did not come, the threat existed. Kharapan wouldn't understand or agree with what she thought necessary. He had a gentle way but was innocent and naïve. He had survived, yes, but it didn't mean that one should not react to the violence of the Church and Rome or try to stop them by any means possible. And yet, although she would not have been able to express it, she felt a softening, as if a light hovered over her thoughts, a light like a thousand transparent dots making everything hazy.

Walking back to the Great Village with Kharapan, Saturnine had many questions and felt much, and hovered near much that could not be said, so that she didn't know how to begin. But Kharapan spoke first. He said he'd heard about Thaddeus. He told her how he'd met Thaddeus in the hills outside of Rome and of Thaddeus's wonder about Saturnine and the story of her life. Saturnine regretted. It seemed that her life had consisted of a series of events that had stolen away time: the time she might have had with Kharapan, the time she might have spent with a mother, the love and life she might have had with Philo, the companionship she might have had with Thaddeus. What sort of person would she have been if she'd had Kharapan as a friend? The question was not new to her. The future, too, seemed to have little room, little chance for her to become what she might naturally and fully be, whatever that was.

Kharapan grew silent. Then, gently, said that he tried to imagine what her life must be like now, the pain over Flavia's death, Thaddeus's death, and having left everything she knew—Rome, her husband, her home. "What must it be like for you now," he said, "here, in a land so strange to you?"

Saturnine couldn't immediately respond. She suddenly said, "I read *Kingdoms*."

Kharapan smiled and shook his head. He remembered that he'd given it to her that night. "And so you've met Metis." Saturnine was about to speak, but he continued. "Metis has a peculiar struggle. She has a power, intelligence mixed with vision, but she hasn't succeeded with herself. There's narrowness in her that blocks out the fullness of the world. She's a lot like Lupicinus," he added.

He wasn't curious about Saturnine's discussions with Metis. He didn't remember that he hadn't told Saturnine his own story involving *Kingdoms*; he'd imagined so thoroughly what he'd wanted to tell her that he'd forgotten he'd never had the chance. Looking at her now, at her pursed lips and determined expression, Kharapan thought that perhaps Metis had said something to Saturnine that had confused her.

"You mentioned Metis last night," he said.

Saturnine, abashed, couldn't remember what she'd said about Metis. His words frightened her, not least his comparison of Metis to Lupicinus.

Kharapan thought he'd embarrassed her and so turned the conversation to Rome. Besides the rest, he told her about Lupicinus's project on the study of myth and his view that Christian religion and doctrine represented a synchrony of the myths of the time and land.

Saturnine smiled. "Even I found hundreds of gospels in your libraries."

"The point," he said, "is that Lupicinus carries out his core in spite of himself and in spite of the self he shows to the world. He prepares a work, probably of genius, that would benefit the rational creature, and in this he touches that sliver of integrity. He has not lost himself wholly and entirely, not his love, the passion that keeps one alive to the highest functions of man. But in spite of this," Kharapan shook his head, "we are all capable of failure. We fail to follow our passion. We become distorted and degraded, depraved. He fears with his whole being following the path of integrity! He thinks it will ruin him, because he has not chosen that path and is already old."

"But what will we do about the threat?" Saturnine said. "How can we protect Chi?"

Kharapan was thoughtful. He said that if the Church came, he suspected Lupicinus would be with them, and he hoped to have a chance to talk to him, even to introduce him to Chi.

Saturnine was amazed: this was his plan?

Besides, he went on, who could say what would happen if armies came. Some people might die. Some buildings might burn. One couldn't stop movements that loomed large and dramatic.

Saturnine was astounded. *Mars*, she thought. Metis's debate. The day would decide everything.

They walked in silence. Kharapan smiled at her and told her how glad he was to find her in Chi. Perhaps he'd believed even then, that night in Rome when Philo died, that she'd go to Chi one day. He felt sorry, however, about the circumstances that made her leave Rome. Saturnine smiled weakly through all of this and didn't contradict him, though his words pained her.

Kharapan found Metis sitting outside her hut in the dry sun. She gave him her peculiar thin smile, filled with irony and bitterness. He knew his gentle looks and words aggravated her. Still, he came. Still he sat with her, now as he had in the past.

"So, you've lived. Do you think you won your challenge?" she said. "We're safe from the Church now."

He sat across from her, knees bent, arms resting on his knees. So she knew what had happened with Lupicinus and the challenge. He hadn't come to talk about his experiences in Rome.

"So. You're keeping informed about your old friend," he said.

She scowled and looked away.

"I have to say it directly," he said. He paused. She didn't look at him. "I heard things. Rumors. Terrible and strange. About murder in the monasteries. I thought you might have heard something. You work there."

She wasn't looking at him, but he could see her suppress a smile.

"What has it to do with you?" she said, staring at him, holding his eyes. Kharapan searched her eyes, her face.

"Everything will be revealed on *Mars*," she said as if suddenly tired. She seemed to turn inward and go still.

"What does that mean? What do you have to reveal?"

"I reveal what I know," she said. "I'll take part in a debate on *Mars*," she added. "My first in twenty years."

A low sun spread across a yellow land. Knowledge played at the edge of Kharapan's awareness without penetrating like the sunlight on the sand. Did he know something that he refused to know? Was she leading him—them—to some terrible place, or teasing him, trying to scare him? He felt he knew her. As strange, as distant as she liked to remain, she had a devotion to words and he guessed that the thing she would reveal had to do with her life work, her study of Christians, her written revelations. She would publish her work. It pleased her to make him think she was a murderer, he thought.

So she'd publish again, he thought, and join in the life of the city. He hoped it wouldn't coincide with the coming of armies, or even one monk, if they came at all. He knew the power of her work. It might incite the people of Chi into a useless, hopeless violence.

For the rest of *Sol* and on *Luna*, Kharapan introduced Saturnine to his country. He took her to an Aristotelian lecture on the study of ants, and a Stoic discourse by the new, well-loved master. They sat in the Epicurean Garden, where Philodemia, an old woman now, charmed Saturnine to tears in spite of her strange mood. They had dinner with philosophers in an intimate setting in the domus of one of Kharapan's friends. On Luna, they swam in the Nile River with children, laughing and playing, and sat in the shade, watching the slow river pass. Time itself in Chi seemed to move slowly, perhaps due to the baking sun, the long days, the vast sky, and the slow, eternal swell of the Nile.

Laughing at something, Kharapan's hand touched Saturnine's. She felt a change within her, a dull surge like the

Nile. He took his hand away, and after a time they went to dinner and remained subdued for the rest of the evening. Saturnine sometimes caught a look in Kharapan's eyes, as if he had a question for her or as if something disturbed him. It caused her chest to hurt, made her look away. But it was impossible for him to know, she thought: he couldn't know of her plan to kill. She wished she could unburden herself of her secrets, even if she had to lower herself in his estimation. In any event, it wasn't possible—some of those secrets were secrets from herself.

TWO

METIS WALKED INTO the Great Hall on *Mars* with a scowl, her defiant eyes taking in the room. She was clean and wearing colorful clothes, her hair neatly arranged in a braid down her back. Many of Chi had come, many of her old Aristotelian masters, but they did not fill the huge room. At the front, she put two thick parchment manuscripts on a small table and waited.

People sat or stood and talked, looking at Metis as if at a strange animal.

"Who'll be the interrogator?" Metis said with an unaccustomed smile, a rare social effort.

"I'll do it myself," Papnute said. "Shall we begin?"

Everyone sat down and were quiet. An old man, a great master, Papnute rarely engaged in debate at the time, although he often led preliminary proceedings. A small man, he stood next to Metis in front of the two chairs that faced the audience.

"Welcome, Metis." She nodded. "I understand our topic is 'moral genius,'" he said.

"Yes, yes."

Saturnine's heart pounded. She could barely concentrate. Metis had a mad look about her. Saturnine wished to sit alone, but Alexis had come in and sat next to her. Saturnine was glad not to see Kharapan.

Papnute began with preliminaries. "Do you agree to be honest and open to possibility, that is, so we might each transcend our own view and reach a better understanding?"

"I agree."

"I agree as well. Do you agree to speak about what you know from experience, and what you believe, and to be clear about what you don't know?"

Metis agreed.

"Good. Tell me, what is the meaning of 'moral genius'? I have no idea." Papnute sat down.

Alexis whispered to Saturnine that this was Papnute's acting position, that he knew nothing.

Saturnine bristled. It was the last time Alexis spoke, however, for events followed that left even Alexis speechless.

"The moral genius," Metis said, a hand on her codex. "The moral genius I speak of is a new character that exists in response to the modern world. This moral genius can't help but recognize great evil. She sacrifices her good life and happiness to fight it. She risks her life and sacrifices the lives of others. This moral genius, unknown to the good people of Chi, is a type of creature engaged in a way of life that must be introduced to you, that must become known." She paused.

"I say it now and directly: this moral genius has an obligation to kill."

Some gasped, others laughed. Saturnine took in a deep, audible breath.

Metis went on, oblivious. "The moral genius recognizes war and undertakes the only means of battle open to her, acting alone and in secret. But she must make others aware of what she can't help but see. Her knowledge, her insight, is so real, so terrible, that she wakes every morning in awe at the enormity of the evil and at what must be done, what she must do."

She looked into the faces of those of Chi, most of whom she knew by name. "She must fight, fight or let her beloved disbelievers be killed by fanatic hatred and rage…." She broke off as her voice rose. She cautioned herself. They must not think her words, her acts, those of a madwoman.

"Can it be…" Papnute said, sitting straight up in the chair, "you describe a kind of misery. Is not good feeling a moral guide?"

"Yes, for most mortals, good feeling, even happiness, is intimate with moral life. Immorality is pain, is the open wound, and leads to dissatisfaction, ignobleness, and unhappiness. Yes, I know!" she cried. She knew their language but had superior knowledge. "Good feeling in the case I speak of, for the type of moral genius I speak of, is not possible. The moral genius I speak of," she said, "transcends the ordinary mortal and can never be happy."

"I wake in the morning," Papnute said. "I go to work with my hands. I take care of my children and my wife and make sure they have food and shelter. I'm careful in my decisions. I avoid acting in ways that'll shame me."

"You're an ordinary mortal. No moral genius."

Many laughed, but it was a tense sound. Saturnine saw Kharapan at the door. He watched Metis with a grave face. Saturnine looked away and didn't look back.

"Was Socrates a moral genius?" Papnute said. "He is wise because he knew nothing. He must have recognized great evil in the world, but I am not aware of his need to kill."

"Ah!" Metis cried. "Yes." A slight ironic smile came to her lips when she noticed Kharapan, but she avoided looking at him. "Socrates is not our modern man. He does not face the threat of a Christian power that wants to control our very thoughts."

"Do we say that a moral man is a happy man, a happy man a moral man, and that Socrates was happy?"

"The happiest man that ever lived."

"And yet, you claim your moral genius can never be happy, she throws away happiness and must throw it away in the face of the evil she sees and the acts she must commit, as you say. Explain: your moral genius and Socrates. I don't understand."

Metis smiled spitefully. "I honor Socrates," she said. "I honor the esteemed philosophers of Chi." She nodded to a few in the room. "But our time is new and terrible! We verge on an evil greater than any that has existed in the history of our species." A hand went out into the air, long spindly fingers spread wide. "The Orthodox Church wants to control the thoughts of rational creatures; it wants to own every mind. Never before have we faced a threat of this kind. The moral genius of Chi, born of Chi, knows—"

"You say 'knows,'" Papnute said gently. "What is this knowing? Is it possible that such a moral genius, as you call her, has too much faith in the power of her ability to know? Where is *agnosis* in her? Can you speak of *agnosis*?"

Metis gave Papnute an indulgent smile.

"Knowledge," she said, "is uncertain and fallible. We people of Chi are well versed in *agnosis*. We are in the unique position to understand, to grow up with, to live with the 'sliver of doubt,' with the illumination of *agnosis*, of what we don't know. We understand how the unknown informs us. *Agnosis* is wisdom and truth and beauty. But *agnosis* should not, must not, make us passive creatures. We must look out into the world, we must see what's before us, and we must act. Some creatures see with a depth that demands that they respond and live what appears to the people of Chi," she waved one thin arm at those present, "what appears to be a strange and tragic life." Her face looked strained as she looked out at their silent, attentive faces.

"As we know," she went on, "one's way of life, even that of the moral genius I speak of, is a model to others, even if she lives in isolation and has no friends, no allies, no one who believes. The moral genius I speak of, her life is harder to decipher. Only she is aware of the truth in the time of her life, but the time of history will reveal the truth of her moral genius."

Silence followed.

"As Epictetus said, in reference to Medea," Papnute said. "'What name do we give those who follow everything that comes into their mind? Madmen.'"

Metis twitched as if pained, her face contorted. "Yes," she said, "but Medea wasn't a moral genius. Medea thought she did right but went wrong. She was lost to passion and made no reasoned assessment of reality." Her eyes seemed to glow as she looked out into the room.

Papnute paused, and his voice sounded dull when he spoke. "Tell me what you know of murder," he said.

The form of the debate demanded this singular question. Metis must speak of what she knew from experience and had to be clear about what she did not know, a question he'd never had to ask nor heard asked in the sixty years or more of his long life.

Metis hesitated. Her heart pounded. "Let's take a hypothetical," she said. "Let's pretend, as a mere hypothetical, that Christian armies are coming to Chi this moment."

Everyone whispered, and nervous glances moved from face to face. Many looked to Kharapan, but he stared straight at Metis with a severe expression. Saturnine felt a guilty pang.

"It's a hypothetical," Metis cried.

She went on when it grew quiet. "Imagine that armies are on the way. What would we be speaking of? Surely not how good we are to our loved ones when we buy bread. People might agonize over what might have been if we'd seen the threat, if we hadn't been blind. Oh we might have tried to stop them, tried to stop war. We might have tried harder to go into the Empire to educate them on *agnosis*."

They stared at her, afraid but silent. Papnute, sensing the debate had become something different, something new, unheard of, went to sit in the front row, his arms crossed as if shielding himself.

Metis continued. "You thought I withdrew from the world. You thought I gave up my ideas about Christians. The truth is I lost faith in you, my people. I lost faith that you would be willing to give up your easy lives to fight." She paused and smiled angrily. "You didn't hear of a monastery in H. where the monks were sick after the morning meal. I poisoned them," she said with a smile, a gleeful look.

Questioning stares, glances between onlookers, horrified expressions. Saturnine watched Metis without expression.

"They thought it was an accident. An old monk was the only one to die," she said. "That was my first Trial. I call them Trials. They thought it was rotten food!" she said. "No one knew I killed." She paused; she noted the silence in the room.

"Is it true?" a man said, looking around. Many stood.

"It's not true," an old woman whispered. "Is it?"

"I'll tell you of the Trials, but I must say something first. You will want to hear what I have to tell you."

She waited for silence; those who had been standing sat down.

In the experience of her life, the future consisted of thought and theory; and the present, the span of a life, was made of the stuff of passion and obsession. In spite of what Metis believed about the future, in spite of her prophecies of a Christian Kingdom, and even a failed Christian Kingdom, she believed she had to do what she must in this life, this war.

"My life," she said, "has been spent in the sole desire and with the single purpose of saving Chi. My life's work is to save philosophy as a way of life. We, humanity, lived in the pursuit of wisdom from the earliest periods of history. We developed ideas of philosophy intimate to the way of life. But that way of life is at risk and, in fact, I believe is likely to disappear. I think it's inevitable. But one might try… one must try, one still has to live, even in the face of such modern evil. An unfortunate age…." She paused.

"I give the first reason for what I've done and had to do," Metis said. "Christians distort the natural morality of the rational creature. No Christian understands the natural morality she is born with as a human animal. I give a second primary reason: their Kingdom will result in oppression and cruelty. It will be a cruel world, full of violence. You know it from *Kingdoms*." She paused. "So I put poison in their food. They had to be sacrificed. The message wouldn't be clear otherwise. I planned how it would end, and I will tell all, but I say first: did murder ruin my life? It did. Planning, carrying out the Trials—yes, all good feeling, and any chance of happiness is destroyed for me. I stand before you, my people, to tell you all before they, the world out there, find out the truth. I want to speak directly, to explain how it began, but it's written…."

Metis smiled at them as if at schoolchildren. "I understood after I finished *Kingdoms* twenty years ago. The necessity became clear when the monk came to our village and Zeno struck him. He killed a monk. Zeno's act was noble. From that moment I understood what had to be done." She paused. "It took time to carry out the first act, before I saw that I must break from our humble unknown and simple ways and take on the fight. I was willing… I had no choice… I've worked in the monasteries most of my life. You claim one can't have absolute knowledge, but who else but me could have such

knowledge of them? I lived in their midst, studied their texts."
She looked out searchingly.

"The knowledge I obtained is here, all written," she said.
She took up a codex called "Theories" and opened it randomly
and read. "'The principal effect of Christianity is to increase
its power over people.' There are several examples in the texts,
but these are technical, and you will read them yourself.... It's
all here. Skipping ahead, 'The word imposes doctrines, and
controls the thoughts and behavior of its people. It threatens
our humanity.'" She flipped to a different section and read,
and then another, but it sounded dry and monotonous read
in this way, disconnected and out of context. Metis closed the
book and set it down.

"Trial Three," she said.

Saturnine couldn't stop herself: her eyes went to the door,
but Kharapan had gone.

Metis told them in mocking bitterness that she'd decided
to rid the Christians of a saint. It suited her purpose. It was
symbolic. Indeed, she said, the saints might call her one of
their devils, one of the devils in the desert, but she was flesh
and blood. We aim to avoid the disaster of the end of religion
and the immorality of Christian atheists, she said. Killing
the emaciated saint in a cave wouldn't do as much as she'd
wished. The mourners were as happy, perhaps happier, with
his bones. "Relics they called them!" She paused. "There can
be no freedom until Christianity is destroyed."

Many stood as if to go.

"Trial four," Metis said loudly, and those who had stood
sat down.

It took over a year to determine and carry out her next act, she told them. She began to stake out the one who upheld the rules, the moral principles, the one called the Delegate. Metis watched him and wandered their halls. "He had a kindly face, a paternal, dignified expression…"

She was a familiar figure in their monasteries, ordinary and polite; she dressed neatly, and they admired her brilliant mind. No one connected her to these crimes. Of course, in the months she was in Chi, she was a different creature, deep at work with her papers, copying and preparing the texts, and devising her Trials, and could hardly bear to speak to anyone.

Metis suddenly felt weak. The room was silent. The silence became like a weight. Those in the room had bewildered, frightened faces. She leaned against the table. "The Delegate's eyes," she said, "his eyes, the look of understanding, those words between us…." She'd had to work two more days after killing him. She'd heard them speak of his murder. Some were glad. The Delegate planned to cut the Monastery's funds. All of the monks were suspects.

As she spoke to the people of Chi, she sounded mad, even to herself. As she spoke, as she described her Trials, her acts sounded both brutal and pointless. Her murders would not affect the course of history. She'd wanted to accomplish more, to kill more. But she'd known all along she couldn't stop them, that the Church would have its Kingdom.

She looked around and smiled.

"You think I'm mad. You'll say that Chi could not have produced me. But I tell you that only Chi could have produced me. I am a moral genius, forsaken by sight, by vision. I'm the pure atheist who alone understands the evil of the Church, and since no one would listen, I had to act alone, and I didn't fail in my duty so much as I shattered and destroyed myself."

People began to stand, but others had come, and the Great Hall began to fill, people standing in the back.

"You'll want to hear the end," she said. Her barely audible voice had great effect, many sat down.

In some of her Trials, as she called them, no one even knew there'd been a murder, as she'd said, such as when she poisoned the monks. In other Trials, the Christians knew someone had been killed but didn't know why or by whom. The conclusion—they had to learn the truth, she said. She had to send out copies of the texts.

"Impossible," someone said. Many spoke at once, others quieted them, saying let us hear.

Metis said that her final plan included speaking to her countrymen. She'd planned the end of her secret war for years, even from the beginning. Of course, a secret war would be meaningless, entirely meaningless, if no one learned what she'd done and her purpose. This "end of her plan," however, never seemed to come. She'd be on the verge of sending out her work when a new Trial would fill her, a new idea that she would be powerless to stop. Each new plan gave her a secret, intense thrill, a new desire.

"But when Saturnine came, a woman of Rome," Metis said. "She provided news of the Church of Rome. It was a sign. I would finally carry out the end of my plan."

Many turned to look at Saturnine. Her body burned and she stared straight ahead.

The people of Chi, Metis went on, believed she'd stopped writing after *Kingdoms*, but she was deep in the *Great Twofold Work*. Metis swatted a fly near her face. There was a deep silence in the room.

She went on. *Theories* contained her ideas, essays, sentences whittled, sculptured phrases under topics such as Mad Desert Saints; Obsequious bishops and popes; The Desperate Worshiper; Lost Monks and Nuns; Monster Jesus; Christian Atheists; The Kingdom; Death of Religion; the Vacuous Future. She unveiled them, removed their disguises, she said. She exposed the so-called saints, how their self-imposed deprivation and poverty disguised their egotistic desire to be the most virtuous of all. She revealed the bishops, to whom Christianity and hierarchy gave an invisible cloak of goodness so that even the jewels they wore couldn't betray their love of money and power. The Church had its monster in Christ, and turned people into monsters who strove, pretended even to themselves to strive, for impossible moral perfection while raging against nonbelievers. "I could hardly breathe as I translated their contemptible texts, as I wrote about their Kingdom of God. But I had my own words, our words, and I laid their monstrosities bare."

The codex she called *Life* was not comparable, she said… for there she documented each Trial.

"But the keystone," she said. The keystone was the act of revealing all, of sending the *Great Twofold Work* out into the world, to Empire, and speaking to her countrymen. She needed to show the world what had been necessary, why those men had had to die.

Metis groaned inwardly and gave a pained laugh. It would have been a miserable irony, she said, if she'd failed to take the last step. The murders would be without meaning. And the people of Chi would never understand, never know her genius, never know how she'd sacrificed and engaged in an impossible struggle for her country, for humanity.

Metis went on, heedless of the pained shocked faces: "You have not been told, but the Church imprisoned Kharapan, and the accusations they made against Kharapan extend to Hellenica. The Church thinks the people of Chi are criminals. They are on their way with armies." She raised a hand to silence them. "There is more. There is still more." She paused, waiting for silence.

"Five days ago," she said, "I sent my *Great Twofold Work* into the world: *Theories* and *Life*. The world will know the truth of what I've done and will understand why Christians had to die. I've sent the *Great Twofold Work* to monasteries, and to the bishop of Alexandria. I've sent it to those who will be sympathetic, too; there will be some who read the *Great Twofold Work* and may join our fight. I've fought this war for you, my people, and all of you will have your revenge before you meet your deaths at their hands. But I wasn't able to stop them." She looked out beseechingly, as if to find some acknowledgement of her sacrifice and good deeds.

Someone asked what she meant. It seemed as if no one could believe or understand what she was saying. Metis put her hand on the manuscripts and said again that the two codices documented the theories and the murders she'd committed and that she'd sent them out with a messenger five days ago. The bishop of Alexandria likely had them in his hands that moment.

"It tells of your murders?"

"Yes! Everything."

"Then you destroy us!" someone said.

They stood, bewildered.

Someone yelled out, "Arrest her!"

Confusion and chaos followed. People surrounded Metis. Saturnine saw two men grab Metis's boney arms. But she didn't resist. She seemed limp, puppet-like in their hands. Saturnine heard, or thought she heard above the din, Metis's voice, "You'll see, you'll see, you'll be glad of me, glad as you draw your last breath."

THREE

THE VILLAGE WAS in uproar. Metis was imprisoned. The people of Chi filled the Great Hall: philosophers, merchants, farmers, the seven officials of Chi. Metis had her crowd. Some argued that Metis wasn't wrong if, in fact, the Church came with an army. Old disputes rose. Some said Metis's life proved that Aristotelians were at risk of being lost to the overwhelming power and seduction of the life of the mind. Stoics and Epicureans agreed. Epicureans advised against pure episteme, knowledge studied for its own sake, and said Aristotelians lacked wisdom, the wisdom that came from paying close attention to the way of life. Aristotelians disowned Metis. Some blamed Epicureans for withdrawing from society and providing an inappropriate model of life. In spite of all the arguments, everyone was pained and afraid, angry and sad.

Looking back at the threads that led to Hellenica's destruction, to the destruction, at last, of that ancient Hellenic culture, philosophy as a way of life, is a wonder to me. I jump ahead, I can't help myself. Theodosius's Edict might be said to be the formal statement that marked the change, a Christian Empire to come, the end of contrary thought, making the end of Hellenica inevitable. On the other hand, one might say, Metis brought the end to Chi. Metis went into Empire and wreaked havoc. Then, Saturnine! the woman of our age, the one who would become Saturnine *atheos* of Alexandria, an icon to disbelievers, known all over the relevant part of the world, exemplifying *agnosis* as a way of life. Like Hypatia, icon of paganism—both violently killed by Christians, destroyed, so to speak, along with their work within decades of each other, events that marked the end of *agnosis* and paganism, respectively. This woman, Saturnine, touched the flaming torch to the pyre laid in Chi, leading Metis to the end of her plan. Saturnine *atheos* of Alexandria might be said to have helped destroy Hellenica and philosophy as a way of life itself. And Kharapan, who dared to speak his mind in Empire, and carry Metis's text there, not to mention Lupicinus's role in events that unfolded.

It is of the latter that I must now speak.

On the ship to Alexandria, Lupicinus had not come to a decision about Hellenica. He might not have gone to General Kastor, might not have led an army to Hellenica. But when he arrived, the church of Alexandria spoke of nothing but Hellenica and Metis, and combined with the events involving Kharapan in Rome—which those churchmen he'd traveled with knew enough about—Lupicinus had no choice. No choice whatsoever. Lupicinus even tried to convince them otherwise: he argued that Metis acted alone and was clearly insane, that Hellenica had been a peaceful country for hundreds of years, causing no trouble to Rome. But the Church would not bend: they feared the wild ideas of Hellenica, a place left on its own for too many years. They wanted to incorporate Hellenica into Empire and establish a church there. And so they did.

But one might say these individuals of whom I speak, whom I write about, we are caught in a web, pawns of history, and who can say why or for what purpose, if any? Individuals are alive, institutions are not, but man's nature seeps into his institutions, *homo homini lupus*.

Church and army destroyed the last vestiges of Hellenism, those people living as philosophers, philosophy a way of life, on the edge of the world. Perhaps lived philosophy is lost to history. In our time, in our institutions, philosophy is a subject one studies; one takes notes and memorizes texts but does not live philosophy as a way of life. To state it more correctly, around the time Chi was destroyed, some in Empire lived philosophy as a way of life. They were outsiders, outcasts, perhaps. But many years later, still in my own time, I do not know and have not heard of any person living that life, living or thinking of philosophy as a way of life, although I heard a rumor of a secret society living philosophy as a way of life in the desert where old Hellenica once stood.

In my time, near the end of my life—it must be near at last, for I am very old—what I've always known, suspected, one might say, has come to pass. Christianity, Orthodox Christianity, is the way of life. There is no other.

Soldiers burned the schools of philosophy in Hellenica along with their libraries, likely destroying many of the last codices to exist in the world. But they might have overlooked the Study.

I will tell what happened in the Study. I mean to reveal all in this chronicle. I do not want to leave room for any misunderstanding, if this chronicle is ever read, about what happened.

Lupicinus, in the Study, holding a codex in his trembling hands, felt his presence before he saw him. He looked up. Kharapan was watching him. In spite of the fires above, schools burning even then, he wore a grim smile, and it seemed to Lupicinus that no time had passed since they'd last seen each other in that other dank underground place. And as if simply continuing their last conversation, Lupicinus raised the scroll and said, "It's an original Josephus. The paragraph about Jesus Christ is absent, must have been inserted by the Church fathers hundreds of years later. And not only this, but I've discovered so much here, so many works we thought destroyed long ago! Here is the source of myth." His thin arm gestured vaguely at the rows of codices and scrolls.

"You only need to stay and finish your work," Kharapan said intently, seriously, with a smile, as well.

Lupicinus smirked, then frowned. He might have thought: here Kharapan and I speak of what isn't spoken in the real world, but here what we say, the fact of speaking, is a fantasy, a menippea. And out there—fires burned.

Kharapan sat down on one of the hard wooden chairs and crossed his hands in his lap. "It's your job to act as you must," he said. "You think you've come to destroy us."

Lupicinus didn't answer, but his thoughts shifted. He

put the codex down. He saw something new in Kharapan—a sense of confidence, of maturity, perhaps; a certain sense of experience and responsibility but also something more: an utter calm.

When Lupicinus didn't speak, Kharapan spoke of Metis's crimes and his shock and said that finding out what Metis had done was like reading *Kingdoms* that first time, an extension of that experience, for here was another life experience, one that shaped him.

"Indeed," Kharapan said, smiling at Lupicinus but with a serious look. "It turns out that you and I are models of our countries. A conversation between us exposes not only ourselves but our worlds. I was internally focused to the point of blindness, ignorantly waiting to be pained and shocked by some external truth, by Metis and her crimes, which had been going on for years. While for you, the outside world is all and directs you, but you fail to know yourself or give weight to feeling, and your inner pain grows. We are blind in different ways, you and I."

Lupicinus sighed, pausing and turning over the ancient document in his hand.

"I once hoped for an integrity that would defy death… but it turns out that life was my challenge," Kharapan said. "I should have struggled for an integrity that defied life. I might have been able to stay in Chi far earlier… But no matter. I am here now."

He went on, as if speaking to himself. "There's a Stoic *askesis*, an exercise: we imagine difficulties in advance—suffering, death. We hope that even the most painful things are lessened by foresight and become old worn-out things. But I who imagined myself prepared, failed, or refused to see…."

Lupicinus watched Kharapan carefully.

"In any event," Kharapan said, suddenly solemn, referring to something deeply important that Lupicinus didn't understand at first. What Kharapan said was something like this: "There is a weakness I have never been able to overcome, knew I never would, and did not even want to, nor did I bother to speak to my closest master about. It is not surprising to me now."

These words disturbed Lupicinus, but he couldn't grasp why until he saw that it was this: Kharapan now spoke as if his struggle were over. Kharapan could not live, did not want to live, without Chi. He was pronouncing his own epitaph.

Lupicinus stood at an angle to the other man, and when he heard Kharapan pause, he walked behind him. He touched the tip of the knife in his pocket, as if to reassure himself of its sharpness. And yet, as he touched his knife, he felt that same dramatic excess, life failing him in not being up to the drama of his imagination, his life consisting of some great and ultimately disappointing illusion. But he could not stop. Even if he'd wanted to save Kharapan in some way, it was too late. Events in the world had gotten beyond him, beyond Lupicinus. He had to finish what he'd come to do, what he'd known all along he had to do. In short: Lupicinus could not let Kharapan be killed by soldiers, strangers, people who did not love him. Nor did Kharapan want to be saved when Chi was destroyed. Lupicinus had a duty, a last terrible duty.

It was a kind of embrace.

Standing behind Kharapan, Lupicinus sensed Kharapan stiffen slightly, but he didn't move or turn to look at him.

"Why don't you stop me," Lupicinus said, his voice high and strange.

Kharapan didn't turn around. "It is up to each man to destroy his life or not," he said. "Still. I don't want to destroy a life, not even yours, but…."

He glanced back, and in his look Lupicinus saw a gentle expression, although later he didn't know if he'd seen anything or only imagined that look. At the time, he remembered thinking Kharapan had spoken his mind. That is, Lupicinus imagined, was certain at the time, that Kharapan had given him, Lupicinus, permission, an acknowledgement of what must be. Hellenica must be destroyed and Kharapan could not and did not want to live without Chi, for without it he had no place in the world. Kharapan acknowledged all of this and chose, specifically chose, to die at Lupicinus's hands, at the hands of the man of Rome, like a mirror of or shadow to Kharapan's life. He acknowledged in his gaze, too, how terribly sad it was for Lupicinus to have to carry out this act, to have to live with what he would do, along with all he had done.

It was so. Lupicinus lived on. All of this in Kharapan's words and expressions might have been in Lupicinus's imagination. He could never reconcile the truth, not even to himself.

After it was over, Lupicinus ordered, or rather suggested to General Kastor, that the Study be destroyed, noting the underground library. Even with the destruction of the Study, the Study and what took place there would never leave his thoughts, and that is how it should be, I do not deny it. Pain and suffering of an almost unbearable kind, arising from a man's terrible acts, is essential to man, that is to such a man as Lupicinus himself was.

Lupicinus watched the thick smoke rising from Hellenica at a distance as he rode up the Nile. He had a book in his pocket: Josephus's manuscript, as if absence, the lack of a few words, could unveil Rome's illusion.

FOUR

THE OFFICIALS OF Chi convened after Metis's "debate," and two agreed to go to Alexandria. They hoped to stop a war. In the hourless night, five officials read Metis's documents and questioned people, including Metis, Kharapan, and Saturnine.

Saturnine told them everything: how she'd read *Kingdoms* and believed she was fated to meet Metis, how she told Metis about the Church and Kharapan's discussions with Lupicinus, though Kenyon had advised against telling. She told them how she'd agreed to join Metis in her scheme to murder the bishop of Rome. The officials asked how much she knew of Metis's Trials, about which Saturnine said she knew nothing. They told her to wait outside. When they called her back, they told her she must leave Hellenica. They said it was for her safety as well as for the benefit of Hellenica. If the Church found her in Hellenica, it might seem as if they, the people of Hellenica, were in conspiracy with her. The pope's church itself might be looking for her. They gave her two days to organize her affairs.

Saturnine returned to the Study. Sitting on her rolled mattress on the floor, standing to pace, sitting again, she fell into deep anguished reflection. So her days in Chi passed like this! She had come to Chi only to play a key role in its destruction! as if she were caught in a terrible world destiny.

At the time, in the Study, Saturnine felt as if she'd been shaken awake. Still, I believe events in Hellenica, and all of what I've related in this chronicle, formed her. She became that woman of Alexandria after the events I relate. Kharapan would likely have claimed that Saturnine had that core, was born with that peculiar passion, as each of us has our own particular passion. I might say, one is born with a certain character, but that character might be crushed by the world, or it might thrive, or it might find a small light, might wriggle through, if some are stunted like a tree in a pygmy forest of which I've heard rumor. Saturnine would likely not have become who she became had she stayed in Rome, married to Victorinus. Tragic events, others, encountering, confronting her own potential for evil, might be said to have saved her, or at least shaped her. She returned to Empire, and she knew how to live her life there.

Metis had startled Saturnine as if from a dream. Saturnine had watched a play, a theater of life in the Great Hall. Sitting in the audience, listening to and watching Metis, she'd felt alive, a sensation she'd perhaps never experienced so vividly. A play watched in the dark of a theater can expose life more vividly than the long slow days of ordinary life. Those vague feelings Saturnine had had since leaving Rome and reading *Kingdoms* on the ship, that perhaps she'd had most of her life, those dreamlike feelings, half awake, half blind, acute after Thaddeus's death—they vanished entirely. Watching Metis, listening to the life before her, imagining Metis's days, the Trials, the writing, the isolation, the obsession—Saturnine had never felt so much at attention, never felt she understood so well.

In this form of expression that perhaps only existed in Chi, Saturnine experienced what her life might have been and might yet be. She felt much confusion and uncertainty, but as she watched Metis, she knew at least this: that she wasn't witnessing a strange, unusual life. She watched her own life, as if she were granted the gift of being allowed to peer into a future life and see what it looked like.

Metis! her whole life! Her so-called Trials had little power to sway the church, little power over history. Her *Theories* might have gathered forces of disbelievers but the Trials…. And yet, in the backdrop to Metis and all she had done, the Empire itself would likely come with forces and violence and murder. Kharapan himself sometimes seemed mad to her, given the state of the world. A part of her felt an angry pride in Metis and what she'd done. It made her burst out in angry laughter. The Orthodox Church, with its claim over the thoughts of men and its right to determine the legality or illegality of thought, was an unbearable evil. And for such a church, such an Empire, to threaten a place like Chi, a man such as Kharapan! But, immediate and powerful in her was a terrible, crushing but also enlivening and humbling sense of her own blindness and faults. This sensation, even the thought of it, would serve to remind her of inner danger for the rest of her life. She had never had such a clear sense of herself and the choices before her for her life, or perhaps to say that she had no choice. She recognized that now.

Baseness, a lack of understanding of oneself, could even lead to murder! to the destruction of entire worlds—so it seemed to her. One man might cause pain and destruction, blunder about in folly, never to know integrity. This shame was of a kind that seeing herself, immersed in a life of weakness and folly, she could barely endure. The failure to have integrity, the disgust with oneself, was, she supposed, the true danger Kharapan alluded to and of which he had tried to warn her about.

She breathed and had some sense of where she started, must start from, knew one might find oneself so deep in the darkness of the sea's depths. Her struggle and immediate aim consisted only in struggling for a chance to see some glimmer of light beneath the waves. Either Rome kills us, or we destroy our own humanity: this was the choice Saturnine faced; this is how she might have framed the question. And she knew the answer, the only possible answer.

She'd only arrived at this understanding when her chance of learning from the way of life of Chi, from the philosophic schools, was likely lost forever. It was unbearable. She believed in her heart that the Church and its armies would come. Yes, they surely would come, and she had played an evil hand in that destruction. Would she lose Kharapan?—she burst into tears. She was so far, far down in the darkness of the sea.

Saturnine feared that when Kharapan discovered her role in events, he would be sick at heart. Still, in spite of everything, in spite of herself and circumstances, she expected Kharapan to come to her at the Study. But he did not.

When the second day had almost passed, Saturnine,

knowing she had to leave and feeling keenly how little she deserved an audience with him, sought out Kharapan. She found him at the Stoic school. His room was filled with people. The people wanted him to explain what had happened in Rome, what his situation had been at the church. They wanted to know what he thought or knew about Metis. They all talked at once, and among themselves, and as some left, still others came. Kharapan saw her and moved through the crowd and stood next to her.

"I need to speak, and they need this from me," he said. "Tonight, in the Great Hall, I will speak. I don't know what I will say. Something. Everything, I suppose." He paused. "Come tonight. We'll talk in private tomorrow."

"I have to leave Chi," she was able to say, unable to stop the tears. "I am supposed to leave today."

"Stay until tomorrow. No one will object or notice. We are all absorbed."

It seemed to her that Kharapan didn't yet fully understand her role in events, and this terrified her. She had to be sure he knew, would not leave without making sure he knew everything. She told him she would stay and hear him speak at the Great Hall. She, like all the people of Chi, needed to listen to his voice, to hear what Kharapan would say. He turned from her and went out. Saturnine watched him and the crowd that followed, leaving her alone in silence.

FIVE

I HAVE A record of the night Kharapan spoke in the Great Hall. The people of Chi were people of the record, of texts, of codices: people of the word. So it happens their records help me tell this tale.

I give only highlights of Kharapan's talk. By now, dear reader, if ever there should be a reader of this text, we likely already know something of what Kharapan said, something of the life and events he spoke of to the people of Chi. Still, in studying these pages, I feel as if I am witness to Kharapan's transformation. One can almost hear and feel the moment when he turns from being that inner-focused man, turns from his inner dream, and takes his place among the people of Hellenica, a man in full. Perhaps he did not undergo a transformation. Perhaps he simply took his place as a natural leader of Hellenica. His inner view, one might say, made him a natural leader of Hellenica, a great man, particularly then, at the end of that way of life. Perhaps, too, he could only be and become this man in this context, at this terrible time. I believe he understood that it was so in the end himself, as fateful or ironic as it might have seemed to him. And yet, the end, his and Chi's together, might have been what he sensed all his life, since he was just a servant boy seeking truth and sitting at his first teacher's feet.

People packed the Great Hall and overflowed out its doors. Kharapan sat in a small wooden chair in front. Someone put a cask of water and a cup on a table near Kharapan, and everyone took their seats or stood at the edge of the room. He remained silent for a long time. He looked out at them. He knew them, had grown up with them, the philosophers he had lived among, the merchants, those who had given him goods to sell. He had tears in his eyes.

At last, he spoke and the room grew quiet. "In Rome," he said, "I challenged a man named Lupicinus, a great church-man. I said our lives, his life, this powerful man of Rome, and mine, if we dared to speak of our lives, would reveal our countries, the places we were born and raised, the places that had formed us. I said our lives would prove which place was best for the rational creature." He paused. "I had a lapse of humility in saying this."

Some laughed. It's a wonder that one can laugh even in the worst of situations. The people of Chi, in particular, had a way of laughing. I witnessed it myself, even in the end.

"I realized it almost immediately," he said. "And yet..." He paused. He rubbed his face with his hands. "And yet, I didn't know then its extent, how true it was, the connection between my life and the life of Chi, in this way: my inner focus, my inability to see, or refusal to face a problem outside myself, even from my earliest years. And I mean Metis in part, or all she represents. Oh, I sensed a potential danger in her. I wasn't so blind or naïve, but I didn't fully see, or let myself see. I let myself fail to act, somehow, which I will explain. And these traits or this character might be the traits or character of our country, of Chi, its essence, and is a part of the luxury of Chi in which we live, which perhaps I will have a chance to speak of."

Someone yelled out: "Is this man, Lupicinus, the one who imprisoned you? How did you meet such a man?"

Kharapan paused. He saw the gravity of their faces and considered how little he knew—about everything, anything. He could give details of his life, of events, and not even a true record, for it was memory, confused and modified by reflection, distorted by his own view of it. But he knew that lies and sentimentality stained the race, like throwing a pail of ink over them. Lies stink and slither as something unnatural on one's skin. The rational creature knows it's day, and knowing it's day, even if not understanding the nature of sun, he can't call it night. It seemed that his whole life was relevant to what they wanted to hear. Perhaps this didn't surprise him. He felt all along, his whole life, that his life was intimate with the life of Chi, his breath the breath of Chi—but he had also ventured into Rome, and Rome helped him too to see Chi, to know Hellenica.

He told them that Lupicinus, indeed, had taken a principal role in his imprisonment. Lupicinus, he said, was the reason he was put into the church's prison, but it was a peculiar event, and he had to explain. He said they'd had a long conversation, the two of them, and then Lupicinus had freed him. He would tell all, he said.

It's here, this moment, or soon after, that I believe I noticed a change in Kharapan. He wasn't practiced in speaking to a crowd, wasn't even so practiced in speaking to his countrymen. His own countrymen could understand his way of life, understand the essential concepts Kharapan lived by, grasp why he believed he had to speak to Lupicinus, and the idea of the challenge between them. They would question him in the language of Chi. Kharapan did not care about position or being a leader of men. But it was precisely this that made him what he was. He had no thought of leading or proving himself. The gravity of events took away any possible self-consciousness in the act and left only substance, the necessary substance of what he needed to say and what they needed to hear. From this night, in spite of the responsibility some felt he had in events, and that he himself felt, Kharapan found himself at the center of Chi. People wanted to hear what he'd say, what he thought, his opinion on everything. Kharapan took his place in his country with seriousness and gravity, as well as a sense of burden and joy, yes joy. He recognized that this, the moment, these events, too, formed him. It seemed to him that his life had been a practice and preparation leading to this place he took among his people, this moment.

No one interrupted Kharapan again that night. I note that what involved Metis was, of course, at the time, a recent wound. The people of Chi couldn't understand, could hardly grasp what had happened. Kharapan himself didn't have an answer or know what he'd say. But he could speak of his experience and tell his thoughts of her. I note that the Great Hall is a huge room, in which voices resonated. I imagine Kharapan speaking that night, sitting on a small hard chair, looking out at the faces of Chi, at those in philosopher's cloaks, and others, listening and watching.

He told them he'd begun his life as a traveler and trader after a conversation with Arminius, the Stoic master, and this way of life, this conversation with Arminius, involved Metis even then.

"Arminius said I had humility," he said. "He said I might guide Metis and that humility had a certain power over hubris. This was when I was fourteen. I could not speak to Metis, not then. I had to leave Chi to become a man, as Arminius defined it, in order to speak to Metis."

Some laughed.

"But I didn't understand the true weight of that admonishment. In years that followed, I hardly spoke to Metis, or even to you, my countrymen, not with seriousness and purpose. I love Chi, and when I return, I feel so at ease, fall into what I love, what I hear and see. I needed Chi, needed to return, needed to hear the way people spoke, the way they laughed, to attend lectures. I needed this in order to be the man I was in Empire, to be able to travel into Empire at all. I never wanted to leave Chi, not when I was fourteen and never since. But I learned to recognize over the years, the way I seemed to fail to exist in Chi. I allowed myself to exist in the background. And so Chi, too, exists in this way, on the edge of the world. And so I had to leave Chi, to travel, so that the world would challenge me and build in me a measure of integrity." He paused, and breathed, looking now within.

"I might have tried harder to know Metis, to understand her strengths and her weaknesses, to argue with her and share myself with her. I might have listened as well to the knowledge and wisdom she offered. Together, Metis and I might have been a whole, we might have been a match, as Rome and Chi might have been as well. Instead, we went forward with the force of our own compulsions."

Kharapan closed his eyes and shook his head.

Earlier that day he'd gone to Metis in her prison cell. They'd been mostly silent, but her view, when she spoke, so confident, so narrow, seemed to him an extreme version of the narrowness of all views. A person might occlude complexity and come to conclusions, and perhaps this was madness, but if so, he'd thought, then everyone was mad. No, he thought, it was not madness but sickness. "There can be no freedom until he is overthrown," she'd said. Kharapan wondered who "he" was: God? Jesus? The pope? Kharapan looked at Metis's bony form, thinking it impossible for her to kill, but her dark eyes stared out with unfathomable rage, and something else more discordant: mirth. When he stood to leave, something changed in Metis. She seemed to see him and to offer him a real smile. "It's done," she said with certain wisdom. "My life has taken form, and who knows what choice we have?" She smiled and shrugged, looking away.

Kharapan told the people of Chi of Lupicinus and their conversations in the cell, even how he'd told him about Monk John's murder, and his reasons for telling. Whether they considered Kharapan a traitor or a hapless believer in some ideal, I don't know. Perhaps they felt, experienced, in this act,

Kharapan revealing Hellenica's guilt at long last, a murder of a monk, to the pope's church itself, as a kind of redemption of their country. That night they were silent. They listened. People rustled, made low murmurs, but remained mostly silent. There would be nights when Kharapan spoke little and many would argue, and they would attempt to make sense of the world, but that night silence filled the Great Hall.

Kharapan told them that he didn't know if Lupicinus would come to Hellenica, and if he did, whether he would come as a friend or with armies. Given what Metis did, perhaps it was even beside the point. He admitted he felt unsure of the tenacity of Lupicinus's mistaken nature. Lupicinus, he said, as mentioned, clung to a certain grand idea about civilization.

I relate a few items of note that Kharapan spoke about, those that might have had an affect on Saturnine too.

In a small country, he said, with inclination for discussion, one came to know or to know about almost everyone. The people of Chi thought they understood crime or knew if someone was likely to commit the same sort of crime, but a murderer had passed among them for some fifteen years. And yet an act of resistance can be right, he said. It might be the negation of a wrong. He paused, and perhaps struggled for a time.

A state is moral, he said, if it acts to prevent suffering, but it is not moral if it goes too far and oppresses its citizens and demands them to think a certain way. In such case, the state is immoral. A man in such a place has no choice but disregard the state and act as he must, think as he must. True, such a man will likely be killed. But that is the sad struggle of a citizen of such an immoral state. Man's moral being reigns supreme above all else, is what truly exists. The good man is a terrifying creature and contains in himself right and wrong itself. All authority bends to the good man and cannot conquer him, cannot even conquer that one man, the good man, the man who trains and prepares and practices. This is why we practice and study and train, to conquer even a terrible force like an immoral state. The good man terrifies the immoral state, and that is why the state must kill him, for he is too powerful, and his words reveal the true nature of the bad state.

But the immoral man, he said, the wrong man, gives the state a right over him. The wrong man is weak and unable to change the course of history or to have an affect on such a state. The church of Empire threatens our way of life. Christians threaten to impose on us. We've seen it and know it's true. But we must consider the individual engaged in the act of resistance and what she has done. Metis called what she did an act of war, but only a state can declare war." He paused.

"I speak beyond my powers—in this. I don't know how to understand or judge all that's happened. I have no doubt that discussions and debates will follow. But I note that in some worlds, people such as Metis and Lupicinus infiltrate the highest spheres of power, and their corrupted cores, corrupted by their failures to be guided by their cores, become the corrupted cores of institutions themselves. That is, a state itself and its institutions become a force of misery and suffering for citizens of that state. I say it's this that might distinguish Empire and Hellenica. Metis acted alone. Lupicinus is, represents, the institution of the Church. He has an institution, an Empire, behind him and his mistaken life. Lupicinus is Empire. Metis is not Chi."

He looked out at them, his eyes filling with tearful pride. "I feel it's deeply true—to come home to Chi is to find the happiest people on earth! Chi," he said, "small, self-absorbed… has the best of life: Aristotelians, heads down, struggle for knowledge. Stoics live the way of life, practice by living ordinary days, doing humble work. They ask us to accept fate. What they ask is beautiful, a beautiful life, and makes us imagine that our lives might also be beautiful. Epicureans engage in the art of friendship and enjoy pleasures in the garden among trees, listening to the river. And look at our systems too! We have the best food, the whitest flour. Our officials help gather the whole of us together in peace. But we do not have armies," he said. "We have not had to protect our way of life." He paused. "Some call Chi the last outpost of Hellenism. In any event, even if we had armies, what good would that be against the force of an Empire?"

Near the end of his talk, he seemed to fall into a kind of reverie. He said, "It's strange that these mistaken creatures, Metis, Lupicinus, formed me. Nothing has been a greater call to the good life than these ill-fated, wrong-turned lives. No one but Metis and Lupicinus taught me more about why I choose my way, why I need to practice and train. Mistake has fertilized my being, my very life, the way I see things." Kharapan seemed to regard this with amazement, hold it in front of his mind's eye.

Regardless of their poor lives, he said, this is what I want to tell you: if you find yourself in a position to die at their hands, then die! It's their work to kill and yours to die—don't waste time judging and don't hate them. Live well. Take care of your own good life. Do what you must to fight them. But die well. That'll take all of you. They have their misery. Lupicinus didn't know the good life he wasted. Those who haven't thrown away the good life, those who follow their core, can look and see that it's so. It's a tragedy that belongs more closely to Romans, this lack of wisdom, this vacuous painful being in the world, this failure to pay attention to the inner life and self. We've been lucky, for we live luxurious lives in Chi. Perhaps all people have that right or should have that right. I don't know. In some sense, this way of life involves a failure to see, a failure to look beyond ourselves, a failure to see the need to protect our way of life.

He stood as if to emphasize his point or show he was done. "Being what we are, we must continue as such to the end. Here's an inner view," he said, in a quiet voice that resonated in the great room.

Silence filled the room.

"We know we'll die. We all die. That is what we face, and we face it in any event, but in the meantime we must live. We must live well, and we must die well."

Kharapan, after a long moment in silence, walked out.

No one said a word. The people of Chi sat quietly for a time and then stood and went out into the night.

Six

AT A SMALL square concrete building in the desert, a guard let Saturnine in to see Metis. As she passed into the shadow of Metis's cell, the guard dramatically banged the door behind her.

Saturnine caught a glimpse of Metis on a hard bench, curled like an animal in pain, but when Metis saw Saturnine, she sat up and bestowed an ironic smile on her. With one thin leg pulled up to her thin chest and the other stretched out on the cold floor, Metis seemed to Saturnine as much a force as the first time she saw her.

"My muse, our Helen," Metis said.

Saturnine stood near the door.

"In truth, we acted a little Christian play, you and I," Metis said. "You invested me with power and wanted me to guide your life." Metis gave a restrained laugh. "I was the all knowing man of God and you the doubting Roman. You wanted to be punished for your sins."

Saturnine's face grew dark. "It's true," she said.

"And yet," Metis said, "It doesn't mean you shouldn't accept my teaching." She paused and stared. "In Rome, be aware of yourself. Never be what Romans call a student. Find your own words." She paused. "Whether wise or foolish, knowing your own words has the beauty of at least being yours. I say this," she said, her eyes on Saturnine, "because I've lived more than you. Whatever people say, I've forged my own life. It is mine."

Saturnine admitted it with a nod.

"We're alike, you and me," Metis said.

Saturnine knew it was so.

"Are we philosophers? No. We engage in the life of the mind, in studies of manuscripts, in writing, not the way of life. We hardly have time for others and constrict our world, monitoring our time, our most precious asset, with great care. You haven't lived this way, but you will."

Metis went on. "Love is the desire for fecundity. As one philosopher says, there are two kinds of fruitfulness: of the body that produces offspring or of the soul when one immortalizes oneself in a work of intellect. True philosophers immortalize themselves in the lived life, which lesser creatures stand by, ready to record. Look at Socrates, at Epictetus…"

Saturnine understood she meant Kharapan, too, but wouldn't say his name.

"Those like us," Metis went on, "we write. That's what we do. And if you dare write, if you dare be man in full, then you might be killed, depending on circumstances. But what choice do we have?"

Saturnine bowed her head.

"In Rome, you'll not escape my fate." She paused. "Unless you choose to be quiet and be married."

Saturnine smiled at what struck her as ridiculous.

Metis sat back. "Am I wise, a master of myself? Do I have wisdom?" She laughed. "You know Chi will be destroyed." She waved a long thin hand. "I act for the Great Unknown, against those who make life a lie, those who have Promethean hubris."

Saturnine felt weak and confused. Metis seemed like sand in her hand. "They hope to show…" Saturnine said and paused.

"That I'm mad?"

Saturnine nodded.

Metis leapt up and groaned and seemed to shrivel. "They'll disparage me and render my ideas, my Trials ridiculous! Don't they see? All will be wasted. Wasted! If they make me mad, they make the acts useless too! They make their own destruction an act of…." She paused. "Mere invisibility. Or strangeness."

Something flashed in her eyes. Metis bent her head and strode toward Saturnine as if absently, but she reached for Saturnine's neck. Saturnine gasped and fell back, but Metis didn't find the vial of poison.

Metis fell away. "Let me have it," she said. Dull wrath flashed in her eyes.

Saturnine had left the poison behind. At least now she might be aware of her acts.

"Chi will not forsake me once the Romans come! But the Romans…." Metis went to the bench with a violent movement and stretched out.

"I want to free you," Saturnine said in small voice. "In spite of everything. But your life might save Chi. That is, if they give you to the Romans. And what choice do they have? Perhaps it will be enough, perhaps it will satisfy them. In any event, I can't interfere. It's not my place."

Metis gave a bitter laugh.

Saturnine thought: the world will see Metis as a decrepit, dirty, mad thing, single-minded, without lovers or friends, a woman who murdered people with her own hands. This was Metis's legacy. Saturnine suddenly felt she understood: Metis wanted Christians and armies to come to Hellenica, it, only that, would justify her work and life. She turned to go.

"Listen," Metis said, sitting up. "I left you a copy of the *Great Twofold Work*, *Theories* and *Life*. You have *Kingdoms*."

Saturnine paused.

"I buried my work in a jar in front of the cactus I showed you. If the Church destroys *Theories* and *Life*, then you must send out copies in Empire. If you do not, the deaths of our people will be without purpose. The life of Chi, if destroyed, will not be vindicated. I leave my life's work to you, solely to you."

Saturnine wasn't flattered. But perhaps she felt a secret thrill, wanted to read that text, wondering if she would dare.

I do not believe Saturnine returned to that spot in the desert, at least not to dig up Metis's work. I suspect Saturnine did return to add her own work, burying it in a jar near Metis's. These are, or likely will be, the only copies of these works in the world. Even if I don't destroy the copies I have, they will likely be found and destroyed by others. Perhaps people of a modern world will dig up those jars in the desert one day. They will discover the work and be surprised to learn how people of an ancient world had thought and lived.

"I prepared a reading list for you," Metis went on. "Of course," she admonished, "know how to take it: decide yourself whether to read what I suggest."

Saturnine suspected this list would contain the very works she most needed and wanted to read.

"You must try," Metis said. "You must never stop trying. This is what we do here."

Silence followed.

"I must go," Saturnine said.

Metis had a supercilious grin. Saturnine suddenly felt that she couldn't breathe. She banged on the door and called for the guard. At last the guard came; the door opened. She glanced one last time at Metis—who glared at her—nodded, and went out.

In the desert, under a vast yellow sky, Saturnine made a vow: she would work to understand herself, would study, practice, be cautious. She'd never sit at anyone's feet. And if she ever saw fit to take someone's advice, she'd consider not just their words but also their lived life, and even then she would not give herself over. She would strive to know her core, and live its ideal, the only guide she might have, regardless of whether or not she believed. She would submit in obedience to that ideal, even if she could never obtain or live it in full.

Later, in one of our encounters, she told me she simply submitted—in poverty, like poverty, in chastity, in obedience to some vague idea of her nature, one she came to know by experience of it, in silence, in work, much of the rest of life in modesty, dress, food, without asking why or even if it mattered. This was the best she could do. A simple, even boring life, she said, from the outside, but within, she had come to know emotion or depth and variation, even moment to moment, the best day as if utterly still, to work alone, not one obligation, to think, to wonder—she hadn't known, she said, that life could be like this, that *life* is this. So rich, at times peaceful, simple, even in the sun, but a great challenge every single day.

SEVEN

SATURNINE FOUND KHARAPAN alone. He stood next to the bed, his back to her. Saturnine made a small sound.

"Come in," he said.

She did and then leaned against the wall. His eyes assessed her. They dropped from her face and lingered on her hands. She felt the weight of the musty heat.

He gave her a confused smile and his words sounded as if they came from a distance. "Strange," he said, "that lives are intertwined and affect countries, empires."

"I need to tell you something," she said.

She told him what she'd told the officials and about everything that had passed between Metis and her. When she stopped speaking, she stared at him with a surprised smile— as if of someone drowning.

"Metis has been a force for both of us," he said after a time. "Lifting the veil of our evil potential." He smiled but wore a serious look.

"Some people make us feel off-balance," Kharapan said,

reminding Saturnine of the night in her library when Khara-pan had come. How different that world! That night! He held his walking stick away from him, looking at it.

He passed her his walking stick with an inward laugh. Saturnine, when she understood, gasped and refused, but he insisted. "No," he said, "this reminds me of the time some-one gave me the walking stick and said the same or similar words. How little I understood at the time. But I learned. I wondered how I'd pass along this walking stick and thought I would know the right time, and here it is. Besides, I won't need it. I don't expect to travel. You are far more aware than I was when I first took hold of this walking stick."

They were silent.

After a pause, Saturnine said that she would go to Alex-andria. Her eyes filled with tears.

"Look at us, Saturnine, creatures so seriously focused on ourselves, we hardly see the sky, hardly dare to smile! We're afraid to insult our own feeling and degrade the worthiness of some great event, but there can be a sliver of mystery, of humor, in the most unbearable events."

He went to his old leather bag and pulled out a worn codex tied with string. "I gave you a codex once." He smirked. "I'm sure this is a better choice."

It was Epictetus's discourses.

The cry of birds in the silence made her look and wonder at the day.

Kharapan did not express regret that she had to go, but she understood and saw what he was in Chi. He came to her—grasped her hands and, as if joyfully, said as he had once before—"Saturnine, live!"

She blushed and smiled and nodded seriously. She understood him.

His last words were modest. He told her that he'd developed far enough on his path to finally stay in Chi. It was, he said with a sad smile, what he'd always wanted.

Saturnine boarded a small boat. A boatman navigated at the back. He pushed along the riverbed with a long stick, moving them to the center of the river and catching the current that would take them to the Mediterranean Sea. A sense of expansiveness filled her. She didn't know if she'd see Kharapan again. She felt terrified for him, for Hellenica. But as the boat moved down river, Saturnine's thoughts eventually turned to Rome. She thought of a name: Saturnine *atheos* of Alexandria. The name would help her to know how to live, help her to stay the path, return to it should she go wrong.

Some called her work Menippean satires, fantastic stories that explored ideas or questions of *agnosis*, of the boundaries of the unknown and unknowable. Some might say that this text of mine is a menippea. Who knows? Saturnine's last work consisted of an original art form in the nature of meditations, questioning meditations. She had a large following, those cats who dared to raise their heads in Empire, indeed, a surprising number of them. Many wanted to sit at her feet, but she would not abide the idea and sent them away. If she had allowed people to sit at her feet, had developed a school, perhaps this willingness to teach might have formed a community. I don't know. In any event, she never had a chance. Or perhaps she, like me, lost faith in a grand idea of civilization.

Perhaps I still can't say for sure which kind of civilization is best for the rational creature. I can't admit Kharapan "won this battle." I think, perhaps, or merely wonder, if civilization, as it is called, is a kind of backdrop posing a challenge, different kinds, to individual character. A challenge (call it that!—the most astonishing difficulty, evil, even a Roman Empire! as if stacked against one, against one lonely nature, character, core, in a world) that will make a man or a woman or fail to make him or her who he or she is, character, chance, all in play. True, the more difficult the challenge, the more likely it will quash one. But in the rare case, one might rise in the face of even the greatest challenge—and aren't they beautiful. Isn't it beautiful—simply to witness. A life, a single human life, unveiling the complexity in man and in the life he leads, a great, shall I say, mystery.

ABOUT THE AUTHOR

Pamela Dickson lives in San Francisco. *Saturnine* is her first novel. She is the author of *Schopenhauer Log* at pameladickson.com.

Made in the USA
Middletown, DE
27 August 2022